The Islanders

The Islanders

A Novel

Meg Mitchell Moore

HARPER LUXE

An Imprint of HarperCollinsPublishers

THE ISLANDERS. Copyright © 2019 by Meg Mitchell Moore. All rights reserved. Printed in the United States of America. No part of this book may be used or reproduced in any manner whatsoever without written permission except in the case of brief quotations embodied in critical articles and reviews. For information, address HarperCollins Publishers, 195 Broadway, New York, NY 10007.

HarperCollins books may be purchased for educational, business, or sales promotional use. For information, please e-mail the Special Markets Department at SPsales@harpercollins.com.

FIRST HARPERLUXE EDITION

ISBN: 978-0-06-291205-3

HarperLuxe™ is a trademark of HarperCollins Publishers.

Library of Congress Cataloging-in-Publication Data is available upon request.

19 20 21 22 23   ID/LSC   10 9 8 7 6 5 4 3 2 1

For Brian and the girls. Addie, Violet, and Josie: you are each my favorite daughter.

The Islanders

PART 1

August, Block Island

Prologue

"It was disconcerting, to see a man cry like that," said Bridget Fletcher.

"Oh, for heaven's sake," said Pauline Morrison, who thought that Bridget could be a bit soft at times. Probably because of her youth, and also because she hadn't grown up on this island, as Pauline had. Growing up on an island toughened you. That was common knowledge. "Why shouldn't a man be able to cry? I'd be crying, in that situation. Anyone would."

"You're not a man, though," said Bridget reasonably. "That's what made it all seem . . . uncomfortable. It seemed like such a private thing. He was just heaving. The sobs were coming out of him in waves. They were wracking his entire body."

Pauline knew that Bridget was enrolled in an MFA course at Boston University that would begin in the fall. It was her private opinion that Bridget talked as though she were speaking lines from a novel she hadn't yet written, and Pauline, who was as well read as the next guy, was used to a more plainspoken way of communicating. That's what years of island living did to you. You learned not to waste anything: not food, not heating oil, not time, not words.

"I don't blame him one inch," answered Pauline stoutly.

"I don't either, of course not!" cried Bridget. Young people were so eager, weren't they? Especially young women. Pauline found it annoying and refreshing in equal measure. Retaining a feel for youth was why Pauline enjoyed her friendship with Bridget, as unlikely as it was. It had only come about because she and Bridget's aunt, Leona, who owned the house on Payne Road where Bridget was staying (rent-free, lucky thing), had been friends at Vassar all those years ago. Leona—she lived in Boston most of the year, running some big-time charitable organization—had asked Pauline to "keep an eye" on Bridget. So dutifully once a week Pauline invited her for coffee at the whoopie pie shop on Dodge Street.

It was a cloudless day toward the middle of August, the wind light and out of the southeast, the water clear as glass. Down on Fred Benson Beach nearly all of the umbrellas were rented out already, and two-thirds of the boogie boards. It was amazing how quickly people forgot there had been a storm.

"I'm not saying he *shouldn't* have cried," said Bridget. "Obviously he felt responsible. So on top of the grief, there was all of that guilt. I'm just saying it's a disconcerting thing to watch. That's all. It was so raw. I can't get it out of my head, the sound of it."

In her own head Pauline began composing the email to Leona. *Checked in with Bridget!* she'd write. *All seems well. We're about cleaned up from the storm.* "Well, you're going to have to get it out of your head and move on," she said aloud. "You've got to be to work in half an hour, right?"

Bridget seemed not to have heard her. "It was just over a week ago. Isn't that hard to believe?" Bridget pressed her palms into the table and regarded Pauline seriously. "You have to admit, it's hard to believe."

Pauline shrugged. Except for the flooding out on Corn Neck Road, really this storm hadn't been as bad as it could have been. Though it seemed like it had come out of nowhere, that was true. For that, people blamed global warming, or they blamed the new president, or they blamed the capricious nature of this particular storm, which had changed direction at the last minute, barreling toward the island without so much as a by-your-leave. Even so, this was nothing like Hurricane Bob, in '91. That had really been something. Pauline said as much to Bridget.

Bridget giggled. "I wasn't even born until '94!"

Pauline snorted. The fact that somebody who was born in 1994 was old enough to be headed to graduate school and hold down a job was just ridiculous. How old Pauline was getting!

Bridget's face turned serious again. "It's just that I'd never seen a dead body before," she said. "I mean, at a wake, sure. But a *recently* dead body. *That* I had never seen. I guess that's why I can't get it out of my head. It was just—life, and then no life. Just like that." She shuddered. "No matter what anyone did or tried to do. The life was just *gone*."

Pauline took a bite of her whoopie pie. Raspberry cream. It was tasty, but this far into the summer Pauline really started looking forward to the fall, when the flavors got more interesting. Pumpkin spice, gingerbread, apple cinnamon. In Pauline's opinion, everything got more interesting in the fall.

"I mean, Pauline, who comes to a summer vacation place and expects to die?"

Pauline regarded Bridget. Her face was so open and unsullied. There was so much ahead of her: she had so much to learn.

"Who ever expects to die, anytime?" she asked.

PART 2

Two Months Ago, June

Chapter 1
Anthony

On the top deck of the ferry from Point Judith to Block Island Anthony Puckett watched a group of bachelorettes drinking from plastic tumblers. They wore identical skintight tank tops—white, of course, bachelorettes always wore white—that depicted a pair of cowboy boots with the words Ride 'Em Cowgirls above and Jennie's Last Rodeo below. Each tumbler was printed with its girl's name in large block letters: ASHLIE, LEXIE, SADIE, etc. (It seemed to be a rule that to attend this party your name had to end in *ie*.) He didn't know what was more depressing: The *ie* factor, or the cowgirl hats each girl wore, here in Rhode Island, so far from Texas or Nashville or anyplace where such a hat might be warranted. Or the orange juice he could see through the clear plastic of the tumblers, which meant they were drinking screwdrivers, the most unimaginative drink of all the drinks.

It was all depressing. Everything was depressing. Not to the bachelorettes, though. They were laughing, laughing, the way you do when you're young and carefree with a weekend ahead of you.

On the other side of the deck, at a safe distance from the bachelorettes, a little boy about Max's age sat pressed into his mother's side. His mother was on her phone, scrolling mindlessly through something, paying the boy no heed.

Don't think about Max, Anthony told himself fiercely. He wouldn't think about the way Max's face transformed when he was about to ask a cosmic, loaded question. For example: *If God made everything, who made God?* (Anthony's parents were staunch Catholics, and Anthony's mother, Dorothy, was indoctrinating Max on the sly, a fact that made Anthony's estranged wife Cassie's normally yoga-calm blood pressure rise.) Or, another example, when Anthony hadn't turned the channel from the nightly news fast enough, allowing Max an accidental glimpse of the aftermath of an ISIS bombing in Turkey: *Why is there evil?*

Anthony couldn't answer either of these questions properly. (Neither, it should be noted, could Dorothy.)

Anthony wouldn't think about Max, and he wouldn't

think about Cassie, and he wouldn't think about Glen Manning, Cassie's smarmy art dealer with whom Anthony was positive she was sleeping. He wouldn't think about his future—financial and otherwise— which was as murky and inscrutable as a churning ocean. And he definitely, *definitely* wouldn't think about his father, Leonard Puckett.

He closed his eyes and dozed. When he felt the ferry slowing he opened his eyes. They were approaching land. He took a deep breath and surveyed his surroundings. Buildings were coming into relief, a jetty, a dozen or so moored sailboats. *To approach a place you'd never been before and to have the privilege of approaching it by boat—well, he supposed there was some sort of magic in that.* He head-wrote that sentence, and then deleted it. It wasn't very good.

He'd told nobody where he was going, and he didn't expect to run into anyone he knew. Cassie certainly hadn't asked: she just wanted him gone. Nobody he knew vacationed on Block Island. They all went to Nantucket or the Vineyard or the Hamptons. It was a stroke of luck that an ancient uncle of a college friend had a Block Island cottage for which he needed a house sitter.

"Couldn't he rent it?" asked Anthony. "For actual money?"

"He could," said the friend. Ryan Fitzsimmons, his name was. In college they called him Fitzy. "But, dude, this place is *old*. It looks like something your great-great-great-grandmother would have lived in. And he can't be bothered to fix it up. But he doesn't want it left alone either. Comes with a car too. A Le Baron. Also old."

"Why don't you stay there?" asked Anthony.

"*Me?*" Fitzy laughed, long, deep, almost insolently. "No way. Charlotte's parents hooked us up with a sweet house on Nantucket for August. And I don't get that much time off from the bank anyway. Gotta keep making the coin."

Rub it in, why don't you? thought Anthony.

Anthony had wanted to go farther away, to a different type of island: Anguilla, Saint Martin, Barbados, someplace where a person could slip in among the beautiful and the glamorous. But his coin was gone. All of his coins were gone.

When the ferry docked he let the bachelorettes lurch ahead of him, pulling their weekender rollaway bags. He now observed that the bride-to-be had a white bow affixed to the side of her cowboy hat—he had missed this before. Her shirt, instead of saying Jennie's Last Rodeo, said My Last Rodeo. Clever.

Have a great bachelorette weekend, Jennie. Have a wonderful life and a happy, happy marriage.

Marriage is the worst kind of heartbreak, he wrote in his head. *That's what the disgraced, lonely man wanted to say to the young bride-to-be. Get out while you still can, Jennie. Run for the hills.*

Before he and Cassie got married she'd gone on a yoga retreat with her four bridesmaids. It was all very civilized and Zen. He'd gone on a bender with his Dartmouth buddies, the details of which were hazy.

He plodded down the ferry ramp and stood for a moment. *The wave of summer humanity undulated around him.* No. Delete.

Just ahead of him was a large white Victorian-era hotel with a sign reading Harborside Inn. Next to it, another one: New Shoreham House. Next to that, another inn, and another one. Any deck attached to any building was full of laughing, drinking people. There were dogs and children and ice-cream cones and sunlight, mopeds and bicycles and Jeeps. And here was Anthony Puckett, dragging behind him his own wheelie bag, holding in his hand a wrinkled piece of paper with an address on Corn Neck Road.

He supposed he'd have to find a taxi to take him to the borrowed cottage, the borrowed Le Baron. Did an island this small have taxis? Ubers? Anything? He could feel sweat dripping down his neck, and his jeans were sticking to his legs. He trudged up the hill that led away from the ferry, and he crossed the street. There his eyes snagged on a sign on a small building next to the post office. He felt a squeeze like cold fingers on his heart.

ISLAND BOUND BOOKS said the sign. And in the front window, of course, inevitable as death or taxes, Leonard Puckett's latest. The cover was fire-engine-red; no images, just the white letters of the title popping out, *The Thrill of the Chase*. Book number nine in the Gabriel Shelton series.

Even here his father followed him.

No, that wasn't right. The book had been here; Anthony had only just arrived. *Revise that, Anthony. Delete. Rewrite.* Once again, he had followed his father.

Twenty-seven Corn Neck Road was a weather-beaten little cottage with a long seashell driveway and, as promised by Fitzy, a large flat rock beside the front porch with a key hidden underneath. From the outside, it could have been any year. On the inside, time had stopped in the early 1900s. Lace, brocade, straight-backed chairs, heavy dark furniture matched only by the heavy dark rugs that lay under them. In the kitchen (small) it was closer to 1942, with ancient silver pulls on the drawers, a laminate countertop in pale green. The stove bore the word *Hotpoint* across it. He had never heard of such a brand. The door to the refrigerator closed completely only when Anthony pushed against it with all of his weight. No matter: there was no food to keep fresh in it, and only a half-empty ice tray in the freezer.

Or was it half full? This was a joke that at one time he might have made to himself, or even out loud. But he no longer felt like joking.

On the kitchen table, which was small and wooden, with four wooden chairs, as if the three bears had put out an extra for a guest, was a note from Fitzy's uncle.

HOUSE RULES, it said.

1. Garbage day is Thursday.

2. No pets.

3. No parties.

"That's it?" Anthony said out loud. He thought he could probably handle three rules.

On a sideboard in the living room sat a crystal decanter flanked by two glasses. Whether this was decoration or invitation he couldn't be certain, but it lent a certain sense of propriety to the place, like he'd just wandered into *Downton Abbey*. There was an amber liquid in the decanter. Brandy. Or sherry. *The lonely man had to stop himself from tipping the whole thing into his mouth, gulping it down like lemonade.*

What a boring story this would make.

He turned from the decanter and into one of the two bedrooms, which contained a four-poster bed whose posts looked sharp enough for him to impale himself on. (Not out of the question.) In his former life, he and Cassie reposed on an upholstered Avery bed from Room and Board on Newbury Street in Boston, chosen, of course, by Cassie. Paid for by Anthony.

Anthony tried not to think of how his wife might now be reposing on the Avery bed—or, more accurately, with whom. The thought that his despicable actions had brewed marital discontent was terrible to consider, but even more terrible was the possibility that the marital discontent had existed long before, like a chapter outline to a book that was yet to be written.

Oh, Anthony, stop it. What an obvious metaphor. You never used to be so obvious.

He wondered what Max was doing right then, right that very minute, and whether he'd been offered a reasonable explanation for his father's absence. But thinking about Max hurt too much, so he rolled up the thoughts like a sleeping bag, tucked them into their matching carrying pouch, and placed them tenderly in a corner of his mind, to be taken out later.

Anthony unpacked his single suitcase into the dark recesses of the dresser drawers. Next he started up the old Le Baron and followed the directions on his iPhone to the Block Island Grocery, a gray-shingled building that smelled of sea air and tourism. Once inside, he saw that the produce section looked like it could fit in the pocket of the produce section at his local Whole Foods. He spent three thousand dollars on four items. (Not really, but it felt like it.) Even to get those four items he had to fight through the throng of people waiting in line at the deli for their sandwiches to take to the beach. They all looked so happy, so hopeful. So sandy! He couldn't stand it.

As he was leaving the store he perused the notices on the bulletin board. Somebody was selling a mini-fridge; seven other people were selling surfboards; a housecleaning crew of six respectable, responsible women was looking for summer housing. But was anyone selling peace? Was anyone selling absolution? A place to live, a career?

He drove to the end of Corn Neck Road, passing three wobbly bicyclists—wobbly, maybe, because the big wicker baskets on the front of the bikes, stuffed with beach towels, set them off balance. The road ended in a small parking lot. Across a vast sea of rocks he could see a lighthouse, and a small pack of people trooping toward it on foot.

He turned the car around. Was this all there was to this island? Was this really *it*? What should he do now? He could go back downtown. (He put air quotes over the word in his mind; one street did not a downtown make.) He could get ice cream, but he wasn't hungry. He could buy a T-shirt, but he'd packed seven of his favorite gray shirts and didn't need one. And anyway those activities might require smiling. They would definitely require interaction with human beings. And for sure they'd require money. No, thank you, to all three.

He proceeded back down Corn Neck Road. In no time at all he came to the seashell driveway, the cottage.

Anthony had come here to hide from the world. But how on earth was he going to be able to hide in a place so *small*?

Chapter 2
Joy

www.DinnerByDad.com

You might think, chili in the summer? Believe me, I know. But trust me. This dish has enough light flavors and summer vegetables (hello, yellow squash!) for even the longest day of the year. And speaking of long days! When Jacqui comes home after a long day in the courtroom there's nothing Charlie and Sammy and I like better than to have a fabulous one-pot meal waiting. Cleanup is a breeze, and we can get right out and enjoy our evening. We wait a long time for summer out here, and when it finally arrives we don't want to miss a minute of it!

Somebody was double-parked, blocking Joy's spot with a well-worn tan Chrysler Le Baron. (Mid-nineties, she guessed.) "No way, mister," she said out loud. "No *way*." Still June, and already this was starting? No way. She didn't live through the long, sometimes lonely winters here, the days when the wind whipped right off the Sound and sometimes the only living creatures you saw were your daughter and your dog, to have her parking spot usurped by a summer person. Joy leaned on the horn.

The guy was on his cell phone, *of course*, and he didn't turn around.

Joy had twenty-five pounds of flour in the back of her Jeep, and the busiest season of the year was upon her. She wasn't going to park in any other spot than her own. "Come on, asshole," she said. Joy had never used the word *asshole* when she was younger. But single motherhood and years of small business ownership on a seasonal island had toughened her right up.

Her phone buzzed. A text from her daughter, Maggie. Want me to cook dinner? Joy's heart expanded, not only because Maggie had offered, but also because she was up before ten-thirty, which meant that maybe she wasn't acting entirely like a teenager just yet. Joy had been a wild teenager herself, given to dramatic emotional swings and inappropriate crushes, which she sometimes indulged in on the streets of Fall River because she had four brothers who were so full of vim and vigor themselves that it was easy for Joy to fly under the radar.

Maggie was thirteen, about to enter the eighth grade at Block Island's teeny-tiny school, where she would have eight classmates, unless someone new exactly Maggie's age moved to town (unlikely). The rising junior class had only five students, so in fact Maggie's class was actually quite large. If such a thing as karma existed in the world, Maggie was gearing up to give Joy a run for her money.

The asshole was still on his phone, so Joy took a second to text back. It's covered today. I'm making veggie chili. She took the time to insert the proper punctuation in the text, apostrophes in the contractions, a period at the end of the sentence. She couldn't help herself, and also Maggie shook her head sternly if Joy used too many abbreviations. Abbreviations, like everything else, were for the young.

Dinner by Dad? texted Maggie.

Dinner by Dad was Joy's favorite cooking blog, and earlier that day she had fired up her laptop to check out the latest post. On Dinner by Dad, stay-at-home dad (SAHD) Leo always had a fresh pot of coffee ready for his wife, Jacqui, before she set off for a day in the city. Sometimes Jacqui left *before dawn*, especially when she was working on a big case. And still Leo had the coffee ready. It was amazing, really, what Leo accomplished. Leo ran four miles as the sun rose, always had a smile on his face and a slice of sprouted wheat in the toaster. Joy hoped his wife appreciated him.

U got it. Joy allowed herself the *U*, for the sake of time.

Chili in the summer?

I KNOW, Joy texted back. But it's loaded with summer veggies. I trust him. Did she ever. She had a substantial crush on Leo. She had been to the Wednesday morning farmers' market behind the Spring House Hotel the day before—she preferred it to the Saturday one at Legion Park, which was always more crowded because of the weekenders—and she was up to her eyeballs in vegetables. If a batch of chili proved too much for the two of them, she could freeze the extra.

Leo and his family, Joy knew from previous posts, lived somewhere vague and midwestern. They definitely had access to a lake. Sometimes Leo caught their dinner, deboned it right there on the boat, etc. Michigan's Upper Peninsula, perhaps? She couldn't be sure—Leo could be restrictive with the personal details, if not the recipes.

Me 2, Maggie texted back. DBD 4ever! This was an uncharacteristically warm response, so Joy left it at that. She leaned on the horn again, and the Le Baron began to move.

As Joy waited to slide into her parking spot she gave the driver the finger, because people had to learn, especially summer people. He was still on the phone, not looking in Joy's direction. "Hey!" she said, leaning on her horn again, until finally he turned. When he did, she lost her nerve; she tucked her middle finger away and pointed angrily at the sign with her forefinger. PRIVATE PARKING: VIOLATORS WILL BE TOWED.

He waved his free hand at her. She couldn't tell if he was waving in greeting or apology or just general assholeness. "Asshole," she said again. He definitely seemed like a New Yorker, but his car had Rhode Island plates, and it didn't seem like a car a New Yorker would drive. It was a *very* old Le Baron. If she had to get more specific within the decade, she'd guess '95. Joy's father had owned—still owned—an auto repair shop that Joy had worked at intermittently through high school and college, so she felt comfortable making a guess.

She watched as the Le Baron pulled into a spot on Dodge Street. Fine, that was allowed, *that* was public parking. She got out of her Jeep and opened the back door to access the flour. But she couldn't help watching as the man inside the Le Baron put his arms down on his steering wheel and then rested his forehead on top of the backs of his hands. Was he laughing? Sleeping? Crying?

She left the flour in the back of the Jeep and moved closer to the car. The guy's shoulders were shaking. He was definitely crying. Oh, boy. She started to back away.

Then she paused. He looked like such a sad sack, sobbing into his steering wheel, and Joy never had been able to resist a sad sack. In fourth grade, she'd been the only kid to be nice to Oliver Wheeler, who had buckteeth and pigeon toes and glasses that got knocked off every time he played four square. In high school, she had volunteered once a week at the Forever Paws Animal Shelter on Lynnwood Street in Fall River because a boxer mix she found behind an abandoned warehouse with the tip of one ear missing had stolen her heart. Her mother wouldn't let Joy keep the dog—five children in that apartment was enough!—so Joy had brought the dog into the shelter and walked out with a volunteer position. Even now she drove her former neighbor, Mrs. Simmons, to the cemetery once a year to visit the grave of her dearly departed husband on the anniversary of his death.

But not this time. She had a daughter and a dog and a business and rent to pay: she had enough on her plate. And it had taken her a good long time and a boatload of mistakes (*Dustin*, her ex-husband, sprang immediately to mind), but finally Joy Sousa thought she'd learned not to borrow trouble.

She turned back toward the Jeep and the flour, and almost ran straight into her best friend, Holly Baxter, who was probably on her way to work for the Block Island Chamber of Commerce. In the summer the island was a lot like Richard Scarry's *Busy, Busy Town* book, with every island resident having a job to do to keep the town running. *I bake the whoopie pies!* Joy could imagine a cartoon version of herself saying in the book. *I help the tourists find their way around!* Cartoon Holly would say.

"We're looking over a new application to the chamber. A food truck," said Holly, without preamble.

"Ooooh!" said Joy. "I hope it's tacos!"

Holly shook her head. "It's not tacos. I wanted to talk to you about this in person." She nodded meaningfully toward JOY BOMBS.

"Me? Why? What are they selling?" Food trucks had come and gone on the island over the past few years.

A worry furrow popped up between Holly's eyebrows. "Coffee," she said. "Salads. Different things."

"So what?" said Joy. "Everyone sells coffee. Lots of people sell salads." But it looked like there was another word trying to come out of Holly's mouth.

"And," said Holly, "macarons."

"Macarons?"

"You know, those little French cookies, they come in tons of flavors, there's an American Girl doll who bakes them . . . I mean, the doll doesn't bake them—"

"I know what macarons are," said Joy.

"I was trying to think of a way I could block it," said Holly. She lowered her voice. "You know, for you."

"For me?"

"Yes. What can I say except you're welcome?" (Holly loved to quote lines from *Moana*. She had a thing for the Rock.) "Except I couldn't do it, so don't actually thank me."

"Why were you trying to block it for me?"

"Think about it, genius," said Holly. "You don't want some food truck selling a baked good practically across the street from your shop, do you?"

"There's no room for a food truck across the street from my shop." Joy gestured across the street, which was small and narrow.

"Hypothetically speaking," said Holly. "This truck is backed by some fancy New York company, apparently they're putting oodles of money into marketing . . . I don't know, the whole thing gave me a worried feeling for you. A little bit of a—" She sucked in her breath and her eyes went squinty.

Joy squinted right back at Holly and opened the back of her Jeep. "Grace," she said.

"Exactly right," said Holly, looking relieved. "Grace under pressure. That's the best way to look at it."

"No, Holly, I mean the doll. Grace is the American Girl doll who owns the bakery." When they were younger Maggie and Holly's daughter, Riley, Maggie's best friend, were obsessed with American Girl dolls.

"Oooh," said Holly uneasily.

"I'm not worried about some macaron truck, Holly. I think it's a crazy idea. Nobody wants to buy macarons from a truck. They'll be gone before the Fourth of July." Sometimes it worked out for the food trucks, sometimes it didn't. This time it probably wouldn't. Block Islanders weren't, as a rule, seeking French food, and she doubted the tourists were either.

"Definitely," said Holly, although still her face wore a funny, inscrutable expression.

"And even if they're not, this island is big enough for both of us. Right?" She hefted one of the flour bags up and wondered if she could handle two at a time.

Joy was in a hurry; the flour was awkward; Holly was rushing off to work—it wasn't until (much) later that Joy realized Holly never answered.

Chapter 3
Lu

Jeremy appeared like a ghost, startling Lu. She closed her laptop furtively, feeling as though she'd been committing a crime.

She was, in a way, wasn't she? Deception was a crime, of sorts. A marital crime, anyway.

Lu looked around the kitchen of the rented house. She was unfamiliar with this particular kitchen, its foibles, the dent in the handle of its metal spatula, its lack of a proper Dutch oven, but she was learning.

"Hey, babe," Jeremy said. "Is there coffee?" He was catching the ferry for a few long shifts in a row—probably they wouldn't see him again until the end of the week.

Is there coffee? was code for, *Are you holding up your end of the bargain?* although neither of them ever said that, because the bargain itself was unspoken. "Let me make you one," said Lu, rising. "Cinnamon?"

"Oh, man, *yes!*" said Jeremy. "Please." He looked at Lu fondly, the way you'd look at a child who picked up a guitar for the first time and tried to strum a few notes. Lu tried to look fondly back, but sometimes when she saw Jeremy dressed for work, cleanly shaven, trailing the scent of a fresh, masculine shower, she wanted to put her fist in her mouth and bite down hard, to disguise her silent, guttural scream.

She was thirty-four years old, and she might be losing her mind.

In fact there was mental illness somewhere in their family, long buried like a dog's old bone. Aunt Vivian, a great-aunt, or possibly even a great-great. Sometimes Lu's mother referenced her—*Oh, dear, I just had an Aunt Vivian moment*—but when Lu probed for the details she got very little information.

When Lu delivered the coffee—she would have poured one for herself, but that would have brought her to a total of three, and more than two made her shaky—Jeremy asked, "What're you up to?" He nodded toward the closed computer. She wondered if he was worried that she might be looking for a job that she could start come fall. Jeremy had grown up in Simsbury and his mother hadn't worked "outside the home," as she put it. They'd had a battalion of household help and as far as Lu could tell she hadn't worked *inside* the home either. But try saying that to her.

"Oh, nothing," said Lu. The lie slipped out easily. "Just getting some ideas for dinner." It wasn't that Jeremy didn't *want* Lu to be working—but, well. When you got right down to it, Jeremy didn't want Lu to be working. He loved having her home with the boys, giving them her full concentration, while he sailed off to the oncology wards, battling the cancerous demons, all courage and energy, in the freshly laundered scrubs for which she was responsible.

That wasn't fair, Lu told herself. She picked up Sebastian's toy tow truck from where he'd left it the night before, on the floor. She put it on the counter and pulled at the boom. She tried not to look at the clock.

Jeremy leaned toward the window, sighing happily. "Smell that sea air?"

"I do," said Lu. "I love it." (She did.)

Jeremy's parents had been coming to Block Island for ages and ages—they'd bought the house on Cooneymus Road back in the seventies, and Lu had visited many times when she and Jeremy were courting. *Courting* was what Jeremy's mother called it—an anachronism wrapped in an old shawl from the attic. Lu used it whenever she could, for kicks.

This was the first time the elder Trusdales had been able to convince Jeremy to bring his family along to Block Island for the whole summer, although they'd been asking and asking since Chase was tiny. At first Lu had resisted the idea with absolute conviction, like a union worker challenging a pay cut, because she couldn't imagine sharing a summer (and she definitely couldn't imagine sharing a kitchen) with her mother-in-law, but when she found out that they wouldn't be sharing the elder Trusdales' house but residing on the eastern side of the island, on Corn Neck Road, she'd eventually acquiesced.

"Our treat," Nancy said smoothly, back in April. "Though I know you'll miss your friends, of course."

Lu, who kept to herself and her computer when the boys were at school, and who did not currently have many friends, had nodded regretfully and said, "I suppose I will."

It wasn't so bad. Jeremy would be gone more, of course, because now his commute to the hospital involved a ferry ride, and he'd have to stay overnight when he had a few shifts in a row. But there was a day camp on the island the boys could attend, and a gym that she herself could pretend to attend while the boys were at the camp. Their own Connecticut suburb was not coastal, and Lu, a native daughter of landlocked (often dreary) central Pennsylvania, was looking forward to an island summer. Plus, the boys went to bed early enough that with Jeremy gone she could do some work at night.

"Don't make anything too good while I'm gone, okay?" Jeremy added now. "You know how I hate to miss your cooking."

"Of course not!" said Lu pleasantly.

"And I'm not sure what time I'll get back on Thursday, I'm in the OR."

"I understand." The schedules on surgery days always got pushed back due to one complication or another, a hazard of the job, nothing anybody could or would complain about, with people's lives at stake. Only a real jerk would make a fuss about that. "I'll save you some of whatever I make, hon. I'll pop it right in the freezer if necessary."

Hon. Oh, lordy. She never said *hon.* Who was this stranger wearing her bathrobe, drinking her coffee? Jeremy leaned against the counter, sipping from his cup. A mean little anxious voice in her head said, *Go, already!*

Still he lingered. "Are you off to the gym today? While the boys are at camp?"

"Probably," she said, cheerfully, deceitfully. "Pilates at nine-thirty!" Lu had never been to a Pilates class in her life; in truth, she didn't actually know what took place in one. Some magical strengthening of the core, she'd heard. "I really like some of the instructors here," she added. (Was she taking it too far?) She made a mental note to find out exactly what classes were offered at the one local, seasonal gym and what some of the instructors might be named.

It was going to be *much* harder to fake things on a small island than in Connecticut.

Which was not to say it couldn't be done.

"That's great, babe," said Jeremy. "I bet you'll get to know people, easy."

Lu said, "Mmmmm." She wondered if the nurses at the hospital considered Jeremy to be the hot doctor on staff. They probably did. Not that all nurses were female, *obviously*, and not that only women were allowed to find her husband attractive. There were probably some male nurses and some lovely female surgeons who noted Jeremy's endearing dimples, his lean torso.

Lu drummed her fingers on the cover of her laptop and smiled her winningest smile and thought, *Please go!* Jeremy liked to walk to the ferry, even though it was over a mile away, because he enjoyed the fresh air and the exercise before being shut up in the hospital and because he could do part of the walk right on the beach if he chose to. For a guy who was often around death, Jeremy had a very wholesome, uncomplicated outlook toward life.

"Maybe when I get back we can start working on that baby . . ." Jeremy said. Before Lu could (had to) respond, she was saved by the ding of his cell phone. A text. Jeremy looked at it and said, "Just my mom. She wants to know what we're up to for the weekend."

"Ungh," said Lu—a sound that she hoped conveyed a friendly interest in her in-laws but not a willingness to commit to any specific plans.

"They have friends coming for dinner Saturday," said Jeremy. "And they'd love for us to join." He glanced at Lu. "But I can tell them we're busy." Admittedly, it was hard to fake busy when you were living on the same very small island, on your in-laws' dime. Hard, but not impossible.

Lu and Jeremy had borrowed a stupid amount of money from Jeremy's parents for the down payment on their home in Connecticut. They'd borrowed, in fact, eighteen of the necessary twenty percent. It made Lu sick to think about. The piddling efforts they made to pay the elder Trusdales back, a couple hundred dollars every month, were never going to be enough. They'd never get that boulder all the way to the top of the hill. Not without Lu.

"Let's talk about it," said Lu, which was code for, *There is nothing I would rather do less.*

Jeremy looked at his phone again, scrolled through his emails, sipped his coffee, until Lu said, "You'd better go! If you don't want to be late." She stood, to encourage Jeremy's exit. Sometimes the boys slept late in the summer; it was six o'clock now, and on a good day they'd sleep at least until seven. "Look at the time." She held out her hand for the empty coffee cup and said wife-ily, "Here, sweetie. You have a long day ahead of you. Let me take that for you."

Lu had worked as a trial attorney before Chase was born and even after—up until she'd been very pregnant with Sebastian. They'd had a top-notch El Salvadoran nanny who took the bus in from the city every morning. By the end of Lu's second pregnancy there'd been complications requiring four weeks of bed rest. Sometimes during those four weeks, Chase would come into her bed, lay his perfect little-boy head on the pillow next to hers, point at her belly, and say, "Baby in dere?" and in those moments Lu's attorney fire felt dampened down, like the oxygen that was keeping it alive was increasingly far away. Then Sebastian had arrived, the nanny had found a job closer to home, and Lu had looked at her husband and said, "I'll stay home with them."

Jeremy, bless his heart, curse his heart, hadn't tried to hide his pleasure—relief came off his skin like heat off an August sidewalk. He had never liked having a nanny. They'd have to borrow more money from his parents while he finished up his surgical oncology residency, and then his fellowship, but his parents would give it to them gladly so that Lu could stay home, because no matter what anyone said about feminism or the new equality in today's marriages or any of that other bullcrap, Jeremy now had what all of them really wanted deep down: a housewife. Lu could hardly blame him. Who didn't want a housewife? She'd goddamn kill for one.

She walked out onto the cottage's back deck, from which she could just see Scotch Beach. There was a solitary man walking close to the water's edge, his head tucked, his hands in his pockets. *That man*, thought Lu, *looks like the loneliest man in the universe.*

Chapter 4
Anthony

The closest beach to Fitzy's uncle's cottage was Scotch Beach, and Anthony could get there in under thirty seconds, but it still took him four days to complete the journey.

For the first three days of his sojourn (euphemism) on Block Island he ventured out rarely, and when he did, it didn't go well. He tried a trip downtown. Just as he was parking, his mother called. She proceeded to describe her most recent afternoon with Max in such detail that Anthony's heart pulsed and throbbed, and if that weren't painful enough he was publicly chastised for blocking an angry woman's parking space. The woman gave him the finger, and after he reparked he laid his head on the steering wheel and allowed the tears to overtake him.

That was his last trip to the center of town.

The next day, he went again to the island grocery store. Eight dollars for toothpaste! Seven-fifty for butter! That was dismaying, but even more dismaying was the display of mass-market paperbacks near the checkout. He waited in line facing several copies of *Downtown Train* and *Child's Play*, both by Leonard Puckett.

At the cottage he kept the curtains drawn because the relentless sun was an insult, the worst kind of affront. In a place where everyone around him was happy and suntanned he was positive he was contracting rickets. He stared at the decanter of mysterious golden liquid on the sideboard and imagined pouring it down his throat, erasing all of his pain. He tried Unisom—first a single dose, then a double—but the medicine made him restless at night and foggy in the morning. It made his legs quiver and shake like an unseen hand had hold of his ankle.

If he were still a writer, he might have described his plight thusly: *Anthony was thirty seconds from the beach and yet he grew paler. He seemed to be drying out, in danger of blowing away, like an old husk.*

There was no momentum in this story, nobody to root for. He stopped.

And so, on the fourth day, he made his way through a bit of underbrush to reach a sandy path bordered by proudly waving beach grasses and some sort of yellow flower he supposed to be indigenous but didn't know enough to identify. He had never been much of a flower guy—he knew only that his mother's favorites were delphiniums, although his parents maintained (with expensive professional help) a substantial rose garden.

The Caribbean of the East! Anthony had seen this phrase plastered on Block Island tourist materials at the Chamber of Commerce the day he'd first arrived. And he'd thought, *Yeah, right,* because from the ferry the water had looked like every other stretch of New England coastline he'd known in his life—somewhat gray, a little bit foreboding, Yankee-proud. But in fact, when the sandy path gave way to the wider stretch of beach, he thought the marketing wasn't too far off. The water here was a pale turquoise, with just a few whitecaps off in the distance. The sand was soft and unsullied by seaweed or other ocean debris, and it caressed his feet in a way Anthony, who so rarely found comfort these days, could only describe as comforting.

He started walking early, but he stayed out so long that the beach began to populate. Off to the right Anthony could see a dad wrestling with a pop-up beach cabana while two little children ran heedlessly toward the water. To the left a clutch of teenagers was beginning to form. The boys were shirtless, lean-torsoed, suntanned, and floppy-haired, and the girls were the same, except bikinied, with long, silky, shampoo-commercial hair and come-hither postures. Anthony was pretty sure they didn't want *him* to come hither.

His phone rang, and the name *Shelly Salazar* popped up on the screen. Without thinking, he answered it.

"Where've you been, Anthony Puckett?"

"Shelly?" said Anthony. Shelly Salazar was the freelance publicist Cassie had hired for Anthony before his career went downhill faster than a German bobsledder. Shelly Salazar was in her late twenties, Anthony guessed, and she possessed a sort of off-color fearlessness that Anthony was both cowed by and envious of. Very millennial. She claimed, when Cassie had hired her, that she'd worked with the Annes/Anns (Tyler and Patchett) as well as the Richards (Russo, Ford?).

"Where. The ef. Have you *been*? I've been calling you, calling Cassie, calling everyone. Nobody answered! Didn't you get my messages?"

"I got them," Anthony admitted.

"We have work to do on the PR front, Anthony!"

As Anthony watched (in, he assured himself, an appropriately avuncular fashion), one of the girls shimmied out of her shorts and waded into the water. Anthony thought it would have been a little bit cold—it was still early in the season, and also early in the day!—but she didn't so much as flinch. Maybe this really was the Caribbean of the East.

"I'm taking some time away," he explained, squinting at the threads of clouds. "Thinking about starting something new."

"Yes," said Shelly Salazar. "That's exactly what you should do! Write something new, write something better, and begin it all with an apology." Her voice took on a different timbre, low and sonorous, like she'd just tasted an exotic fruit and was reporting on the sensation. "If you start with an apology, and if *that* becomes the thing, we can get you into every magazine, on every read-this list. Bustle, Lit Hub. Lenny Letter! The *Times*."

At the mention of the *Times* Anthony shuddered.

"Well," said Anthony. "I don't know if I can write something better." *Simon's Rock* had been good—it had been really, really good, he'd funneled all of himself into that book, until— "But I can definitely write something new. I think."

"Doesn't have to be better." Now Shelly sounded like a forties lounge singer hopped up on cigarettes and absinthe. "It's the apology we're going to sell. If people buy the apology, they're going to buy the book.

So you'd better make sure that apology is a goddamn piece of art."

"Right," said Anthony. He sighed. "Okay."

"Holy shit," said Shelly. "I just had the Best. Idea. Ever. Do you think we can get a picture of you and your father together?"

"I don't know . . ." said Anthony. "We're sort of on fragile ground right now, I don't want to push it—"

"Seriously, Anthony, I'm dead serious. I can't believe I didn't think of this before. This could be the answer to everything. I can see it in my mind's eye." Shelly's voice flew up an octave. "And my mind's eye is pretty prescient, always has been. If he was sort of, I don't know, laying his hands on you, on your shoulders maybe, like he was giving you *absolution*. Oh, my God. We could get Annie fucking Leibovitz to take that photo, it would be so big."

"Shelly," said Anthony. "No. I really don't think so."

"The golden child, tarnished, fallen. And risen again."

Anthony begged to differ on two of those points, but could find neither the energy nor the vocabulary to do so. "Shelly—"

"Remember when Michael Phelps got busted for DUI? And then he won all of those gold medals in Rio? People eat that shit up."

Anthony winced and held the phone a little bit away from his ear, but he could still hear Shelly. "They really eat it up," she added.

"I don't think he would go for that," said Anthony. We never really knew about the inner lives of our parents, did we? But Anthony knew enough about his father to know that a photo shoot with Annie fucking Leibovitz and his own tainted son would fall at least in the bottom third of his wish list.

"I bet Cassie would go for this. I bet she could help convince him! I can't get her to call me back, though—"

"Trust me," said Anthony. "Cassie is not the way into this." The night before, during the few wretched hours the Unisom had lurched toward its goal, he'd dreamed about his wedding day. For Anthony and Cassie's wedding somebody had woven wildflowers in Cassie's hair and braided the whole mass together, and she'd worn a simple silk sheath that could have doubled as a nightgown. No shoes. (His mother had been horrified.) Her bouquet had been wild and green, more fern than flower. She'd looked wholesome and stunning, like a woodland fairy in a glossy magazine layout of woodland fairies. They'd been married under a wildflower archway. Last night Anthony had dreamt the wildflower archway was falling down during the vows. "Anthony!" cried his mother. "Anthony! Move out of the way! *Move out of the way!*" But Anthony was confused and paralyzed. He remained where he was, while Cassie ran barefoot into the crowd, saving herself.

He woke sweating under Fitzy's uncle's sheets, pulling at the air above him. But even awake he could find no peace: He couldn't stop thinking about Glen Manning. He imagined Cassie and Glen in bed together, the article in the *Times* spread out beneath them. "What did he think, he wouldn't get caught?" said Imaginary Cassie. She threw back her head and laughed long and hard, showing the perfect white pearls of her back molars. "I mean, what was he thinking? Right, Glen? *Right?*" Laughter, laughter, so much laughter. "Oh, baby," said Imaginary Glen Manning, the rustic, masculine-yet-artsy stubble on his chin gently catching the nascent sunlight. (It was morning in this scene, but where was Max? Asleep? *Awake?* Probably with Dorothy.) "You get me so hot when you laugh like that." He rolled over and made mad, passionate love to Cassie on top of Anthony's stupid grinning photograph. "Harder!" cried Cassie. She took a fistful of the newspaper and crumpled it. "More, Glen, more!"

"Anthony?" said Shelly now.

"Here," he said. "I'm here."

"Let's just keep it on the table for now," said Shelly.

Anthony pictured the table: farmhouse, distressed dark wood, seating for twelve. The kind of table Cassie had been seeking for their dining room. Maybe she'd found it by now—maybe Glen Manning had bought it for her. "Fine," he said resignedly. "We'll keep it on the table."

"I'm so glad we caught up, Anthony!" Shelly Salazar actually did sound glad, which heartened Anthony a bit. "Now, you go start writing that apology."

Anthony imagined himself sitting at the dining room table in Fitzy's uncle's fusty living room. *The disgraced novelist sat for a long, long time, staring at the golden liquid in the crystal decanter. The temptation was great, and yet he resisted, aware, always, of the importance of the task at hand. Pen to paper, he began to write.*

No, that wasn't a realistic scenario. He had nothing to write: nothing to say. His writing days were over. That scene belonged in the fantasy genre. Anthony Puckett didn't read fantasy, and he certainly didn't write it.

He took one last wistful look at the beautiful water, the beautiful teenagers who presumably had the worst of their mistakes ahead of them. Then he walked back up the little sandy path and pushed back through the underbrush and made his way to the cottage, where he found a woman standing outside his front door wearing a pair of ripped denim shorts and flip-flops and holding an empty measuring cup. She smiled at him.

"Sorry!" she said, with such familiarity he wondered if he knew her. "I know, it seems so old-fashioned, coming to a neighbor for this. But I thought I'd give it a try. I'm making an essence-of-summer cobbler and I don't have enough sugar. So, I said to myself, I'll ask my closest neighbor."

"Sugar," said Anthony. He peered at the woman. A little younger than he was, probably. Across her nose was what, if it had not been a giant cliché, he would have called *a smattering of freckles*. She had a small gap between her front teeth, all very girl-next-door. Which she was, literally.

"It seems like something neighbors in *Mad Men* would do—you know, the depressed housewives living in the suburbs." She thrust out the measuring cup. "But anyway. Do you have any? Just half a cup?"

"I'm not sure if I do," he said.

She switched the measuring cup into her left hand and stuck out her right. "I'm sorry," she said. "I should have introduced myself first. I'm Lu." Her face was open, easy, nonjudgmental—the opposite of most of the faces surrounding Anthony these days. There was something about her that reminded him of Amanda

Loring, who had been his best friend in fourth grade. Fourth grade was paradise; fourth grade was before puberty, before middle school and girls in lip gloss and everything that came after, before his dad got famous, before he learned that women like Cassie could guile you with their beauty and charm and then leave you to roast in the juices of your own mistakes.

Ever so slightly, his spirits began to lift.

But then he remembered that he was shunned and probably toxic. He remembered that the only people in his universe who would talk to him were his mother, whose pity and concern he couldn't bear, and Shelly Salazar, who wanted him to do a photo shoot with his father and Annie fucking Leibovitz. He remembered that he wasn't even fit to be a good father to his son, and he felt his heart close up like a crocus after sundown. He didn't deserve a new friend.

"Sorry," he said gruffly, trying not to look in the woman's eyes in case he had hurt her feelings. "No sugar."

Chapter 5
Joy

As they walked to the eleven-fifteen ferry, Joy watched Maggie carefully for signs of confusion or stress. Maggie was going to visit her father, Dustin, and Sandy (his newish wife) and Tiki (their two-year-old daughter), as per their usual arrangement. One weekend a month Maggie would don one of her clever T-shirts—Never Trust an Atom, They Make Up Everything; I Don't Want to Taco 'Bout It, It's Nacho Problem—and cross Block Island Sound to spend the weekend with her father.

Joy knew from Holly, whose mother was a child psychologist in Boston, that childhood stress could manifest itself in unrecognizable ways, and even though Maggie had been making this trip for nearly two years now, ever since Dustin had resurfaced, taken up residence in Newport, and expressed a desire to reconnect with Maggie, Joy wanted to be watchful. Thirteen was a vulnerable age.

Did Maggie possibly have a stomachache that she was trying to hide from Joy? No, she was just brushing some confectioners' sugar from her T-shirt. (Lemon ricotta pancakes, Dinner by Dad, ab-so-freaking-lutely phenomenal.)

Was she showing signs of reluctance to leave the island? No, she had merely stopped in front of Mia's Gelateria to tie the laces on her Converse. New England, read today's shirt. Because Old England Was Wicked Stupid.

Pickles walked between Joy and Maggie, looking eagerly from one to the other. "Sorry, Pickles," said Joy. "No ferry ride for us." Pickles, like many island dogs, loved the ferry.

The girl working at the ferry terminal was a soon-to-be senior at the high school (one of seven): Madison Blevins. She had a cast on her left arm from wrist to elbow. "Hey, Madison," said Maggie, and Madison said, "Hey, Maggie." Madison wore a dark blue polo shirt with the ferry insignia on the upper left side. Joy tried to unremember the story about Madison Blevins getting drunk at a house party the evening of the last day of school and falling down on her wrist, because this was a tiny island and even teenagers who made mistakes probably deserved more privacy than they got.

Unless that teenager was someday Maggie, in which case Joy would want to know about any bad behavior immediately.

"You don't need to bring me *on* the ferry," said Maggie, after Joy had bought her ticket. "I can find a seat on my own."

"I know," said Joy. "But I want to know where you're sitting. I want to be able to picture you."

Maggie rolled her eyes.

Joy got Maggie settled into a seat, and then she hugged her goodbye, and then Maggie hugged Pickles, and then Pickles licked the side of Maggie's face. Maggie was a tremendous hugger, always had been: enthusiastic without being needy, confident while still being warm. Now the hugs, if they came, came intermittently, no rhyme or reason to them, like shooting stars or thunder.

Joy didn't like leaving Maggie like this. She knew that Dustin and Sandy and Tiki would be meeting Maggie on the other end, at Perrotti Park in Newport, to take her home for the next forty-eight hours. *To their home*, she corrected in her head. Because Maggie's home was with Joy, in the little cottage with the crooked kitchen. But what if Sandy caused some delay that made them late for the ferry? What if Tiki had a dirty diaper or a temper tantrum or did that thing that two-year-olds sometimes did where they went bone-less when somebody tried to pick them up? It could be really difficult to get a boneless child into a car.

"It's okay, Mom," said Maggie. "I've been on this ferry a million times."

"But not as much as the Point Judith one."

"It's the same thing."

"It isn't. It's a whole different dock! What if you get lost?"

Eye roll from Maggie, the second of the day. (Joy thought with trepidation of Madison Blevins.) "I'm not going to get lost," Maggie said. "There's only one way down from the boat."

Joy put her hand on the purple streak in Maggie's hair. "I thought you said this washed out, by the way. It sort of seems permanent."

"I did? I said it washed out?"

"You definitely did."

"Hmmm. That's really weird. I don't remember saying that."

By now many of the ferry seats were claimed. There were families and young day-trippers and people with large suitcases who were either leaving for or returning from longer vacations, and Joy realized that she'd better get off the boat before it departed with her on it, because wouldn't that be a hoot, for her to come off the ferry in Newport with Maggie, Pickles prancing between them. Wouldn't Dustin and Sandy love that.

"Make sure your dad calls me," she said. "The minute he has you in his possession." While she understood on an intellectual level that Dustin had grown up and matured in the years since their marriage had ended, and while she understood too that with an upgraded wife (skinnier, and definitely taller than Joy) and a toddler in his life he was probably a responsible person who wasn't likely to lose Maggie, and while she further understood that part of the reason Dustin had moved to Rhode Island was to nourish and water the dormant relationship with his eldest daughter, she still felt the finger of worry leaving a bruise on the tender underside of her arm. "The *second* he has you," she said. "I mean, before you even get in the car, you have him call me."

"O*kay*," said Maggie. Then, "What are you going to do while I'm gone?"

"I have a meeting with Bridezilla," said Joy. Bridezilla, whose real name was Kimberly, was a cranky bride-to-be from Boston who was due to be married at the Narragansett Inn at the end of August. Joy had met her a few times and she'd never seen the young woman smile. Her mother, Linda, a nonconfrontational woman with a prodigious J.Jill collection who'd been a regular at the shop for years, was as lovely as Kimberly was unlovely. Linda had put in an order for a thousand whoopie pies to be served at the two-hundred-guest wedding and also to be boxed up as wedding favors, three per guest. It was a significant order, especially since the pies for the wedding would have specific, island-themed decorations—sailboats and seashells—which raised the price by almost a dollar per pie. For these reasons, Joy was trying to overlook Kimberly's unpleasantness. "After that," Joy told Maggie, "I'm not sure. Pickles and I might go out and paint the town."

"Oh, please, Mom."

"What? We might. Pickles likes to get out as much as the next dog."

Maggie rolled her eyes a third time. "Just don't do anything embarrassing. Seriously, okay?"

The hours before Joy had to meet with Bridezilla stretched out endlessly. The shop was in the capable hands of Olivia Rossi, Joy Bombs' summer assistant manager. Early in the season Joy could manage well enough alone, but as tourist traffic picked up she always needed someone to help at the counter while Joy baked or to oversee the ovens or fill the pies. This was Olivia's first day on her own, and as tempted as she was, Joy knew it would be too Type A of her to stop by and see how Olivia was doing. Olivia was capable and mature, with a level head that belied her sixteen years.

The day was enchanting, and Joy knew the beaches would be wall-to-wall. She could wander down to Fred Benson on foot or hop on her bike and cross the island to Stevens Cove.

"I don't feel like doing *any* of those fun things," she told Pickles when she was back home from the ferry, sitting on her couch, resting her feet on the coffee table. "I just feel like sulking." What she wanted to do was indulge the insidious worry she felt every time Maggie was with Dustin. What if, now that she'd been visiting regularly for almost two years, Maggie decided she liked it better at Dustin's house? What if Sandy was more patient than Joy, and kinder? Dustin had somehow secured a job that allowed Sandy to stay home with Tiki; what if Maggie realized that what she was missing in her life was a mother figure who didn't have to go to work at dawn every day?

What if the most important person in Joy's life fell in love with Dustin's second family?

After she'd had a very brief conversation with Dustin confirming that he had Maggie in hand, Joy wandered around the cottage. She dialed Joy Bombs and hung up before Olivia Rossi could answer. She spent more time than she should have in Maggie's room. First she lay down on Maggie's bed, on top of the black (black!) comforter Maggie had asked for on her twelfth birthday. She sniffed the pillow to see if she could locate the scent of Maggie's shampoo. She couldn't. Had she forgotten to remind Maggie to wash her hair? She dialed Maggie's number, then hung up before she could answer. She was becoming a stalker.

She opened Maggie's closet and studied the neatly hung jeans, the collection of Converse sneakers in multiple colors, the tidy piles of T-shirts: I'm Not a Monday Person and I'm Not Short I'm Just Concentrated Awesome and the one that Joy would only let Maggie wear inside the house: Cute but Psycho. Joy's personal favorite featured a hedgehog and the existential question Why Don't They Just Share the Hedge? It made her laugh every time.

On Maggie's nightstand was her iPad, which she used in the olden days, before she got a phone. The messages on the iPad were synced with those on Maggie's phone, and Joy picked it up, punching in the passcode, which she knew to be the month and day they'd adopted Pickles, and studied the messages. Pickles eyed her reproachfully.

"Don't judge me, Pickles," Joy said. "You know the rules as well as I do." The rules were that as long as Joy paid the cell phone bill she was allowed to look at anything on the devices.

Do u rly think i should go 4 it

Riley's reply: Yes

Maggie: Hes so much older

Riley: Not rly

Then the next text from Riley: T:)T

(What did that mean?)

Joy checked the time on the messages. Maggie and Riley had been texting when Maggie was on the ferry. Joy's stomach turned over. What did it mean to "go 4 it" when you were thirteen years old? What did "so much older" mean when you were thirteen? Did it mean fourteen, or forty-five?

Chapter 6
Lu

Chase and Sebastian were in rare form at the grocery store. That sounded like it might be something good—rare form, like a rare painting or a rare coin—but it definitely was not. Because Jeremy was staying at the hospital after all, Lu had let the boys stay up too late watching *Lego Batman*, hoping they'd sleep a little later and allow her to get some work done. But the late bedtime had thrown off their rhythms and they'd woken up earlier than usual. In fact, they'd woken Lu up by jumping on her bed at seven minutes past six, so she'd lost on both ends.

Also she'd taken down half a bottle of her favorite inexpensive white wine—Josh Sauvignon Blanc—and had woken with the beginnings of a headache. Now Chase was hanging off the edge of the cart, and Sebastian, who was really too old for such things, was riding inside. Lu hadn't wanted to come shopping at all, but her attempt to borrow sugar from the neighbor had been unsuccessful and she needed a few other items too.

She was getting behind, and soon people would start to notice. She had to knock it out of the park with the essence-of-summer cobbler.

She examined a package of strawberries. Her grocery costs were going to triple this summer, and that was no small consideration. Jeremy would notice. He'd want her and the boys to eat meals with his parents more often. People thought that doctors were rich, but it took years and years and years to start making real money. Jeremy had only completed his fellowship two years before. Rich was a long way in the future. Even out of debt was a long way in the future. Lu took a deep breath, thought about the money in her secret account, and felt immediately better.

Just then she heard someone say, "Lu *Trusdale*?" She whipped her head around to see a woman with a strong, square chin, indented with a perfectly round dimple. "You're Lu, aren't you?"

Lu looked at her warily. Her insides felt jumpy. She nodded.

"I'm Jessica!" The woman leaned toward Lu, like she expected to be congratulated. "My mom is super-best-friends with your mother-in-law, and we're here for the summer too. You probably don't remember this, but I was at your baby shower!"

"Of course," said Lu. "Jessica, of course." Lu didn't remember a single thing about her baby shower except for a feeling of near panic that came over her in waves. Jeremy's mother had planned the whole thing, and there were so many people there that it took two full hours to open the gifts. The day had made Lu feel unnecessarily extravagant and spoiled. Also, she hated to be the center of attention, unless there was a judge and a jury involved, so by the end of the event her face hurt from smiling so hard and so insincerely.

Jessica wasn't shy about looking in Lu's shopping cart. "Oooooh!" she said. "Artichokes! How brave of you. What are you making?"

Lu didn't say, *Broken artichoke heart salad to go on the side of pasta puttanesca*. She said, "I don't know. Something very simple. Truth be told, I'm not much of a cook."

"Yes, you are!" said Chase. He was kicking at the wheel of the shopping cart. "You cook all the time!"

"Oh," said Lu, growing flustered. "His definition of cooking and mine are a little different." She could have stopped there, but something made her go on.

"You know kids! You throw some chicken nuggets on a sheet pan and they think you've cooked for them!"

Jessica nodded appraisingly. "Well," she said finally. "We should definitely hang out. I'll get your number from your MIL." She actually said the letters, not the words: M. I. L.

OMG, thought Lu.

"Great!" said Lu. "Definitely do that." She waited until Jessica had turned in to the frozen food section and then she allowed herself to exhale in relief. She *hated* not being anonymous while she shopped or cooked. She didn't like surprises in any form: she liked to be the one who doled out the surprises, controlled them. She told Chase to hold on to the cart so he wouldn't get lost and she hightailed it toward the register and paid as quickly as she could.

There was a man in a gray T-shirt perusing the display of mass-market paperbacks near the register. From the back, she didn't recognize him, but when he turned slightly to reach for a book she saw that he was her neighbor, the grumpy one who didn't have any sugar and didn't invite her inside and hardly said two words to her. Lu watched as he picked up a book and flipped through it. As it turned out, Lu, who read everything, had read that book. Because she believed in second chances, she said, "That one was good. You should get it."

The man looked up at her, startled. "Oh!" he said. "Hey, it's you. The sugar lady."

"It's me," she said. She gestured toward her cart. "But don't worry, I bought sugar."

"Leonard Puckett," said the man thoughtfully, massaging the cover. He chewed on the side of his lip and finally said, "I've heard he's overrated." He looked for a long time at the book and then he turned it over in his hands and studied the author's photo, which took up much of the back cover. The photo was of an older man with a head of white hair and eyebrows that were full and stern and foreboding.

"I mean, I *guess* you could say that," Lu conceded. "Those kinds of books do start to blend together after a while. But they're pretty reliable entertainment if you just want to sit on the beach and read."

"You're probably right," said the man. He smiled; he had a very nice smile, which almost disguised the fact that his eyes drooped down at the corners in a way that made him look either sad or tired. He put the book back, then picked it up again. "I apologize for being rude the other day. I—I wasn't myself. I should have been friendlier. I usually *am* friendlier. I didn't even introduce myself. I'm Anthony."

"Lu Trusdale. And this is Chase, and this is Sebastian." Chase and Sebastian were engaged in a thumb war, so she said, "*Boys!*" until they looked up and smiled. "Do you have a last name, Anthony?" Lu asked. She always liked to get the full story.

He looked down at the book again and then back up at Lu. "Anthony Jones. I'm Anthony Jones." He slipped the book back inside the rack. "I'm not going to get this. I don't really even like to read!"

"Oh, too bad," said Lu. "I love to read. I'm pretty undiscriminating—mysteries, literary, biography. Cookbooks!" Her new neighbor seemed nice enough, but she'd never understood people who didn't like to read. When Lu was in college she thought she might go to graduate school for English literature, until her favorite disgruntled professor told her there was neither money nor glory in that path. The law, if pursued correctly, promised both.

Sebastian was starting to move around impatiently inside the shopping cart, making it rock dangerously.

"Hey, buddy," said Lu's new acquaintance. "Careful in there. I wouldn't want to have to send the PAW Patrol out." Sebastian grinned and stopped moving around.

"You know your way around four-year-old boys," said Lu. This guy didn't present like a dad. Maybe he was an uncle.

"Lucky guess," he said. "See you around the hood." And he was gone as quickly as he'd appeared.

In the grocery's small parking lot, Lu watched Anthony as he hesitated, then crossed the street and entered a place called Poor People's Pub. A surprising feeling of envy washed over her. When she worked at the law firm, every Friday she and the other young attorneys would step across the street after a long day to sip martinis and unwind. She had loved the camaraderie of those evenings, the fatigue that came after a day worked to its fullest. If the boys weren't with her she might have called to her neighbor to see if he wanted company. It would be nice to have a new friend.

But new friends—new male, childless friends who were heading into bars—weren't practical in her current circumstances, under her current agreement with Jeremy, the way they would have been in her former life, so there was nothing to do but pack the boys and the groceries in the car and head back to Corn Neck Road.

Where she saw her mother-in-law's car in the driveway. "Fuuuuuck," she said, under her breath.

But not under her breath enough. "*Mommy!*" said Chase.

"What?" She glanced in the rearview mirror. His face was screwed up in appraisal and, well, for lack of a better description, disapproval.

"You're not supposed to say that word."

"What word?"

"*I'm* not allowed to say it," Chase said staunchly. "*I* won't."

"Fuck," said Sebastian pleasantly. He was tracing a shape on the car's window and lounging in his booster seat. "You're not allowed to say *fuck*."

Lu massaged her temples with two fingers of each hand. "I was about to say *funny*, boys. I'm not supposed to say something is funny?"

Chase squinted at her and shook his head strictly.

"Look!" said Sebastian, pointing. "It's Grandma." Lu's MIL's face appeared in the front window, and she began to wave in a friendly (or frantic) manner. Had Lu not locked the door? Or did Nancy have her own key? Perhaps, as the person paying the rent, she felt entitled. Maybe she'd marched herself down to the Island True Value the minute she'd signed the lease for Jeremy and Lu and made herself a set. Or maybe Jeremy had made Nancy a copy and not told Lu. Either scenario was very possible.

"Fantastic," said Lu, trying to work some false cheer into her voice. "A visitor!"

She was really, absolutely, definitely, *no question* going to need to find somewhere else to go to work.

Chapter 7
Joy

Joy was on her way to the meeting with Bridezilla and Bridezilla's mother when she got a call from Harlan Nichols, the landlord who owned the building on Dodge Street that housed Joy Bombs. Joy was ever so slightly peeved that Bridezilla had insisted that they meet at the venue—the storied Narragansett Inn—instead of at Joy Bombs. It seemed like one of those small and irritating ways that an unhappy person with money tried to keep control over others with less. And Kimberly, Joy was certain, was not a happy person. How she could find anything to be *unhappy* about was anybody's guess: she was a gorgeous, well-pedigreed, successful digital marketing manager for a restaurant group based in Boston, and she and her fiancé, who happened to be swimming in family money *and* worked in the front office of the

Red Sox in some capacity, lived in a brownstone on Commonwealth Avenue. Had Joy known about Kimberly's Bridezilla tendencies beforehand, she might have turned the job down, but she liked her mother so much.

And there was the money, of course! A thousand whoopie pies was a lot of pies, but even more tantalizing was the prospect of all the referrals a wedding like this could generate. Out of two hundred high-powered, heavily monied guests there were sure to be more than a few with sons or daughters getting married or showered or bar- or bat-mitzvahed or otherwise feted. Rich people were always feting each other.

A phone call from a landlord was almost never an indication of good news to come. Before Joy answered Harlan's call she ran through her monthly mental to-do list to make sure she'd paid the June rent. She knew she had, because she remembered running into the high school basketball coach, Bernie Bowman ("Double B") in the post office. Double B was mailing two Block Island sweatshirts to his grandsons in Traverse City, Michigan, and Joy had helped him figure out that the priority flat-rate box was a better deal than paying by weight. And then she'd put the rent check to Harlan through the slot. She was positive she had.

"Harlan!" she said, trying to make her voice sound

carefree and non-worried, even though she was neither. She parked on Ocean instead of behind the inn because she enjoyed the walk up the vast green lawn; she liked pretending she was a summer person from the early 1900s, just emerged from her carriage and on her way to an elegant dance. Or would she be emerging from an automobile? Didn't matter.

"Joy," said Harlan. "There's something I gotta talk to you about. And I'm not sure you're gonna like it." Harlan's voice had the gravelly, overworked sound of a longtime smoker. He was a property developer who lived in Providence, and Joy imagined that he could have been part of the murky political underworld occupied by Buddy Cianci back in the day. Possibly he still was.

"Okay," said Joy. She braced herself. She'd never known a person to say, *I'm not sure you're gonna like it*, and then follow those words with a lovely surprise.

Harlan went on to tell her that he'd be increasing the rent for Joy Bombs by seven hundred and fifty dollars per month, effective August 1.

"Harlan!" cried Joy. "That's a lot of money!" Her pulse started to race.

"I'm really sorry," said Harlan. "But it's a business decision."

"Out of the clear blue sky, though?"

"Not really. Your lease is up for renewal."

"But—"

"It's like this. We're moving my mother into High-lands on the East Side, one of those long-term care places. They have, what is it, yoga and tai chi and all of that."

"Tai chi?" said Joy.

"Right. Also Halloween parties, that sort of thing. Memory care. My wife and I can't help her on her own anymore. She's got a touch of the dementia. So we've got to find a place for her to live, and with those places you get what you pay for. She's got—what? A little bit of my dad's pension. But basically nothing. So . . . I had to make some decisions. And this is one."

"I'm sorry to hear that," said Joy. She really was. "But, with all due respect to you and your mother, an increase like that is outrageous! With no warning."

"This is your warning," said Harlan. "If you read the fine print in your lease you'll see that you're en-titled to a forty-five-day notice regarding rent increases or other changes as you come up for renewal. Now, if I'm doing my arithmetic correctly, this is forty-eight days." She pictured Harlan counting laboriously on his thick fingers, moving his lips as he counted.

Suddenly the hill to the inn seemed long and steep. How was she going to get all the way to the veranda with the phone, the cooler bag with samples of sixteen different whoopie pie flavors, and the additional weight of her financial panic?

"Joy?" asked Harlan.

Joy shifted the cooler bag. She'd never been the type to be outdone by a small setback, but seven-fifty more a month was really going to sting. Maggie was thirteen and Joy, as hard as she'd tried, had put away only a pittance for college. She'd been paying rent on the cottage *and* the shop for all of these years and was basically just keeping her head above water. She'd never be able to save enough to buy her own place. She'd die an old lady in a rented cottage, alone except for the cats she'd end up adopting. Not that she'd be able to afford cat food. All this work, all this time, and nothing to show for it.

"You with me, Joy?"

But what was she supposed to do? She couldn't move! She'd outfitted Joy Bombs with the industrial ovens, the walk-in, tons of heavy equipment. She was still paying back the small business loan, monthly payment by meager monthly payment. And where would she find another location, anyway? The truth was the new rent Harlan was quoting reflected the fair market value. She'd have to suck it up. She'd have to grit her teeth and pretend that Bridezilla was a lovely young woman whose nuptials Joy was very much looking forward to. If Joy could score just a few more events each year maybe she'd be able to absorb the rent increase.

"I'm with you," she said. "Reluctantly, I'm with you."

"Joy?" said Harlan. "You need an official letter for that? I can put Stacy on it if you do." Stacy was Harlan's longtime secretary. You were supposed to say "assistant" nowadays but Harlan still called her his secretary. Stacy still wore her nails long and painted red; she still frosted and permed her hair.

Joy would just work harder, like she always had. That was the only solution. "No need, Harlan," she said. "August first, I've got it. Save yourself a stamp." She hung up and tucked the phone in her pocket.

She could see that Kimberly and her mother were sitting in chairs on the inn's wide veranda. There was a third woman with them whom Joy did not recognize. Most likely a wedding planner trucked in from Boston. Everybody but Joy was wearing sundresses. Kimberly's was off the shoulder. Her shoulders looked fantastic, tanned and toned, but even before she got all the way to the veranda Joy could see that her Bridezilla mouth was set in a sneer. Joy knew from this that Kimberly had had her heart set on a Boston wedding—the Taj, the Ritz, the Four Seasons. An urban hotel, not an inn on an island that Kimberly obviously thought was second-rate.

Just before she walked up the inn's steps Joy turned and looked out toward Great Salt Pond, which connected to Trims Pond, which connected to Harbor Pond. Block Island was lousy with ponds—365, one for every day of the year. She took a deep breath in then exhaled slowly. This was her *home*. Her island, her business. She wasn't going anywhere.

Joy debated what to do after the meeting when she remembered that Peter Womack, Maggie's fourth-grade teacher, was bartending at Poor People's Pub this summer. She'd known Peter for years and years. Peter was also divorced, and Holly was always after Joy to date him. But Block Island had just under a thousand year-round residents: the problem with dating was that you only had so many false starts before everyone in town would know the things you wouldn't do in bed and—sometimes worse—the things you would do after two and a half glasses of Chardonnay.

She went home for her bike, then rode to the pub and locked it up outside.

"Make me something," she told Peter, sliding onto a stool.

Peter raised his eyebrows. "Yeah?" he asked. "Something besides the Decoy Sauvignon Blanc? You always order the Decoy." Before taking the job at Poor

People's Pub, Peter had bartended at Ballard's, and before that at Captain Nick's; he'd served Joy a lot of glasses of Decoy Sauvignon Blanc.

"I know," sighed Joy. "I'm a creature of habit. It's not my favorite of my personality traits, believe me."

"Nothing wrong with habits," said Peter.

"Especially if you're a nun," said Joy.

"Ha!" Peter laughed, loud and genuine. "I always forget how funny you are, Joy Sousa. What do you want me to make you?"

"Something fun," Joy said. "Something summery and fun." She looked carefully at Peter. He was cute, if a tiny bit pudgy, and he was single. Also, he thought Joy was funny. Maybe she should overlook her rule about on-island dating. Then she remembered that she wasn't looking to date anyone at all, because she was a self-sufficient modern woman who did not need a man to be happy. Peter drew his eyebrows together, thinking. "Summery and fun, no problem."

It was only four-thirty. The summer sun was still ridiculously high in the sky, shining like crazy, almost bragging, and the sunburned tourists were only just coming off the beaches and starting to think about cocktails and appetizers. The bar was mostly empty.

"Maggie's with the ex-husband," Joy said. "And the

newish wife. And the two-year-old." She appreciated that Peter winced on her behalf.

"That's okay," he said. "Good for Maggie to spend time there."

"I'm just worried . . ." Joy paused. What exactly *was* she worried about? "I'm just worried Maggie is going to feel like she's been replaced." Tiki *was* cute, even Joy had to admit that. She had Dustin's piercing blue eyes and Sandy's full lips.

"Nobody could replace Maggie," Peter said, loyally and also accurately. "I saw her the other day, you know. She's looking so grown up!"

"Don't say that, Peter. I'm not ready for that." Often Joy still thought of Maggie as a six-year-old with a missing tooth and a little-kid version of a beer gut; sometimes it downright shocked her to see Maggie's long limbs and watch the face of a young woman, the new dips and hollows in her cheekbones, start to emerge.

Peter smiled. "I know. Time marches on, the bastard."

"Where'd you see her?"

"She was hanging out with some summer kids. Here and there." Island kids always hung out with summer kids: the infusion of new blood was part of the reward for the long winter. "Just be careful she doesn't get her heart broken."

Do u rly think i should go 4 it, thought Joy. Her mind contracted. She wanted to put Maggie's own heart inside a UPS box with plenty of bubble wrap and Styrofoam peanuts. She wanted to keep it there forever. Safe.

"Let me ask you this, Peter. You're a teacher. You speak Text, right?"

"I have a passing knowledge of it. I wouldn't say I'm one hundred percent fluent."

Joy took a cocktail napkin and pointed at the pen behind Peter's ear. When he gave it to her she wrote T:)T and pushed the napkin toward him. "What's this mean?"

He squinted at it. "Oh!" he said finally. "Think happy thoughts."

That was a nice sentiment. Joy could live with that.

"How strong do you want this drink?"

Hes so much older, she could not live with. A strong drink was in order.

"Strong, but with the strength mainly masked by tropical fruit flavors," said Joy.

"Got it," said Peter. "The wheels are turning. Give me just a minute. But don't watch. That spoils the magic."

Joy moved her eyes away from Peter and allowed her gaze to roam the length of the bar, where she was surprised to see a solitary figure slouched on a stool. How had she not noticed him when she came in? The more she squinted at him, the more familiar to her he was, and after a full minute she realized that he was the man who had parked the Le Baron so obnoxiously in front of her parking space the week before. The sad sack! His shoulders were slumped forward in the same way they had been that day, and his head was down; both of these positions suggested an attitude of supplication or defeat.

Who *was* this guy? Looking at him was enough to make Joy feel depressed herself. Or maybe it was her own life that was depressing her. Maybe it was the thought of lonely year piled upon lonely year, and the starkness of the realization that in five years Maggie would be gone, and, let's face it, probably Pickles too, that made Joy do what she did next: crook her finger at Peter and, when he bent toward her, whisper, "Make two of whatever it is you're making, and send one down to that guy. He looks like he could use a lift."

"You sure?" said Peter. "Because that guy—"

Joy didn't let Peter finish. She could be a creature of habit every other damn day of the year. But today it was summer, and she was free of her usual obligations, and the sun was shining with a vengeance, and she would not let herself turn into a person whose own daughter would feel sorry for her when she was in college. No, today Joy would dispense a small act of kindness on a stranger who looked like he might need it.

"Nope," she said, holding up a hand to Peter. "No arguments. Just do it." Then, because that sounded bossy, she added, much more gently, "Please." The sad sack was wearing a gray T-shirt, which, if Joy remembered correctly, was the same thing he'd been wearing when she'd seen him crying in the Le Baron. Was he too sad even to change his clothes? Oh, boy. What a thing.

Peter made the drinks, served Joy hers, and carried the other one the length of the bar and placed it in front of the downtrodden man. Joy took a sip of her cocktail. It tasted like a sunset and a tropical vacation and a ride on a catamaran all rolled into one. She saw Peter say something to the man and gesture toward Joy and she put her head down, studiously inspecting her fingernails. She felt strangely self-conscious; she never bought drinks for random people. But the guy seemed *so very sad.*

Because she was looking down she didn't see the man push away the drink. It was only out of the corner of her eye that she saw him get up. She felt his departure behind her, so rapid that she had the sensation of a dry desert wind blowing at her back.

She looked at the man's empty barstool, then back at Peter. "What the hell?" she asked. "What the major hell?"

"I was trying to tell you," said Peter. He shook his head. "I didn't think he would want it."

"*Why?*"

"He was drinking seltzer."

Joy sighed. This was ridiculous. "Who comes to a bar to drink seltzer? Alone? At four-thirty in the afternoon?"

"Actually," said Peter, "he's been here since around three."

"Even worse."

Peter shrugged. "People do funny things all the time."

"Did he sip it?"

"The seltzer?"

"No, *Peter*, the cocktail."

"No."

"Not at all, not even one sip?"

"Not even one sip."

"Bring 'er back, then," said Joy. "I'll have them both. Unless you want the second one."

"No way," said Peter. He winked. "Those drinks are way too strong for me. I'm working, Joy."

Chapter 8
Anthony

Anthony was gazing at the ocean from the back deck of the cottage. *The disgraced writer, surrounded by beauty from every angle, beauty he did not deserve to see, much less partake in, was deep in thought.*

Christ, what a load of crap. This would be the most boring book in the world if he ever wrote it. He couldn't even head-write anymore, and he'd *always* been able to head-write, even as a kid. How did he expect ever to get any sort of traction again if the best stuff he could come up with was pat and overly sentimental?

There was a rusty grill on the deck, an old-fashioned Weber, charcoal, and a set of mid-century patio furniture, black, wrought-iron, the kind that leaves designs on the backs of your legs. Anthony sat down. It was extremely uncomfortable furniture. He got up again and scanned the beach. There were a few surfers, though the water was flat. You had to appreciate that they were out there anyway. Three families were setting up camp for the day. They had pop-up beach tents and coolers and trolleys that had giant wheels on them and bags of sand toys. Looking at the sand toys made his soul ache. The previous summer he and Cassie and Max had spent a week on Nantucket and Anthony had helped Max build an entire sand village on Children's Beach. They'd spent a whole afternoon on it.

Aside from the families there was also the same (or a similar) knot of teenagers that had been there almost every day: girls in bikinis tossing their hair around, slim-chested, hairless boys goofing around in front of them. The bizarre mating rituals of the young. *The disgraced writer observed the bizarre . . .* No, never mind. It was so uninteresting to read about somebody watching somebody else. Unless you were reading a thriller and you knew the person watching was either going to murder or get murdered. Just ask Leonard Puckett. (*House with a View*, a stand-alone.)

Anthony could also see one towheaded boy of four or five, wearing green pajamas, marching toward the ocean like a man on a mission, arms swinging, knees high. He looked an *awful* lot like— Who did he look like? Anthony wracked his brain while he waited for one of the parents to go after the kid. All of the parents were too busy setting up their elaborate beach homes-away-from-home; nobody was watching the boy. The boy was getting just a little too close to the water. (Also, who brought their kid to the beach in pajamas? Every other kid there was wearing a bathing suit and a sun hat.)

"Hey!" called Anthony. "Hey, the kid!" The calling was futile—the wind snatched away his words as soon as he uttered them. "Hey!" he called again, louder this time. "The kid! Watch that kid near the water! *Watch your kid!*"

Oh, hell. They couldn't hear him. Anthony ran down the deck stairs and pushed his way through the path that led to the beach. Once there, he scanned the sand. No small boy. His heart was thumping against his rib cage; his breath was ragged in his throat. He was out of shape, that was for sure. He searched the beach again. The families were to the left. He thought he saw a flash of green far to the right. He took a deep breath, and he ran.

"Dude!" said one of the teenagers as he sprinted past. "Where's the fire?"

"Go to hell," Anthony said, or would have, if he'd had the breath. He could feel his un-taut belly bouncing. He kept running. When he got to the flash of green, he saw that it was the pajamas, and he saw that the pajamas were on the boy, and that the boy had waded out to his knees—almost to his waist. He saw also that the waves had picked up, and that the water was no longer flat. Out in the water, a surfer was optimistically paddling out. Anthony ran into the water and grabbed the boy under the arms, lifting him onto dry sand.

"Okay," he panted. "Okay, there you go. It's okay. You okay, buddy?"

The boy screwed up his face and started to cry, and now Anthony saw that this was the boy from the grocery store, the one who lived in the cottage next door, with the mother who wanted to borrow sugar and liked to read books by Leonard Puckett. The boy looked to be about Max's age. Tiny baby teeth, no spaces yet where any had fallen out. Pudge in his cheeks. He cried like Max cried too, as though the world had done him a grave injustice.

"What are you doing out here all alone?" Anthony asked. Panic made his voice sharper than it would have been.

The boy sniffled and stared at Anthony. His nose was running and he wiped at it with his pajama sleeve. The pajama shirt had a picture of a Minion on the front. Stuart, or Kevin? Anthony wasn't sure. When the boy's breathing became more rhythmic, he said, "I was following that seagull." He pointed with a chubby forefinger out toward the horizon. "But now it's gone."

"Okay," said Anthony, as much to himself as the boy. "It's okay now. Everything is going to be okay. Let's get you back home. I think I know where you live. I think you live right next to me. Do you know where you live?" Anthony wondered how much this boy had been taught about talking to strangers. He and Cassie had told Max if a man you didn't know tried to take you somewhere you were supposed to scream. He looked carefully at the boy. He didn't look like he was about to start screaming.

The boy shrugged. "In Connecticut, my house is red."

"That's a good piece of information," said Anthony. "But how about here? Do you know what color your house is here, on Block Island?"

"In Connecticut," said the boy importantly, "my friend Colin has a dog named Hooper."

"Also good to know," said Anthony. "My name is Anthony. Do you remember that I was talking to your mother recently, at the grocery store?" The boy shook his head. "Okay, that's okay. Well, I know your mother, and I'd like to take you home to her now."

"Okay," said the boy affably. He reached up and slipped his little hand inside of Anthony's. The trust in that gesture, and the warmth of the hand, nearly stopped Anthony in his tracks. An unfamiliar sense of peace and comfort spread through him.

They reached the cottage next to Anthony's and Anthony rapped sharply on the back door. When the woman—Lu, he remembered—came to the door she looked from the boy to Anthony and back again, confused. She took in the wet Minion pajamas, and she probably also took in the fact that Anthony and her son were holding hands like a couple of besties.

"He was all the way down the beach," said Anthony sternly. "Up to his knees in water. I happened to see him, so I ran after him. And brought him back to you."

"He was *what*?"

"I was chasing a seagull," explained the boy. "But he got away."

"Are you serious?" said Lu. "I can't believe it. I thought he was upstairs." She knelt down and folded the boy to her chest. "Come in," she said when she rose, and Anthony followed the boy into the kitchen. "He's only four!" Lu said. "He doesn't know how to swim yet. He can swim in a Y pool, but not in the ocean . . ." She put her hand to her chest and exhaled. "Sebastian, I thought you were in your bedroom!" Of course, Sebastian. Anthony should have remembered that. "You can't leave this house without me. Geez, when I think about what could have happened. Where's Chase? Is Chase upstairs?"

Sebastian shrugged. Anthony shrugged.

"Chase!" called Lu. "Chasecomedownhererightnow!" Footsteps thudded down the stairs. The older brother appeared in the kitchen and Lu gathered him into the hug. "Thank God everyone's okay," she said.

"Mommy, I can't breathe," whispered Sebastian.

Anthony felt like he was intruding on a very private moment, but it didn't seem right to slip out the door with no official farewell, so he let his eyes wander around. This kitchen was much more updated than the one in Fitzy's uncle's house; it was painted a cheerful light green and had modest but modern kitchen appliances and a small center island. On the island was an open laptop. Something propelled Anthony toward the laptop, and suddenly Lu was slamming the computer closed before Anthony could see what was on the screen. *Interesting*, thought Anthony. Lu had a secret. He filed that information away for future consideration.

"I don't know how to thank you," Lu said. Her face had gone pale and her freckles stood out like dark spots. "I have no idea how that happened, and I don't know how to thank you. You absolutely saved his life. He's a total space shot. If you hadn't come along when you did, he would have walked in over his head, chasing that seagull."

Anthony found himself at a loss for words. It was an unusual situation; he'd never saved a life before. *No problem* seemed inadequate. *Glad I could help*: too insouciant. He studied Lu. Once again Anthony was reminded of Amanda Loring in the fourth grade, with her open, honest face, her pigtails and freckles, her prowess on the four square court. Finally he settled on, "You don't need to thank me." Then he added, "Just . . . be well."

Be well? He chastised himself later, back in his own cottage. Who talked like that? Citizens of the Victorian era? Now he was unsettled. The image of the boy, so close in age to Max, walking to—not just to, but *into*—the water, untended. Children could slip past adults so easily. The menaces in the world were so many, so varied and numerous, that it was a wonder any of them made it to adulthood unscathed.

He thought about Lu and the way she'd slammed down the cover of her laptop. Well, people did things online they weren't quite proud of. They shopped too much; they cruised pornography sites; they got caught up in headlines that said things like, "You Won't Believe What This Star from the Eighties Looks Like

Now!" and spent a three-hour stretch falling down a rabbit hole. And sometimes their young sons took a walk on the beach all by themselves while people weren't paying attention.

Anthony was tired. Partly he could attribute his fatigue to the unaccustomed exercise. In another time, another life, he could finish a five-mile run in thirty-five minutes, easy. But not anymore. Also, it was exhausting, interacting with other people after so many solitary hours. He cast one longing look at the decanter.

But, no. He wouldn't. Instead he lay on the couch and fell into a deep sleep in which he dreamed Max was falling over the side of a boat. Max was wearing his red T-shirt with the alligator on it, the Max-o-Saurus shirt that Anthony had given him. It was Max's favorite shirt; he wore it all the time. When it was dirty, he pulled it out of the laundry hamper and wore it anyway. (It made Cassie crazy when he did that.)

In the dream, Max had no life jacket on. Who put a child in a boat with no life jacket? Even in his dream state Anthony paused to wonder this. Anthony was in the boat with Max, so he must have been responsible for the lack of a life jacket. When Max fell over the side, Anthony grabbed at the T-shirt, but it slipped through his fingers and Max disappeared into the water. The water swallowed him so quickly: he was there, and then he wasn't. *Max!* screamed Anthony. *Max! Max!* He jumped over the side of the boat—it was a small boat, something low, close to the water—dove down, and opened his eyes. But the water was murky; he couldn't see anything. He kicked his legs and flailed his arms, feeling with all of his limbs for Max's body. Nothing. *Max!* he screamed. But his mouth filled with water and he had to push himself to the surface, sputtering and choking, before going back under.

Anthony woke up sweating and terrified, the sunlight streaming in through the cottage's windows. His mouth was dry, his T-shirt was soaked, and he was completely disoriented. When he stood and walked into the kitchen his legs were shaky.

He reached for his cell phone and called Cassie. Voice mail. He disconnected and called again. Again, voice mail. So Anthony called again. And this time she answered! "*What?*" she said peevishly. "What's going on, Anthony? Why all the calls?"

"Where are you?" he asked. "Why didn't you answer?"

"I was in a barre class. I had do not disturb on but you called so many times it disabled and the phone started ringing. Geez, Anthony. I had to leave during ab work. It's a major infraction, to have a cell phone ring in there. People have been blackballed for less."

Anthony didn't care about Cassie's barre class. "Where's Max?"

"He's at home, with Hallie."

"Who's Hallie?"

"The sitter. You know her. That high school girl across the street?"

"Okay." Anthony remembered Hallie. She had a rose tattoo on her forearm and always wore a baseball cap. She was nice. "Okay, I was just checking. I had a bad feeling, that's all."

"Anthony." Her voice softened a touch. "Get ahold of yourself, okay? Just—get ahold of yourself. You're starting to scare me."

Later, Anthony opened his front door. He was thinking of taking a bike ride. On the stoop he found a sturdy paper plate. On the plate were several giant blueberry muffins dusted with cinnamon sugar. And taped to the plate was a note. Trying out a new recipe, it said. I know I can't thank you enough for saving Sebastian today but I thought this might be a step in the right direction. —Lu

It was ridiculous—over the top!—how quickly a feeling of goodwill spread through his body from this small kindness. And that was before he took even a single bite of muffin.

Chapter 9
Lu

Lu found a lovely little café to work in. It was called Joy Bombs. The coffee was phenomenal, the Wi-Fi was free (password: makingwhoopie), and the specialty, small whoopie pies that came in a variety of flavors, were to die for. She bought a sampler plate, coffee for herself, juice for the boys. After the incident with Sebastian and Anthony, Lu wanted the boys within sight even while she was working, so Chase had the family iPad and Sebastian had Lu's phone. Jeremy didn't like the boys to be on electronics at all, not at their ages—he didn't think it was good for their brain development. In fact, he'd brought it up just the day before, before he'd left again for the hospital. Lu didn't think it was good for the boys' brain development either, but it was easier to have a zero-tolerance policy about electronics when you worked sixteen-hour shifts and sometimes slept at the hospital.

They spread out at the table, and Lu began to write.

Readers! Let's talk mozzarella and tomatoes. I don't know if you're lucky enough to have fresh tomatoes where you are. It's early in the season for many. Here in the Midwest we're still waiting for our first batches. My garden is telling me that July looks promising. If you have 'em, by all means use 'em! But remember what Dinner by Dad always tells you: a good canned tomato (and there are some, see my affiliate links) is waaaaay better than one of those waxy-looking villains from your produce section.

Lu wasn't sure if she'd do the mozzarella and tomatoes for dinner tonight, but she'd definitely make ice cream for dessert. She'd brought her ice-cream maker with her for the summer. The boys would go ballistic. Leo churned his own ice cream, of course. Fresh strawberry in the summer, peppermint stick closer to the holidays. Everything was seasonal on Dinner by Dad. And local, whenever possible. Maybe she could use the balsamic vinegar from the tomatoes to make a glaze to go on top? *Yes.*

Lu had begun the blog as a hobby, sort of a lark, when the kids were really little, a way to pass the time and keep her mind sharp while they napped. She'd tossed up a few recipes, written a little bit of background for them, talked about her kids, her home. The usual. Yawn, yawn. Then she'd searched some other mommy blogs and realized that stay-at-home mom bloggers were a dime a dozen. Cheaper, even. You could probably get a dozen for a nickel.

Stay-at-home dads, though! Less common. Stay-at-home dads were sexy, warmhearted, exotic. And a stay-at-home dad who could cook, who laid a warm and nutritious meal before his two sons and his fingers-to-the-bone attorney wife each night? A dad who took the bacon his wife brought home, fried it up in a pan, broke it over an arugula salad topped by a perfectly poached farmhouse egg and homemade parmesan croutons? A dad who discovered (and then wrote about) such creative ways to conceal shredded zucchini and chia seeds that his sons never even *for a second* guessed they were there? That guy was worth real money. So she became Leo.

Leo was super-upfront with his readers about his struggles as a SAHD. The loneliness! The loss of identity! The insecurity! The way he felt after school drop-off when the moms clustered together and never thought to invite him in on their conversations! Sure, they waved and said hello, but he never really, truly felt a part of things. He was an interloper, an intruder, an outsider.

In the kitchen, though, he felt as at home as a duck in water.

The blog started to take off. The page views grew and grew: fifty thousand a month, then a hundred thousand, then *two hundred thousand*. Advertisers started approaching. A few brands popped up to gauge interest about sponsored posts. Then it was more than a few; it got so that Lu could pick and choose among them, agreeing to a sponsored post only when she thought it was something Leo's readers would genuinely believe in.

After a time, Dinner by Dad's family felt as familiar to Lu (sometimes more) than her own. She learned how to use Lightroom software for editing food photos. Most bloggers photographed themselves, their kitchens, their children, but Lu decided to do something different: simple charcoal drawings of Leo's children, his wife Jacqui, occasionally himself. (There was a time, in high school, when Lu had considered art school over a traditional college; she'd been doing charcoal drawings for almost as long as she could hold a pencil.) She was active on social media: Instagram, Twitter. And now—

well, Lu wasn't making quite as much as she'd made as an attorney, not yet. But she could see her way clear to a time when she'd surpass that. It happened. Look at apinchofyum.com; look at smittenkitchen.com.

Lu opened a bank account in her own name at a different branch in town and squirreled away her earnings. She hadn't yet spent a penny of her blog money. She was just letting it grow and grow, and when she had enough, when she was ready to step out of the blogging closet, she was going to write a big fat check to Jeremy's parents for every dollar they owed them. And then, at last, she'd be free.

"What's this?" the Trusdales would cry. "However did you—?"

"Oh, it's nothing," Lu would say, smiling gently, eyes modestly downcast. "I've been doing a little free-lance work on the side, that's all."

You're so lucky, Lu's mom always said. *To be able to stay home with your kids.* Lu's mom had worked for forty years as the office manager for a dentist; Lu and her sister had been latchkey kids, eating Doritos straight out of the bag after school and inhaling un-limited quantities of *Santa Barbara* and *Days of Our Lives*. There had been no vegan chili: there had been no chili at all, not unless they cared to open a can of Hormel and dump it into a bowl themselves. In fact, that's why Lu had become a good cook in her mid- to late teens. Necessity really was the mother of invention.

Lu sighed. Tomato and mozzarella had been done and done again by every food writer in the blogosphere. She'd have to do better. Cube it? Add farro, salami, grill the bread? Make the bread first, and *then* grill it?

Leo and his family lived near a beautiful clear lake in an unnamed state. Somewhere vague, midwestern. The lake had glorious sunsets and offered lots of water sports. Leo was teaching the boys to paddleboard. He was a trained lifeguard, of course, and they kept the paddleboards in shallow water, so there was no real danger. Leo was really careful like that. You could trust him with anything.

Some summer nights, when Jacqui wasn't kept too late at work, Leo packed up one of his delectable dinners and the whole family walked down to eat at one of the picnic benches near the lake. What a blessing it was to live somewhere so civic-minded, where taxpayer dollars went to keeping the town so beautiful and user-friendly. You could even recycle your plastics right there at the lakefront.

Sometimes they stayed to see the sunset, if the boys weren't too tired. Oh, those boys did get tired! Outside all day, helping in the vegetable garden and (yes!) swinging from the tire swing Leo had hung from a branch of the old oak tree in the yard. Gosh, that tree must have been there for generations.

And of course Jacqui rose so early to get to work, and had to look so very presentable. Sometimes it was difficult for Leo to keep up with the dry cleaning. He didn't let it get him down, though.

Lu scrolled through Google Images, wondering if she could find a photograph of a lake that would look anonymous enough that she could claim it as her own, as Leo's own.

"You got a text," said Sebastian. He'd come around to stand beside her, holding her phone. Lu chewed her lip. She'd only gotten—what? Four minutes of work done? She took the phone from Sebastian and glanced at it. Jeremy: rough here hows it going there? (*Definitely cube the mozzarella*, she thought. *And farro . . . that could work. That could really work. Remember how Leo's son Charlie had loved farro the first time he'd tried it?* Nobody had expected that! But children were full of endless surprises.)

Lu tried not to feel like knives were scratching at her vertebrae. She loved her family to the moon and back, of course she did. She just didn't need to be around them all day, every day. For—how many more years? Chase was six, Sebastian four. Fourteen years until they'd both be away at college. She was a terrible person for thinking that.

She wondered what would happen if she texted back, Im losing my fucking mind. Jeremy didn't want to hear that; when he was at work he wanted to think of Lu and the boys packaged up nicely, tied with a bow, the perfect family.

Great! she texted back. Just packing up for the beach.

Wish i could be there with you!

Lu watched a family of five, two parents and three daughters—maybe college age down to ten or eleven—crowd around a table made for four. The youngest daughter said, "Cecily, you're not giving me any *room*," and the father, maybe catching Lu looking, smiled ruefully and said, "The magic of family vacations!"

She smiled back and returned to her phone.

Me too, she typed to Jeremy.

In theory, yes. In theory more time together would be wonderful. In practice, well. If Jeremy were there right now he'd be another person to make lunch for and clean up after, another person to hide her laptop and her secret life from. He might want to talk about Baby Number Three; he'd probably want to start working on Baby Number Three! She knew it bothered him that

Sebastian was already four—he'd wanted the children parceled out every two years.

She should have added an exclamation point.

Me too! she revised. He'd be happy to get it twice. She added a smiley emoji.

Fourteen more years of picking up dropped towels and unloading the dishwasher and loading it right back up again so the next day she could unload it yet another time: a Sisyphean task if ever there was one. Her mother would be horrified if she knew that Lu was thinking this way—what she wouldn't have done to have no responsibilities other than the home and the kids. Lu could never reveal her dark thoughts to her mother.

"Is that a lake?" Sebastian asked, pointing at the computer screen with his toy tow truck. The thumb of his other hand was hooked into his mouth. They'd let him get too familiar with the pacifier, which he'd then traded for the thumb, and they hadn't been able to break him of the habit. She was supposed to be working on that.

"It is," Lu said. "Isn't it pretty?"

Sebastian nodded, his little face grave. "I want to go to there."

"Yes," said Lu. She pulled him toward her and stuck her nose deep into his hair. "Yes, baby, I want to go to there too."

She heard the tinkling of the bells on the door and then a voice said, "Hey, girl!" but Lu was facing away from the door and she didn't turn to look; she didn't know enough people here to get hey-girled in public. (Or private, really.) But then a shadow fell across her computer screen and suddenly Jessica, the daughter of Nancy's friend, was sitting down across from her, and Lu was caught remembering that she hadn't texted her back about going out for drinks. "Fancy meeting you here!" Jessica said. She was head-to-toe lululemon, sweating tastefully, and as Lu watched, she reached (with some nerve, Lu thought) out her arm and helped herself to one of the whoopie pies Lu had bought. "Ohmygod, these things are *so good*," said Jessica. Her eyes rolled back in her head in an exaggerated display of pleasure and she picked up her phone.

"I grew up eating these, in Pennsylvania," said Lu, when what she really wanted to say was, *What the hell? I was saving the raspberry for myself.*

Jessica was tapping away at her iPhone, but she glanced up long enough to smile politely. Chewing.

"That's where these came from, you know," said Lu. "A bigger version of them. Long ago, they were called 'gobs.' Coal miners brought them in their lunch buckets." She was visited by an overwhelming sensation of nostalgia, though she had never worked in a mine (probably a good thing). She might think about a gob-inspired post.

"Funny!" said Jessica absentmindedly. She was scrolling through Instagram, tapping the photos with what Lu thought was indiscriminate haste. "I'm going to have to run, like, three extra miles to make up for this indulgence," she said, when she looked up. "Hey, we should totally run together! Do you like to run?"

"Er," said Lu. "Not really."

Jessica nodded. A little crater popped up between her eyebrows. It disappeared when she smiled. "I see. More of a gym girl?"

"That's it," said Lu. "That's exactly it. Gym girl."

"Then you must have taken Tommy's class. I just came from there."

Lu gave a half nod. "I think so . . ."

"Oh, you'd know it if you had, girlfriend. You'd know it if you had." Jessica tapped the side of her hip. "You'd feel it *right here*."

"Yes!" said Lu, tapping her own hip in the same spot. "Exactly. Tommy."

"Anyway," said Jessica. "I've got to zip on out of here. We should totally do this again."

"Totally," confirmed Lu.

Jessica waved at Chase and Sebastian on her way out. "Bye, boys." The boys didn't look up from their electronics. Lu knew she should also be working on their manners.

Lu looked around the shop. A young teen with a purple streak in her hair was giving a vigorous, robust wipe to the counters. Lu told the boys she'd be right back and went in search of cinnamon. She didn't really need the cinnamon but she wanted to ask a question.

"What's reinventing the whoopie pie mean?" she asked the streaky-haired girl. She had seen the phrase on the sign, and was intrigued.

The girl turned her attention to filling the napkin holders. Her shirt read That's Too Much Bacon, Said No One Ever. "It just means whoopie pies used to be made with all sorts of crappy things, like Crisco and stuff. My mom makes them with all-natural ingredients, and they're smaller. So you can have, like, ten of them." She smiled. Her smile was charming, with a mouthful of metal that announced, *My body is growing in crazy ways over which I have no control.* Lu had wanted braces when she was a kid, but her mother couldn't afford them. Jeremy said he liked the space between her two front teeth. Lu hated it. Chase and Sebastian, of course, would be given sets of braces along with their middle school locker combinations, the way children of means were.

"I see." Lu filed this information away for the future. "So this is your mom's store?"

The girl nodded. She moved along in a calm, unhurried manner—relaxed while being efficient. She reminded Lu of Lu's sister, who taught at an inner-city high school in Baltimore with metal detectors at each door and not enough pencils to go around. Lu's sister would probably kill to stay home with her children, but she was married to a cop and they needed both incomes. Which made Lu a privileged jerk for wishing she could work when she didn't technically need to. Lu couldn't reveal her dark thoughts to her sister either.

Before Lu could really sink her teeth into her guilt sandwich she heard a crash, a little scream of dismay. She whipped around to the table to see that a mug was broken and the family iPad was sitting in a pool of coffee. Chase, who was normally a pacifist, had his little fist raised like he was about to punch Sebastian. "Mommy!" said Sebastian, his eyes big and scared. "*Mommy!*"

Lu grabbed a handful of napkins from the newly filled dispenser and hightailed it over. The iPad's screen was dark: not a good sign.

"Let me help," said the girl, who brought industrial-sized rags and soaked up the coffee puddle almost immediately. To Sebastian she said, "It's okay, buddy," which was something Lu hadn't yet thought to do. "This case looks pretty solid, it's probably going to be fine." The case was one of those indestructible rubber ones, so Lu had done at least one thing right, anticipating a liquid tragedy.

Lu took a deep breath. She felt like she was falling. Jeremy wouldn't like this—he wouldn't like this at all. She wasn't supposed to need help.

"Is there any chance you're looking for an additional job?" Lu asked the girl. "Because I'm hiring a mother's helper."

Chapter 10
Anthony

T. S. Eliot might have told us that April is the cruelest month, thought Anthony, but sometimes June is no great shakes either.

It was a surprising but welcome discovery for Anthony that Fitzy's uncle had a meaty cable television subscription and a cable box attached to a small but impressively modern flat-screen television hidden inside a dusty armoire. He turned it on and flicked through the saved programs, out of curiosity. The uncle's taste was eclectic and somewhat bewildering—he recorded *NBC Nightly News with Lester Holt* every evening, but also *America's Got Talent*, *Halt and Catch Fire*, and reruns of *Friends*. Also: *Keeping Up with the Kardashians*.

It was early morning; the networks were still running their usual shows. Anthony stopped on one of them, thinking he should probably catch up on some current events. He'd been so wrapped up in the implosion of his own world he sometimes forgot there was a wider one out there. The climate was changing, nuclear dangers were proliferating, immigrant children were suffering. In comparison, his own troubles were minuscule.

"Up next!" said the announcer. "This month's book club pick is one of the summer's hottest thrillers, an instant number-one *New York Times* bestseller. Stay tuned—after this word from our sponsors, we're going to tell you all about it."

"Oh, no," said Anthony. "No, no, no." He wanted to push the off button on the remote but his fingers wouldn't move. On one side of the split screen appeared the cover of *The Thrill of the Chase.* On the other, his father, freshly shaven, wearing a tweedish jacket, giving a coy little wave to the television viewers.

Anthony sat on the uncomfortable sofa for three minutes, while he learned about Ultra Soft Charmin and fresh-squeezed orange juice and gummy vitamins for those over fifty-five.

His phone buzzed: his mother. He ignored it. He knew she was calling to tell him to turn on the TV.

Turn it off, he told himself. *Turn it off, walk away. Go to the beach, look at the waves.*

But of course he couldn't, he didn't. He sat there, and he watched as the host—Travis Weaver—announced the presence of *New York Times* bestselling author Leonard Puckett, and the finale of the Gabriel Shelton series. When the camera panned back, all the world could see that next to Travis on the studio sofa was Anthony's father, one foot casually resting on the opposite knee, a little smile playing at his lips, his fingers tented together.

They shot the shit for a while, Travis and Leonard, and caught up the three people in the world who had never read a Gabriel Shelton book on who the guy was and why he was so consistently out for blood. (Gabriel Shelton was a con artist who traveled the world, conning people, sleeping with supermodels, staying in one glossy, hard-edged penthouse apartment after another, engineering successful heists, and forever eluding his nemesis, CIA agent Rex Chapman.) When they were done with that, Travis said, "Leonard, I'm sure I speak for our live audience and the folks at home as well—what everybody really wants to know is, how do you do it? How do you keep going, year after year, book after book after book?"

"I can answer that," Anthony told Travis. "I can tell you the whole history. There he was, a mid-level corporate accountant . . ."

"There I was," began Leonard, "a mid-level corporate accountant . . . but what I really wanted to do was write. So I wrote in the mornings, and I wrote in the evenings."

First came *A Pirate's Penance*, which sold modestly, but well enough to secure a contract for a second book. *Murder by Moonlight* built respectably on the audience of the first book. Then *A Sea Change*, which catapulted Leonard Puckett from the fringes to the core: a household name.

After sales of *A Sea Change* reached a million, Leonard's publisher set up a long-term contract, and Leonard agreed to write two books a year: like clockwork, like magic, or some unknowable combination of the two. Four months to write, six weeks to revise, two weeks off in between. A pattern was established from which Leonard never wavered. Work began at nine. Lunch with Dorothy at noon, four more hours of writing, and then scotch at five, while he fiddled around with what he'd written that day. Dinner at six-thirty sharp. He averaged twenty-five hundred words a day, which meant he could complete a draft of one of his one-hundred-and-twenty-thousand-word books in forty-eight working days, taking the weekends off. While his editor took a red pen to that draft, he began the next one. He chugged along and along, the Energizer Bunny of the publishing house, as reliable as the tides, a man whose work habits you could set your watch by.

They moved out of their condo and into the five-bedroom home on Marblehead Neck when Anthony was eleven. Anthony's sense of his father became the sound of the heavy oak door to his office closing, the tinkle of ice in a rocks glass, the Puccini he played at full volume when he was stuck on a plot point.

But in truth Leonard Puckett was so rarely stuck on a plot point. He was rarely stuck on anything! The ideas kept coming, as if to a river fed by an endless supply of tributaries. The Gabriel Shelton series. The Delgado Marina series. The series that took place entirely on board a Navy submarine in the Indian Ocean. There were foreign editions by the bucketload, film rights and audio rights and large-print rights and mass-market editions. You couldn't take a plane, a train, a goddamn Greyhound without being offered the chance to buy the latest Puckett.

Leonard Puckett, in the reviews he never read ("Those who can't, review," he said), had been called both formulaic and thrilling. He'd been called a genius and he'd been called a cad. Talentless and overhyped and underhyped and a faker and a realist. None of it mattered, none of it. The books kept selling.

"I've got one word for you, Travis," Leonard said on the television screen.

Travis leaned forward, riveted, almost drooling. He looked like he might start making out with Leonard right then and there.

"Discipline."

Travis sat back, disappointed. Discipline wasn't magical; it wasn't even interesting.

"You don't write a book if you don't log those hours in the chair," Leonard added. "You certainly don't write fifty-nine of them."

"Fifty-*nine*," breathed Travis, his disappointment tempered by grudging respect.

"A cup of strong black coffee in the morning," Leonard went on, "a scotch at exactly five o'clock. Lunch with my wife every day. Those are the things that keep me going."

"You heard it here!" cried Travis. "Right out of the horse's mouth."

They went to another commercial break; Anthony's phone rang again. This time he answered. He owed his mother that.

"Your father is on the television, Anthony."

"I know. I watched. Are you with him?"

"Oh, no. I stayed home. He did a nice job, didn't he?"

Anthony sighed. "He always does."

"Please call your father, Anthony. Tell him you saw him. Tell him he did a nice job."

"He doesn't want to hear from me."

"Of course he does."

"He doesn't! Or he would have called. Emailed. Something."

"He wasn't sure how to handle it, that's all." There was a pause, and he pictured his mother's pristine silver bob, her classy pants and blouses. She was a woman who dressed up to go shopping, who never left the house without lipstick and perfume. After a beat Dorothy said, "Can you blame him for that?"

Anthony didn't answer. *Yes,* he thought.

"How long are you going to hide out there, Anthony?"

"Mom. I'm not hiding out."

"Of course you are."

"I had to leave! Cassie threw me out." His voice cracked. "She doesn't want me around right now, and I can't say I blame her. I had to find somewhere to go."

"You could have come here."

He thought about the study door, always closed, the Puccini, the heavy silence of the great man at work. "You know that wasn't an option."

"It's always an option. This is your home." When Anthony didn't answer, Dorothy said, "I have to tell you about what Max said the other day. Such a funny thing."

Anthony's pulse picked up. "You saw Max?"

Dorothy paused, then said, "Yes. I had him for two nights."

"Two nights? Where was Cassie?" His mother had had Max for two nights and Anthony couldn't even get five minutes on the phone with him? Every time he asked, Cassie said he wasn't available. He was four years old! Of course he was available! No, said Cassie. He was at camp. He was at a playdate. A swimming lesson. A birthday party. Some of this was true, probably (Cassie kept him remarkably busy), but it couldn't *all* be true. Cassie thought Anthony was a bad influence on Max; Cassie wanted to keep him to herself.

"She had to go away for work," Dorothy said cagily.

Right, thought Anthony. Because art that sat in an expensive boutique in Boston's South End (and really, if they were being honest, didn't sell a hell of a lot) required so much business travel. Could his mother be so naïve? "Where'd she go?"

"I'm not sure," said Dorothy.

"Interesting."

"In the end, I didn't care," said Dorothy. "Because I was so happy to have Max."

Again he thought of their wedding, on the grounds of an old horse farm in Shelburne, Vermont. Cassie's blond hair was in those braids with the wildflowers woven in. Her dress was held up with the aid of two slender straps that looked like pieces of braided ribbon. She was paler than dawn, with minimal makeup. Her skin was luminous; everything about her was luminous. She walked down the cedar path that led to the wild-flower arch completely barefoot, her toenails painted a pearly pink. The irony must have struck Dorothy immediately; after the ceremony she pulled Anthony aside and whispered, "Your new wife is already barefoot and pregnant!"

The reality was that though Anthony had flicked Dorothy's comments away like they were a fly, she had seen Cassie's true colors long before he had. Cassie was in it for the money and the prestige. They'd written their wedding vows themselves; Cassie had insisted they use none of the usual, hackneyed phrases, no *'til death do us part*, no *for richer or poorer*. Anthony had thought that was further proof of Cassie's stylishness and charm, but in retrospect it just seemed prescient.

"Well, what did Max say?" Anthony asked now. "That was so funny?"

"We were baking cookies, and while the cookies were in the oven he asked me if they were loading! Can you imagine? Loading! Cookies!"

Anthony smiled. That was a very Max-like question.

"It reminded me of when you were about his age and you asked what wist was," Dorothy continued. She laughed. "Somebody had used the word *wistful* in front of you, and you, precocious boy that you were, assumed that if one could be wistful, there was something called *wist* one could be full of."

(It made sense to Anthony, even now.)

"Anthony? Maybe *I'll* come and visit *you* sometime soon."

"Here?"

"Yes. There's something I'd love to talk to you about."

"Ah . . ." Anthony looked around the cottage. It was a two-bedroom, but, still, he couldn't imagine his mother in the other bedroom. "Maybe not quite yet, Mom. I think I need to get my head on straight first. Alone."

He was glad he couldn't see his mother's face; he didn't want to know if he'd hurt her.

"Well, we'll talk about it. It would be good for us to spend some time together. I'll speak with you soon, okay? Hang in there."

"Hanging in," he said.

When they disconnected he texted Cassie. Can I talk to Max? If I call, will you answer?

Immediately the little bubbles popped up to tell him Cassie was writing back.

Not here. At camp.

But he's alive though?

Of course he's alive. Why wouldn't he be alive?

On the screen, Travis was asking Leonard about the program he'd started to bring creative writing programs to state prisons across the country. Writers Unbarred, it was called. *Give me a break,* thought Anthony. He hadn't known about the program.

"I just think everyone should have a voice," said Leonard, shrugging. "Right? Maybe we've made mistakes, slipped off the path, but that doesn't mean we shouldn't all have a *voice.*"

"There he is," said Travis, as the transitional music began to play, indicating the end of the segment. No questions about him, then, about Anthony. That must have been part of the agreement beforehand. "Leonard Puckett," said Travis. "A great man, and a good man."

"Bullshit," Anthony told the television. "Bullshit, Travis. You can't be both of those. Good or great. You have to pick one." Anthony threw the remote at the television, but gently, more softball pitch than major league curveball, because he knew he couldn't afford to replace the television or the remote.

He looked at the decanter with the beautiful golden liquid. He wanted it so badly, so very, very badly—he wanted the scorch, the burn, the slow warm ease of forgetting. But he couldn't; he wouldn't. Drinking, after all, was one of the things that had gotten him into this mess in the first place.

Chapter 11
Joy

On the twenty-fifth of June each year Joy drove her former neighbor, Helen Simmons, to the Island Cemetery to place a wreath of flowers on the grave of her husband Jack to mark the day of his death. Jack Simmons had died in 1997 at the age of sixty-four. This year Mrs. Simmons was eighty-four; she had been Joy's first friend when Joy and Maggie moved to the island all those years ago, before they moved to their current cottage.

"When are *you* going to get married, Joy?" Mrs. Simmons asked about thirty seconds after she got into the car, accompanied, as always, by a great cloud of perfume. She always wore a summer dress to the cemetery, along with thick-soled orthopedic shoes ("Bunions!") and pantyhose. Mrs. Simmons didn't believe that a woman should show bare skin on the lower part of the body unless she was at home. Joy always put on a sundress out of respect but she drew the line at pantyhose. She had worked for two hours in the shop that morning in order to free herself up, and she had Maggie in there helping Olivia. Maggie could practically run the shop on her own.

Joy turned on Chapel Street, braking for a horde of jaywalkers.

"Summer people," said Mrs. Simmons.

"I know!" said Joy, hoping she could steer the conversation away from marriage. "Just the other day I couldn't get into my *own* parking space—"

"So when?" said Mrs. Simmons. "When will I be going to *your* wedding?"

"I've already been married, Mrs. Simmons. It didn't work out. You know that." They had some version of this conversation every year: Joy told Mrs. Simmons how Dustin had left the marriage to pursue his dream of becoming a rock star. "I really need to focus on the band," he'd said. "If I'm going to get anywhere."

To that Joy had said the cruelest thing she could think of, maybe the cruelest thing she'd ever said to anyone: *Whether or not you focus, Dustin, you're not going to get anywhere. You're not going to get anywhere. Because you don't have any talent.*

He left anyway.

"Dustin," said Mrs. Simmons. "I don't know how he let you go."

"Well, he did," Joy said. "Somehow he managed."

"His loss."

"Thank you." Joy paused. "It was a long time ago. I'm over it now, really I am. And anyway, if that marriage hadn't ended, I wouldn't be here! I wouldn't know *you*."

"That's true," Mrs. Simmons conceded. "You came here to heal something that was broken. A lot of people come here for that."

This was a surprisingly insightful comment from Joy's passenger, and it was also true.

When Joy was nine years old her father's older sister, Branca, who had no children of her own, had rented a house on Block Island and invited Joy's parents, Joy, and her brothers to stay for a week. The house had been near Vaill Beach, backed by a dramatic cliff, reached by walking down a path through Snake Hole Road. It had been one of their only family vacations; closing the auto repair shop for that many days was too great an expense for her family to absorb more than that one time. Joy had never been as happy in her life as she'd been that week on Block Island. When Dustin's departure punched a hole in her heart and she felt something substantial and essential leaking out of it, she'd come back.

"You can't be married to those moon pies, you know."

"Whoopie pies, Mrs. Simmons. They're whoopie pies."

"Either or," said Mrs. Simmons.

Joy set her lips together and said nothing. Joy's mother's mother, Fionnula, whose family had settled in Roxbury after leaving County Offaly, Ireland, worked as a young woman at the Berwick Cake Company, where the whoopie pie was first manufactured. (This statement was *super-controversial*, Maine and Pennsylvania also claiming provenance.) Fionnula had a special liking for Joy; Joy was the youngest, and the only girl, and the most *Irish-seeming* product of her middle daughter's marriage to a Portuguese Fall River auto mechanic. (Her snub nose. Her feistiness. Her tendency toward sunburn.) And so, when the rest of the family was at the shop—the boys working on the cars, Joy's mother keeping the books—Fionnula and Joy baked and baked and baked.

The pies were so big, though! Sometimes the size of a hamburger. Too big. Too unhealthy, with the Crisco in the filling. Too much like a rock that had fallen accidentally into your stomach.

Joy stopped baking in college. She worked at her father's shop; she worked at a questionable Olive Garden. She scarcely cooked when she was in her early twenties (wrapped up in Dustin) and also when Maggie was an infant (exhausted by motherhood). But when Maggie turned one and her afternoon nap became long and predictable, when Dustin started disappearing to who-knew-where, Joy began experimenting with her own version of Fionnula's whoopie pie. Smaller—the diameter of a cucumber slice—with more palatable fillings, interesting flavors, and no trans fats. The whoopie pie: reinvented.

"Holy crap," said her brother Erico, when she presented him with a sample plate. "These things are amazing. They're like little joy bombs."

Bingo.

With the money Dustin gave her when they split—she had no idea how he'd managed to acquire it, they'd been *so poor* for the entirety of their brief marriage, there had to be something illegal about the funds with which he finally supplied her (drugs? Joy didn't want to know)—she rented a tiny bungalow off West Side Road. Then she took out a small business loan and opened Joy Bombs, the island's first and only whoopie pie shop.

Screw you, Dustin, she thought, as she shopped for commercial ovens, perfected her recipe, experimented with different seasonal fillings: pumpkin, peppermint, mocha. More salt in the salted caramel, or less? (Always more, was the correct answer.) *Screw you and the horse you rode in on, Dustin.* It was an expression her aunt Branca had favored, uncharacteristically crude words, yes, from someone normally so genteel. But effective. Joy's anger kept her going. She was a *wronged woman!* With a *little girl to care for!*

Then one day she woke up, fed Maggie and dropped her off at the little day care on the main street, unlocked the door to the bakery, looked around at the five small tables, the restaurant-grade espresso machine, the spoons lined up like soldiers awaiting orders, and realized that she didn't need her anger anymore. In fact, she didn't even *have* her anger anymore. It had floated away on an island wind.

Maggie turned three, then four, and so on. She was a delight: aggressively freckled, curious, funny. Joy made friends. She began to understand the rhythms of island life. The way you worked your fingers to the bone during the summer in order to make enough money to survive the winter. Which of the island's ponds offered the best ice-skating. Where to look for barn owl nests along Mohegan Bluffs. She was too busy to be angry, too consumed and (dare she say it) too happy to feel wronged.

But there were times that two-thirty in the morning found her wide awake, staring into the vast darkness, wondering about growing old alone. Wondering what would happen when Maggie went off to college. Would Joy one day become a crazy old lady who talked only to her cats?

To guard against this possibility (and because she didn't like cats) she took Maggie one day when Maggie was eight to the animal shelter in Warwick to pick out a puppy. They ended up with Pickles, a whitish beagley mix with a black eyebrow-shaped patch over one eye.

"I love her," said Maggie. "She looks like someone interrupted her when she was putting on her makeup."

And just like that, they were a family of three.

"But you're all alone!" continued Mrs. Simmons now. "You should get married again. You should at least have a beau." Joy giggled inwardly at the word *beau*. It was a wonderful word, really. It deserved to come back into circulation.

And it would be nice to have a beau, Joy agreed. It would be even nicer, perhaps, to have sex again. With the exception of three summer flings and that awkward business a couple of years ago with Bob Herbert, who ran the auto repair shop, Joy lived like a cloistered nun. If cloistered nuns had daughters to raise and small businesses to run.

"I'm not all alone," she told Mrs. Simmons. "I have Maggie. I have Pickles. Tonight, Maggie and I are making a dish from our favorite food blog: it's a new twist on spaghetti with clam sauce. Maggie's going to dig the clams herself, today! You should come for dinner!"

"Shellfish allergy," said Mrs. Simmons primly. "And you won't have Maggie and Pickles forever."

"I know," said Joy regretfully. "It's a real shame that dogs' life spans are so much shorter than ours."

"You lose the daughters, is what I meant. That's how it goes. My two daughters I never see. My son: All the time. I can't get rid of him." Mrs. Simmons always wore lipstick for the cemetery visit, and never mind if she colored outside the lines. At least she was trying. Joy thought that was very brave.

"Well. I have my business too, you know, Mrs. Simmons."

"You need a beau," she repeated staunchly. After a beat she said, "What's this I heard about a food truck coming to the island? Who wants to eat food that comes off a truck? That sounds very dirty, if you ask me."

"It's not a pickup truck, Mrs. Simmons, it's a— Think of it as a mobile kitchen. Like an ice-cream truck, but with different kinds of food. Anyway, they'll never get the permitting, not in time for summer. How'd you hear about it?"

"Same way I hear about everything. My Thursday night card game."

"Bridge?"

"A little bridge, a little canasta. Speaking of. You know where you should take me sometime? That Mohegan Sun. Barbara Galveston's daughter took her there two weeks ago and she won eighty-five dollars at the craps table."

"Okay," said Joy. "Okay, why not? Let's do that someday." She could probably get Holly to go along on an adventure like that.

At the cemetery, Joy pulled up the paved road to where it started to become a dirt path. "Here we are," she said. "You remember where you're going?"

"Of course I remember!" Mrs. Simmons shook her head at Joy and reached for the shopping bag at her feet, in which Joy knew was a wreath made out of the same flowers she'd had in her wedding bouquet (roses and peonies). She had held her handbag on her lap like a pet the whole ride. "Thank you for the ride. I will be ready to go home in half an hour."

Mrs. Simmons always needed half an hour, which seemed to Joy like quite a lot of time, but she didn't question it. Perhaps Mrs. Simmons needed to catch Mr. Simmons up on the events of the year. Usually Joy walked across the street to Ball O'Brien Park to watch the children playing on the town playground or the skate punks doing their tricks in the skate park. Sometimes she brought a mug of coffee or a snack and sat at one of the picnic tables in the pavilion. She used to bring Maggie to this playground quite often, so she watched the young mothers pushing small children in the baby swings, and the older kids pumping their legs to make the big-kid swings go as high as they could, and she tried not to feel too nostalgic about the inevitable and soul-crushing passage of time, because after all, children couldn't help that they grew up.

This year, Joy didn't feel like sitting at Ball O'Brien Park and watching the children. She turned off the ignition and got out herself, took a look around the cemetery. Some of the graves had flags waving beside them. Some had freshly planted flowers or dying bouquets. Some (most) had nothing at all.

She watched Mrs. Simmons bob and weave her way through the graves, clutching her handbag in one hand and the shopping bag with the wreath in the other. Finally her bobbing head disappeared from view. Joy looked at the set of gravestones closest to where she stood: the Starr family. The father had lived from 1919 to 2010; the mother from 1923 to 1995. But the children! Two sons, one dead at age sixteen, one at age twenty-six. UNFINISHED WORDS AND MUSIC read the gravestone on the latter.

Imagine being those parents, outliving both sons. Imagine being the dad, outliving his wife too! Joy turned away and walked toward where she knew Mr. Simmons's stone to be, just to make sure Mrs. Simmons had arrived safely. For a moment she couldn't locate her. Then, as she drew closer, she saw that she was kneeling by the gravestone. No, more than kneeling, she had two hands on it and she was bowed over it. And she was sobbing. Joy turned away quickly. To mourn like that! After all these years! Joy couldn't help but wonder, who would she mourn in such a manner? Only Maggie. And there was no way—*no way in hell*— she was letting Maggie die first. If Maggie died, Joy would Romeo-and-Juliet herself right next to her, no question.

But what a world it was. You could lose your husband when you were in your sixties, and you could live out the rest of your days a widow, appearing quite content, and yet one day a year you could put on lipstick, crooked though it may be, and pantyhose, and you could cry over the grave of someone who had been dead for twenty years. What a world.

"You're married to those moon pies," Mrs. Simmons accused again on the way back. "That's who *you're* married to." She had wiped her eyes and brushed off her knees and by the time she bobbed and weaved back to Joy the only trace of her sorrow was a smudge of her lipstick line.

"Whoopie pies," said Joy. "And I'm not married to them."

"You may as well be," said Mrs. Simmons resentfully.

"Oh, Mrs. Simmons," said Joy.

Unfinished words and music: Didn't they all have those inside themselves, at the end?

She chose a different route back this time: Center to Beach to Corn Neck, skipping Ocean altogether. Why not? It was a summer morning, and she had a little time to be adventurous.

"Are you lost?" asked Mrs. Simmons, peering out the window.

"Mrs. Simmons. Of course I'm not lost! I've lived here for eleven years!"

"Well, this isn't the route we took on the way there."

"Don't worry," said Joy. "I'll get you home."

As they rounded the curve toward the end of Corn Neck Road, Mrs. Simmons said, "Careful, now!" and Joy slowed down, because there was a large crowd of people standing in line for—something. The line was encroaching on the road.

"What's *this* crowd?" asked Mrs. Simmons. She rolled down her window and stuck out her head. "'Grand opening,' that sign says. 'Free samples.' Slow down, Joy! I want to see."

"I'm hardly moving," grumbled Joy. There was a pretzel of anxiety baking in her stomach. There must be at least fifty people in the line.

"Ooo la *la*," said Mrs. Simmons. "The Roving Patisserie. It's *French*!"

"French-*ish*," corrected Joy. "I mean, really I think it's basically a cookie truck."

"It must be good!" cried Mrs. Simmons. Her face was alight with hope and possibility. "Look at that line."

"People aren't lining up because it's good, they're lining up because it's free, and people love free stuff."

"Can we stop? I'd like to see what they have."

Joy set her lips together and tightened her grip on the steering wheel. "I'm sorry, Mrs. Simmons," she said. "I'm very sorry, but we can't stop. I'm afraid I'm due back at the store ten minutes ago."

"Well, then you should have taken the other route home. It was faster." A note of petulance crept into Mrs. Simmons's voice, and she folded and refolded the shopping bag that had held the wreath.

Joy's phone pinged. A text from Maggie: I got a job.

Joy used Siri to text back: You have a job. Maggie's job was helping at Joy Bombs. Her other jobs were wearing her funny T-shirts and her Converse sneakers in all different colors, and being a stepdaughter to Dustin's second wife, Sandy, while being careful not to like her as much as she liked Joy.

"Talking to a phone," grumbled Mrs. Simmons. "With no one on the other line."

Another job, Maggie wrote back. Mother's helper.

Great, texted Joy. Can't wait to hear about it. But all the way back home, after she drove past the blasted food truck (she might have to talk to Holly again about the permit, see if everything really was completely up to snuff), as she navigated summer foot traffic and summer bike traffic, she felt the force of Maggie pulling away so strongly it felt like they were the poles of two magnets, repelling each other. She couldn't help imagining a time, not too far in the future, when Maggie would be gone from her and she wouldn't even know the first thing about her daughter's life.

And she couldn't help thinking, *Mother's helper? What about this mother? What about this mother right here? Who's going to help this mother?*

Chapter 12
Anthony

Anthony found an ancient map in a kitchen drawer and discovered that if you followed Lakeside Drive to Center Road, which basically bisected the island, you'd get the lay of the land. He started up the Le Baron and set out. He accidentally turned off Lakeside before he should have (he was notoriously bad with directions) and found himself on Cooneymus Road.

He tried to head-write the scene, just to see if he could. Here there were oodles of honest-to-God farmland, most of it bordered by low stone walls, and houses tucked away at the edges of vast green hills with glimpses of the ocean beyond.

But there didn't seem to be any point to writing, in his head or otherwise. There was no story here. He thought about Max's little-boy smell, which reminded him of fresh-cut grass and baseball. He thought about the way Max followed along with his forefinger in a book when Anthony read to him, because that's what he'd seen grown-ups do. He thought about the way Max nodded to himself before attempting some difficult task—he was learning to tie his own shoes—as if he were saying, *Okay, buddy, let's do this.* Anthony's soul felt squished, trod upon. He imagined calling his father, asking for money so he could somehow fix all of this, start over, make it up to Max. No. Never. His mother? Maybe. But how much? And how would he ever be able to pay her back?

He pulled over to the side of the road. There wasn't much of a shoulder, but there wasn't much traffic either. He texted Cassie a variation of the same text he'd been sending every day.

Call me please. I dont need to talk to you but let me talk to Max.

Nothing back.

He sent another: Did you get my last text. You don't have to talk to me. Just put Max on the phone.

Still nothing.

Please, he texted.

What if Max forgot the sound of Anthony's voice? What if he forgot what Anthony looked like? What if

Max's enduring memory of Anthony was one of the last images he'd been presented with, that of his father crying over *The Runaway Bunny?*

Anthony's phone blinked ominously: LOW BATTERY. He sighed. When he got back to the cottage, he'd charge his phone, then he'd call Cassie. If Cassie didn't answer, he'd call his mother—maybe Max was there again! If not, he might work up the courage to talk about money.

The only problem with his plan was that he didn't exactly know where he was; the wrong turn had thrown him off. And even though Block Island was only seven miles long, Anthony's familiarity with its geography was almost nonexistent. He started the car again. Was there a *tick-tick-tick* noise coming from the engine? He cocked his head, listening. Maybe he'd imagined it. Anthony's knowledge of the inner workings of cars, when written out in long form, could fit on one side of a dime.

He eased back onto the road, figuring that if he reached the water he'd probably be able to work out how to wind his way around the island and back to the cottage.

The Le Baron shuddered and shook and came to a cranky halt.

"No!" said Anthony. "No no no no no." He turned the key in the ignition. Nothing. "No!" he said. "Don't do this to me." He hit the steering wheel with the palm of his hand. The car was smack in the middle of the road.

Anthony got out and struggled for a good long time with the hood. Even this simple task was a challenge. Mortifying. From off in the distance he heard the deep lowing of a cow. "I know, buddy," he said. "I feel the same way."

When he finally had the hood open, he stared at the engine, as though the car might reveal the source of its problems in word form, so that Anthony could read it. He felt himself turn red with humiliation, even though there was nobody there to watch him.

He looked again at his phone and began to google. He'd google *Le Baron* and *tick tick tick noise*. The LOW BATTERY message blinked twice, then darkness fell over the screen.

The day was hot and cloudless and the sun glinted off the asphalt like an insult. In town, from the little Anthony had seen, this place was wall-to-wall people and tank tops and ice cream and noise. How could an island that seemed so overpopulated—the crush of humanity where the ferries docked, the intolerable moped traffic, bikes everywhere—also be so empty?

He waited, and waited some more. His unease deepened. At last a bright yellow Jeep, top down, came along the road and stopped behind him, pulling over to the side. The license plate read JOYBMBS and the driver was a woman who looked vaguely familiar to Anthony, although he didn't know why. She had long dark hair and pale smooth skin. She was wearing giant sunglasses, which she pushed on top of her head when she said, "Need some help?" Her eyes were dark brown.

Anthony wiped the sweat from his brow. He didn't like being in a position of need, and there was such shame clinging to his lack of car knowledge. But the truth was the truth. "Yeah," he said, ducking his head. "I guess I do."

The woman hopped out of the Jeep. In the back, there was a dog, tongue out, wide-mouthed, practically smiling. Anthony was not a dog person, so he couldn't have said what kind it was. He'd wanted a dog when he was a kid. He'd wanted one *so badly*. But his father had said no. He wasn't interested in the mess, the noise, the potential for distraction. His mother had bought him a consolation prize: a hamster.

Where had he just seen a Jeep like this?

The woman was somewhere in her thirties. When she smiled, lines shot out from the corners of her eyes. They disappeared when she stopped smiling. She peered under the hood alongside him. She smelled like vanilla, and he noticed a white smudge along her temple. He had a sudden and disconcerting urge to wipe it gently away. *Get ahold of yourself, Anthony.* It had just been so long since he'd touched another human being, that was all.

"Maybe you could give me a ride, if it's not too inconvenient?" he said. "I'll have to get someone to look at it. Maybe get it towed. I'm not sure what happened. It just—" He made an exploding sort of gesture with his hands. "It just shuddered and stopped."

"I'm someone," said the woman. "I'm looking at it right now. Hang on." She nodded crisply, then went back to her Jeep, rummaged around, and returned with a tool case. "Was it making sort of a *tick-tick-tick* noise?"

"Yes," said Anthony, amazed and mollified. "*Tick-tick-tick* is exactly the way to describe it."

"For how long?"

"Well," said Anthony, "I guess I don't know. It's not my car. I'm borrowing it. It came with the house I'm staying in. I haven't been driving it long. And I haven't gone very far." His discomfiture gained strength.

The woman proceeded to use a wrench of some sort to pry off a black piece of plastic. Her confidence and grace put Anthony in mind of the guy who worked the oyster bar at Island Creek in Boston. "Yup," she said, pointing. "It's your timing belt." She rummaged around inside the engine and held up a piece of broken rubber. "Broke right in half. Must've been ticking for a while? You had some oil coming out of the motor, maybe? Those were all warning signs."

Had there been oil coming out of the motor? Anthony strained to remember. "Like I said, it's not my car. So I don't know."

"Hop in." The woman gestured toward the Jeep. "I'll run you wherever you're going. This car isn't going anywhere until it gets a new belt." She closed the hood and peered at the front of the car. "What is it, anyway? A '95?"

"I don't know," Anthony said. He hadn't thought to wonder about that. He'd just thought: *Old.*

She tapped the hood. "Well, that's what I'd guess. A '95. Give or take. We'll give Bob Herbert a call, have him tow this to his shop." She gestured toward the passenger door, and Anthony climbed inside. The dog reclined toward him affably, its head hooking over the passenger seat. Anthony leaned away.

"That's Pickles," said the woman. She pushed the dog back by the chest, but the dog sprang forward again in a boomerang motion and licked her ear. She giggled and said, "Oh, *Pickles!*" and rubbed vigorously behind one of the dog's ears.

For heaven's sake, thought Anthony miserably.

"Where are you headed, anyway?" the woman asked, pushing the dog back again (successfully, this time).

"Corn Neck Road."

"I'll get you there on one condition."

"What's that?" He felt wary and on edge, a fox guarding a vast den of secrets. His head ached. It was so hot.

"I want to know why you sent back my drink," she said. "The other day. At Poor People's Pub."

Chapter 13
Joy

"Corn Neck Road," said Joy. "That's my favorite road." It wasn't, actually; her favorite road was Coast Guard Road—one of the most coveted, most private roads on the island—but she wanted to be polite.

"Is it?" said the man.

"It is," she said firmly.

After that, a silence fell, and Joy thought about how she might as well become an Uber driver and make some money for her efforts. The bill from the dairy in Vermont that supplied her with cream had just come due, plus there was the impending rent increase, and the threat of the macaron truck. The fact was that she could probably use the extra income from driving an Uber.

Joy stole small, furtive glances at her passenger. She wondered if he was going to keep his end of the bargain. He was wearing a gray T-shirt, just as he had been the other times she'd seen him. No wedding ring. Finally she said, "Well? The drink? Why'd you return it?"

"I . . ." Long pause.

"It was a really good drink."

"I'm sorry."

"I had to drink mine and the one I sent to you. I had a headache the next day."

"I'm sorry," he repeated.

She glanced again at him and thought he might be blushing. She couldn't remember the last time she'd seen a grown man blush. It was kind of adorable. She wondered briefly if Leo of Dinner by Dad ever blushed; it seemed like just the sort of thing he might do, given the proper circumstances. There was that time when the four-year-old had pulled a can of beans from the bottom row of a bean-can pyramid in the grocery store and that older lady had said that awful thing to him . . .

Her passenger said, "I'm not—I'm not drinking."

It occurred to her that this man might be a recovering alcoholic—after all, Peter said he'd had seltzer at the bar. Joy scolded herself for what might have come across as insensitivity. She'd known plenty of alcoholics in her life: Dustin's mother, her first roommate out of college, half of her mother's extended family. "Did you come here to dry out?"

He coughed. "In a way. Sort of."

"I'm sorry. I'm sorry I tried to tempt you."

But *I'm not drinking* was different from *I don't drink*. *I'm not drinking* implied a past, and maybe also a future. So Joy was intrigued.

"It's okay—it's fine." A moment passed. The silence resumed. The Jeep bumped along. Finally her passenger spoke again. "Thanks for the ride," he said. "I really appreciate it. I didn't know what I was going to do, all the way out there, with a dead phone battery."

"No problem," said Joy. "I was heading this way anyway." This was a lie; she'd been heading to Stevens Cove to walk Pickles, and after that she was going to head back to the shop. Maggie was helping out until eleven a.m., and Joy had told her that after that she was free to go to her mother's helper job.

"Really?"

"Sure." No. Corn Neck Road was about as far from Stevens Cove as you could get and still be on the island. "I'm Joy, by the way. I guess I should have mentioned that." She turned onto West Side Road and gestured toward the back of the Jeep. "And you've already met Pickles."

"Hey, Pickles," said the man cautiously.

"You can pet her. She's really friendly."

"That's okay."

"Not a dog person?"

"No." A pause. "I wanted one, when I was a kid. But I never had one." His face twisted. Then he said, "I noticed your license plate. What's it mean?"

"Oh," she said. "I wanted it to say JOY BOMBS. That's the name of my bakery. Because my name is Joy. But it was too many letters, so I couldn't have the O. I mean, I guess I could have picked another letter to leave out, but the O made the most sense."

"Okay," he said.

After that he said nothing, so Joy waited a beat and asked, "And you are . . . ?"

"Oh. Anthony."

More silence enveloped them: this one seemed deeper, more complicated than the first, and Joy decided not to worry about it and instead spend some time appreciating the view. They were surrounded by farmland now, with the ocean barely a blue slash in the distance.

Joy's thoughts trotted toward dinnertime. Dinner by Dad's last posted recipe had been a broken artichoke heart salad with pasta puttanesca, but she didn't know if she felt up to dealing with artichoke hearts. Maggie had a mature palate and an adventurous attitude; even so, artichokes were a lot of work. But then she thought of what Dinner by Dad always said—a good meal was almost always worth the effort it required—and she'd already bought all of the ingredients. She'd wrangle the artichokes.

Just when it seemed the silence might crack under so much pressure, the man—Anthony—spoke again. "How do you know so much about timing belts?"

Joy flicked on her turn signal, turned onto Center Road. "My dad owns an auto repair shop," she said. "Off-island. My brothers worked in the shop, and in high school I worked the phones, but every now and then they'd let me help out back there."

She felt him hesitate, even bristle. This was common—a man did not like to depend on a woman for car advice, she'd learned that years ago. But clearly he didn't know a broken timing belt from a broken heart.

She forged ahead. "Anyway. Bob Herbert is the best on the island, and he can tow you to his shop. I'll call him for you. But I don't know if he'll have a timing belt for a '95 Le Baron in stock. He might have to get it off-island, order it for delivery. It could be a couple of days." She looked back at the road. They passed a young couple on rental bikes with big wicker baskets bobbing. They wore sunglasses, no helmets, and the girl had blond hair that swung back and forth as she pedaled.

"Just my luck," said Anthony. "Stuck in a place with no timing belts." Joy rolled her eyes. Nobody was *stuck* on Block Island; people, in her opinion, should feel lucky to be here. But just as she'd known plenty of alcoholics in her life, she'd known plenty of people who considered Block Island second-rate. Lesser.

When Joy was a girl, growing up in a crowded three-bedroom apartment in Fall River (one bedroom for her parents, one for her four brothers to share, if you can believe it, and the smallest one for her), she'd craved space more than anything else. Everything was so *crowded* in Fall River—the smells from people's cooking intermingled, cars parked so close to one another that their bumpers kissed, tempers wound around each other like snakes. It never ceased to amaze Joy that here she could look out from every edge of the island and see nothing but land, space, and water. Long ago she had promised herself that she'd never take it for granted, and she never did. "Well," she said, "in the island's defense, a '95 Le Baron is not exactly common these days."

She cut across Old Town Road. Traffic! She should have stayed on West Side the whole way.

Her passenger didn't seem to have heard her last sentence. "What's that line for?" he asked, looking out his window. "Is that a food truck?"

"Oh, come *on*," said Joy. "Are you kidding me?" The line for the Roving Patisserie was even longer than it had been the other day, and she didn't think they were giving out anything for free this time. These were paying customers, wallets at the ready.

"What's it sell?" asked Anthony.

"Nothing," said Joy quickly. "Just some silly . . . promotional thing. Nothing important." But she slowed down, because from the back she thought she saw . . . no, it couldn't be . . . yes, it was. Maggie and Riley, heads tipped close to each other, probably bent over some Instagram video of a kiwi growing inside a banana or something. "No way," she breathed. Maggie was a customer of the Roving Patisserie. Not only that, she'd left Joy Bombs before Joy had given her permission.

"What?" asked Anthony.

Pickles, sensing drama, lifted her ears.

"Nothing," said Joy. She shook her head, hoping to dispel the sight. Maybe she'd imagined it, after all. Then her phone buzzed. She glanced down. Can I eat at Rileys after I babysit. Maggie. She sighed. She looked again at her passenger and thought about the artichokes. Maybe . . .

No, he was potentially abrasive and possibly an island snob. She couldn't.

Then she saw him reach a cautious hand out to pet Pickles. Okay, maybe he was trying. And he had been so sad the last two times she'd seen him. Maybe he was a good guy in a bad situation, a guy who deserved a break.

Her mother said Joy always saw the good in people who didn't deserve it. But didn't that mean she sometimes also saw the good in people who *did*?

She made up her mind. "Are you free for dinner tonight?" she asked. "I'm making a pasta puttanesca with a broken artichoke heart salad. I've already bought the ingredients, and now my daughter isn't going to be home. It's too much for one person, and I wouldn't mind some company. I promise I'm not creepy or pathetic. I just don't like to waste good food."

He eyed her warily at first and she regretted her question almost instantly. How many times did she need to be turned down by a grump in a gray T-shirt before she got the message? But just as she was starting to say, *Never mind, forget it*, his face opened up and he smiled. "Sure," he said. "Sure, that sounds delicious. I'd really like that."

She felt her insides relax. "You would?"

"I would."

"You have a bike?"

"Yes. There's one in the garage of the place I'm staying in."

"Great. You can ride it over. It's not far. Hopefully the bike is in better shape than the car."

"Here's hoping." The smile really did transform his face.

She turned in where her passenger indicated and pulled up the long driveway. The cottage was set back, not far from the water. It was a shabby little place but the location was killer. She could see where a path from the house connected to one of the main trails down to Scotch Beach. "How long are you staying here?" she asked.

"Up in the air," he said.

"I see." This was unusual: most rentals had a start date and an end date. "Are you here alone?"

"Definitely alone," he said. "Most definitely. My wife, ah—she couldn't join me."

Wife. Married. She deflated, recalculated. Maybe it wasn't worth the artichokes after all. Not that she'd been planning to jump him. But it seemed inappropriate, to invite another woman's husband to dinner, a stranger at that. She glanced quickly at his hands. No ring, just as she'd thought. Well, not all men wore them. Dustin hadn't.

"Where's your wife?"

"At home, in Newton."

"I see." She didn't.

"We're— It's complicated." He stopped and wrinkled his nose. Then he said, "I guess we're separated."

"I see," said Joy again, but what she was thinking was, *You guess?* Seemed like being pregnant, or drunk: you either were, or you weren't. She turned off the Jeep. Outside the cottage next door she saw a pretty blond woman getting into a car with two little blond boys. One boy was holding a toy tow truck, driving it through the air. (Joy remembered when Maggie was young enough to drive things through the air—wasn't it only yesterday?)

Then she realized she knew this woman; she'd *met* this woman! This was Lu, the woman who had hired Maggie (away from Joy), and these boys were Maggie's new charges. They were probably going to pick up Maggie now! Maggie had better hurry back to the shop. Go figure, the recovering alcoholic Joy had tried to force a drink on and then picked up by the side of the road was living right next to the woman who was stealing Maggie away from Joy. She sighed and turned her attention back to Anthony. "I'm sorry. I am, really." Separated. That's probably why he'd been crying. "Is this a new situation?"

He nodded. "Very new."

"I've been through it. It's awful, I know. But it gets better, with time. I promise you, it gets better."

"In my case, I don't think it will. For a lot of reasons. But thank you." He opened the door, stepped one foot out. Pickles popped up and over from the backseat, panting. "Are you staying?" he asked.

"*What?* Of course not. Why?" She put her hand on Pickles's chest and gently returned her to the backseat.

"You turned off your car."

"Oh. No, I'm not staying. It's just that we care about the environment here on our island, so we don't idle. Locals don't idle."

He was standing outside the Jeep now. "That would be a good book title," he said. "*Locals Don't Idle.*" He looked pensive.

"I guess," she said. "I'm not much of a reader." Joy pulled a business card out of the Jeep's side-door pocket, wrote something on it, and handed it to him. "My card," she said. "My address is on the back. And now you have my number. In case Bob Herbert has any trouble getting the timing belt. I can always call my dad. Also in case you decide not to come to dinner tonight."

"Why would I decide not to come to dinner? I accepted your invitation."

"I don't know. Sometimes people change their minds." Maggie, for example. Maggie had been planning to eat dinner with Joy, and then she changed her mind.

"I won't," he said. "Thank you for the ride. See you later."

"Sure thing," she said. She started the ignition and watched him walk toward the cottage, crouch down, and remove a house key from underneath a flat rock. She started to turn around, stopped again.

"Hey!" she called. He had the key in the lock; he turned. "Hey. We forgot to do last names. Mine's Sousa."

"Okay," he said. He seemed to be struggling with the key.

She waited. "So, that makes you . . . Anthony what?"

"Oh," he said, looking from the lock back to her. "Anthony What will be fine."

"Why don't you come at seven o'clock for dinner," she said. "Anthony What."

Chapter 14
Lu

Lu was driving Maggie and the boys home from Ball O'Brien Park. After Lu and the boys picked up Maggie outside of Joy Bombs, Maggie had watched the boys on the playground while Lu sat at one of the picnic tables in the pavilion and worked out a new salad dressing. She would test it the following day, when the boys were signed up for a summer program at Nancy's club.

The boys had been entranced by the skaters at the skate park, who looked to be about Maggie's age or maybe a little older: suntanned, shirtless, with the sinewy muscle, the narrow shoulders, the eight-pack abdomens of the athletic prepubescent or just-barely-pubescent male.

"Did you know them?" Lu asked Maggie as they left.

Maggie shrugged. "Nope," she said. "Summer kids."

"That must be fun," said Lu. "To have a whole new population of boys come to town for the summer!"

A half smile flashed across Maggie's face, gone as quickly as it had come. "I guess," she acknowledged. "Sort of. Yeah, it can be."

What Lu wouldn't have given for an infusion of fresh summertime blood in her dreary town when she was Maggie's age!

"I'm hungry," said Sebastian, a touch whiny, and Chase echoed him, taking the whining up a notch. Proper lunchtime had come and gone while they were at the park.

"We'll be home soon," Maggie told them, turning toward the backseat. She sounded like a miniature mother, and Lu was very proud of her.

"We could go to Joy Bombs," suggested Lu. She knew whoopie pies weren't exactly a well-balanced lunch, but it would hold the boys over and maybe she could go straight to an early dinner. The day after tomorrow Jeremy would be home, and she wouldn't be able to get away with that. In addition, she could go for a cup of the coffee. It was the best on the island.

"No!" said Maggie. "No, I don't want to." Lu glanced at her, surprised by the vehemence. "It'll be crowded in town," said Maggie.

"Okay," said Lu. "Home, then." Although she couldn't think what she had to feed the boys at home. She'd spent such a long time on her last post, she'd completely forgotten to plan or shop for regular meals. It was the curse of the food blogger, she supposed—like the cobbler's children having no shoes, here were her kids, with empty bellies.

"No!" said Sebastian. He kicked the back of the seat. "I don't want to go home!" He kicked the seat again.

"Sebastian!" cried Lu. "Stop that right now. *Right now.*"

"I want a whoopie pie!" said Chase.

"We could stop at the Roving Patisserie," Maggie ventured.

Lu said, "The what?"

"It's a food truck," said Maggie. "It's new this summer." She took out her phone and tapped on the screen. "Let me just see where it is now. It moves during the day."

"Oh, I get it," said Lu. "It roves. Clever."

"It's at the Southeast Lighthouse," Maggie reported. "That's kind of far away. It already moved once today."

"No problem." Lu readjusted the route, proud that she now knew enough about the geography of the island to figure out the way without asking.

They joined the (considerable!) line at the food truck, and Lu studied the menu. She'd left her notebook in the car, but she wished she hadn't: she wanted to take notes. The Roving Patisserie's menu was sophisticated (salade Niçoise, croque monsieur *and* madame, macarons) and the presentation was cute without being cutesy. The sandwiches came with a toothpick-sized French flag, and the *pommes frites* arrived in tasteful paper cones. "Get whatever you want," she told Maggie, rooting in her bag for her wallet.

A girl came up to them, whom Maggie introduced as her friend Riley. Riley had honey-colored hair wound around her head in a complicated braid. She had wide hazel eyes. She was wearing micro-shorts and flip-flops and a strappy tank top; she clearly held an advanced degree in attention-getting. Maggie, meanwhile, was wearing a shirt that said Fluent in Sarcasm.

"Does your mom know you're here again?" Riley asked Maggie.

"No," said Maggie. Was that a touch of defiance in her voice?

"Oooooh-kay," said Riley. Lu could tell by the way she drew the word out that there was something about the situation Lu wasn't understanding.

"Why wouldn't your mom want you to be here?" Lu asked.

Maggie rolled her eyes. "My mom thinks the truck is taking her business."

Lu glanced behind her—the line had filled in, and was snaking around the parking lot. "Oh!" she said. "Oh. I should have thought of that. I don't blame her. Should we leave?"

"No!" said Chase and Sebastian at the same time. They had their eyes, Lu knew, on the fries.

"No," said Riley, giving Maggie a meaningful look that Lu couldn't interpret. "No, you shouldn't leave."

Maggie set her pretty lips in a straight line. "No," she said. "Definitely not."

As they drew closer to the truck, and after Riley had left to join whoever it was she'd come with, Lu sensed something change in Maggie—a shift in her posture, an almost unnoticeable rise of color in her cheeks that could have been attributed to the summer sun and Maggie's lack of a hat.

Then Lu saw the boy in the truck, taking orders. "*Oh*," she murmured. She understood. This boy wouldn't have been young Lu's type—she'd always gone for the brawnier boys, the football and rugby players—but his hair was adorably floppy, and when he said, "Can I take your order?" his accent was just accent-y enough. He was older than Maggie, and he was French, so therefore he was exotic, and clearly he was bored. For all of these reasons Lu could see the appeal.

"I like your shirt," he said to Maggie, when they finally reached the front of the line.

"Thank you." She broke into a wide grin that made her look at once six years old and twenty-one.

Well, if you were a thirteen-year-old island-reared girl, well, then, yes. This boy. Of course.

"I'll have two orders of *pommes frites*," said Lu. "And a croque madame. And whatever Maggie here is having."

What Maggie seemed to be having was a small anxiety attack. She ordered a Coke and three macarons, and she fumbled in the pocket of her denim shorts.

"Oh, no," said Lu. "My treat."

Maggie shook her head, apparently rendered mute. It was almost funny, except that it was also painful. Lu wanted to cry, *Be careful with your heart!* But she wasn't Maggie's mother. She wasn't exactly her friend. All she could really do was pay for her Coke and her fancy French cookies.

To: dinnerbydad@hotmail.com
From: mississippimom357@gmail.com

Dear Dinner by Dad:

Why don't you have a photo of yourself on your blog? I follow a lot of food blogs and most of them have the blogger's photo! A lot of us moms out here in the blogosphere want to know if you're as adorable as you sound. :)

To: mississippImom357@gmail.com
From: dinnerbydad@hotmail.com

Thanks for writing! I appreciate your mail. For the sake of my kids' privacy, I prefer to remain unseen. You'll notice that although I post plenty of photos of my food I never post family photos. It's part of the deal I made with my amazing wife, Jacqui, when I started the blog. It was important to her, so automatically that means it's important to me. I hope you get a sense of who we are from my charcoal drawings. I also hope I am as adorable as I sound, but it's hard for me to say for sure.

Yours in home cooking,
Dinner by Dad

To: dinnerbydad@hotmail.com
From: kkjohnson4321@me.com

DbD:

I'd love to hear your thoughts on our current president.
I heard he really likes his ice cream! #Twoscoops

—Kate

Dear Kate:

While I wish I could share my political views with
you, I've made a deal with my advertisers and my
very own soul to keep all that stuff off my blog. It's
not that I wouldn't love to talk politics, but I do very
firmly believe that part of the beauty of food is that
it exists so nicely on its own plane (and I don't mean
Air Force One, ha ha ha). I want to keep it that way.
Thanks for reading, and happy food prep!

Dinner by Dad

To: dinnerbydad@hotmail.com
From: ophie167@microinvestments.com

Dear Dinner by Dad,

I just picked up my CSA share and these goddamn vegetables are coming out of my ears. What do I do??

—Ophelia

Dear Ophelia,

Can we all say what we really think about CSAs? Yes? No? Okay, I'll say it for us. We feel really freaking good about ourselves when we're signing up for them and really freaking bad about ourselves when we're watching a bunch of kale die a slow death in the back of the bottom fridge shelf, behind the hummus.

First of all, throw that shit away. It's not going to get less wilted as time goes on. Nobody is looking. I promise. Go ahead.

There. Feel better? Me too.

Second, Just because your neighbor and three ladies from your book club are going gaga over the CSA pamphlet doesn't mean you have to too. If you want to sign up? Go right ahead. But if you don't, don't sweat it. Cooking shouldn't be about that. Go to a farm stand when you need something fresh and local. Get what you need from the grocery store if that's easier. This is a judgment-free zone.

That said, pickling is a perfect way to use up those veggies in a way that makes them last and last. And it can be the perfect way to introduce your little ones to preserving fresh food. In addition, the fermenting process brings some super-healthy bacteria to your food and your gut. Now that you've brought up this idea, I'm going to plan some pickling. Please stay tuned, and thank you, Ophelia!

Dinner by Dad

To: dinnerbydad@hotmail.com
From: mommieslittlehelper2@interlink.net

Dear Dinner by Dad,

I love how you write about your wife and your boys. I hope they know how lucky they are to have you. Even so, I wish you were single! Hey, if things ever don't work out between you and Jacqui just PM me . . .

Anon in Alabama

Dear Anon,

I'm flattered. Truly, I am. I consider myself the lucki-
est man on the planet, and I wouldn't jeopardize
my family for anything. But thank you for the kind
words, and keep on cooking!

Dinner by Dad

To: dinnerbydad@hotmail.com
From: dancerlaur2020@aol.com

Dear DbD:

How do you stay so cheerful all of the time? Don't
you ever feel like throwing in the towel? The dish-
towel, that is. I do.

—Lauren

Dear Lauren:

Abso. Freaking. Lutely. Sometimes being at home is
hard. The average toddler cries between four and
six times a day. Dishes SUCK. Always: they always
suck, I don't care who you are. It takes forty-five
minutes to make a meal and four seconds for a kid
to throw it on the floor. I get it! Just yesterday, the
dog threw up, the coffeepot exploded, and Charlie

fell off his skateboard and opened up a crater in his knee. I almost lost it. I haven't ended the day with a clean shirt since Britney had a song on the Billboard 100. But I'm here for you, readers, and we can all be here for each other. Let's make this work. Let's make some food.

DbD

Chapter 15
Anthony

"Anthony Puckett! Huxley Wilder here."

This was his agent, who, once the nitty-gritty details had been dealt with, had commenced dropping Anthony like everyone else in his life had dropped him. There was something so . . . well, so *unaccidental* about Anthony's misfortune. It really stopped people in their tracks. He hadn't fallen ill or lost a parent, he hadn't been summarily fired, his house hadn't burned down, he didn't even have anything as interesting as a drug addiction that might have been discovered to be chemical in nature. He had simply been dishonest. He had cheated. He had stolen.

"Huxley!" Anthony said. "Great to hear from you." It *was* great to hear from Huxley, especially after the thing with the car earlier that day. He had thought he was stranded before, just by virtue of being on an island, but now, with the Le Baron temporarily out of commission, the word *stranded* took on a new meaning. Hearing Huxley's voice, which had its very own swagger to it, something vaguely Clint-Eastwood-meets-Harrison-Ford-meets-Bryan-Cranston, gave Anthony a brief flash of hope. Maybe all was not lost. Maybe Huxley had some good news for him. Maybe the publisher had had a change of heart.

"Yeaaaah," said Huxley throatily. "Maybe not so great. So listen, buddy." Huxley and Anthony were close to the same age. How had Huxley earned the right to "buddy" him? *Buddy* was what a father was supposed to call a son. It was what Anthony called Max. Last Anthony had checked, Huxley Wilder was not his father.

"I'm listening," Anthony said warily.

"What do you want first? The bad news, or the bad news?"

"Just give it to me straight," said Anthony. "Please, Huxley." Anthony was sitting at the little formal table in Fitzy's uncle's living room, his bare feet on the ornate carpet. He stared at the decanter, the two glasses sitting next to it. "You're making me nervous."

"You probably should be nervous. There's been a miscalculation."

"A what?"

"We owe more to the foreign rights agent. They miscalculated."

"They *what*?"

"They miscalculated, something about the advance from Turkey, I don't know how it happened, but anyway I had to cut them a check for twenty grand today, which means *you* have to cut *me* a check for twenty grand."

"Shit, Huxley." Anthony stared hard at the piano. IVERS & POND, it said. BOSTON. Who was Ivers, who was Pond? Anthony sighed and stood and walked over. He hit one of the keys. The piano let out a weary, malnourished plink.

"What's that noise?" asked Huxley. "What are you doing?"

"Just tickling the ol' ivories," said Anthony morosely.

"The what?"

"Never mind."

"Where you hiding out, anyway?"

"Who says I'm hiding?"

"Word on the street," said Huxley. "I ran into Shelly Salazar the other day when I was at lunch with an author."

Both the word *lunch* and the word *author* hit Anthony where it hurt. *He* used to eat lunch; *he* used to be the author. He wondered what bright young thing had taken his place, but was too proud to ask.

"If you must know . . ." said Anthony, "I'm in an undisclosed location."

"Oh, come on, now."

"I'm in a cottage where time stopped in the 1820s."

"Ha!" said Huxley. "Ha, ha!" The sudden, barking laugh startled Anthony like a gunshot. "Very funny."

"I'm not joking, exactly," said Anthony.

"The Old West?"

"Something like that. The Old East."

"Well, wherever you are, I hope you've brought your checkbook. I'll need it by September first."

It didn't cost Anthony anything at all, not a penny, to hit the end button and bring the call to a stop. Huxley might have been in mid-sentence; hell, he might have been in mid-word! Anthony would never know.

Outside the window the beach grasses were dancing up a storm. Personification. Also: cliché. *Whoosh, whoosh, whoosh.* Onomatopoeia. How far he had fallen. Once he had been "a young master of both plot and human emotions" (*Kirkus*, starred) and "a writer not only to watch, but one to savor, word by word" (*Publishers Weekly*, starred) and even "simply put:

simply stunning" (*The Washington Post*). Now he was a recreational grammarian.

Anthony took two steps toward the decanter on the sideboard with its mysterious golden liquor. Brandy? Sherry? Nectar of the gods? The two glasses set out beside it looked so inviting, so much more inviting than just one would have looked. He supposed this was why staging by realtors was so effective.

He couldn't cut Huxley a check for twenty grand, because he didn't *have* twenty grand. Was this the time to fall on the mercy of his parents? His mother might give it to him; his father might not. He dialed his parents' number, and when his mother answered he said, "Mom, hey."

"Anthony!" his mother said. "I'm so happy to hear from you. How are things in . . . where are you again?"

"Block Island," he said. "And things are, well . . ." He couldn't get it out. His parents were swimming in money, practically drowning in it, and yet he couldn't say the three simple words: *I need money.* "Not so good."

"Anthony?" said Dorothy. "Send me an address. I'll be there tomorrow. I'll bring lasagna!"

"No, Mom," said Anthony. "Thank you, but . . . no. I don't need any lasagna."

"It might be good for us to spend some time together. There is something I've been meaning to talk to you about. For a long time, really." There was a pause. "It's about your father. In a way."

"About *Dad*? Is he sick?"

"Sick? No! Of course, the doctor is keeping an eye on his blood pressure, always, because of that nasty family history, but, no—nothing like that." She cleared her throat. "Maybe this matter *is* better discussed in person. Maybe I should come there."

Anthony closed his eyes. "No, Mom. I'm really not ready for visitors. I'm sort of . . ." He glanced at the decanter again. *Rehabbing* wasn't the right word. Recovering? Re-something? He glanced at the clock. Nearly six-thirty, and he had to unearth the bike from the garage and stop by the grocery store for something to bring too. The last thing he felt like doing was eating some sort of pasta with a stranger. But he had said he'd be there, and it seemed like the least he could do was not let someone else down.

"Mom?" he said. "I have to go. I've actually got somewhere I need to be."

"Well, imagine that!" said Dorothy. "A social life already!"

"It's not exact—"

His mother interrupted him. "Off you go, then, my tale will keep for another day."

He would get a bottle of wine for his hostess—a Sauvignon Blanc, maybe, or a Sancerre—and, as much as he'd want to partake, a bottle of Perrier for himself. For just one evening he'd pretend to be a regular guy with an almost-ex-wife and no kids.

So tonight he'd eat the artichokes—he'd choke them down if he had to. He'd sip a seltzer, make polite conversation, and he'd begin the long process of clawing himself back to humanity.

Chapter 16
Joy

It had seemed like a harmless idea at the time—invite someone new to dinner—but now, released from the confines of the Jeep and faced with the realities of a stranger (and a man, and a nice-looking man, at that!) in her home, eating at her table, Joy began to feel very nervous.

She'd read Dinner by Dad's blog post three times, smiling each read-through over his story of the origins of puttanesca sauce as a favorite of long-ago prostitutes who used the aroma to lure in customers. (*Not a story for the kids!* Leo had said with an electronic chuckle, and Joy imagined Leo sitting at his computer, shaking with private mirth.) She carved out the artichokes ahead of time, obviously, because who wanted to do that in front of guests, and by the time the doorbell rang she had the sauce simmering on the stove and the artichoke hearts boiling companionably on the burner next to them. The rest of the ingredients were prepped, sliced, whisked, measured, and awaiting their turn.

But she was nervous about being alone with a man. That was understandable. Wasn't it? He didn't *seem* murdery but maybe he was. Maybe she shouldn't have invited him to her house. As an extra precaution, she texted Holly: If you don't hear from me by 10 p.m. please come by and check on me.

Holly texted back, ??

The wine he brought was a Sancerre, a good one, and although she felt funny opening it for just herself she didn't feel funny enough *not* to do it, so she poured a healthy glass. Then she poured Anthony a glass of the seltzer he had brought and sliced up a lemon to go along with it.

The elements of the meal came together beautifully, if she did say so herself. (She did.) The artichoke hearts were tender and flavorful and the puttanesca had just the right amount of zing to it.

And the conversation came together almost as well as the meal!

Anthony was a freelance journalist. He'd told her his last name: he was Anthony Jones, not Anthony What. His marriage had been brief, the split fairly amicable, although he preferred not to talk in depth about it. His wife had cheated on him. "Not much to tell," he said, shrugging. "It's the oldest story in the world. And *this*"—he pointed with his fork at his plate—"is the best meal I've had in months. Maybe years."

She smiled. "Just wait until dessert," she said. She'd made a simple banana chocolate bread pudding with mint crème anglaise. This was not a Dinner by Dad recipe, because, as any avid reader knew, Sammy, the younger of the two boys, did *not* like bananas. (Oh, how Leo lamented that fact; bananas were so easy, and so portable.)

"You have parents, don't you?" she asked. "What are they like? What do they do?"

He hesitated and said, "My father is an . . . an entrepreneur."

"Oh!" she said. "That sounds interesting. In what area?"

"It's hard to explain."

"Try me."

"It's . . . sort of complicated. And boring."

"Ah. Technology?"

"Of a sort."

"What about your mother?"

"My mom keeps up the house. She brings my dad a scotch every night at five o'clock. He works in a home office most of the time. My mom never . . . had to work. Never wanted to work, I guess?"

"How old-fashioned," Joy said. Then, because it felt like a judgment (privately it was), she added, "And sort of adorable." She didn't really believe that.

He stiffened and said, "Depends on how you look at it. But that's enough about me. Tell me about yourself."

Maybe it was the wine, or maybe it was the fact that nobody had asked her about herself for a long time, but Joy found herself opening up like a properly steamed mussel. She told him about her business, and about the very real threat posed by the Roving Patisserie. She told him, because he asked, about her divorce. She told him that she had been twenty-six years old, the mother of a two-year-old, married to a guy who truly thought he was Kurt Cobain without the mental illness, when Dustin had come to her one day and said, "I'm out."

"Just like that?" said Anthony, appropriately horrified.

"Just like that," she confirmed. "He said that he really needed to focus on the band, if he was going to get anywhere."

"And did he? Get anywhere?"

"*No.* That's the worst part, or maybe the best part. Of *course* he realized it was never going to happen. Of course he grew up. Of *course* he got a regular job, with health insurance and a 401(k). And when he got remarried, of course he did it better the second time around. He was more ready for it. I mean, we were so young! Just kids."

She kept going. There was more to say!

She talked about her parents and her grandmother, the late, great Fionnula, and about her four brothers and their wives. All of her brothers had married their high school girlfriends, and all of Joy's sisters-in-law still teased their hair the way they had in high school and vacationed for one week each summer on Cape Cod. They favored deep and unhealthy tans, had no problem fighting with their husbands or children in public, and would fall on their swords for any member of their family. The sisters-in-law didn't understand Joy at all, she told Anthony. Who would move so far from family? Who would get a *divorce*? Who would let themselves become a single mother?

"I guess I'm sort of the lone sheep," Joy said. That wasn't quite right. "The black wolf." She was mixing her animal metaphors. She blamed that on the Sancerre.

She told him about the first time she took the ferry to Block Island with Maggie to start their new life. She couldn't work out how to back the car onto the ramp. Everybody else seemed to know how to do it perfectly and she was holding up the other cars. She'd started crying, and a ferry worker had said, "Hey, miss, step out of the car. Let me do it for you."

"I'm not even sure I should go!" she'd sobbed. In the car in front of her a middle-aged man poked his head out the window to see what the holdup was. If he hadn't been blocking her way she would have driven off the ferry, back to Fall River.

The ferry worker couldn't have been more than eighteen, with wide, white cheeks and an official Block Island Ferry hat and the loveliest green eyes. "Of course you should go," he said. "Why wouldn't you? You bought your ticket, didn't you? Come on out, come around, and sit in the passenger seat so your girl doesn't get scared. I'll back you up." Thinking about it now, Joy could have cried. "The kindness of strangers, I guess." The Sancerre was half gone already. The edges of the evening were going from softly blurred to downright out of focus. She said, "Are you *sure* you don't want a small glass?" She pointed at the bottle.

He was sure.

A pall fell briefly over the evening when Maggie called to ask permission to stay overnight at Riley's. Joy walked into the other room to take the call. "You just spent the night there last night . . . oh, okay, yup, sure, no, I get it." She tried not to let her deflation show in her voice. *Don't act desperate around your child*, she reminded herself. *Desperation makes you pathetic, and teens can smell pathetic for miles.* Even so, she was astonished by how quickly the tears sprang to her eyes when she thought about Maggie sitting on the couch with Holly and Holly's husband, Brent, and Riley, watching a movie, perhaps passing a bowl of popcorn back and forth, laughing at the funny parts the way Joy supposed all nuclear families did.

In reality, of course, she figured that Riley and Maggie were in Riley's room with their phones, Snapchatting the summer kids, or out for ice cream at Mia's Gelateria, or just wandering downtown like a couple of hooligans, looking for some excitement. Joy had done the same sort of thing when she was young, and admittedly the streets she had wandered had been far more dangerous than these.

She returned to the kitchen, feeling prematurely alone.

"Sorry," she said. "Just my daughter." While she'd been gone Anthony had rinsed their dinner plates and stacked them by the sink. A tear leaked out and she turned away. Wine did tend to make her weepy, and she'd had a lot, but no need to turn her heart inside out in front of her dinner guest. Hopefully he wouldn't notice the tear.

"Hey," Anthony said. "Hey, hey. Everything okay?" Anthony wiped at the tear with his thumb. Instantly a charge went through Joy's body. *Wow*, she thought. *Wow.*

After that there was a new energy to the evening, Joy was sure of it. Over dessert, which they ate at the small kitchen counter, Anthony's bicep pressed close to hers, and neither of them moved away.

She drank more of the wine. She thought of Mrs. Simmons saying that Joy would be alone forever. The skin on her face felt very alive where Anthony had touched her. She thought, *Can something like that happen this fast?*

She thought, *No way.*

She thought, *But maybe.*

After dessert, Anthony declined Joy's offer of coffee. He said he'd better be getting on his way. Joy wondered if he meant that to be code for, *Do you feel it too?* She hadn't said that Maggie wouldn't be home, but the knowledge definitely opened up options.

"Okay," said Joy. She meant that to be code for, *Yes, I definitely feel it.* She stood. The air was positively singing with possibility. She leaned in and closed her eyes.

She met empty air.

Anthony let three of his fingers fall against her cheek. He whispered, "I can't. I'm sorry." Joy's eyes flew open. "The dinner was amazing," he said. There was something complicated in his eyes, something inscrutable.

"I understand," said Joy. That was code for, *I don't understand at all. I am humiliated but I am going to play it off.*

Well, thought Joy, *that's that.*

She packed the leftovers into Tupperware and stacked them in the fridge. She texted Holly to let her know that she wasn't murdered. She poured just the teensiest bit more wine into her glass—why not?—and drank it standing up, shocked that she could have misread the signs so completely. She could blame part of it on the wine, but really, couldn't she put some blame on her own inexperience? Why had she gone on and on about her sisters-in-law? Why had she made a dish that prostitutes used in order to lure in customers? Why had she had so much Sancerre?

And why did she care? *You don't need a man,* she reminded herself. *You are a strong and independent woman, a business owner who scratched out her own living on island soil, and who will continue to do so, no matter what the Roving Patisserie is up to. They are fleeting, and you are for real, forever. You don't need anyone! You just need Maggie and Pickles and Joy Bombs. It's the four of you against the world.*

When the doorbell rang ninety minutes later Joy had already brushed her teeth, walked Pickles, spoken to Maggie on the phone to say good night, set her alarm for the morning, put her hair in its messy evening bun, paid the electric bill, and cleaned out some old food from the refrigerator. She was trying not to miss Maggie too much but, really, the silence when she was gone was deafening. Thank goodness there was nothing for teens to do on the island in the winter—once October came, she'd have Maggie back to herself.

"Oh, for the love of Pete, Pickles," she said. "Who could that be?" Maybe it was Holly, with more wine. Maybe it was Maggie—she'd changed her mind, she wanted to sleep at home (bless!). She opened the door. And there, on her doorstep, wearing the same gray T-shirt and a sheepish expression, was Anthony Jones.

"Hey," he said softly. "I came back."

"You came back." She held the door open, and he stepped inside. Joy reached for her messy evening bun and released her hair. Her heart was beating very, very fast. Her cheeks felt warm. "I thought you couldn't," she said.

"I didn't think I could." His face was so close to hers. He had brushed his teeth: she smelled mint.

"But now you can?" She was whispering.

He nodded. "I regretted saying that. And I realized that I actually can." He put his thumb on her cheek again. Something about that thumb.

It was hard to say, after that, who kissed whom first. Did it matter?

Pickles sighed and flopped onto the floor, turning her face away, giving them privacy, which Joy appreciated, because it had been a long time, and she was worried she was a little rusty, and she certainly didn't need an audience.

Chapter 17
Anthony

Anthony awoke once in the night to a cacophony outside an open window. He lay there for a moment, confused. This wasn't Fitzy's uncle's cottage; this wasn't the four-poster bed. This wasn't the quiet and isolation of Corn Neck Road. Then he remembered the artichoke hearts, and the banana bread pudding, and quite soon after that he remembered his own fractured heart, which he could feel opening and turning toward the light, like a heliotropic flower.

There was a throb of disco music from down the street. Outside the open window a drunken fight was playing itself out.

A girl: "You did *too*, Sully, you did *fucking too!*"

The answering voice (presumably Sully): "Come on, Mariah, why you gotta go and do that? Why you gotta do it every time . . ."

The voices faded; Sully and Mariah went on their un-merry way.

He thought, *Is this really happening? Am I really here?* He felt in the darkness for the body next to him. He thought, *Joy.* He turned on his side and fell into a sleep like he hadn't experienced in months, since before Huxley Wilder called him to tell him about Anonymous Source.

Sometime after dawn there was a shifting on the mattress, a kiss on his forehead. He said, "Whaa?"

"Shhh," said the voice of an angel. "Shhh, back to sleep."

Hours later, he awoke again. He was alone. His limbs were heavy after so much sleep. He felt clearheaded and wonderful, as though his brain had been infused with some magical elixir.

In the kitchen, Pickles was sitting politely, wearing an inquisitive, slightly reserved expression. Anthony reached out a cautious hand. Pickles licked it. Anthony fought the urge to pull away, and Pickles stopped licking and lay on the floor near Anthony. She sighed, possibly with contentment.

There was a note on the counter, along with instructions on how to work the French press.

I'm at the shop. Get yourself out of here by noon. Take this note with you, or eat it. And make the bed if you don't mind, Maggie'll know something is up if it's not made.

Anthony looked at the clock on the microwave: ten-thirty. He didn't want to leave.

He let his eyes roam around the kitchen, taking in the cabinets with paint peeling in the corners, the dings in the cheap metal sink, the slightly tilted floor. If Anthony were still a writer, this would be a home he'd love to describe.

The cottage was not fancy, but it was tidy and well kept, he would have written, *with a large window in the front room, out of which he could just see a slice of the cobalt sea.*

He couldn't really see a slice of the sea; he was employing poetic license. Was *cobalt* being generous? This was New England, after all. But Block Island's water *was* very blue, in a non-New-England-like way.

His phone rang: his mother's number showed on the screen. He'd call his mother back. Later, he'd call

Cassie, again, ask to speak to Max (again). But just at that moment he didn't want to talk to anyone. He was experiencing a sensation that had not visited him in so long that it took him some time to put a name to it.

Contentment.

He thought, *Plot twist*, and turned off his phone.

Chapter 18
Lu

www.DinnerByDad.com

Stay tuned, folks, because in the next few days we're going to get serious about pickling (s/o to Ophelia). We're going to do the obvious and pickle cucumbers. We're going to pickle onions and carrots and peppers and we're even going to pickle peaches. We're going to talk expensive vinegars and how not to overheat your pickling liquid and why pickling is a fantastic activity to do with kids, and I'll share some stories about my first pickling experience with Charlie and Sammy. We're going to talk about why splurging on one bottle of Huilerie Beaujolaise Vinaigre de Citron might just make your life better. The only thing we're going to stay away from, readers, is asparagus. Some things just aren't meant to be pickled!

Lu was starting to feel excited. She'd never pickled anything before! And why not start now? She was already imagining the antics the fictional Charlie and Sammy would get up to with the vinegar, and the photos she'd take of their labeled mason jars. Maybe she'd even have her own real live kids decorate their own real live mason jars, and she'd photograph those. Jeremy might be happy when he returned from the hospital and saw the fruits of their labor. The vegetables of their labor, more accurately. Jeremy loved pickles. He always scarfed down the pickled radishes at the sushi restaurant, and he piled bread-and-butters high on his hamburgers.

Maggie couldn't come today because her mother needed her in the shop. But, stroke of luck, Lu had spotted a sign for a one-day, four-hour camp at the club on Corn Neck Road. (Nancy and Henry were members.) She'd dropped Chase and Sebastian off at nine. They were going to learn to clam!

She spent some time reading other food bloggers' pickling posts. You could pickle with or without sugar; you could pickle with high-end vinegar or good old inexpensive white vinegar, the kind Lu bought in giant jugs in case she had to build a last-minute volcano with baking soda. Lu wanted to be able to report to her readers if it really did make a difference. Would they have high-end vinegar on Block Island? She wasn't sure. But if she found it, she could set up an experiment, try a few of the veggies with the cheap stuff, a few with the expensive stuff.

When Jeremy came home next, he could do a taste test! Blindfolded, because all of the best taste tests were, and Leo could write about Jacqui doing the taste test after work one night. He'd feed the different options to her, forkful by forkful, which wasn't quite as sexy as feeding a woman strawberries by hand, washed down with champagne, but it might be enough to get the more romantically deprived of her readers a little bit excited.

Shower, and then shop for vinegar, or the other way around? She was standing in the middle of the kitchen, weighing the pros and cons of each, when she heard a car drive up. She hightailed it to the bedroom, which offered a clandestine view of the driveway.

Shit shit shit shit shit. Nancy was descending from her beautifully maintained silver Cadillac coupe (the Cadillac of Cadillacs). She was wearing, on this summer morning, which was already hot and humid, a tan pencil skirt, a smooth light yellow blouse, and a pair of dark green pumps. Pumps! Dark green! On an island! In summer!

Could Lu pretend not to be home? No, her own car was in the driveway; there was no escaping. If only they had a dog, she could pretend to have been walking it. Was it too late to procure a dog? Could she walk Sebastian's hamster, which had traveled all the way from Connecticut with them?

The doorbell rang once, then twice. When it rang a third time—this time Nancy was depressing the button for several seconds, obviously *making a point*—Lu descended the stairs and opened the door.

Her mother-in-law looked surprised to find Lu there, although who else would she have been expecting? "Hi, Nancy," Lu said, stepping aside and ushering Nancy in. She kept her voice noncommittal, easygoing, at an appropriate level of polite daughter-in-law-ness. She was the picture of a woman not a bit bothered by being disturbed on a summer morning.

"I hope I'm not interrupting anything." Even though, of course, she wasn't wearing gloves, Nancy somehow gave the impression of whisking them off. "Is Jeremy at the hospital through the weekend?"

"He is!" Where else would he be? "He had to stay longer than he thought."

"I don't know how he does it," sighed Nancy. "All those hours, working so hard."

"I know how he does it," said Lu. "He has a wife." She hadn't meant to say that out loud.

"Well," said Nancy. "Yes. But you don't see his patients for him, do you? You don't perform his surgeries?"

Lu thought, *Everything but!* She chortled gently and said, "No, of course not." Then, because she had the impression that this was what Nancy wanted, she added, "I could never."

Nancy nodded crisply and made her way, uninvited, to the kitchen, while Lu followed behind, explaining apologetically that the boys weren't home because of the clamming camp. Too late Lu saw that she'd gotten so caught up in the pickling plans that she'd forgotten to clean up after breakfast; she watched Nancy take in the constellation of morning toast crumbs, the Rorschach blot of orange juice. Under Chase's stool, she could be certain, was an entire meal's worth of surrendered cereal bits. She pictured them being carried off by an army of industrious ants. *Look what we've found*, one ant would say to another. *Look at this, it's a goddamn gold mine!* And then they'd motion to all of the other ants to join them.

Lu swiped as many of the crumbs as she could into the sink without being too obvious about it. "Would you like some coffee?" she asked Nancy.

"I had mine hours ago." Nancy was a competitively early riser.

"Me too," said Lu. "But I'm going to have more."

"I suppose I could have another."

Lu made herself busy with the coffee maker. She couldn't bear to be idle in front of Nancy; it made her feel naked.

"Were you . . . exercising?" Nancy took in Lu's apparel. "While the boys were gone?"

"I was," said Lu untruthfully. "Yes." She pretended to wipe some sweat off of her forehead. "Just got back, in fact. Spinning. Really tough class." She shook her head as though she could scarcely believe it, how tough it had been. "One of the teachers here . . . man, oh, man . . ." She let her voice trail off and she looked into the middle distance. Her legs positively ached with the memory of that class. "Tommy, his name is."

Lu had been fourth in her class at Stanford Law. How she'd loved the *gleamingness* of the Stanford campus, the umbrellaed tables set out in Crocker Garden, the *thinking* that went on. Advanced Supreme Court Litigation, American Legal History, 21st Century Skills and Practice Management: she'd loved it all. Later, when she was working, she'd loved wearing suits every day, heels, ticking her way down the hall at the firm, her mind ticking too, keeping up with her heels. She'd never minded the long hours. She'd thrived on them. And now an imaginary spin class made her tired.

"I was thinking of doing some pickling," Lu said.

Nancy sniffed. "*Why?*"

"I thought it might be fun. I thought it might be something I could do with the boys when they get home this afternoon."

"It sounds messy," said Nancy.

"I don't mind a little mess."

Lu watched Nancy's eyes roam around the kitchen. "No," Nancy said finally. "I guess you don't."

Lu had to get Nancy out of here. She peered at the clock on the microwave and feigned shock. "I'm so sorry!" she said. "Is that the time? I need to jump in the shower."

"Now? I've only just arrived. I thought we could visit." Lu wondered if she could use Jessica as an excuse, but surely a lie like that would get back to Nancy.

The coffeepot was gurgling along happily, like it had not a care in the world. Lu was searching her mind for other places she could reasonably pretend to need to be when Nancy asked, "When do you pick them up?"

Lu checked her watch. "One o'clock."

"I could get them."

"Really?" Lu approached this offer with care. She didn't want it to run away, like a frightened animal. "Would you really do that?"

"I would. I'll take them to lunch after. We'll sit somewhere by the water, look at the boats. When Jeremy was a boy he used to love to eat over by New Harbor."

The boys had brought bagged lunches to camp, but Lu wasn't about to divulge that piece of information to Nancy. She hoped the boys wouldn't either. They were growing children: they could eat twice. This would give her at least ninety extra minutes, maybe enough time to shower *and* put on actual clothes *and* buy the vinegar and the vegetables *and* set up the mason jars, so that when the boys got home she'd have the project ready to go.

"That's settled, then," said Nancy. She wiped her hands together as though she were wiping away a problem. "Do you need to call someone at the camp, let them know I'll be collecting them?"

Did she? Lu couldn't remember. "I don't think so," she said.

"Maybe you'd better, just in case."

"Right. You're right. I will." (She wouldn't.)

Lu poured the coffee into two mugs and placed one in front of Nancy. Once they'd had their coffee maybe she could usher Nancy toward the door.

"How are things in the bedroom, Lu?"

Lu choked on her coffee. "I'm sorry?"

"In the bedroom. Between you and Jeremy?"

Lu's face grew hot. Something about Nancy turned her into a compliant child who felt like she had to answer any questions put to her. Her own mother didn't have that effect on her. Nobody else in the world did! It was just Nancy. Once, when Sebastian was a newborn, Nancy had inquired into the specifics of Lu's violent case of mastitis. And Lu had told her!

"They're fine," she said, inaccurately, now. The truth was that Jeremy was so often working, and Lu was so often up in the night with Chase and his vicious nightmares, that they sometimes seemed more like office mates on rotating schedules than like husband and wife. Coworkers.

Nancy nodded her approval. "Good. It's a busy time for you all," she said. "But it goes so fast, the boys are only little once. You blink and you miss it."

Lu gritted her teeth. "How come nobody ever says that to a man?" she asked.

"Excuse me?" said Nancy.

"It goes fast for everyone, how come people don't tell the dad that? They tell the mom, always the mom. I have never heard a single person say that to Jeremy." She looked deep into Nancy's eyes and then, without waiting for an answer, she said, "I need to take my shower now. Please, help yourself to more coffee."

Lu ran the shower super-hot and stepped inside, letting the steam engulf her. She had read somewhere that cool water was better for your skin, but hot water felt *so good*, like it was washing away all of the evil parts of her. All the resentment and bad temper and terrible thoughts of wanting to be elsewhere. Leaving her cleansed and motherly, ready to pickle.

When she returned to the kitchen Nancy was, impossibly, still there. She was holding Lu's cell phone.

"Your phone rang," said Nancy. "While you were in the shower."

What Lu thought was, *Please don't tell me you answered it.*

"I answered it," said Nancy.

"You answered it?" Lu tried to convey with her voice what an appallingly inappropriate thing to do this was, but she feared that instead she still came off as the same compliant child, waiting patiently for the grown-ups to tell her the answer. "Who was it?"

"It was a wrong number."

"What do you mean?"

"They were looking for someone named Leo."

Lu's hands got instantly sweaty. "Well, who *was* it?"

Nancy gave Lu a shrewd look. "How should I know? It was a wrong number, and I told them as much."

Later, when she checked her blog email, Lu found this, from aknowles@wla.com.

Dear Leo,

I tried to track you down by phone but it was a #fail. Whoops! My name is Abigail Knowles, and I am a new agent with the Wilder Literary Agency in Manhattan. I'm looking to build my list of clients. I'm a new and VERY BIG fan of your blog, and I think we could put together a fabulous cookbook proposal to shop around. If you are interested in talking more, please respond to this email at your convenience. I know a publisher will *gobble* this idea up, ha ha.

All best,
Abigail

Chapter 19
Anthony

In the afternoon Anthony returned to Joy's house with a bouquet of flowers he'd bought at the farmers' market at Legion Park. It had been a heck of a bike ride out there, but worth it. The flowers were stunning. He planned to deliver them with an apology. He'd let Joy do more of the talking the night before, and he hadn't been completely truthful about his own background. He hadn't been honest about his father. He hadn't mentioned his son. He hadn't expected to fall for her! He hadn't expected to sleep with her! But sometime during the night the universe had reordered itself. Everything was different now.

He rang the doorbell: no answer. Gingerly he tried the knob, which gave way immediately. He could just sneak inside and leave the flowers in the kitchen. From inside the house he could hear strains of the *Hamilton* soundtrack: "The Room Where It Happens." He closed the door again—the house wasn't empty. He rang the doorbell again.

Back when his star was on the rise he and Cassie had second-row seats to *Hamilton*; he loved that song.

A girl opened the door. She had a purple streak in her hair and green gum in her mouth. She was wearing a T-shirt that depicted an ear of corn and said I Know It's Corny But You Are AMAIZEing. She tilted her head at Anthony and said, "Are you a robber?"

"No," Anthony said. "No, I'm not a robber. I come in peace. I'm a friend of your mom's. You must be Maggie." Joy's genes had to be pretty strong, the Navy SEALs of genes, because her daughter was basically a carbon copy of her.

The girl looked at him quizzically.

"Hold up," she said. From the pocket of her jean shorts she produced an iPhone. Without asking, she took his photo. "I'm just texting your picture to my mom," she said. She waited, then her phone dinged. "Okay," she said. "She verified that you're not a robber. Come in, so Pickles doesn't run out the door." Anthony hadn't noticed that Pickles had appeared, panting and smiling. He entered the cottage and held out his hand. Pickles licked it. Apparently this was their new routine. If so, he could dig it.

"We're acquainted," he told Maggie. Pickles moved her head—was the dog *nodding*?

Anthony shook the flowers a little bit and held them out to Maggie. "These are for your mom."

Maggie considered him, then took the flowers and placed them on the counter, then jumped so she was sitting on the counter. It was a look that wasn't quite a scowl but it wasn't quite a smile either—it lived somewhere in between, in the netherworld of human expression.

His editor would strike that last sentence. Chronic bestsellers were carried on the back of snappy dialogue and plot. Just ask Leonard Puckett. *Write like you have a knife to your throat*, Leonard Puckett was fond of saying.

Don't be silly, Anthony. You don't have an editor anymore.

"Did she say anything else?" he asked. "Your mom?"

Maggie studied Anthony and blew a green bubble. He thought it was going to pop all over her face but she had a nifty trick, allowing it to deflate quietly so she could suck it back into her mouth and begin the whole process over again. "Nope," she said. "She didn't."

She watched Anthony implacably.

"Nothing at all?" He felt a little part of him begin to wither and wilt.

"She was busy, at work."

Joy's soft hair, Joy's collarbone. The rest of it—oh, the rest of it! The things he'd done, the things he still wanted to do.

"All right, then. I'll catch her later." Anthony gestured toward the flowers on the counter. "You should probably put those in water." He'd almost said *we* but he caught himself. Seemed too familiar, too presumptuous.

"I'm on it," said Maggie authoritatively. She hopped down from the counter and scooped up the bouquet.

"I think there's a little packet of flower food tucked inside there." Early in their marriage Anthony had brought Cassie a fresh bouquet of roses every Friday evening; he knew his way around the care and feeding of flowers. He'd stopped once Cassie started sleeping with Glen Manning. Or maybe it was the other way around. Maybe Cassie had started sleeping with Glen Manning because Anthony had stopped bringing her roses.

But Maggie was way ahead of him. She was already cutting open the packet and dissolving it in a vase full of water. "Got it," she said.

"Okay, then," he said. "Bye, Maggie. Bye, Pickles."

The former writer reluctantly left the house. And the lovely child with the purple streak in her hair turned the music back up and didn't give him a second look.

As he was un-leaning his bike from the gate that separated Joy's tiny yard from her neighbor's, his phone rang. He thought, *Joy!* He answered without looking. But it was his mother.

"You never called me back, Anthony. I thought we were going to talk."

"I'm sorry, Mom. What did you want to talk about?" He stuck his phone between his shoulder and ear and began to walk his bike.

"Your father started his book tour," Dorothy said. "He's in Madison, Connecticut. RJ Julia." When Anthony was young, some of his favorite times were when his father was on book tour, and it was just the two of them in the house, him and his mother. They ate grilled cheese for dinner and played endless games of Spit and Crazy Eights. The very house seemed to breathe more easily, freed from the confines of Leonard's needs, Leonard's schedule, Leonard's heavy footsteps.

Through the window he could see Maggie dancing and lip-syncing. If he really strained, he could hear the music too—the soundtrack was playing in order,

"Schuyler Defeated" now. An island girl, wise and funny, with an open heart and a purple streak in her hair.

"Mom?" Anthony asked. "Did you have something *specific* you wanted to talk about?" He wouldn't be able to ride a bike and talk on the phone at the same time. But if he told his mother he was about to get on a bike, it would sound like he was on vacation, not in exile, on his own personal Elba.

"I do," she said. "I do have something specific. But it's not a quick thing. If you don't have time now . . . another time."

"Okay," he said. "Another time. Are you sure, Mom?"

"Another time," she repeated. "Soon."

Chapter 20
Lu

Lu read the email that had come through on her blogging service twice before she let herself believe it was true. A literary agent named Abigail Knowles, who worked at an agency in Manhattan called WLA, wanted to talk to Dinner by Dad about putting together a cookbook proposal to shop around to publishers.

I know a publisher will gobble *this idea up*, was the line Lu kept reading over and over again. The big bloggers all had cookbooks. A legitimate cookbook could raise the profile of a food blog exponentially. Abigail Knowles had sent a follow-up email with more detail. She *loved* Dinner by Dad's charcoal drawings of his family. She loved that he was a mystery, but he also was not. She felt like she knew him, like she'd like to have a drink with him at a barbecue, and she was positive zillions of home cooks would feel the same.

"Don't get excited," Lu told herself. You had to be careful with good news—you had to hold it gently, like a glass ornament, or else it might shatter. *Good news is for other people*, Lu's mother used to say grimly. (In her case it was usually true.)

Nancy had taken Chase and Sebastian out for bagels at the Old Post Office Bagel Shop. (In some ways it was turning out to be sometimes quite handy to have a mother-in-law around.) Lu sat outside on the front porch of the cottage for a few minutes, savoring the email, wondering what it would be like to call or text Jeremy and say, *You'll never believe what happened!*

Just then Anthony rode up to the cottage next door on the rickety old bike she'd seen him depart on the evening before. She'd wondered where he was going but she hadn't asked. She hadn't felt cheerful and expansive the day before, because the boys had been cranky and it was hot and she hadn't just gotten enough work done and she hadn't just had an email from an agent in New York. But now she had Abigail Knowles tucked inside her like a present she hadn't opened all the way. Lu called, "Hello! Hi!" waving until Anthony turned in her direction.

Anthony waved back. She couldn't help noticing that he was wearing the same clothes she'd seen him in the day before. He always wore a gray shirt, but the shorts were plaid, and distinctive. In college they'd called this the Walk of Shame, when you returned home the next morning in the same clothes you'd left in. Was Anthony doing the Bike of Shame? Well, good for him if he was.

"What's with the bike?" she called.

He made a face and walked toward her. "Car broke down. Had to get towed." But he didn't look too upset about it. He actually looked pretty happy. He was smiling more openly and more sincerely than she'd seen him do yet. When he smiled that way he looked so familiar—where had she seen his face before?

"You know," she said, "I just can't shake the feeling that I know you from somewhere."

Almost imperceptibly, his smile changed. "I doubt it. I have one of those faces that people think they know. This happens to me all the time. I look like people's uncle or their vet or the guy at the supermarket who gathers up the carts . . ."

"Noooo," she said slowly. "Hang on, I'm really good at this, actually, I just need to concentrate." Ex-boyfriend of one of the girls she lived with after college? Character actor in a Netflix show? Med school friend of Jeremy's? No, no, and no. But wait. "Did you ever work as a bartender?"

He shook his head. "Never."

"Hmmm." She stepped closer and considered his features, squinting the way you might squint at a piece of art. She sighed. "It's driving me crazy. What I feel like is not so much that I've seen you in person before, but that I've seen your picture. In a magazine or something."

"Weird," he said. His smile grew thinner. "I dunno. Listen, it's been great chatting, but I've got to—"

"It was a newspaper!" she cried. "I'm positive it was a newspaper."

He seemed to deflate. The smile disappeared altogether.

"Is that it? Do you write a newspaper column or something?"

She had the sense he was engaged in an internal struggle. Finally he pointed to the two rocking chairs on the porch and said, "Mind if I sit down?"

"Of course not. Please, help yourself." She gestured toward the chairs, and when he was seated she sat in the other one. They both began to rock slowly, like an elderly married couple.

He said, "I'm going to tell you something. But you have to swear you won't tell anyone else."

"Yes!" she said. Someone else with a secret; here was a kindred spirit. "I swear. You saved the life of my child. We are bound together forever."

Chapter 21
Anthony

The New York Times

MacSimon Brown has announced that it is scrapping plans to print 250,000 copies of Anthony Puckett's second novel, *Simon's Rock*, after it was discovered that passages in the book were lifted directly from a little-known novel published in 1951 by the Irish writer Kieran O'Dwyer.

Anthony Puckett, whose debut novel, *A Room Within*, spent thirty-seven weeks on the *New York Times* bestseller list nearly five years ago, was set to release his much-anticipated second novel in June. He is also the author of a book of short stories, *The Temptation of Adam*.

Mr. Puckett is the son of mega-bestselling thriller writer Leonard Puckett, whose novels have been translated into more than forty languages and have sold at least 200 million copies worldwide.

Charles Graydon, head of MacSimon Brown, said in a statement that the company "takes this matter very seriously. We were very much looking forward to the opportunity to promote Mr. Puckett's second novel under our auspices and we are greatly saddened to learn that we will no longer have the opportunity to do so."

Some industry watchers have speculated that the pressure to produce a second book that would sell as well as Mr. Puckett's debut—perhaps propelling Mr. Puckett into the stratosphere currently occupied by his father—placed undue strain on Mr. Puckett and may have factored into his decision to plagiarize. Bestselling debut novels are notoriously difficult to follow up. The author of the 2009 bestseller *The Help*, Kathryn Stockett, was said to be working on her second novel as long ago as 2012, and has yet to publish it.

Others in the publishing industry took a more sanguine approach to the accusations. "I bet if you checked twenty books you'd find that at least six of them contained some sort of plagiarism," said Shelly Salazar, a freelance book publicist based in Manhattan who claims to have worked with several top-selling authors. "Maybe seven. I mean, seriously? *Simon's Rock* is an amazing book. Amazing. And Anthony Puckett wrote almost every word of it himself."

"Some degree of plagiarism ought to be considered part of the publishing process," said Richard Posner, a former judge on the United States Court of Appeals for the Seventh Circuit in Chicago and author of *The Little Book of Plagiarism*. Posner acknowledged that the practice is more rampant in the academic world than in the world of fiction. "Academics are particularly concerned with and prone to plagiarism," said Posner. "It can be difficult to publish in academia without drawing on previously published work." For novelists, the practice of plagiarism is both more unusual and more difficult to refute when discovered, if, as in the case of Mr. Puckett, exact sentences and paragraphs are copied word for word.

In the end, the copied passages add up to a little less than 1,200 words of a 120,000-word book, but that number will prove little help to Mr. Puckett, who, despite numerous attempts, did not return calls seeking comments. The publishing house declined to disclose how much of Mr. Puckett's well-publicized advance, said to be in the two-million-dollar range, the author was asked to return. Thomas P. Campbell, a Manhattan-based attorney who specializes in cases of plagiarism, speculates that MacSimon Brown will want to recoup most, if not all, of the advance.

To some in the industry, Puckett's situation recalls that of Kaavya Viswanathan, who, in 2004, as a seventeen-year-old, received an advance reported to be $500,000 for a two-book deal for two young adult novels. When excessive similarities were later found between her work and that of an already published book by Megan McCafferty, her publisher pulled the first book and canceled the contract for the second. Viswanathan claimed that although she had read McCafferty's books, any similarities between the two were subconscious.

The elder Mr. Puckett, whose fifty-ninth novel, *The Thrill of the Chase*, is due out in June, could not be reached for comment. The estate of Mr. O'Dwyer, who died in 1998 in Castlebar, County Mayo, Ireland, also had no comment on the charges. The book in question, *There Comes a Time*, O'Dwyer's fifth and final novel, sold fewer than 5,000 copies worldwide. It is not known how

Mr. Puckett might have become familiar with the work of Mr. O'Dwyer, whose popularity, though considerable at its height, was mainly confined to his native country.

It is also not known publicly how the plagiarism was discovered. Calls to Leonard Puckett's publishing house went unanswered.

Along with the article, they'd published Anthony's author photo, in which he was leaning against a distressed piece of wood, perhaps meant to resemble the wall of an old barn. He was wearing a collared shirt, one button casually open, and he looked smug. In fact, he looked sort of like an asshole. He was *smiling*. Which was fine, of course, for a book jacket photo, but definitely not for a photo to go alongside an article detailing his shame and humiliation. Anthony hadn't even wanted to use that photo on the book jacket. He'd preferred the photo that had appeared on the jacket of *A Room Within*, in which he looked more somber, more literary and pensive. But Cassie had insisted on a new photo; she'd insisted on the smile. "You're a different person now than you were then," she'd said. "You're a star, Anthony! You need to play the part." She'd called his look "approachable."

Looking at the photo now made him feel nauseated. It didn't even help him to write his feelings down in novelistic form, though he tried it anyway. *Anthony Puckett could see right through his stupid fucking Cheshire grin, all the way to the black heart that lay beneath.*

PART 3

July

Chapter 22
Joy

One of Joy's suppliers, who was supposed to send fifty pounds of butter from a Vermont dairy farm, had missed the ferry, and Joy was in a minor panic. An image of Bridezilla loomed; before that wedding, she had several other large orders to fill. She tried to keep her cool with the supplier—she usually built in an extra day on either end for emergencies, the way you had to when you were an islander. But still she was incensed, and she let the manager of the dairy farm know it. Geoffrey Billings, his name was.

"I'll make it up to you, Joy," Geoffrey was saying. "You know we really value your business. I'll see what we can pull together for the very next shipment."

Joy had never met Geoffrey Billings, and when she talked to him on the phone, which she did often, she imagined him in farmer's overalls, freshly emerged from his stool in the milking shed. Of course, all of the milking was done by machines, and Geoffrey was probably sitting in an office, surrounded by invoices and coffee cups and pictures of his grandkids at a swim meet, no more an actual farmer than Joy was.

"And I value your products, Geoff," said Joy. It was true. If you put the word *Vermont* in front of the word *butter*, your pies instantly tasted better. Put *organic* in front of *Vermont*: even better, and they cost more. "But this can't happen again. Not in the summertime."

Sometimes when she heard herself on the phone like this, strict and businesslike, she thought of her father, who had spent most of her childhood chewing out somebody for something—the compressor that didn't arrive, the pipe bender he was overcharged for. It was funny how you could think you were leaving your past behind when part of it always traveled right along with you. A stowaway.

"I'll figure this out, Joy," Geoff said. "Give me ten minutes, I'll call you back."

"Fine. I'll be here for twenty minutes," said Joy sternly and untruthfully. (She was going to be in her office all afternoon.)

Her text noise sounded. She had put on the bird chirp because she thought it would be peaceful and relaxing. But really it was startling. Her startle morphed into a smile when she saw the text was from Anthony. Are you free later today?

She started to text back, What do you have in mind? But tone didn't translate in text, so that might come off as coquettish. Thinking about two nights ago, she actually started to blush. That was the Irish side of her, her mother's legacy—the Portuguese side didn't blush.

The day before, Anthony brought her flowers and left them with Maggie. Dustin had never, ever brought Joy flowers. Not even once. On their wedding day he and two of his band buddies were supposed to stop by the florist to pick up the order Joy's mother had placed and paid for, and even that he couldn't manage. They'd been given a funeral arrangement by mistake and *didn't even notice.*

Invoices, Joy told herself. *While you wait for Geoff Billings to call you back you need to think about invoices. You don't think about Anthony.* Who did she think she was, starting up a relationship with a recently separated stranger? After work she had to walk Pickles and check in with Bridezilla's mother and stop by the grocery store for orange juice and call Holly back and figure out dinner for Maggie. Joy wasn't free, not at all. She ignored the text.

But his eyes. His *back muscles.* The way he brushed her hair out of her eyes . . . his thumbs.

No. It was a one-night stand, that was all. That was fine. She was entitled to that. It was summer! She was an adult! She'd been tipsy!

Joy's "office" wasn't so much an office as it was a small section of the shop's kitchen that she'd claimed for herself. No walls separated her desk and filing cabinets from the baking area, where right now Olivia Rossi was walking two of the newly hired college kids through how to fill the pies. When summer really ramped up, Joy would need the extra bodies. "It might seem easy, but it's not," Olivia was saying. Olivia was the only person Joy knew who actually looked good in a hairnet. "For one thing, it's really easy to get tired. And it's no joke making sure you scoop the same amount into every pie." Joy smiled. Olivia was only sixteen, but she'd worked for Joy the previous summer and she was preternaturally diligent. Who said the younger generation had no work ethic?

Maggie was handling the counter, though she'd already told Joy that with her new nannying job she might not be available as much as she'd planned on. Joy didn't correct her, though she knew she'd been hired as a mother's helper, not a nanny. Lu had told her as much, when she'd introduced herself to Joy. "I'll be there with her almost all the time," she'd said. "I'm just looking for an extra set of hands so I can get some things done around the house."

Joy tried hard not to resent women like Lu, who spent their days at the beach with their children while their husbands ferried back and forth to work.

These were the same women who spent ten or more dollars a day at Joy Bombs, so in fact she had to be careful about how much to resent them. It was just that sometimes Joy watched these women herding their children around and showing off their toned shoulders and, sometimes, having the gall to complain about it. That made her want to scream.

"I'm so excited about my job," Maggie had said right after Lu and Joy had met. "Lu is *so nice*. And the boys are super-adorable. Her husband is gone all the time at the hospital. She's alone so much! She really needs help."

I've been alone for a decade, thought Joy. I *really needed help*. Joy had been one hundred percent on her own since the day Dustin walked out. Her family, close-knit as long as you were within a ten-mile radius, had released her like a kid letting go of the string on a helium balloon—they were sad at first, but once she was out of sight they sort of forgot about her. Sometimes Joy had to remind herself that that's why she was strong. Every solitary challenge she'd surmounted had added to her strength, muscle fiber by hard-won muscle fiber, until she was rock-solid.

"Isn't she so nice?" Maggie had said.

"Definitely," Joy said, and bit her tongue so hard the act became actual rather than rhetorical. "So nice." Maggie was genuinely excited. And these days she opened the window to her soul only so often; if Joy didn't clamber through it at just the right time, it shut again. *Bam.*

When Maggie walked back to the office now, Joy could see that the soul window was definitely closed. "Can I spend the night at Riley's?" Maggie jutted her chin forward just the way she had when she was three and wouldn't try sweet potato.

Joy squinted at her and said, "Who's behind the counter?"

"Nobody's here," said Maggie. "If the bell dings, I'll hear it and I'll go out. So, can I?"

"You were just at Riley's two nights ago. Why don't you spend the night at our house? We can watch *Pitch Perfect* again. I'll make caramel popcorn!"

Maggie's eyes narrowed. "I knew you'd say no," she said viciously.

"I didn't say no! I just said you were . . ." But Joy didn't get a chance to finish the sentence because

Maggie said, "*I knew it!*" and huffed her way out of the kitchen.

"*What's happening, Mags?*" Joy whispered. For years and years it had been the two of them against the world, shoring up to face the island winds. Now talking to Maggie was like walking through a minefield. No, it was worse—it was like walking through a minefield at night when someone had taken your night-vision goggles and given them to Riley *because they looked better on her.*

Her phone chirped again. What do you say? We'll do something summery. Show me something on this island I haven't seen.

Maggie was back, like a whack-a-mole that kept popping up. "Well, can I or not?" she demanded.

Joy picked up her phone. She texted, I'm in. I'll text you when I'm done here. Then she summoned all of her patience and smiled sweetly at Maggie. "Of course, darling. Since you asked so nicely. Of course you can spend the night at Riley's." She was trying for a joke but the tone was off, and she could see that she'd irritated Maggie.

Her phone rang. She answered without looking. "Joy Sousa." She heard the bell signaling that somebody had come into the shop and she motioned to Maggie to go back to the front. The caller was Geoff Billings, and the news wasn't good. He wasn't going to be able to get the replacement shipment out when he thought he could, because someone else in his office had mistakenly promised Joy's order to another customer. Instead of being two days late, the butter would be five days late.

Joy said, "Five days?" She closed her eyes and inhaled. She'd have to rethink everything about the next week. She'd get behind on production, and she had three large orders scheduled to go out to Boston on Monday. Almost as bad, what if people on the island came in search of whoopie pies and, finding none, flocked to the Roving Patisserie for macarons instead?

"This is unacceptable, Geoff," she said. Her words sounded sharp and she thought, *Good. Let them.* "I'm going to have to figure a few things out here. I'll be in touch." She might have to find a new supplier. She might have to get her own cows! (Obviously not practical.) She ended the call and laid her head down on the desk, the way she remembered doing in second grade during mandatory rest time, when Mrs. Willingham was her teacher. Mrs. Willingham had long chestnut hair and wore big hoop earrings and had a tinkling laugh. Maybe Joy could go back to second grade, before she had the weight of a business and a rental increase and a teenager on her shoulders. In second grade, her biggest worries had been how to improve her dismal four square skills and who to invite to her eighth birthday party at Forrest's Family Fun Center in Taunton.

"If you'd stayed close to home, sure and I'd be helping you out too," Joy's mother had told her when Maggie was four and Joy called to tell her Maggie had caught the flu at preschool. (Her mother's lilting brogue and many of her native phrases had never been snuffed out on the streets of Fall River.) "Come home and I'll help you now," her mother had said.

Maybe she should have gone back home that day, thought Joy. The punishment for wanting total independence was the same thing as the prize: total independence. She was about to dive headfirst into a big vat of self-pity when suddenly there was a touch on the back of her neck. She looked up, startled. Anthony. Her cheeks warmed.

"Hey," he said. "I decided to wait. Maggie said you were back here. You look like something happened. How can I help?"

Joy felt a sudden prick of tears. It wouldn't be a good idea to cry in front of the man she'd just slept with. She would come off as mentally unstable. But. They were four simple words, and nobody ever said them. *How can I help?*

She lifted her face to him, and it felt like she was lifting it to the sun after a long, dark winter. His body somehow seemed to carry all of her favorite scents: cinnamon, vanilla, nutmeg. (Maybe she was attracted to him because he smelled like a bakery. Was there such a thing as whoopie pie pheromones?) When he bent down to kiss her she didn't even look around first to see if Olivia Rossi or the newly hired college kids could see her. All of a sudden she didn't care.

Chapter 23
Anthony

Joy said she needed some time to get a few things done and walk the dog. Anthony could go home, and she'd pick him up in ninety minutes. She'd drive, because he still didn't have a car, and anyway his house was right on the way to where they were going. When she pulled up in the yellow Jeep she gave two successive short honks, but he was watching out the window—he didn't need the honks.

"Hey," she said, smiling, when he hurried out. "Hop in. It's really close, where we're going." The top was down. The sun was still up.

He buckled his seat belt, suddenly shy. He felt like he was on a high school date—excited and anxious, almost sweating, certainly uncertain. His eyes fell on the Jeep's door. In the little pocket there he saw a cherry

ChapStick and a pack of Trident spearmint gum, along with a package of tissues. The cherry ChapStick also reminded him of high school; his first girlfriend, Tricia Sanders, had been a prodigious user.

Joy turned down a narrow road across from a large yellow farmhouse. Anthony had been up and down this road many times by now, but he hadn't noticed the house or the road. Not long after, she pulled into a parking lot, where there was a wooden sign reading CLAY HEAD TRAIL.

"A hike?" he said doubtfully. He wasn't dressed for hiking—he was wearing sneakers without socks, and he'd put a long-sleeved plaid shirt, unbuttoned, over his usual gray T-shirt.

"Just a tiny one," she said. "Not even a hike. A small walk." She slung a backpack over her shoulders and pointed east. "The ocean is right over there. But you won't know it until we're right up on it. These trails are twisty. We get a lot of migratory songbirds out here. And if we're lucky, we'll see a yellow-crowned night heron. They've got these plumes that come out of the back of their head, makes them look like balding men."

He said, "I hear the night herons are *much* cooler than the day herons," and then held his breath until she laughed. This modest joke had been a risk—in the past six months, he'd given up on both laughing himself and encouraging laughter in others. But she laughed, and he exhaled.

It wasn't a long walk, nor was it arduous in any way: Joy had told the truth (another point in her favor). About a third of a mile in, they came to a fork. Joy hesitated. "Sea level?" she asked. "Or up?"

"Up," he said, immediately regretting it—he was prone to vertigo. The trail twisted and turned some more, and now they were headed up, up, up, until at last they stood on top of a bluff overlooking the ocean. Joy indicated a labyrinth of trails winding away from the water. "You can wander on these paths forever," she said. "It's called 'the maze.'" She pointed. "And if you look all the way down there—see? It's the North Lighthouse, which you can also get to by following Corn Neck Road to the end and then parking and walking along the rocks. This"—she stomped her foot—"is all clay. That's where the trail gets its name. Maggie used to make little clay figures when we came up here." She seemed to be lost for a moment in a parental reverie, so Anthony remained quiet and enjoyed the view. He avoided looking straight down, because of the vertigo.

He thought about a young Maggie building clay figures, and the image made him smile. He wondered if Maggie had had stripy hair and funny T-shirts back then; he wouldn't put it past her. Then he thought about Joy, hiking up here, knowing that if Maggie fell ill or scraped her knee or broke her finger it would be up to Joy and only Joy to take care of her. It must have been difficult and sometimes scary for Joy to hoe that lonely row alone.

His thoughts turned to Cassie. "Look at Mommy," Cassie said once, trying to get Max's attention for a photo at the playground. And Anthony found himself standing just off to the side, saying, "Look at Daddy!" They weren't working together. They were competing, volleying Max back and forth like a tennis ball.

In the final, rotten days of their cohabitation he and Cassie had given up saying hello to each other—they'd let go of all of the casual niceties that you'd bestow upon a virtual stranger. Cassie had begun to speak to him through Max: *Look at that, Max! Daddy is having another drink.* He started to do it back: *Max, is Mommy just getting back from meeting with her art dealer? That meeting took a very long time.* Obviously the barbs from their words flew over Max's head, but it wasn't fair or right for either of them to throw them.

"Look!" cried Joy. "Down on the beach. See that? It's a baby harbor seal."

Grateful for the interruption, Anthony steeled himself and looked down. He imagined that he was swaying, then falling. He reprimanded himself. All he could see was a gray lump of rocks. "I don't see it," he said, unbelieving.

Joy pointed. "There!"

He saw just the lumpy rocks. He peered and squinted. At last one of the rocks began to move toward the water, and it turned out it wasn't a rock at all. "What do you know," he said. The seal seemed awkward and uncomfortable, like a slug with flippers, though it moved quite quickly. "How *old* is it?" he asked. "Is it old enough to be out on its own?" He felt concerned for the seal.

Joy chewed her lip. "Probably over six weeks, at least. If the mother isn't with it. After around that age, the baby sticks with the mother, but the mother mostly ignores it." Almost under her breath she added, "Which is the opposite of my experience."

"How do you know so much about seals?"

She shrugged—she looked delightfully sexy when she shrugged, and he felt his pulse race. "The harbor seal is our state mammal," she said. "Knowing the details is in the residency requirements."

They stood on top of the bluff and watched the seal's progress. There was something so optimistic about its shifting, unrefined locomotion that Anthony felt a sudden spring of hope. *You go, girl*, he thought. He was guessing at the gender, but the sentiment was exact. Shouldn't they all, once beached, get the chance to make their way back to the water? Shouldn't *he*? He had made a mistake he'd been led to believe was unforgivable. But maybe it wasn't. Maybe, in fact, forgiveness could take an unexpected form. The seal— bumbling, yes, but stalwart and somehow proud—was a testament to possibilities. He reached for Joy's hand and realized that she was reaching for his at the same time. The vertigo he felt now wasn't uncomfortable or frightening so much as it was bracing, restorative.

"What are you doing after this?" he whispered.

"I'm free," she said. "I'm free as a yellow-crowned night heron." She pressed her body close to his and moved one hand up until it was covering the back of his neck. Her hands were small, but somehow she seemed to be holding his entire body with just the one.

Chapter 24
Joy

For the next three and a half weeks Joy had one of the best summers of her life, and this was including the summer she was sixteen and dating Tad Formosa, which was the same summer her best friend Krista's grandmother allowed the use of her unoccupied house near Craigville Beach in Centerville.

Was it because of the sex? Maybe. Yes, definitely it was partly because of the sex! She wasn't going to lie about that. But there were many more things too.

They hiked Clay Head Trail again; this time they did spot a yellow-crowned night heron. ("Endangered!" said Joy proudly. She felt like she'd given birth to the heron herself.) They biked up Corn Neck Road and then walked out to North Lighthouse at sunset. They kissed leaning against Settlers' Rock and Joy thought her stomach might drop right out of her body. Joy had always wanted to kiss someone at sunset leaning against Settlers' Rock.

Maggie taught Anthony how to clam. All the island kids knew how to clam, and Anthony was exactly the right amount of impressed. For all of his professed non-experience with dogs, Anthony was a top-notch dog walker, and Pickles had taken to him like a border collie to a Frisbee. Anthony fixed a hinge that had been loose in Joy's kitchen cabinet for months. Joy knew how to do that, but somehow she never got around to it.

Anthony didn't talk much about his life before coming to the island, or of his plans for after he left. Joy didn't press him. She understood that island life was transient and that you were allowed to leave part of yourself behind and forget all about it once you approached the breakwater. Hadn't she done the same thing, all those years ago?

One day, when Anthony had gone to sleep at his own cottage because Maggie and Riley were sleeping at Joy's, she woke up in the morning, forgetting he wasn't there, and reached for him. She felt a little surge of panic when she found his side of the bed empty. *Uh-oh*, she thought, frowning at the panic. *You, Joy Sousa, are getting attached.*

She got behind on keeping the books at the store.

When she finally took an afternoon to catch up, she was startled to see how much lower this summer's sales were than last summer's. She'd *felt* busy. She felt busy all the time! Thank goodness for Bridezilla's wedding. Even so, she was going to have to put the money she'd started to put away for Maggie's college toward the rent increase. She was going to have to ask Dustin to chip in to replace the college savings.

She texted Dustin. There's something i need to talk to you about. Call me when you can, and then she put it out of her mind.

They went to Tiger Fish for dinner with Holly and her husband, Brent, leaving the girls at Holly's house watching a *Gossip Girl* marathon. They booked a horseback ride that took them on the beach and right into the surf. One night they watched the moon rise from Beacon Hill. They cruised the stalls at the farmers' market at Legion Park.

Fun, yes. Sex: definitely, yes, please. Love? Nobody said love. Why should they? It was a summer romance, that was all.

But every so often now, kissing Anthony goodbye, or waking up next to him on the nights when Maggie was at Dustin's or sleeping over at Riley's, she found herself thinking, *Well, maybe.* And then, finally: *Yes.*

Chapter 25
Lu

Lu knocked on Anthony's door. "I made way too much summer vegetable lasagna," she said without preamble, when he opened it. "And Jeremy is doing a double shift. Could you find it in your heart to help me? Tonight?" It wasn't like she could have made less lasagna—a lasagna pan was a standard size. But the boys didn't like all the summer vegetables (Chase eschewed mushrooms in all forms, and Sebastian harbored a grievance against eggplant) and Lu loved this dish; she hated to see it go to waste. She would roast a pan of broccoli too, since the boys would eat that and she could throw the leftovers into a salad the next day. "Unless you have plans with Joy," she added hastily. "But I thought Maggie said that she and Joy had something to do tonight—"

"They do," he said. "Dinner with friends. I'll see Joy later, and in the meantime I'd love to have dinner with you and the boys."

It made Lu feel useful to have another adult to cook for. Her mind had actually formed the phrase *to have a man to cook for*, but she knew how politically incorrect that was, so she pushed it right back into the recesses of her brain. Was there a name for that, the part of the brain where you put inappropriate thoughts? Jeremy might know.

It wasn't only about the lasagna, though. Now that she knew that Anthony wasn't just her summer neighbor who was dating the mother of her mother's helper but that he was *in hiding* and that his father was *the one and only Leonard Puckett*, she wanted to know more about him. She was intrigued!

When Anthony showed up two hours later, he was carrying a small bouquet of wildflowers—a lovely touch. Lu put them in water and cut up the lasagna. She served the boys at the kitchen island, and she and Anthony sat at the little table in the kitchen. Chase had found a chopstick and was using it to pick out all the mushroom pieces.

"So," Lu said, once they were settled. "I have so many things I want to ask you, now that I know who you are." She still couldn't quite believe it. She had read *A Room Within* when it had come out, after that fabulous review in the *Times*. Everybody had read that book when it came out! "For one thing, are you close with your father?"

Anthony started. "Not really—not anymore."

"Not since you brought shame upon the family name? Chase, put that *down*." Chase was holding the chopstick alarmingly close to his brother's nostril. Lu caught the look on Anthony's face and said, "I'm sorry." She had overstepped. It was a bad habit of hers, assuming a familiarity with a new friend that she hadn't yet earned.

"No, that's okay. It's not that. It's more that—well, it happened *before* I brought shame on the family name. When I was a kid, we were close. But when I was in college we sort of lost that. It was like, my whole life, my dad was this icon, you know. A star! In the book world, anyway. And in our house, for sure. I revered him."

Lu nodded and speared a piece of broccoli. She'd finally gotten the hang of this oven, and of the too-shiny rimmed baking sheet. (So many times she wished she'd brought her own from home; she'd written a whole post once on the joys of roasting vegetables on a stained, blackened sheet.) But this time she'd nailed it; the broccoli was lightly charred on the outside and still tender when you bit into it. Little bit of sea salt. Just the way she liked it: it was better than popcorn.

"A lot of people feel that way about their parents." He sighed heavily. "And then at some point, he became human. I guess when I became a writer myself. Then, after what happened earlier this year—I mean, *what I did*, not *what happened*—he didn't want to talk to me at all. He must be so ashamed."

"I'm sorry," she said.

"It's my own fault."

"But I'm still sorry. At the same time, I can imagine it being hard on him. He's *so* big-time. I've been reading your dad's books . . . forever! In college . . . man. I used to avoid studying so I could read them. They were like crack."

"It wasn't like being Mick Jagger's son, but it was still a big deal. He sells *a lot* of books. He makes *a lot* of money. He has a lot of fans. He was interviewed by Travis Weaver earlier this summer!"

"I know," said Lu. "I actually saw that." She thought Travis Weaver was a little pompous, but she watched him anyway because she liked his hair and sometimes they did a decent cooking segment. The day Leonard Puckett was on she'd learned a new trick to try with gazpacho: soak the bread before adding it to the blender. "He was great! So charming. It's so funny that I didn't know then that that was your father."

"Can I be done?" asked Sebastian and Chase at the same time. They must have planned it ahead of time.

"You two can skedaddle," Lu told them. "Just put your plates in the sink first." They'd done a passable job on the broccoli but had made a poor showing with the lasagna, as expected. Charlie and Sammy were much more reliable vegetable eaters. "I always wanted to be a writer," she continued, turning her attention back to Anthony. "I guess that's why I—"

(She almost said it. Out loud.)

"Why you what?" He seemed genuinely curious, which Lu appreciated.

"Why I liked law school so much," she recovered. "There was lots of writing. Everybody else got tired of it, but I never did." That was true. "In college, I was an English major. I was crazy for Virginia Woolf. Money and a room of one's own, and all of that."

He nodded approvingly. "Good choice," he said. "From one English major to another."

"My senior year my housemates and I adopted a cat and I named her Lily Briscoe."

"I love it. Lily Briscoe the cat." He laughed sincerely.

His laughter felt like an achievement to Lu. She didn't feel like she'd made Jeremy laugh at all lately, either because he hadn't been here or when he was she was too busy covering her tracks to indulge in humor.

And they used to laugh so much! All the time, laughing until they got stitches, laughing until the cows came home. Even during sex, they used to laugh.

Chase's and Sebastian's plates rattled as they went into the sink—Lu knew she was walking that fine line between teaching them table-clearing manners and risking broken dishes she'd have to replace. They were very excited because Maggie had seen a notice for an event at the Island Free Library. The library was having an exotic-animals person in, which was exactly up Chase's alley. Lu imagined the exotic-animals person might bring a lizard or an iguana; perhaps, if they were lucky, a chinchilla or a nonthreatening but impressively long snake the children could take turns wearing on their necks. She knew, of course, that Chase, having glimpsed the poster downtown, was hoping for a wallaroo or a Siberian tiger.

Once the boys had disappeared into the living room and turned on the television, Lu asked, "So, really, what was it like? Being the son of someone like that?" Jeremy would have disapproved of television time immediately after dinner. He wanted them to play wholesome board games, but he was never here to play them.

Anthony moved the last bit of broccoli around his plate. It was extra-charred, and if Lu had known him better she might have asked him if she could have it. "It was all I knew," he said. He squinted at his plate. "I don't really have a point of comparison, you know? I mean, I guess what I would mostly say is that our worlds revolved around him, my mother's and mine. We traveled where he needed to go, we stayed quiet when he needed to work, we ate dinner at the same time every night because he worked best when everything around him was really controlled. He was like a god to me, you know? And then . . . I don't know. I showed him my first story, and everything changed."

"Probably he was jealous." To Lu that seemed obvious. When she'd first read *A Room Within* she'd been blown away.

"No," said Anthony. "Not of me. Never. Leonard Puckett doesn't envy anyone."

"Of course he does. Everyone envies someone. Even Virginia Woolf! She envied Katherine Mansfield."

"She did? I didn't know that."

"She did. It was a whole thing. I wrote a paper on it. Anyway, look at your father: he had all this commercial success, but then you came along and wrote, essentially, the Great American Novel."

Anthony shifted uncomfortably. "I wouldn't go that far," he said.

"No, really. *A Room Within* is amazing."

"Thank you," said Anthony. "I really appreciate that, I do. But then I went and did that stupid thing, and ruined all of it."

It had been a really unwise thing to do, Lu agreed. "Why'd you do it?" she asked. "You're so talented on your own."

Anthony took a long time to answer. Finally he said, "It was a bad time for me. A real low point. I didn't—I didn't have my head on straight. I'm just starting to feel like I do now, a little bit. Don't judge me. I mean, if you can help it."

"Don't worry," Lu assured him. "I don't judge anyone." This was untrue. She judged Nancy. She'd judged the heck out of Jessica. She judged careless food bloggers who didn't test their recipes enough before publishing them. But she wouldn't judge Anthony. She needed a friend, and he was turning out to be a good one. She wasn't going to judge her way out of that. "Also," she said, "I have my own secret. Want me to tell you?"

Anthony's eyes grew wide. "Of course," he said. Lu lifted her wineglass, took a generous sip, and told Anthony everything about Dinner by Dad. *Everything.* The talking felt invigorating and purifying, like the middle stage of a juice cleanse, and when she was done Anthony said, "*Wow.* Holy cow. I can't believe it. I'm so impressed! I'm going to go home and read all of your posts."

Lu was secretly delighted, and also scared. A writer like Anthony Puckett reading her posts! "You don't have to read *all* of them," she said. "That would take you a while. I've been doing it for two years. Don't tell Joy, okay? Maggie doesn't know. Nobody knows. Really! I've never told anybody the whole story, except for you, right now."

"I won't tell anyone," said Anthony. "Scout's honor."

"Were you a Scout?"

"Never."

"Me either." Lu's mother hadn't been around to drive Lu and her sister to afternoon activities, so they'd been limited to those that took place at school.

"Wait," said Anthony. "Your *husband* doesn't know?"

She shook her head. "No. He— I can't tell him. He has . . . a very firm idea of how things should go. And this isn't in his plan."

Anthony nodded. "Okay," he said. Then: "To secrets," lifting his seltzer can.

Lu raised her wineglass. "To secrets." They tapped, and they smiled at exactly the same time, and Lu felt like she'd found something she hadn't even really known she'd been missing.

Chapter 26
Anthony

All through the better part of July, every time Anthony started to tell Joy the truth, something stopped him. He hadn't been this happy with a woman since . . . since when? He was going to say since he'd first met Cassie, but the truth was he hadn't ever been this happy with Cassie. He'd never been himself with Cassie, from whom he had no secrets, and yet he felt completely himself with Joy, who knew only half the story.

Joy made him laugh. She was so passionate about everything: sweet pickles versus dill (dill, always, unless on a cheeseburger), gelato versus ice cream (gelato), thick-cut fries versus shoestring (oh, always, *always* shoestring). In bed, they were—well, it was going *very well*. One night *When Harry Met Sally* came on television, and they watched it, both ridiculously riveted. It turned out they both liked romantic comedies: *Sleepless in Seattle. You've Got Mail. While You Were Sleeping.* "But this one's the best by far," she said. He concurred.

He loved to watch her cook in her tiny, mismatched kitchen, even though, by her own confession, she was more baker than cook. Without the help of her favorite food blog (a coincidence so fantastic he, an erstwhile novelist, would never have dared to construct it in fiction), she said she'd be nothing. Maggie had the true culinary talent in the kitchen. Maggie's face took on an earnest look—almost pinched—and when she was really concentrating the tip of her tongue slipped out of the side of her mouth. He would never be able to tell them about the kitchen he and Cassie had put in at their Newton home, about the six burners on the range, only one of which was ever used, mostly to boil water for tea or the occasional hard-boiled egg. (To Cassie food was more about subtraction than addition.) Joy was an enthusiastic eater—even voracious.

Anthony learned that the island had an ecosystem he hadn't understood, couldn't have understood if he hadn't met someone like Joy. Bob Herbert fixed the Le Baron; it ran like a dream. The locals fed on the tourists, and the tourists fed on the locals. Both sides were unapologetic about their parts in this arrangement. And underneath it all thrummed a vibrant and teeming community. The islanders didn't, as he would have imagined, wait through summer to get to winter. Nor did they wait through winter to get to summer. They took each season in stride.

You could only be a part of this ecosystem if you were relentless, optimistic, resourceful, and self-sufficient, and if you taught your offspring to be the same. So Anthony found himself captivated by all of the island tricks Joy and Maggie knew. If you wanted any beach to yourself, you walked the dog at sunrise. If you wanted a good table at Eli's, you went on a Wednesday. If you wanted clear water and soft sand, you braved the crowds at Ballard's, but if you wanted to hunt for shells and sand dollars, you went to Surf Beach.

He was smitten. He might love her. He would tell her the truth soon.

It turned out Anthony Puckett was a dog person, after all! Finally he understood what all the fuss was about regarding dogs. They asked for almost nothing, and when you gave them even the little that they asked for, they looked at you with such adoring eyes that you felt loved as you'd never felt loved before. You got so you always had a sense of where the dog was: under the table, sitting by the door, sleeping on the deck, chewing a bone. He took to walking Pickles mornings on the beach. Pickles had lots of local friends: a Lab mix named Titan, a boxer named Sadie, a beautiful golden retriever named Olive.

Maggie was remarkably independent. She was perfectly capable of making a meal for herself or for the three of them. She disappeared into the bathroom and came out with streaks of different colors in her hair. She did her own laundry. When she wasn't being industrious, she was having a childhood Anthony would have killed for. She went off on a bike with her friend Riley, when she wasn't helping in the shop or working for Lu. She was learning how to sail a Sunfish. Once she sat all day on the deck of the cottage and read from a battered copy of *A Wrinkle in Time*.

"Yours?" Anthony asked Joy, pointing to the book, hungry for a little piece of the girl she had once been.

"Oh, *no*," she said. "I wasn't much of a reader."

He couldn't tell her the truth.

Once, Maggie said, "Anthony, did you have a favorite movie as a kid?"

The answer was right there, as though it had been waiting only for the question to be asked: *The Karate Kid*. Cassie didn't know that. Nobody had ever wanted to know that before.

Anthony dared to order Maggie a shirt from Amazon with a pun about a bear and a deer, holding his breath when she opened it. "I *love it*," she proclaimed. "I really love it. Thank you, Anthony."

The only thing marring Anthony's happiness was the absence of his son. There was always a part inside of him crying out, *Max! Max! Max!*

He called Cassie again and again.

"Sorry," she said. "He's at camp."

"He has a playdate."

"I'm working, Anthony, he's with the sitter."

Once: "He's staying with your mother. Call him there."

He did, and nobody answered.

He tried getting tough: "You can't keep me from our son!"

"Oh, can't I?" And then silence. His bluff had been summarily called. He couldn't go home to the house where he wasn't welcome.

But occasionally she yielded and he was permitted short conversations with Max. It was enough—just—to sustain him.

Once he had a ghastly dream wherein his father was standing over him with an unabridged copy of Merriam-Webster's dictionary. *I'm sorry*, Anthony croaked up at his father. *I'm so, so sorry.* His father lifted the dictionary, and Anthony covered his head with his hands.

Another time it was his mother, cutting the crusts off of his peanut butter sandwiches at the kitchen counter, her back to him, her hair perfect. But when she turned around there was a giant hole in her dress where her heart should have been, and her eyes were flat and empty.

In a panic he tangled himself in the sheets; he thrashed and kicked, trying to get out.

"What?" said Joy. "You okay, baby?"

Nobody had ever called him *baby* before, except maybe when he was an actual baby, and if that had happened he didn't remember it. He sank back into the pillows, sweaty and relieved. He rummaged around under the sheets until he found her hand, and when he had it he didn't let go.

He had to tell her. But if he told her and he lost her, he'd die.

He couldn't tell her.

His mother called him every three days. More often than not he was too busy to answer her.

Ready for a visitor? she texted.

Not a good time, he replied.

We still have to talk, came her answer.

Once he and Joy walked by Island Bound Books after returning a moped they had rented to ride out to Charleston Beach for a picnic. Anthony couldn't help but steal a glance at the window. Was *The Thrill of the Chase* still there? Front and center. Not only that, there was a poster now in the window, with his father's photo and big red letters proclaiming AUTHOR EVENT! AUGUST 7. The photo was a three-quarter shot. Leonard had his arms crossed over his chest and an extremely satisfied smile on his face.

Oh, brother, thought Anthony. *You've got to be kidding me.*

Now would be a good time to tell Joy, he thought. *You have a natural entry point.* He gave it a feeble try. "You ever read that book?" he asked, tilting his head toward it. He thought he might do it. He might say, *That's my father.* He might say, *I'm that guy's son.* He could say, *There's more to the story.*

"Which?" Joy was distracted: Olivia Rossi had texted about a message Bridezilla's mother had left at the shop.

"That one. In the window. *The Thrill of the Chase.*"

"Oh, that?" She glanced up at the poster quickly, then back at her phone. She muttered something about a dairy in Vermont. "Not my kind of book, mysteries." Really, most books weren't Joy's kind of book. She wasn't a reader, just as she'd said! It was actually very refreshing. In the evenings when they were home together she went over accounts from the shop or suggested that they watch something on cable or Netflix or Hulu. *Ray Donovan* was supposed to be good, or how about *The Handmaid's Tale*?

"Thrillers," he corrected her, about Leonard's genre. "I believe they call those thrillers."

But she was already talking into the phone, turning away from him.

"I love you," he said experimentally one night, when Joy was putting together a simple caprese salad with grilled tuna. She looked so startled that he quickly revised: "I mean, I think I'm falling in love with you." And a second revision: "I think I might be."

The sentence hung there, an uninvited guest.

"I'm low on olive oil," she said, her eyes wide, almost feral. He'd gone too far, too fast. "And I'm due to pick up Maggie in twenty minutes. Do you think you could run to the grocery?"

He went to the grocery, his pulse racing. When he returned they spoke no more about it.

They went to Mohegan Bluffs. One hundred and forty-one steps down, the same back up! Anthony noticed he wasn't out of breath when he got to the top, the way the people in front of them were. Day after day with no alcohol, the biking, the sunshine and sea air: he was losing the Depressed Man softness around his midsection. He had a tan!

They hiked out to Rodman's Hollow. Anthony read the sign out loud. PLEASE RESPECT IT SO THAT ALL— HUMAN, CREATURE, AND PLANT ALIKE—MAY SHARE IN ITS PEACE AND BEAUTY. Now he was also smitten with Rodman, whoever he may have been.

They went to the 1661 farm and petted the alpacas and met the star-horned sheep. They ate calamari at Poor People's Pub and ice cream at the Scoop Shack.

They ate at Eli's: tomato and burrata salad, ginger-rubbed swordfish. After, they sat on a bench near the ferry terminal, watching the drunk people. A young woman in stilettos and a bright blue sundress wobbled into her companion.

Joy leaned over and kissed him. She'd had two glasses of Sauvignon Blanc at Eli's.

Now, he thought.

"I have something to tell you," he said in a small voice.

Joy pulled back and looked at him. "Are you a murderer?"

"What? *No.* Of course not. Why would you think that?"

"You look so serious all of a sudden."

"It's not that."

"Okay, then," she said. She resumed kissing him.

"It's just that I—I'm not . . ."

She stopped again. She whispered, "Let me guess. *You're not who you say you are.*"

His palms started to sweat; his ears started to sweat.

"Oh, boy," she said. "I got you, huh? You look terrified. I'm kidding, of course."

"You know what?" he said after a beat. "Never mind. It's nothing we can't talk about another time."

"You sure?"

He couldn't tell her.

"I'm sure," he said. He put his hands on the sides of her face and pulled her gently toward him.

Chapter 27
Lu

Jeremy was home for dinner. It was a real treat! Lu had made a Thai mango salad with peanut dressing. It was very simple, but the mangoes made it feel exotic. In fact, that's what she'd be writing in her post.

You know how passionate I am about eating foods that are fresh and local. The butter lettuce I used in this recipe, for example, came from my local farmers' market. So you might be surprised to see that this dish also features succulent, ripe mango, which is not exactly indigenous where I live. I admit it, these mangoes caught my eye in my local grocery store and I couldn't help myself. Did you know that almost half the mangoes in the world are grown in India?

Both boys were devouring the salad—a win! Also, it was versatile. She'd made hers with chicken, but her vegetarian readers could easily substitute grilled or stir-fried tofu, and the pescatarians could use shrimp or even salmon. Provided the salmon was wild. Leo was very into sustainable seafoods, and he'd done a post about the dangers of farm-raised salmon that had generated a slew of reader mail. Though of course Leo's preferred seafood was always the lake trout that he caught himself.

In between bites the boys were tripping over each other trying to tell Jeremy about their past few days. It was adorable, how happy they were to see him. And he seemed to be in a good mood, relaxed, smiling. Now they were telling him about the salmon pink bird-eating tarantula, native to Brazil, that had come to the library on exotic animal day.

"But you're terrified of spiders, Lu."

Lu only half heard him. She was wondering if it was worth creating a peanut-free version of the salad too, with a different kind of dressing. Maybe soy nuts to retain the crunch. She was also dreaming about a trip to India she'd create for Leo and Jacqui, something that would inspire a new twist on a chickpea curry. Maybe they'd gone before they were parents. Maybe they'd gone on their honeymoon! Yes. They also went to Thailand and visited an elephant sanctuary. Phuket Elephant Sanctuary. She'd do all of this tomorrow, plus the charcoal drawings to go with it. She also had to go to the bank and get cash for Maggie. For the first time since she'd been accumulating it, Lu had started to dip into the money in her private account, to pay Maggie. Once every few days she walked to the ATM at the Washington Trust Bank on Ocean Avenue. It wasn't much—Maggie had quoted her a rate of eight dollars an hour, a steal—but still Lu cherished the feeling of withdrawing the cash that was her very own, and using it to pay her very own mother's helper that she'd hired so she could run her very own business. Her own bur-geoning empire.

"Spiders," said Jeremy now. "You must have hated that."

She had made the boys promise not to mention Maggie to either Jeremy or Nancy. Neither one would see it the right way. Nancy would wonder why Lu hadn't just asked her to help if she needed some free time "to shop or exercise" (there were a hundred an-swers to that question), and Jeremy would see Maggie's presence as Lu shirking her duties to the boys, Lu being dishonest, Lu spending money they didn't, technically, have. For some reason Jeremy had no problem accept-ing a free summer home from his parents as well as a huge loan for a house down payment but would never dream of taking their money for small, day-to-day expenses. It didn't make any sense to Lu, but then she hadn't grown up with family money, so she supposed there were invisible rules she'd never understand.

Jeremy couldn't know about Maggie: it simply wasn't an option. "Maggie is our special little secret," she'd told the boys. "She's like a magical fairy; if we tell anyone about her she might fly away!"

They nodded solemnly. They promised. They *adored* Maggie. She was young enough that she was still mostly a kid herself, so she'd get down on the floor with them and pretend to be an elephant, or she'd arm-wrestle Sebastian, always letting him win, or she'd watch *The Lego Movie* with them and enjoy it every bit as much as they did. "Come with me if you want to not die!" she'd say, and the boys would roll around, laughing, saying with her things like, "We are from Planet Duplo, and we're here to destroy you." (Lu didn't understand any of these references; the first time the boys had seen the movie she'd been answering reader mail on her laptop.) They'd do anything to keep Maggie from flying away.

"They didn't bother me," said Lu. "Maybe I've grown out of it." She shot warning looks to both boys.

Jacqui went crazy over this salad, she'd write. Should she come up with a fictional case for Jacqui to be working on? Some of her stay-at-home mom readers relished the details of Jacqui's professional life; big-time jobs were like porn to them. Office porn.

She didn't notice that the whole table had gone silent until suddenly they were all staring at her.

"Who's Maggie?" Jeremy asked.

Instantly, Lu flushed. She glanced at Chase and Sebastian and said innocently, "What?"

Chase hit Sebastian and said, "You weren't supposed to *say.* Mommy told us not to tell, you're an *idiot.*"

Sebastian began to cry. Jeremy paid no attention to the boys and fixed a cold, clinical gaze on Lu. Was this the gaze he fixed on his patients right before they were put under? How terrifying. "They said that *Maggie* has been showing them how to bodysurf."

Lu cleared her throat. "No, no," she said. "They're not really bodysurfing, of course. They're just in the very shallowest water. More like skimboarding, without the boards. It's not even ankle-deep!" This was the wrong answer, of course. She knew that. It wasn't about the dangers of the ocean.

"That's not my question," said Jeremy slowly. He put down his fork. There was still a piece of chicken on it. She'd cooked the chicken on the grill on the back deck, which was an old Weber, not as good as the Napoleon they had at home. Nevertheless, Lu was happy with how the chicken had come out. She'd done it on skewers, and she'd taken a decent photo. She'd use the photo in tomorrow's post too.

"She's our babysitter!" said Sebastian, through his tears. Chase hit him with an elbow. "She has lots of freckles," Sebastian added.

"She's a good dancer," Chase said, reluctantly joining in.

Jeremy said, "I see." He smiled at Chase and ruffled Sebastian's hair. "Isn't that nice." He took a second helping of salad and chewed the chicken. He didn't meet Lu's eye.

The boys had scarcely finished their food when Jeremy said, "Boys. Go upstairs and build that Lego kit."

"What Lego kit?" Sebastian asked.

"Any one. The Batman one."

"We already built that one," said Chase.

"We did," Sebastian concurred. "We already built all the ones we brought."

"Go rebuild one, then."

"Well," began Sebastian reasonably, "once you build one you really can't rebuild it because of the way the—"

"Just go," said Jeremy. "Just *go.*" They went. "I'll make sure the grill is off," said Jeremy.

"It's off," said Lu. "I always turn it off."

"I'll just make sure," said Jeremy quietly. He stood and made what Lu thought was a great show of walking onto the deck and checking all of the burners. Upstairs, she could hear Sebastian doing his politically incorrect imitation of a cop about to arrest Chase.

When Jeremy returned he regained his seat and said, "You never said anything about needing a babysitter. Are things too much for you around here, Lu?" The words were almost kind but the sentiment behind them was not.

Lu said, "Sometimes." It was true.

"In that case," Jeremy said, "you can ask my mother for help."

"I don't want to ask your mother for help." Lu was suddenly, violently enraged at the situation she'd put herself in. It looked to Jeremy like she couldn't handle the children without help when really what she couldn't handle was children plus a burgeoning career without help. (And who, realistically, could?) But she couldn't balance the scales without telling him everything.

"My mother loves to help, Lu."

"She doesn't love to help! She just loves to see me need help."

"That's not fair." Now Jeremy sounded peevish. "She wanted us here because she enjoys spending time with the boys, you know that."

Grudgingly, Lu had to admit that might be true.

"Besides, once we have another baby we'll be outnumbered. We'll need her help then."

Lu gritted her teeth. She couldn't make this argument be about another baby. She had to keep dodging the baby question; if she dodged it long enough, maybe it would go away.

"I want you to fire her," Jeremy said. "I don't want a stranger here with the boys. Isn't that why you left your job, so we wouldn't have a stranger here with the boys?"

He's tired, Lu reminded herself. *He's always tired when he comes back after a few long shifts in a row.* The commute to and from the hospital was wearing on him. Jeremy didn't get enough sleep, that was a big part of the problem. It was a scientifically proven fact that lack of sleep impeded your memory retention, your overall health, your sense of well-being and happiness. She'd heard a podcast about it. His circadian rhythms called to him, but he couldn't answer.

Lu understood that she had to speak carefully. "She's not a stranger," she said. "The boys love her.

She's young, and she plays with them. She's funny. She can cook! One time she—"

"She's a stranger to me," Jeremy interrupted. His mouth was set in a line that said he'd brook no arguments.

Even so, Lu tried again. "You should get to know her. Then she won't be a stranger anymore. She's delightful."

"That's enough, Lu." Jeremy put his hands to his temples and rubbed hard. "I don't want to talk about this anymore. I don't want to get to know her. We don't need to be spending money we don't have when my mother is right here, and when you're home all day. I want you to fire her."

The words were right there on the tip of her tongue. *I have money. Sort of a lot of money, actually.* More sponsor money had come in recently, and her affiliate sales for the Instant Pot had *really* picked up after that macaroni-and-cheese post from May. If things kept going at this rate, by next year she'd be earning almost as much as Jeremy did, especially if the cookbook worked out. If she really focused, if she really worked hard, if she could squeeze more working hours into every day, she could earn legitimate money.

Tell him, Lu. 'Fess up now, tell him. Maybe he won't be mad. Maybe he'll be proud, just the way you want him to be. Maybe he'll be relieved.

But she knew he wouldn't be any of those things. She knew if she brought up Dinner by Dad now, they'd have a fight not only about that but also about a third baby. She wouldn't be able to hide how she felt about that.

Readers, wrote Dinner by Dad the next day, *do you ever just feel like giving up on everything? Do you ever feel like it's just not worth it, any of it?*

Three hundred and seventy-six readers posted follow-up comments. Leo needed to keep his chin up. Leo was doing important work. Leo had only to look at Sammy and Charlie to see how much what he was doing mattered. Leo couldn't give up on them, not now, not anytime!

Chapter 28
Joy

Olivia Rossi had the day off, one of the college kids was sick (read: hungover), and the other was mixing a batch of filling in the back. That meant Joy was in the shop all day. Off-season she would have ducked out to meet Maggie at the ferry after her visit to Dustin's, but in the height of summer when the ferry was due in, Joy Bombs had a good-sized line. Instead of walking down to greet Maggie, Joy was working the cappuccino machine like it was a cello and she was Yo-Yo Ma. She was cutting up sample whoopie pies to put in the case. She was making change and running credit cards.

Joy and Anthony had a seven-thirty reservation at Winfield's. Joy was beyond excited; she was going to have the seared scallops to start and then the grilled swordfish. Or maybe the halibut.

When the bell on the door tinkled she glanced up, prepared to give her signature I'm-the-owner-and-I-want-to-make-you-feel-welcome hello, and her eyes fell on . . . Dustin.

Dustin? Joy hadn't seen Dustin in more than a year. They'd communicated about Maggie's visits, of course—they'd texted, they'd emailed, occasionally they'd talked on the phone. Joy followed Sandy's Insta-gram account, where Sandy posted (too many, in Joy's opinion, one per day would have been quite enough) photos of Tiki at the beach, Tiki wearing a Santa hat, Tiki and Sandy together on the back of a horse. Joy refrained from liking or commenting but she couldn't help but notice that Maggie did both. Maggie was profligate with her smiley faces and her hearts. Dustin never appeared in the photos. He must have been hold-ing the phone.

"Hey!" said Dustin. "Joy. I decided to take a ferry ride back with Maggie. You said there was something you wanted to talk to me about, so I figured—why not in person?" He looked around the shop—was he angling for free food? Maybe Sandy didn't feed him. Maggie said Tiki was more of an all-day snacker and that neither Sandy nor Dustin ever seemed to prepare or eat a regular meal. When Maggie offered to make them Dinner by Dad's black bean tostadas they looked at her like she'd offered to sing an aria from *The Marriage of Figaro*—and then they'd declined.

"What a nice surprise, Dustin," said Joy dishonestly. The truth was that even after all these years she didn't like to see Dustin, because seeing Dustin forced her to remember a time when she'd been very unhappy. But she did need to talk to him about the money. "Where's Maggie?"

"She took right off," said Dustin. "She said she had to babysit?"

This was news to Joy, but she let it pass. When the line had dissolved, Joy put together a plate of whoopie pies and brought it over to a table, motioning with her free hand for Dustin to take a seat.

"Awesome!" he said. "Food!" Joy noted that Dustin's admiration of free stuff hadn't changed any.

"Listen," said Joy. "I hate to bring up money."

Dustin's hand paused over the plate.

"But," said Joy.

Dustin returned his hand, empty, to his lap.

"I've been thinking," she continued, "about setting up a college account for Maggie. You know, one of those five-twenty-nines? And I thought if we both contributed, then in five years, when she's ready to apply, we might at least be able to look at some decent state schools." Her cheeks were flaming. She hated talking about money, hated being anything less than one hundred percent free of Dustin.

But she had to. She feared Maggie would end up attending the Community College of Rhode Island, Flanagan Campus, returning home every weekend to stay with Joy because the eighteen roommates with whom she was sharing a two-bedroom in Lincoln made it impossible to get any work done. And of *course* community college was a viable option and she could always transfer to a four-year college at some point, but Joy had always believed that Maggie was meant for a four-year private liberal arts education—the kind that Joy had been unable to afford for herself. She could see Maggie at Williams or Amherst or Mount Holyoke.

Dustin said, "Hmm." He picked up a whoopie pie and put the whole thing in his mouth.

Joy studied him. Sure, he was skinny, but so many other changes had occurred since Joy had known him well. His flat stomach might scream, *I HAVE THE METABOLISM OF A HUMMINGBIRD*, but his thinning hair, the lines around his mouth, his old jeans: these things screamed, *I AM APPROACHING MIDDLE AGE!*

"I thought you were doing well!" said Dustin, talking around the whoopie pie. "The place is always crowded. That's what Mags said."

Ugh, thought Joy. *Don't call her Mags. You don't deserve to call her Mags.* "It is doing well," she said defensively. "But it's not that simple. There's some competition this summer . . ."

"That food truck?" said Dustin. "Mags told me about that. Sounds awesome!"

Joy thought, *Shut up, Dustin. And stop saying* awesome. *You're not a teenager.* But she said, "And the rent on the building went up." She tried to hold her voice steady. "It's just hard to get ahead, that's all."

Dustin nodded with what Joy at first mistook for genuine sympathy. Then he said, "You know what, Joy? I wish I could help. I really do. She's such a great kid." (*No thanks to you*, thought Joy.)

"But," said Joy.

"But. I just don't have any extra right now, you know? Man, little kids are *expensive*. You wouldn't believe it."

"Oh, I would," said Joy. She thought about the year Maggie turned six and had a growth spurt that caused her to outgrow all of her clothes in one winter. She thought about the year the roof leaked in the shop and she'd had to replace the mixer. She thought about the time three years ago when Pickles broke her leg and had to be treated by an off-island vet.

"And Sandy's whole family is out in L.A., so plane tickets back and forth a few times a year, you know? It adds up. It really adds up. Sandy's not working anymore, to be home for Tiki."

"How nice for her," said Joy. She squeezed the sentence out from between gritted teeth.

"So, man, I'm really sorry I can't help in, like, a regular way, you know? I mean, I'll do what I can, but I just can't guarantee anything." Dustin ate two more whoopie pies in rapid succession. "Hey, where do you think that food truck is today? It's always in a different place, right?"

"Yes," said Joy. "But I don't know where it is today." She actually did know, but she wasn't telling.

"I'd love to bring back some of those cookies for Sandy and Teeks." (Apparently *Tiki* was not enough of a nickname; it had to be further shortened.)

Joy's phone, which she had set on the table, buzzed. Dustin glanced at it and said, "You have a contact named Bridezilla?"

Joy sighed. "It's a long story." She didn't owe Dustin *anything*, not even an explanation. She let the call go to voice mail and she stood to indicate that she had many important matters to attend to. She knew that the next ferry back to Newport wasn't for another ninety minutes and she didn't want to be charged with babysitting her ex-husband. She had pies to make and Bridezillas to call back. Where, by the way, did Dustin come up with the money for an extra round-trip ferry ticket if he was so destitute?

"Hey," said Dustin, all smiles now that he wasn't being shaken down for a monthly 529 contribution. "Mags says you're dating someone? That's great, Joy. That's really great."

The last thing Joy needed was to be condescended to by the man who'd once crushed her spirit. She said, "Yes," and nodded crisply. She picked up the plate and Dustin's crumpled napkin. She almost ate the last whoopie pie, but then she remembered that she was saving up her appetite for a delectable dinner at Winfield's with Anthony.

Three nights before, Anthony had said *I love you* while she was grilling tuna. She'd pretended not to hear him. But now she wondered why she'd done that. Why was she holding back? What did she think she was waiting for? Why had she sent him out for olive oil, of all things? (She wasn't even out of olive oil, it was just the first thing that came to mind.) She was an adult who had been more or less single for a full decade. Her ex-husband was so far out of the picture he couldn't even cough up a couple of bucks for college tuition. She was on her own. It struck her now like a punch to the stomach that it was a very lonely place to be.

Chapter 29
Lu

Lu, in the kitchen, could hear the soft murmurings of Maggie playing a game of Sorry! with the boys upstairs. Maggie had come straight from the ferry—she'd been visiting her father. Lu had only asked her to come at the last minute, last night, after the fight with Jeremy, who had left again this morning.

She was working on a skillet cornbread, trying to figure out how to incorporate jalapeño peppers without making the bread too spicy to appeal to young palates. Honey would help. And definitely cheese. She chewed on her lip and wondered if she could simply swap out the ingredients from one of Dinner by Dad's sweet cornbread recipes—maple cranberry, maybe. She had boiled the corn earlier that morning and now was slicing it from the cob. Very satisfying. She loved a task whose margins were clear: now the cob is clean, so now you are done.

"Sorry!" rang out from upstairs. It sounded like Chase. He was gloating, so he'd probably knocked one of Sebastian's pieces off. She listened carefully to find out what would happen after that. Sebastian wasn't good at losing. That was why Lu didn't play board games! It wasn't worth the headache, even though she knew that lessons about winning and losing were crucial for children to learn at a young age, etc. She found it much easier to take the boys outside and let them run off all of their joys and frustrations until they were just well-behaved, tired boys, just shells. Lovable shells, of course. But shells. It was the same principle she'd seen applied to dog-rearing. Although they didn't have a dog themselves, their neighbors in Connecticut owned a fearsomely energetic border collie named Gus, and much of the neighbors' time seemed to be spent getting Gus tired enough so that he behaved like a regular dog. (Why not, then, get a regular dog? That's what she always wanted to ask the neighbors.)

"Sorry!" came again. This time it was Maggie, and the word sounded more gentle coming from her, as though she really did feel sorry. What a funny word: *sorry*. You could toss it around so casually when you accidentally cut somebody off in the grocery store or wanted the waitress to repeat the specials. Or you could scream it at someone, like she had last night at Jeremy, lying through both syllables.

"What do you want?" she'd screamed finally, once they'd allowed the fight to escalate to the level they both secretly wanted it to be.

"I want you to stop sneaking around behind my back! I want you to say you're sorry! I want you to fire her."

Oh, it had been awful, the rage she'd felt. She'd felt like she could hurt someone.

"Lu!" he said, when she didn't answer. (His voice was so sharp!) "Did you hear me? I want you to fire her."

Lu understood that on the surface the fight was about Maggie, but on a deeper, more insidious level it was about the baby. A third baby would require resources; Jeremy didn't want those resources going somewhere else. Jeremy didn't want Lu physically or emotionally separated from the boys because he wanted her in the maternal mind-set.

"Did you hear me, Lu?" His voice had turned gentler, but her ire was reaching toward the ceiling.

"I heard you," she yelled. "Fine! Okay! I'm sorry!"

That was all he'd needed, it turned out, the word, not the actual meaning behind the word. How easy it was sometimes to fake it.

When Jeremy was sleeping she'd slipped out of bed to text Maggie. Can you come tomorrow too? Something came up.

Sebastian came down in tears, complaining that Chase had knocked back his blue piece with the red piece and he'd had to go *all the way back to the blue circle at the start.*

"But that's how the game is played," said Lu, though three-quarters of her mind was on the cornbread. (Was buttermilk absolutely necessary?) "If *you* landed on a space that *Chase* was on, you'd be able to do the exact same thing to him."

Lu and her sister had played endless board games when they were little, because they were so often alone while their mother was at work. Clue. Risk. Yahtzee. Trouble. Pre-Internet, of course.

"Well, I didn't like it," said Sebastian. "Chase was being mean."

Lu sighed, turning her attention from her cornbread to her son. Maybe Sorry! was too complex for a four-year-old. Sebastian was too little to understand how much of it was just due to chance. Also it took a long time to get through a complete game, if she recalled correctly, probably far too long for his teeny-tiny attention span. He did look despondent. "Maggie!" she called up the stairs. "I think maybe a different game, if that's okay!" Then she thought for a fraction of a second and added, "Sorry!" She didn't know if Maggie would get the joke but she had given herself a little chuckle.

"I want to stay with you," Sebastian said.

Lu hesitated and looked around the kitchen. "Sure, yeah, okay," she said finally. "You can help me measure."

"No problem," called Maggie. Lu could hear her making a game with Chase out of picking up the pieces and the cards and putting them back in the box, which was not something Lu would have thought to do. She would have left the pieces scattered upstairs and tripped over them later, crushing the cardboard box in the process.

"Sebastian, come play with us!" Maggie called. "You'll love this game, I made it up!"

This seemed to pique Sebastian's interest: he dropped the empty measuring cup he'd been holding and was gone without so much as a backward glance.

Was everyone better at mothering her own boys than Lu was?

Lu was in between years in law school when she met Jeremy, on Main Street in Hyannis, near the Puritan Clothing Shop. She'd been thrown from her bike because a man in a parked car had opened his door just as she flew past. She wasn't hurt badly, but the shock of it had been something terrible, and she'd lain immobile on the street for a moment, trying to work out if she was going to cry or not.

The man from the car was kneeling beside her, but Jeremy, who'd been parking his car when the accident happened, pushed him aside, almost roughly. "I'm a doctor," he'd said. (That was a lie, it turned out; he was a second-year medical student.)

"Don't you worry," Jeremy had said, once the driver had left them. "I'm in medical school. I can fix anything."

"Well, I'm in law school," she'd answered. "So don't mess up. I can sue anyone."

He had laughed at that. And while he was laughing he looked at her knee where the skin had shredded off, and then he swabbed at it with a square of sterile cotton that he seemed to have pulled out of thin air, and by the time he was finished she was perfectly bandaged and there wasn't a trace of blood anywhere. He'd wheeled her bike carefully from the street to the sidewalk and then he said, "You're lucky you didn't bang your noggin. You should have been wearing a helmet."

"I know," she said, touching her miraculously unharmed head, charmed by his use of the word *noggin.* "I know I should have been."

What if Lu hadn't fallen off of her bike that day—what if she hadn't even gotten on her bike, or had a bike to begin with? Lu rewound the tape in her mind all the way back to when she was a girl of five, the training wheels just off her pink Barbie-themed bike. One thing happened, then another—a seemingly random series of events—and then there was your future, sealed to this other person's for such a long time, maybe even forever.

Poor thing, she chided herself, *your marriage isn't what you expected it to be.* She remembered a middle school joke where you would rub your thumb and forefinger together. *What's this?* you'd say. *It's the world's smallest violin, and it's playing just for you!* If her mother, her sister, any of the destitute people living in inner cities and third world countries could hear her, that's what they'd do. They'd play the tiny violin. And she deserved it. *Marital dissatisfaction is a problem of wealth and privilege,* she reminded herself. *You are lucky to have this problem, because you are lucky to have the leisure to worry about such things as you sit in the summer home that you did not arrange or pay for.*

Even so! She thought about a cookbook with her name on it. She thought about the Pioneer Woman and her empire (a boutique hotel! a housewares line!) that had all started with a blog. And she couldn't help it: She wanted. She wanted.

––––––––

"What are you baking?" asked Maggie now. "It smells delicious!" Lu hadn't actually begun baking anything yet, so that made her smile; either Maggie was having a Pavlovian response to the sight of the ingredients all laid out, or she was just really, really a nice kid. Her shirt said If History Repeats Itself, I'm Getting a Dinosaur.

"Cornbread."

"I *love* cornbread!"

Lu thought about Jeremy saying, "She's a stranger to me." She thought about the cookbook proposal she was working on, and she thought about the money in her secret account.

"I'll take you as many days next week as you're free, by the way," she said to Maggie.

Chapter 30
Joy

Dinner at Winfield's went extremely well. Joy had thrown all caution (and wisdom) to the wind and ordered the spaghetti carbonara with duck confit instead of the swordfish or the halibut, and Anthony had the grilled beef tenderloin. A seltzer for Anthony, and two glasses of Prisma Sauvignon Blanc for Joy. She was ready, if Anthony produced another *I love you.*

Over the appetizer (they shared the seared scallops and the Narragansett Bay mussels), Joy pulled out a few of her favorite family stories—the time all four of her brothers got kicked out of Scottie's Pub for fighting *with each other*, the time her sister-in-law Tina packed up her family after a day at Sandy Beach and drove a quarter of a mile away before she realized she'd left one of her kids behind, the time one of the Halla-more Clydesdales pulling Santa's sleigh pooped on her father's shoe before the annual Christmas parade. For dessert they shared a crème brûlée that was to die for.

But Maggie was sleeping at home that night, no sleepover at Riley's, no Dustin, so after dinner they parted ways, Anthony depositing a chaste peck on Joy's lips. Joy's entrée had been heavy on the garlic—was that to blame?

Later, the cream from the carbonara wreaked havoc on Joy's system. She came down with a case of heart-burn. She tossed and turned for much of the night. It was too warm in her bedroom, but when she opened the windows there was so much street noise that she couldn't fall asleep. She walked around the upstairs, checking on Maggie, checking on Pickles. (Both were slumbering soundly in Maggie's bed.) She took three Tums and drank a glass of water. She returned to her own bed and tried every sleep aid app on her iPhone—Calm, Brain Waves, Sleep Genius, Sleep Pillow. Noth-ing worked. Everything seemed to make her brain race faster.

Just after dawn she gave up and made coffee in the French press. When she looked in the mirror she saw that her eyes were puffy. Her head hurt. Her heart hurt. It was ridiculous. What, specifically, was wrong with her? Was she simply too full of rich food and wine, or was she in love? Was she *heartsick*? Pickles appeared from Maggie's room.

She sat on the deck with her coffee and watched the first streaks of light begin to swoop across the sky. Pickles sat on her feet. As she sipped, she felt the truth float toward her like an island breeze.

She loved Anthony.

She did.

She'd been a fool to respond so cagily when he'd told her he was falling in love with her. (Out of *olive oil?*) She'd been scared, that was all. But despite all of her proud status as an independent woman, despite all the years-old disappointment with her marriage and the bitter taste it had left her with, it was time to stop hiding from the truth. She was a woman in love. You could be independent *and* be in love, couldn't you? Could you?

Maybe *she'd* tell *him*. Yes, that was exactly what she should do: Life was short and summer was even shorter. Why wait for him to say it again?

Olivia was opening the shop, so before Joy went in to work she took Pickles out for a walk through Rodman's Hollow. Maggie, who was awake uncharacteristically early, came along—a rare treat. At the end of the walk they took Mohegan Trail to Spring Street to get back into town, and Joy's organs constricted only a little when she saw that the Roving Patisserie was parked near the post office, a little too close to Joy Bombs for Joy's taste. There was already a line. Joy looked the other way. Soon it would be the end of July—summer was flying.

Now it was just after one and Joy was dragging with a capital *D*. She made herself an espresso and knocked it back. Olivia was in the back of the shop overseeing the filling of six trays of pies. The door opened; the bell tinkled. In walked a woman, definitely not a local, not your typical Block Island tourist either. She walked up to the counter and shook her head so that the colored tips of her hair, which were blonder by half than the rest of her hair, swung back and forth. Joy watched the hair for a moment, fascinated, almost hypnotized. Swing, swing.

"Hey," said this creature, "I'm looking for Anthony. I heard I might be able to find him here."

The woman was wearing a positively ridiculous outfit, a fitted summer dress and heels that, if Joy had known anything about shoes, she was sure she would have been able to identify as a four-hundred-dollar-plus set. Jimmy Choo or maybe that Italian guy, Ferra-whatever. Her eyeliner was perfect (tattooed? didn't people do that?) and her arms were uniformly smooth and bronzed. She wore perfume that Joy, who knew even less about perfume than she did about good shoes, would only have described as expensive. She looked like she could be Bridezilla's slightly older sister.

This, of course, must be the estranged Cassie. Who else would show up here, looking rich and well attired, acting presumptuous, asking for Anthony? Having such ridiculously long eyelashes? *Wearing lipstick?* People didn't wear lipstick in the daytime on Block Island—they wore Banana Boat lip balm, or nothing at all. They wore flip-flops, they wore beach cover-ups or shorts and tank tops, and they wore a light coating of sand.

"Anthony?" A low drumbeat of panic began to play in Joy's ribs. Did Cassie want Anthony back?

"Anthony Puckett."

"I don't know an Anthony Puckett." This couldn't be Cassie. The last name did sound familiar, though— where had Joy heard it recently? *Puckett,* she thought. *Puckett, Puckett, Puckett.*

"He's here for the summer," said the woman. "Or, ah, maybe longer, I don't know. Sandy hair, about this tall . . ." She indicated with her hand. "*Super*-cute."

Then again, *could* this be Cassie? The physical description of Anthony was spot-on.

"I know an Anthony *Jones*." Super-cute was absolutely right. But something else felt very wrong.

The woman sighed. "Fine. Whatever. I'm sure it's the same guy. He might be incognito." She narrowed her eyes at Joy.

"Why would he be incognito?"

"Do you know an Anthony or don't you?"

Now Joy was certain this was Cassie. She was caught exactly halfway between feeling threatened and feeling angry. If she'd had the guts, she would have smacked Cassie across her gently made-up face, smearing her lipstick. How dare she leave Anthony for another man! How dare she make him sad? How dare she, how dare she, how *dare she*? And also, what did she want with Anthony now, after all this time? Joy didn't like feeling threatened.

Joy raised her finger and said, "Yes. I think I do. Do you need his number?"

"I have his number. I've been trying to call him since I got on that ferry. He's not taking my calls."

Joy picked up her cell phone from behind the counter. "Let me give him a try."

Anthony answered on the first ring. "Joy!" he said. "I'm so glad you called. I was just thinking about last night. It was such a strange ending to a great night, and

I know that's because Maggie was home, but I never got to say—"

"Not now," interrupted Joy. "Anthony, not now. I have to tell you something. Cassie's here."

"She is?" said Anthony. "*Cassie?*"

At the same time the woman with the colored tips to her hair said, "What the fuck are you talking about? Cassie?"

"Aren't you Cassie?" Joy asked. She was definitely very confused.

"Absolutely not," said the woman aggressively.

"You're not?"

"I know Cassie, Cassie hired me. But I am definitely not her. She— Whatever. I can never remember how that goes." Not-Cassie sighed and held a business card out between two fingers. Her nails were cut square and painted an extravagant turquoise, like they were trying to match the color of the water off Scotch Beach.

"Scratch that," said Joy into the phone. "It's not Cassie after all. My mistake." She took the business card and squinted at it. "It's Shelly Salazar, book publicist."

"Oh, *God*," said Anthony. "Really?"

In a quick and decisive motion Shelly Salazar took the phone from Joy and pressed it to her own ear. "I heard that, Anthony," she said. "And I don't know where you are on this tiny island but you'd better get yourself down to where I am, a place called . . ." She looked around. "What is this place called?" she asked Joy.

"Joy Bombs," said Joy. She tilted her chin up in a small display of pride and ownership.

"Joy Bombs," she said into the phone. "You know it?"

"He knows it," said Joy. "He definitely knows it." Out the window she saw Maggie pull up on her bike. *Reinforcements, thank goodness.* She watched as Maggie steered the bike into the bike rack and wound the lock carefully around it, locking not just the tire but the body of the bike to the stand, the way Joy had shown her. *Good girl.* During the winter they wouldn't dream of locking anything on Block Island, but in the summer you just never knew.

"Cute title," Shelly Salazar said, when she was off the phone. "Joy Bombs."

"It's not a *title*," said Joy. "It's a name. Aren't titles just for books?"

"Or movies," said Shelly Salazar. "Or magazine articles."

"Not for bakeries, though."

"A bakery," repeated Shelly. "You guys sell gluten-free chocolate chip cookies?" She turned to scrutinize the display cases.

"No," said Joy. "We sell just one thing. Whoopie pies. Here, try one." She put a classic chocolate cream on a plate and held it out over the counter. Normally she cut samples into small pieces but she gave Shelly a whole one.

Shelly Salazar reared back like a spooked horse. "Oh, I couldn't," she said. "Gluten."

"Allergy, or preference?" That was something you had to ask, in case ingredients got mixed.

Shelly blinked at Joy and said, "Both."

Joy wanted to say, *You have to pick one*, but she held herself back.

Joy hadn't heard Maggie come in. Maggie liked to use the back door, the one that led into the kitchen, because she said it made her feel more legit. Suddenly she was there, and she was saying, "We have gluten-free whoopie pies," and when Joy turned around she saw that Maggie had already donned an apron and plastered on her best customer-service smile. Her purple streak was pulled back into a ponytail, along with the rest of her hair. Her T-shirt said My Other T-Shirt Is a Ferrari. She looked fresh and wholesome, like a Swedish milkmaid.

Shelly Salazar nodded and said, "Do you have gluten-free sugar-free dairy-free?" Her expression was optimistic, as though she actually expected that they might have something so *useless* and *ridiculous* in a *bakery.*

"Absolutely not," said Joy, under her breath.

"No," said Maggie. "I'm sorry, we don't. Maybe try, uh—the farmers' market? I can give you directions." She met Shelly's gaze square on, and she smiled.

Shelly handed the whoopie pie back to Joy and for a split second she looked legitimately disappointed. "I'm sorry," she said. "It looks delicious. I wish I could, I really do."

Then the door opened: Anthony. He was wearing faded jeans and a plain gray T-shirt that looked exactly like the T-shirt he'd been wearing that day at Poor People's Pub and really almost all the other days of the summer. Joy could feel a faint blush rise to her cheeks. All of Anthony's T-shirts were the kind of T-shirt that tried to pretend they were from Target or Olympia Sports but really cost ninety-five dollars and were made from silk spun by a thousand exotic caterpillars. That was why they were such a butter-soft place to lay one's head.

"Anthony," said Shelly. Big smile, open arms.

"Shelly," said Anthony. Smaller smile.

Joy watched them closely as they embraced and did that New York cheek-kissing thing. She didn't observe any kind of spark between them, any chemistry.

Anthony looked her way and—what was that? Some kind of a *salute*? Then he turned back to Shelly and said, "You be careful of these things. You eat one, you want to eat ten. They're little joy bombs, just like the name claims."

A section of a moment passed and then Shelly said, "Ohhhh!" She smiled. "Joy bombs. I get it."

"Also my name is Joy. It's a play on words, you see."

"Ah. A *double entendre*, if you will."

"Oh, I will."

Shelly laughed a little, not insincerely, and then said, "Anthony Puckett, *you* are a hard man to track down."

Anthony glanced at Joy again and then back at Shelly. Did he look a little panicked? And *what* was going on with this last name?

"Wait," said Joy to Anthony. Where had Joy heard the name Puckett? She searched her memory and came up empty.

"Hang on," said Anthony to Shelly.

"Mom?" said Maggie to Joy.

"Anthony?" said Joy.

"We have to talk," said Shelly to Anthony. "I came all this way to see if we could finally do that thing with your fa—"

"Not now," said Anthony, cutting her off. Not since that first car ride had Joy seen Anthony blush, not even in the heat of, well, in the heat of the moment, but now she thought she saw some color rise to his cheeks, visible even through his impressive summer tan.

"What?" said Joy, miffed.

"Not *you*, not now," said Anthony, looking at Joy. He turned to Shelly. "I mean, *you*, not now."

"Oh, come *on*," said Shelly. "This is ridiculous. I came all this way! That ferry trip takes fifty-five minutes, you know! To go what, thirteen miles?"

"Why does she keep calling you Anthony Puckett?" asked Joy.

Shelly ignored her. "My feet are killing me, Anthony. I'm not leaving unless it's to go to a bar and figure this thing out once and for all. I've got five different publications lined up for this, ready to rock."

"Publications?" said Joy. "What kind of publications?"

"Nothing," said Anthony. "No publications. Shelly, why don't you come back in a little while? I want to talk first to Joy here."

"No *way*," said Shelly. "We've been talking about this all summer. I want to lock this down, Anthony."

"All summer?" said Joy.

"Joy—" said Anthony.

There were prickles on the back of Joy's neck and up and down her arms. "You know what?" she said. "You guys go to your bar. Maggie, Olivia is in the back.

You call her out here the minute things get busy. I've got to run home for a few minutes."

"Joy—" said Anthony again.

"Anthony?" said Shelly. "What's going on here? I'm getting a vibe."

"*Joy,*" said Anthony, more urgently.

"Uh-uh," said Joy. "Nope. You, not now."

Chapter 31
Anthony

It was still daylight but inside Poor People's Pub it was perennially twilight. Anthony called Joy six times as they walked over; she didn't answer even once. His heart was hammering, and he was sweating through his gray T-shirt. He felt the same smoldering fear and regret he'd felt when Huxley Wilder had called and said those five words: *Puckett. We have a problem.*

"What do you have for tequila?" Shelly asked the bartender, whom Anthony recognized as Joy's friend Peter. Peter rattled off a list of names, most of which were unfamiliar to Anthony, who was not by nature or habit a tequila drinker. It had always seemed so unnecessarily complicated, the business with the lime and the salt: one more thing to figure out in an already abstruse world. "Ohmygod, you have Herradura?" She grasped Anthony's arm. "Have you ever tried Herra-dura?"

Anthony had not, and said so.

"You. Will. Fucking. Love it. I promise." To Peter she said, "Two," and also held up two fingers; Anthony supposed this was in case the word *two* was somehow unclear.

"Ah," Shelly said when the bartender put the shots in front of them. "God, I love the smell of a tequila shot, don't you, Anthony?"

Anthony hadn't done any kind of shot since the night before his wedding, when his groomsmen had taken him to Three Needs on Pearl Street in Burlington and gotten him inauspiciously loaded on Jack Daniel's. "Sure," he said politely. "Tequila. Love it."

The bartender brought over a small plate with two slices of lime, a saltshaker, and two cocktail napkins; Shelly waved him away. "We don't need the chasers," she said. "Not with Herradura." She lifted one of the shot glasses and handed the other to Anthony; she tipped hers into her mouth and indicated with one hand that Anthony should do the same. She closed her eyes and lifted her chin slightly: a gesture of ecstasy. "God, that's good," breathed Shelly. "It's bold, I mean, you can *taste* it, but it's so smooth. Doesn't leave you cringing." She flagged down the bartender. "Two more."

"I'm all set," said Anthony, who hadn't done his first shot. Shelly shrugged and made no corrections in the order. She seemed entirely unaffected by the tequila. She was so very thin, he didn't understand how this was possible.

When the next round arrived, Shelly dispatched her second shot as efficiently as she had her first and smacked her lips together. "So," she said. "This place. Block Island. It's so funny. What's it like, for real?" She pushed his shots closer to him.

Anthony took a deep breath and let it out slowly. "It's . . . amazing," he said at last. "It's really an amazing place." *Amazing* was such a vague and banal word, and it didn't begin to describe the blue-green water, the juxtaposition of the farmland with the ocean, the beach grasses blowing on the way to Scotch Beach. Mohegan Bluffs at sunrise. North Lighthouse at sunset. "Amazing," he said for the third time. His father would have been ashamed of him. *Specificity over vagueness* was one of Leonard Puckett's tenets. You had to be specific, when you were writing two thrillers a year. Your readers wouldn't stick around otherwise. "I mean," he finished lamely, "it's a really nice place to take a break. Let's put it that way."

Shelly nodded. She twirled some hair around the tip of her finger, and when she let go the hair maintained a curl. She did the same thing to two more sections of hair and then let her hands fall to the bar, tapping it twice as if to say, *There. That's done.*

Anthony needed to get to Joy. By now she would have plugged his real name into Google. She'd know everything. His heart had taken up residence in his throat. His insides were churning. "Listen, Shelly," he began, "if you came all the way here to talk about the photo shoot, I really don't know if I can—"

"Oh, *that*," she interrupted him. "That's okay, we'll get to that later. I mean, I really think it could be a game-changer for you, I have absolutely no doubt, but I totally get it if you're not ready to do it right now."

"Okay," he said, thrown by the *later.* What did Shelly think they would get to *before*? "Yeah, I guess I'm not ready."

"Let's just talk," Shelly said, as if Anthony hadn't spoken. "For now. I've never really talked to you, Anthony Puckett. I mean, I've *talked* to you, about the book stuff and whatever, but we've never *really* talked. You never told me, for example"—here she paused to twist one of the many giant rings on the fingers of her left hand—"what it's like being the son of *the* Leonard Puckett. The one and only."

"Oh," Anthony said. "Gosh." Same question Lu had asked, but decidedly different circumstances.

"You're so adorable, Anthony Puckett. I can't believe you just said *gosh.* We've got to get you out in front of the public again. Now, tell me what it's like to be a Puckett."

"It's . . . hard to explain, Shelly. And honestly not all that interesting."

"Or, we don't have to talk, you know," Shelly said. "I have a room at the Spring House Hotel."

Oh, God, thought Anthony. He excused himself, walked to the bathroom, and called Joy again. No answer. When he returned, Peter asked, "Another round?"

"Yes, please," said Shelly.

"Just a seltzer," said Anthony weakly.

"If you don't want to go to the hotel," said Shelly, "I could just . . ." She let one of her manicured hands fall into his lap.

Anthony could feel his skin burning. He glanced at Peter to see if he could see where Shelly's hand was. Peter was drying glasses with one of those little bar towels and didn't seem to notice. There was a young couple sitting at a high-top in the middle of a fight. Anthony heard the girl say, "This is just such fucking bullshit, Michael. I can't even." At a nearby table a group of bachelorettes were drinking frozen daiquiris and laughing. He shifted and gently lifted Shelly's hand from his lap, placed it on top of the bar, and gulped his seltzer.

Shelly Salazar took Anthony's hand and flipped it over so that the palm faced up. She traced the lines on his palm with her manicured finger, closed her eyes, and breathed in deeply.

Anthony glanced around the bar. "What are you doing, Shelly?" he whispered uneasily. "Are you reading my palm?"

"Yes! Look at mine." She opened her hand. "My left line is higher, which means I prefer a passionate or fiery kind of love. Let me see yours. Put your hands together, Anthony. Line up your little fingers."

Anthony put his hands together and lined up his little fingers. Shelly frowned and studied his hands. He couldn't believe he was indulging this. He needed to leave, to hunt down Joy, but he felt bewildered, adrift, and completely incapable of moving out of the way of the whirlwind that was Shelly Salazar.

"How do you know all this?" he asked.

"I read it online. You know, when you're looking for some random thing, like the weather for some vacation you're about to take, and then all of a sudden you're clicking links that say 'Top Ten Ugliest Celebrity Public Fights' or 'This Man Cured His Toenail Fungus with This Ancient Chinese Remedy'? Well, I came across a link that said 'Become a Palm Reader in Ten Minutes.' So I did."

"Wow," he said. "Ten minutes. So fast."

"Anthony," Shelly said. "I know you've split with your wife. But I have to tell you, your love line is really strong. Very active. So . . ." She looked at him meaningfully.

"I'm not interested," he said quickly. "I mean, I think you're a really pretty girl, Shelly."

"Girl?" She sat back. "I am twenty-eight years old, Anthony Puckett. I am practically an old maid."

"*Woman*," Anthony corrected. "I think you're a really pretty woman. I'm simply not looking for that right now."

"Looking for what?" Shelly rested her chin in the palm of her hand and studied Anthony.

"You know what I mean. For that." He nodded significantly at her other hand, the one that had been on his groin. "I'm not looking for that," he repeated.

"Ohmygod," she said, sitting back. "You all take everything so *seriously*."

"Who is we all? Men?"

"Your *generation*. I dated a guy your age—what are you again, like forty-five?"

"Thirty-nine!"

"Whatever. This guy was forty-five. Forty-six, maybe. Divorced. Just like you."

"I'm not divorced," he said. He had, in fact, been honest with Joy about that part. It was just everything else he'd held back on. He wished he could walk the summer backward, all the way to the day the Le Baron broke down and the Jeep pulled up beside him. If he had to do it all over again he'd tell the truth right from the beginning.

She shrugged: same difference. "He had a couple of kids, I don't know, two, maybe three, I'm not sure, I never met them. Anyway, everything was *Let's talk about where this is going, Shelly,* or *I need to know what you're thinking about, Shelly.* It was *exhausting.* I was just in it for some good sex, and also he had this *amazing* apartment on the Upper West Side, and this was when I was living with a completely psycho roommate down in the East Village in a total shithole. I would have slept with almost anyone to get out of that place."

Anthony winced. He felt six hundred years old. He missed Joy: he wanted Joy.

"I said, *Why's everything have to be so serious?*" Shelly continued, either ignoring or missing his wince. "I mean, the places he took me to! Atla. Fairfax. Le

Coucou. I kept asking him, *Why can't we just keep going out to these amazing dinners and fucking?*" She paused. "Actually," she said pensively, "the sex was just okay, if you want to know the truth."

"I don't need to know the truth," said Anthony.

"But seriously, the dinners and the apartment were amazing." She was lost for a moment in a glassy-eyed reverie, and then she snapped out of it and turned her laser gaze on Anthony. Anthony flinched. "Everyone is too serious about everything these days," she said. "I just don't get it. So you copied a couple of paragraphs from some book by some dead writer nobody's ever heard of. Does the world have to end?" Her gaze shifted, and she indicated the shot glasses in front of Anthony. "You going to do these or not?"

"Not," said Anthony. "Definitely not."

"Well, I'm not going to waste two shots of Herradura." She lifted the glasses, one by one, and tipped them into her mouth. Then Shelly Salazar smacked her lips together, held out her hand, and said, "Goodbye, Anthony Puckett. It has been a pleasure working with you."

"Goodbye, Shelly," Anthony said. "Thank you for everything."

"When you change your mind about that thing with your dad," she said, "which I know for a fact you will, you pick up your phone and you call me immediately. Okay?"

"I'm pretty sure I won't," said Anthony. "But if I do, I will."

Shelly Salazar slid off the barstool and straightened the skirt of her dress and left the bar. Anthony turned to watch her go; a slight wobble on her super-high heels was the only indication that anything had gone on in that bar, anything at all.

Chapter 32
Lu

www.DinnerByDad.com

Did I ever tell you about the first meal I made for Jacqui? We'd been dating for three weeks and four days. She was in law school, stressed and exhausted and beautiful. I invited her to my apartment. I sent my roommates out for the night. That part was easy. I cleaned the bathroom! That part was hard. But I was halfway in love with Jacqui already, so I took my toothbrush and I went at the sink with it until the residue of four post-college young men was eradicated.

I went to the store. I bought spaghetti, cheese. I bought a new toothbrush, because the one I'd used to clean was my only one. Lettuce for a salad.

It was iceberg! That's how little I knew, back then. I had sauce in my fridge. When I got home and opened the jar I saw a bit of mold furred on the inside of the lid. I went back to the store. I got a new jar of sauce. This was before it was easy to find good sauce in a jar. I'm sure there were some, but I didn't know enough to look for them. I think I bought Prego.

I started cooking. My mom called. I told her what I was doing. She said, "Whatever you do, do not serve that woman powdered cheese. I raised you better than that. Grate it fresh."

I said nothing.

She said, "Leo? Do you hear me? Buy a good block of Parmesan."

I went back to the store. I bought a good block of Parmesan. I bought a grater. At this point my grocery budget for the week was gone, maybe even for the month. The cheese was really expensive. I started grating. I grated the first layer of my third finger along with the cheese. I threw out the cheese, all of it, because I couldn't tell where the cheese ended and my finger skin began. I went back to the powdered cheese. I poured it into a little bowl I found in the back of the cupboard, hoping it looked classier that way. It didn't.

My finger kept bleeding. Did we have Band-Aids in that apartment? I'll let you guess.

I served the woman who became the love of my life the most boring, most predictable, least home-made meal there is with a hunk of toilet paper wrapped around my finger and held there with a piece of duct tape. When Jacqui ate every bit of that meal and asked for seconds, I knew I loved her. When she heaped the powdered cheese on and gamely used the back of her fork to flatten a cheese ball, I knew I loved her more.

Flash forward. Tonight I am serving my taco salad with vegetables I grew myself in my back-yard garden. I might make a summer cocktail to go with it: something with tequila and jalapeño. (Recipes to follow.)

I learned to cook as my gift to Jacqui and our family. This is what I could do for them to make all of us happier and healthier and give us all a reason to come together. You can do it too, readers. It doesn't have to be hard. But it does have to be better.

When Maggie was finished at Joy Bombs and ready to help Lu, she toted the boys off to the beach, taking extra care with their sunscreen. Due to Sebastian's near miss earlier in the summer, they were under a strict no-swimming order when Lu wasn't there. But they could build sandcastles, run footraces, play tic-tac-toe in the sand.

Lu was trying to figure out how best to photograph the tequila cocktail when the doorbell rang. She started, then took cover behind the living room curtain so she could peer out at the driveway without being seen. Shit: it was Nancy.

"*Lu!* Yoo-hoo! Lu!" Nancy rang the doorbell and knocked at the same time. Nancy was the only person Lu knew who actually said, "Yoo-hoo!" with a straight face.

Lu watched the doorknob turn slowly; she was cursing herself for not locking it, but Lu had confirmed that Nancy had an extra key, and she definitely had enough gall to use it, so it was hopeless either way. She took a sharp left turn and tiptoed quickly up the stairs, bringing her laptop with her. She needed to save everything she'd been working on and keep it out of Nancy's sight.

Nancy pushed open the door.

"Just a sec!" called Lu. "Just coming down!" She ran down the stairs and threw herself in front of the door, blocking Nancy from entering. She'd left some of the cocktail fixings out on the counter; she didn't think Nancy was going to be on board with the idea of day drinking, especially if Jeremy had told Nancy about their fight.

Nancy peered around her, trying to see what Lu was keeping her from. "Jeremy said you might need some extra help, so I thought I'd stop by. I would have come yesterday but I had an engagement."

"Extra help?" Lu wondered if Nancy came in, Lu could shuttle the cocktail glasses into the sink before Nancy had a chance to see them.

"He said you've been worn out lately." So he'd told her something. Nancy smiled conspiratorially. "Ooooh, maybe you're pregnant!"

"Definitely not," said Lu. *Definitely* not.

"Soon, I'm sure."

"Here's hoping." Lu manufactured her own smile and plastered it to her face. "Chase has been having nightmares, that's all. I haven't been sleeping well."

Nancy's face fell. "Oh. Well, soon enough, I'm sure." Lu wasn't quite sure how she'd gotten caught up in this third-child conspiracy. Two children had always seemed exactly right to Lu: one for each hand. Maybe that was because she had grown up in a small family, while Jeremy had two brothers. Whatever the reason, he was gung-ho to go for the bigger family. He always said "go for," like a new baby was a tricky soccer shot. It was easier for Jeremy to talk like that because if a new baby came along he'd be mainly watching from the sidelines while Lu ran up and down the field.

"Where are the boys?" Nancy bobbed and weaved; there was a second when Lu thought she was going to duck right under her arms to get past her.

"They're upstairs."

"Maybe I'll just come in and say hi."

"Oh, gosh, I wish you could, but they're napping!"

Nancy looked at her shrewdly and said, "Chase doesn't nap."

"Not at home, he doesn't," said Lu. "But something about the salt air here, all the sun—he gets really wiped out. I was just checking on them, they're out like a couple of lights."

"Call me when they wake up," said Nancy. "Maybe I'll come back."

"That would be so great," said Lu. "They'd love it."

She hustled Nancy out the front door and made her way back to the kitchen. Before returning to the cocktail scene she checked her email. She had seventy-eight new messages, one of which said, *Invitation!* in the subject heading. Lu got a little fluttery feeling in her stomach just as she used to as a girl when she got asked to a birthday party.

She read the email, then reread it. She was invited to Sapor!, one of the biggest food blogging conferences in the country. Sapor! was huge; it was the conference that had launched a thousand bloggers. It would take place over five days. In San Francisco! Not only was Lu invited, she was invited to be a panelist. The topic of her panel: "Infusing Your Blog with Real-Life Stories."

She would be speaking on the third day, though she was invited and encouraged to attend for all five. How was she going to manufacture a five-day trip? She couldn't call it a girls' trip. She didn't have enough friends to go on girls' trips, and anyway girls' trips of more than two nights were frivolous, everybody knew that.

Equally pressing, how was she going to present herself as a stay-at-home dad in front of a live audience? Necessity being the mother of invention, she'd have to figure it out. Later.

I'd love to, she wrote back. *Thank you so much for the invitation.*

A text came in: Jeremy.

Mom says you were acting funny. Everything OK?

How perfect that Nancy had gone right to Jeremy with news of Lu's erratic behavior. Nancy probably suspected Lu of something trite, like an affair. Normally this would have bothered Lu, but just now, with the invitation in front of her, she didn't care.

Everything's great, she texted back. Couldn't be better.

Chapter 33
Joy

It didn't take long to find it. Some simple googling. Of course, the *Times* article came up right away, followed by more articles in other papers: the *St. Louis Post-Dispatch*, the *Washington Post*, the *Boston Globe*. ("Carbon Copy." "Hometown Boy Humbled.") And more besides that, in industry publications. *Publishers Weekly*. *Shelf Awareness*. *Writer's Digest*. All Joy needed, of course, was the first one; no mistaking Anthony in the photo.

She tracked down Anthony's wife via her Facebook page, a public page that linked her art to a studio in the South End of Boston. Willing herself to close the browser, and unable to do so, Joy stared for a long, long time at Cassie's photo. Both her hair and her shirt were silky. She looked like a model for an expensive skin care regimen, an advertisement for not eating. She looked like someone who would run fast in the other direction if she saw a whoopie pie.

Joy had never felt so short, so brown, so curly and curvy, so well fed—so wrong about everything.

On the publisher's website there was an author bio that nobody had had the sense to pull: *Anthony Puckett lives outside of Boston with his wife and their young son.*

Son? thought Joy.

Joy's phone rang a lot the next morning. The seventh time that day and she didn't pick up, but the eighth time, she did. She was on her bike by then; she'd ridden as fast as she could, as far as she could.

"What?" she said aggressively. *Anthony Puckett lives outside of Boston with his wife . . .*

"Listen, Joy. It's me."

With his wife and their young son.

"I know."

"Can we talk? Can I come over?"

Anthony Puckett had never told Joy Sousa about his young son.

"I'm not home."

Anthony Puckett had stood with Joy and looked at a poster of his own father and pretended not to know him.

"Where are you?"

"I'm out."

"Out where?"

She sighed. "Not that it's any of your business, *Anthony Puckett*, but I'm on a bike ride."

"Where? I'll meet you."

"I'm halfway around the island. You'll never catch me."

"So wait for me."

She huffed and sighed again. "I don't know if I want to see you. I'm pretty sure I don't."

"But I want to explain things to you. Where are you really? You can't avoid me forever."

"I bet I can."

"You can't."

"I'm at the end of Corn Neck Road," she said finally.

"At the lighthouse? At Settlers' Rock? Where?"

"*Fine*," she said. "We may as well do this now." This was the Portuguese side of her talking, a lifetime of brawling brothers who poured their emotions out like milk from a pitcher. "I'm at the parking lot before the lighthouse." She had leaned her bike against the sign that said WELCOME TO THE BLOCK ISLAND NATIONAL WILDLIFE REFUGE and was standing with her arms folded, looking out at the Sound.

The parking lot was almost full, but nobody was around. Everybody must be walking out along the rocks to the lighthouse.

When she saw the Le Baron coming down the road she walked closer to the water. Let him come to her.

"Hey," Anthony said as he approached her, wobbling over the stones that covered the beach. His gray T-shirt had a stain on the front of it, and his hair was blowing in the breeze off the Sound. Joy tried to fixate on the T-shirt and not on the hair; she used to love seeing Anthony's hair messy like that. Used to: it was already in the past. She wished her heart could hurry up and be finished breaking so it could start to repair.

She pointed toward the lighthouse and said, "Did you know that in 1831 a schooner wrecked on Sandy Point here?"

"No." If Anthony was taken aback by the unexpected history lesson, he didn't show it. "I didn't. Joy—"

"The ship was called *Warrior.* Can you imagine it? Twenty-one people died. Not too far from where we're standing now."

"No . . ."

"Do you even know how Block Island got its name?"

"I guess I don't." He didn't seem to be getting the extent of her anger.

"Typical," she spat. "Most people who come here don't bother to find out. This island was charted by the Dutch explorer Adriaen Block. Did you know that the Narragansett tribe first called it 'Manisses'?"

"I didn't."

"That name translates to 'Island of the Little God.'"

"Okay. That's very interesting, Joy—" He put a hand out as though to touch her, or calm her, but she backed away.

"And, yeah, the sunsets are amazing and the beaches are fun and the cocktails are really good, but you people, you people who come and then leave again, you don't realize that there's a whole history here. You don't realize that you leave your messes behind for the rest of us to clean up. You come from outside, and you change what's here, and then you leave again, like it's nothing."

This time Anthony didn't respond. After a beat, Joy continued. "So let me get this straight. According to the *New York Times*, and many other publications, which I found with the help of my favorite search engine, you have a son."

Anthony nodded. "He's four. His name is Max."

"And your *father* is the guy with the gigantic display in the window of Island Bound Books, am I correct about that? Leonard Puckett?" When they'd stood in front of the poster he'd asked her if she'd read anything by that guy.

"Correct," said Anthony.

"*And*. Furthermore. You yourself are an author, not some freelance journalist. Only, your second book, for which you got paid, like, a bazillion dollars, got yanked before publication because you plagiarized part of it. And you got caught."

He nodded. "Such a tiny part, though," he said. "It wasn't even a—it was such a—I mean, most of the book was . . ."

"Uh-huh." Joy crossed her arms over her chest. Her heart was beating so hard she could feel it slamming into her hand. "I should have known," she said. "That it was all too good to be true. That you were too good to be true."

"But I'm not too good to be true," he said. He sounded desperate now. He raked his hands through his hair. "I'm here, I'm me, I'm the guy you've spent the better part of the summer with. *It's still me*, Joy. If I could just explain to you, if I could just tell you, it was all such a mistake, one stupid move that got blown way out of propor—"

She cut him off. "You are the biggest bullshitter I have ever met in my life, Anthony Jones." He winced. "Puckett, I mean!" she corrected. "Anthony Puckett.

Basically everything you ever told me was a lie. One big fat stupid lie."

"No! Not everything. Some of it. Well, not so much a lie as a—as a withholding of some of the truth."

"What a pretty way to put it," she snapped. "I can tell you're a writer!" She picked up a stone and hurled it toward the water.

"I'm sorry. I'm sorry! I don't know what else I can say, Joy. I came here at the beginning of the summer and I was broken. Completely broken. My ex-wife wouldn't—" He was trying to persuade her now, but she wasn't going to let herself be persuaded.

"Not ex. You're not divorced, remember?"

"You're right. Not yet. I will be, but not yet. Anyway, I came here just to hide, to lick my wounds, and to figure out what was next, and I didn't want to meet anyone. I didn't want to talk to anyone. I was hiding. That's why I chose this place, I thought I could be invisible for a while, until I got enough strength to return to the real world."

This made Joy even angrier. How dare he consider her world, her island, not the real world? She hurled another stone. "This is the real world, for some people. This is my real world. This is Maggie's real world. You can't just step into it and . . ." She put her fist to her mouth and bit down hard on her knuckles.

She wanted so badly to stop herself from crying, but she was just so, well . . . so *disappointed.* "You can't step into it and play with it, and step right out like it's nothing."

When Anthony spoke again his voice was gentler, conciliatory. The desperation was gone, and he was speaking tenderly. "I know I can't," he said. "I mean, I know I did, but I shouldn't have. I know it's bullshit. If I could just make you see, Joy, how broken I was at the time. How heartbroken."

"Well, bully for you. Everybody is heartbroken." She couldn't hold back the tears anymore. She turned her face away and swiped at her eyes with the back of her hand.

Anthony stepped closer to her. "Not you, Joy. You're not heartbroken."

"Says *who?*"

"You're the strongest person I know. That day my car broke down and you drove up and you were this beautiful vibrant person, so alive and strong, zooming around in your Jeep, with your *delicious* little whoopie pies . . ."

No. She wasn't going to let him bring the pies into this. That made it all seem too easy. There were still moments that Joy's heart felt like an open, weeping wound. Dustin had found another wife, had produced another child, and in those momentous gestures plus plenty of smaller ones that came before and after, he was saying, *I tried you, Joy, and you weren't good enough.* She knew heartbreak as well as anyone. She said, "You don't own heartbreak, you know."

"I never said I did!"

"You're acting like you do."

He bristled at that. The tenderness was dissolving. Good. Let it. Joy wanted Anthony to feel bad, just as she felt bad. "I am not," he said.

"You are too, Anthony not-Jones. You walk around here with your head low, like the world has dealt you a bad hand, all hangdog, like we're all supposed to feel sorry for you."

Something in his face changed, got harder. "I'm not *acting* like anything. Maybe I actually *am* sad. Maybe I've had a pretty shitty year and when I got here the only person who wanted to talk to me from my old life was *Shelly Salazar,* of all people . . ."

Joy snorted.

"And I've destroyed my relationship with my father, my wife, and my son, and probably also my mother, who called me every day until she gave up on me too . . . All I did was make one stupid mistake. I have to lose everything over it? *Everything?*"

"I'm sorry," Joy said, "if I didn't RSVP to your pity

party, but I'm having a very, very hard time with all of this."

He raised his eyebrows. "That's a great line," he said. Then, more softly, like he was whispering a secret, he repeated, "*I'm sorry if I didn't RSVP to your pity party.*" He patted his pockets—was he searching for a notebook?

"*Don't,*" she said. "You can't use it, you don't have permission. That's my line." Joy inhaled deeply. It was a lot to take in, all at once. "Let me see if I have this straight," she said. "Your wife left you when you got caught for plagiarism?"

"No." Anthony rubbed his eyes: he suddenly looked very tired. "My wife started sleeping with someone else long before I got caught. Probably even before I plagiarized. But she officially kicked me out after I was caught, yes. And the money dried up, and everything dried up. I'm in a deep, deep hole. Yes." He shook his head. "I knew you wouldn't understand. That's why I didn't tell you."

"I'm sorry?"

"I said, I knew you wouldn't understand. I knew you wouldn't get it."

"And why not?" She breathed in deeply. She felt her anger crystallize. "Why wouldn't I get it?"

"Nothing." He shook his head again. "It's just . . ."

"What?"

"Your divorce was amicable. The relationship you have with Dustin, the way you handle Maggie together—it's different. It's smooth. You wouldn't get what it's like for me, not really. You have it easier."

This made Joy seethe on both the inside and the outside. "Are you kidding me? The nerve you have!" She thought about all the lonely nights when Maggie was asleep and the winter wind was howling. "You think it's been smooth sailing the whole way, that it was just no problem to have a two-year-old and no money and be on my own, starting over in a new place? It's taken me a decade to get where I am, Anthony. A decade. And almost none of it has been easy."

"Well, but . . ." His face twisted; she could tell that he was struggling to say what he wanted to say the right way. "What I mean is, you're tough. You know what you want, and you just . . . go after it. In that way I think it's been easier for you. Because of who you are, the kind of person you are. Which is what I admire about you, Joy."

He might be trying to flatter her, but every word was just making Joy more angry. "Then you don't understand anything," she said. Growing up wealthy with a famous father, having his own path mapped out for him, then willfully throwing it away—no, he didn't deserve Joy's sympathy, and she wouldn't give it. "Maybe instead of acting like such a victim, you should figure your own shit out. That's what I had to do. And it hurt plenty along the way. You don't *own* pain, Anthony Puckett. You don't own the whole world of pain."

He was silent for a minute. She could see her words settling in.

"You're right," he said finally. His voice was more conciliatory and he stepped toward her. "I'm sorry. Joy, I really am. I'm sorry I disappointed you. I'm sorry I didn't tell you the whole story. I'm sorry I didn't have everything figured out when I bumped into you. I never meant to get attached to this place, or anyone here. It never seemed . . . real to me."

Couldn't he see that with every sentence Anthony was only getting himself deeper in the hole? "Excuse me all over the place," said Joy. "But like I said before. This *is* my real world. This is mine and Maggie's real world every day, year-round. And you cannot come into it and make me fall in love with you *under false pretenses.*"

His mouth twitched; she'd almost made him laugh. But Joy had no more patience for this. Why had she opened her soul, her home, her bed to this man, who wasn't who he said he was? She should have known it was too good to be true. Everything was. Joy walked back to the wildlife refuge sign and un-leaned her bike.

Dangerous Riptides! said the sign. *No kidding,* thought Joy.

Anthony followed and opened the door of his car.

"Joy—" he said.

"No," said Joy. Her heart was breaking into a thousand little pieces. "No, Anthony. No more. We're all done here. Forever." She turned her back while he got in the car, and when the Le Baron pulled out of its parking spot she gave no indication that she knew the car was there at all.

If Anthony said anything out the window, she didn't let herself hear.

She did hear one sound, though. The sound of her foot crunching on something—what? A phone. Anthony's phone, which must have fallen out of his pocket. Well, served him right. She picked it up and put it in her own pocket. She buckled the strap of her helmet under her chin. And then she pedaled away, with the Sound on one side of her and the Atlantic on the other, and the long, sometimes hilly Corn Neck Road ahead of her.

Chapter 34
Lu

The Block Island Airport was a pretty gray building that made Lu think of a fancy highway rest stop. She'd heard the restaurant there was very good, with prizewinning chowder and fantastic omelets, but she knew Nancy wanted to take the boys there for the first time, so she abstained, even though they were driving right by and they were all hungry. Maggie had to help her mother out at the shop, so Lu and the boys had gone to West Beach to hunt for sea glass. They hadn't found any, which made Lu feel like a loser. Maggie had told her a person could *always* find sea glass at West Beach.

Lu was hoping to stick the boys in front of a nice long movie when they got home so she could get some work done. She'd try to get them not to tell Jeremy. He wasn't a fan of daytime movies; he'd want them learning a foreign language or taking a stab at pre-algebra. If she put on a movie Chase might even nap; even now he was doing the head-jerking, almost-sleeping of the overtired child. She was tired too, but she wasn't allowed to do the head jerk while she was driving. Obviously.

She heard her phone ping in the console next to her—the text sound she'd set for Jeremy. She resisted the urge to check it. The boys were all over her about looking at her phone while she was driving.

When they were younger, and first dating, before they lived together, Jeremy called Lu at the end of every shift, no matter the time, and Lu lived for those phone calls, no matter how disruptive. Now there were times when a call from Jeremy felt like an intrusion or a reproach. She felt like he was checking up on her.

She looked quickly at the text once she'd made sure the boys weren't watching her.

How r u holding up, Jeremy texted like a teenage girl.

If she hadn't been driving she might have texted back, I feel like crap. Was there an abbreviated version of that? Probably CRP.

It was a sweet text, really. He meant because of Chase's nightmare the night before. Lu had been up for hours with him. She knew she could have and should have been grateful for Jeremy's concern but instead she was irritated: irritated that she'd been the only one

Chase had wanted, irritated that she was *always* the one Chase wanted, irritated that it was only one out of approximately seven nightmares that Jeremy witnessed so that even when he was trying to be kind he never really saw the whole picture.

The evening had started benignly enough. Dinner, bedtime for the boys, a little television. In bed, Jeremy reached for Lu, rubbing her back, the back of her neck, the space behind her right ear. Lu recognized his classic seduction moves, but had an anxious feeling about being behind on the blog. If she was being honest with herself she'd been hoping instead that Jeremy would fall asleep early so she could sneak down and get some work done.

No such luck.

What had Queen Victoria's mother told Victoria? *Close your eyes and think of England*? Okay, fine. Lu closed her eyes and thought of avocado-and-cucumber salad with a light balsamic dressing; of homemade lassi and tikka masala; of her author photo on the book jacket of her very own cookbook.

After, she lay in the dark, listening to Jeremy's breathing, waiting for it to even and deepen so she could sneak downstairs for her laptop. Out of nowhere came the noise that meant Chase was having a nightmare. It always started long and desolate, like the lowing of a disgruntled cow, and progressed from there to a wail, and sometimes a shriek.

"I'll go," she said, already starting to rise from the bed.

Jeremy grasped her hand. His fingers were soft and warm against hers. "Don't," he said quietly, half asleep. "Stay here with me. He'll go back to sleep in a minute."

"He won't. I can tell." When Chase got really revved up he sounded like a fisher-cat caught in a fox trap; if he got to that point he'd wake Sebastian, and then nobody would get any sleep. Better to go now.

"Want me to go?" Jeremy was half mumbling—he had the medical school survivor's gift of being able to sleep in any situation.

"That's okay," she whispered. "I know the drill."

She was able to quiet Chase quickly, but she had to climb in bed with him to do it, and he threw one arm across her chest and kept it there before falling into a deep sleep. She thought again about her laptop. Every time she tried to slide out from under Chase's arm he tightened his hold on her, and she didn't think she could get out without waking him. It felt not so different from trying to work herself loose from Jeremy's hand earlier so she could go to Chase. If she freed herself from Chase, would somebody else grab her next?

She felt tricked, but the truth was she'd been tricked for years. After Sebastian was born she'd fallen under the spell of his steady infant gaze and the feel of his tiny hand grasping her thumb. *Stay with me*, his gaze had said. *Don't let us ever be parted.* She'd acquiesced, and in acquiescing she'd joined the long line of women who had laid down their work and picked up their children.

She wondered if Chase might one day tell his therapist that when he was young his mother had one eye on him and his brother and the other on the screen of her laptop.

In the end, anyway, she'd fallen asleep on her side of the twin bed and had woken with a crick in her neck, Jeremy gone.

"Hey!" said Sebastian now, pointing to the airport parking lot. "It's the cookie truck! Can we stop?"

Lu glanced over. Yes, the telltale French flag, the even more telltale line of people.

"Not now, sweetie, okay?" She had posted only once in the past three days; she knew if she didn't get something up soon her readers would start to wander. It was the relentless pace of the really good blogs that made them successful: the relentless pace, and the fact that they made it look easy. (Sort of like motherhood.) "I really need to get home," she told the backseat.

Chase was fully awake now. "I see Maggie!"

"No," said Lu. "You can't see Maggie, Maggie is helping her mom at Joy Bombs."

"But I do. She's right there."

"She is," confirmed Sebastian. "I see her too."

Lu slowed to a crawl and squinted. There was a knot of teenagers off to the side of the food truck, and, yes, there was Maggie. There was the French boy who worked in the food truck; there was Maggie's friend Riley. There were clouds of smoke rising around them, and a flash of black as Maggie handed something to Riley.

"Oh, Maggie," Lu said. "Maggie, *no*."

"What are they doing?" asked Sebastian.

"Nothing," said Lu sharply.

Chapter 35
Joy

Joy was in a wretched mood, tired and out of sorts, when Lu, Maggie's employer, came into the shop. She replayed her fight with Anthony again and again. In romantic comedies, the false start always led to the Big Epiphany, the Grand Declaration. But they'd stopped at the false start.

Because life was not actually a romantic comedy, she reminded herself. Their false start had been a real end.

They sat. Joy listened to everything Lu told her, and then she shook her head and said, "I'm sorry . . ." Her head was all cobwebby; maybe she'd misunderstood. "I'm sorry . . . are you telling me you think Maggie was *vaping*?"

"I don't know if *she* specifically was vaping," said Lu. "I just know that the kids around her were."

Joy was not going to admit that she wouldn't recognize vaping if vaping walked up and tapped her on the top of the head. She'd do Google Images when she got back to her office. "Who was she with?" She felt a panicky feeling rise. "Maggie doesn't know any kids who do vaping."

Lu smiled. "It's just called vaping," she said. "Not *doing* vaping. Maggie doesn't know any kids who *vape*." Joy found the smile a touch condescending even as she understood that Lu probably meant for it to be inclusive. "Anyway, I'm sure it's going to be all right. I didn't mean for you to get all worked up. I just wanted you to know."

"I'm not all worked up!" cried Joy, who was feeling very worked up. In her mind she was already texting Holly. Call me, she'd say. Right away.

"It's just that . . ." Lu leaned forward conspiratorially and put her hands on the table. "When you're young, it's easy to make yourself vulnerable. Didn't you ever make yourself vulnerable when you were young? Especially when you had a crush on someone?"

Ha! Had Joy ever! When she was twenty-two and Dustin was the lead singer of the Chiclets she'd spent fourteen nights straight tossing her hair around at venues up and down New England. Club Babyhead and Lupo's in Providence. The Paradise in Boston.

T.T. the Bear's in Cambridge. She would have jumped off a bridge for Dustin, off a cliff, out of a moving train. *Vulnerable* was an understatement. But she'd been twenty-two, not thirteen!

Out of the corner of her eye Joy noticed Olivia Rossi pause in the wiping of the counter, the way you pause when you don't want to miss a word of what someone around you is saying. "Olivia," said Joy, in a slightly fake voice, "could you just run into the storage closet and see how many boxes of coffee stirrers we have? I forgot I have to put in my order by four o'clock today."

Olivia disappeared into the back—was she walking more slowly than she needed to, maybe a little reluctantly?—and Lu said, "And especially when the crush is on someone older . . ."

"Right," said Joy, because she couldn't very well say, *I don't know what you're talking about and I'm worried my daughter likes you and your nuclear family more than she likes me.*

"I mean, he's adorable," Lu went on. "I don't blame her. She's got great taste! But we don't want her to get her heart broken."

"Of course not," said Joy. Her voice was her regular voice, but inside she was roiling. She had forgotten all about the text she'd seen earlier in the summer, but the memory came flooding back to her now. What had it said? *Do u rly think I should go 4 it.* How could she have forgotten?

The lack of a male role model in the household meant that Maggie was looking to older boys—she shuddered—for affection, and who knew what else. Joy had been distracted this summer, with the business, with Anthony, and she'd taken her eyes off Maggie. And now Maggie was telling Lu things she wasn't telling Joy.

She let her pride fall to the floor, where it landed with a thud that was almost audible. "I'm sorry," she said. "But I'm not sure I know exactly who you're talking about."

"Oh!" said Lu. "Oh. No, I'm sorry, of course I thought if I knew, you'd know. How funny." It wasn't funny. Lu felt sorry for Joy, Joy could see it right there on her face. Poor single Joy, couldn't keep track of the one child she was lucky enough to have. "It's Hugo! The boy who works at that food truck, the Roving Patisserie? I think his parents must own it. He has floppy brown hair . . . super-cute. Have you tried the salade Niçoise? It's to die for!"

A clattering sound came from behind them and both Joy and Lu turned to look. Olivia Rossi stood there, with narrowed eyes and a hand on her hip. On the floor in front of her was a small pile of spoons that had been knocked from the counter. Olivia looked stern and disappointed, like an English nanny. Had she heard the conversation? "No backup boxes," she said. Her expression turned sphinxlike, unknowable. "We're completely out of stirrers," she added. Her voice was low and even, giving nothing away.

Just then a shadow fell over the table. Joy looked up to see Maggie turn away from the table. Where had Maggie come from?

"Figures," Maggie said. "Figures you'd do something like this. I knew I couldn't trust you." A flash of yellow Converse, and she was gone.

Joy and Lu sat for a moment in stunned silence. The shop door closed behind Maggie. In the back, they could hear the clattering of pans as Olivia Rossi prepped for that afternoon's baking.

"Is she mad at *me*?" asked Lu finally. "Or . . ."

"Or me?" whispered Joy.

"I'm not really sure," said Lu. "Maybe both?"

Chapter 36
Anthony

Anthony returned to Fitzy's uncle's cottage. For a little while he tried to comfort himself, as one does, by falling back on one of the most basic of human instincts: self-righteousness. Wasn't Joy, after all, very attached to her dog, going so far as to *brush Pickles's teeth with a toothbrush*? And at the same time didn't she let Maggie run a little wild around the island, coming and going as she pleased, riding her bike at night, chopping with very sharp knives? And also, who did she think she was, shoveling an endless number of calories into Anthony? (Didn't she understand that *not every night had to be a dessert night*?) Wasn't she a bit unnecessarily hung up, all these years later, on the wrongs that had been done to her by her ex-husband? Did she possibly worry too much about the competition that had come to the island in the form of the Roving Patisserie, and was it possible that she talked about it *a little too much?* Everyone knew that whoopie pies and macarons were not the same thing.

It didn't work. He didn't actually believe that any of Joy's quirks were flaws. If anything, they caused him to love her even more. He wanted to bury his face in her hair, her neck.

At the same time, an unwelcome guest visited Anthony: the thought of the twenty grand he owed Huxley. August was nearly here; he had to come up with the money by September. This was a fact Anthony had managed to push down all these weeks, to bury under Joy's bed, but now it crawled out and reared its ugly, ugly head.

The liquor in the crystal decanter caught Anthony's eye. He'd managed to avoid even a sip of tequila with Shelly Salazar, but now the contents of the decanter called to him with the force of a Siren. *Hear my music,* sang the tawny liquid. *Launch your ship upon these rocks.*

To distract himself, he thought he'd try to call Max. He hadn't talked to him in—what was it? Four days? Longer? He'd lost track.

He patted his pockets. No phone. He checked the kitchen, the bathroom, the deck. Negative. He went out to the Le Baron and searched under all of the seats. Nothing.

Plot twist, thought Anthony glumly. *Extremely inconvenient plot twist.*

The next time he passed the decanter, he reached for the stopper, and for one of the glasses that sat on the tray waiting for the guests who never came. He poured. He sniffed. He drank. The liquor went down easy, warming him from the inside out. How much harm could just a little bit do? Hardly any. And if a little bit did hardly any, a little bit more surely wouldn't hurt. He had poured such a small portion the first time around.

Chapter 37
Joy

When Maggie got home, Joy was at the door waiting. In her hand she held an e-cigarette, as small and innocuous-looking as a flash drive, that she'd found in Maggie's backpack. Part of Joy, the detached part, was curious to see how Maggie would react when presented with the incontrovertible evidence. The rest of her was just mad.

Maggie's face went white, and her freckles stood out like sentinels. "I don't know what that is," she tried.

"Of course you know what it is. *I* know what it is."

"You do?"

"I do." Joy wasn't going to tell Maggie that she'd googled an article called "What Every Parent Should Know About Vaping." "I know way, *way* more than you think I do. This is a vape pen, and I'd like to know what it was doing in your backpack."

Maggie blinked. "I think it's Riley's," she said, after a long pause. She leaned closer to the pen, as if looking for a name tag. (*Interesting*, thought Joy. She hadn't thought Maggie's first reaction would be to toss her best friend under the bus.) "Yes, it's Riley's. She must have put it in my bag."

"Where did Riley get it?"

Maggie shrugged. "I don't know." She furrowed her brow and looked pensive. "Maybe from Hugo?"

"Who's Hugo?"

"Just this kid."

"Just what kid? I know everybody on this island. I don't know anybody named Hugo."

"He's here for the summer. From France."

"France, like *macaron*-ville France?"

"I think so," said Maggie in a tiny voice.

"Fabulous," said Joy. "Really wonderful." Not only did Maggie have vaping equipment, it could be traced back to Joy's mortal enemy, the owner of the Roving Patisserie. Lu had been right.

"Don't tell Holly, Mom, *please*. Riley will kill me."

"I'll worry about what to tell Holly later." (She had already told Holly.) "Right now I'm going to worry about you. Have you used this?"

Maggie hesitated.

"*Maggie!* Answer me." Joy hated the way her voice sounded, loud and shrill, and she also hated the way she felt, on the precipice of a severe panic attack, filled with a burgeoning rage.

"Once or twice," said Maggie finally. "Okay, and now you're going to freak out."

"I'm not freaking out!" Joy could feel her blood pressure skyrocket, and she almost couldn't see for the anger. She was definitely freaking out.

"You are. You're freaking out all over the place. What's the big deal? Everybody vapes. The summer kids all do it."

"The big deal! It's a gateway drug, and I'm sure not everybody does it. I'm *positive* not everybody does it."

"It's not a drug. It's just, like . . . flavored air."

"It's not just flavored air. And it's a gateway *activity*. It leads to other activities. Regular cigarettes. Pot. It can make it harder for your body to fight germs. You can get popcorn lung!" She had learned that from the same article.

Maggie blanched. "You made that up. There's no such thing."

"I did not. There is." Joy reached for her phone, to prove it. *Siri*, she wanted to say. *Help me raise my daughter.*

"You don't have to show me. I don't really want to know." Maggie then treated Joy to some statistics about everybody in France smoking and four-year-olds drinking wine and eating beurre blanc sauce. "French people are so much more sophisticated," Maggie finished.

"I don't care what French people do," said Joy. "I care what you do." She realized this was a completely unoriginal version of what mothers had been saying to their daughters since the beginning of time, but she couldn't help herself.

"You are completely and totally overreacting," said Maggie. She folded her arms over her chest. "This is so typical."

"You're thirteen years old, Maggie! If anything, I think I'm underreacting." How was Maggie managing to make her feel old and stodgy? It wasn't fair. She wasn't stodgy. Hadn't she, Joy, smoked a bunch of weed junior year in high school when she was dating that pothead Marco Brotelho? You bet, but she'd been sixteen her junior year, almost seventeen. *Maggie was thirteen.* Joy had brought her beautiful baby girl, heart of her heart, to live on this beautiful island so she could breathe the purest air, be surrounded by some of the world's most natural beauty, protected by miles and miles of ocean and within glimpsing distance of any number of endangered species. Now that beautiful baby girl was letting some summer assholes fill her young, unsullied lungs with poison. And her mind with who knew what. No, Joy wasn't overreacting. She was reacting exactly right. Confident in her rightness, she was figuring out what to say next when Maggie pulled out the big gun. And aimed. And fired.

"You're just mad because Anthony doesn't want to be your boyfriend anymore. Because you're mean and boring, and he finally figured it out."

Joy could see right away that Maggie regretted that. But the barb had lodged deep, right away, right in the middle of her ribs, where it took Joy's breath away. There was no way she was going to be able to pry it loose.

She had never really punished Maggie before. She'd never had to! Maggie had always gotten along so well in the world in general, and on the island in particular. Maggie knew how to put air in the tires of the Jeep, and how to make a cheese soufflé. She had been ten when she'd learned how to gut and fillet a fish. She could swim out of a rip current and get herself home from anywhere on the island on her bike. She'd always taken excellent care of herself, like a baby lizard or an infant snake.

But this. This was too much.

"You're grounded," said Joy.

"What?"

"You heard me."

"For how long? I have to babysit tonight."

Joy hesitated. She didn't know how long groundings typically lasted, never having doled one out before.

"How about for the rest of the month?" asked Maggie. (It was the last day of July.)

Normally Joy would have appreciated the humor in that. But she was *so angry*. And she was scared.

"Indefinitely," she said. "You can babysit, but except for that, you're grounded. Maybe forever."

Chapter 38
Lu

When Maggie came that evening there was no trace of the surly girl from the day before. Lu had set her up with a picnic dinner to have with the boys on the beach.

When I was a boy, wrote Lu, *times were different.*

I know this seems like a very basic, very obvious thing to say. Members of each generation think that their own growing-up years were a simpler time. But I don't think you can argue with the fact that ours really, truly was. When I was the age my boys are now we played baseball and kickball on summer nights like these. The games went on forever. The nights went on forever. Am I waxing too nostalgic for you, readers? I apologize if I am.

There's something about summer evenings that makes me feel that way. The word "nostalgia," as any Don Draper fan knows (please see Season 1, Episode 13, "The Wheel"), comes from a Greek compound consisting of the words "homecoming" and "pain." And when I'm feeling nostalgic, the thing that eases that pain is comfort food. I'm talking fried chicken. Meatloaf. Mac and cheese. Chicken potpie. Food that sticks to your ribs, and sticks to your heart.

Lu paused. Too corny? Well, she could adjust it later if necessary. Anyway, her readers tended to respond well to corniness. Again, she was willing to bet that was because they believed she was a man. Too much emotion from a woman was, well . . . expected. Unsurprising. Sometimes annoying. But from a man? Charming, of course. Attractively vulnerable.

She was working on a recipe for mini–chicken potpies. Both her fictional boys and her real boys went crazy when their food came out small; they ate twice as much overall when it was a third the size. It was an elegant equation.

She stretched her arms above her head and rolled her head from side to side, easing the tension in her neck. Lu had been able to work so much more with

Maggie here to help that her body was starting to complain about all the sitting. Maybe she should actually start taking some of the exercise classes she'd been pretending to attend this summer. (She wouldn't.)

She'd have to figure out the proportions for the mini-pies—and, oh, dear, would there be any proper ramekins in this kitchen? She knew she'd seen a pot big enough to boil lobsters out in the garage, and boiled lobster meant butter, and butter typically required ramekins, so she rooted around in the very back of all of the cupboards, and there she found them, under a half-used package of lobster bibs and next to a jumble of crackers. Her mind raced briefly ahead to lobster potpie, but she reminded herself to focus on the recipe at hand. Maggie was a huge help, but Lu didn't have unlimited time.

When she returned to her computer she saw that a new email had come in from Abigail Knowles of the Wilder Literary Agency.

I love the sample cookbook pages you sent over, thx! I think it's going to be really easy to pull together a proposal from these. I've spoken to my boss Huxley and he's totally on board. I am currently out of the country on vacation (Italy!) so we might have to wait to talk. When I'm back, we'll set up a phone call to discuss strategy and timing. As soon as I found you, I knew I had to have you. Can I have you?

Could Lu reasonably expect to become a man, to acquire a man's voice, while Abigail Knowles was in Italy? Unlikely. Because she had the house to herself she tried it quickly, deepening her voice. "Hello," she said. "May I have Abigail Knowles's office, please?" It was ridiculous. At best she could maybe come off as a prepubescent boy, but certainly not a mature man, a married father of two. Why, exactly, had she let herself get into this situation in the first place?

She looked at the kitchen clock; she looked out the window. She rechecked her post-in-progress and hit save. Then she got up to stretch her legs and check on the laundry.

Lu was only in the laundry room for two minutes, maybe less, but in that time Maggie and the boys returned from the beach. It was amazing, Lu thought when she came back down, the way it took no time at all to transform a scene of peace and tranquillity into one of utter chaos. A sand pail was upended in the entryway just outside the kitchen, and shoes and towels were thrown every which way. Sebastian's nose was running.

"Mommy, I need you!" called Chase from the downstairs bathroom. He was using that singsong voice that, try as Lu might, she could not keep from grating on her nerves; he sounded like a child on a bad television commercial, not like his true, authentic self. Sebastian was beginning to pick it up too.

"Just a minute," she called combatively. She fixed her eyes on Maggie, who was staring at Lu as one would stare at a friendly apparition that had appeared unexpectedly.

"I hope you don't mind," began Maggie slowly, and, because she guessed what was coming, Lu, in her head, said, *I peeked at your computer.*

Lu stared hard at Maggie's T-shirt, which showed a gravestone with a water droplet on it and the words RIP Water You Will Be Mist.

"I peeked at your computer," continued Maggie. "Which I know I shouldn't have done."

Lu had a queer sensation in her stomach.

"And I can't believe . . . you are . . . are you . . . are you *Dinner by Dad?*" Sebastian had wandered off; there was nobody to hear, but Maggie lowered her voice anyway.

"Maybe," said Lu carefully, assessing. "Possibly." Her first instinct was to chide Maggie for looking at something that wasn't hers. For snooping. That was against the rules of general civility and the rules of being in someone else's house as well.

But something stopped her, and later, when she had time to think about it, she figured out what it was. It was the ghosts of girls from time immemorial being told to follow the rules, stay quiet, not make a fuss, never do anything that might get them in trouble. Don't speak up, don't have an opinion, and if you have one please express it very quietly and in a way that won't offend anyone around you. *Be good girls, now,* her mother used to tell Lu and her sister. Or: *The way you're sitting/standing/eating/thinking: that's not very ladylike.*

When Lu excelled at Stanford Law she heard her mother once confess to an aunt her concern that Lu might never find a man if they all thought Lu was smarter than they were. "Men don't like that," she'd whispered to the aunt. At the time, listening from the kitchen, Lu had felt herself swell with outrage and indignation. But as time went on she came to see her mother as the product of her own background and upbringing. Two daughters, no husband, the responsibilities of their little world all squarely on her shoulders. Her mother had worked her whole life at the same job, nine to five as a receptionist at a dental office, fifty weeks a year, while her heart grew unhealthy and her ankles got thick and her vision went blurry and time ticked away and her daughters watched soap operas after school. She didn't know any better—who on earth would have taught her?

But there was Maggie, looking at her with her eyes bright and hopeful, and she was so interested in what Lu was going to say next, and she was so young and unsullied and her potential was vast and untapped, so there was nothing for Lu to do but to meet her gaze levelly and say, "Yes. You're right. Yes."

"Ohmygod." Lu watched Maggie take all of this in—she watched her understand the help Lu needed with the boys, the time she spent on the computer, with the drawing pad. The inordinate amount of cooking for a family with one-quarter gone most of the time. "That's my very favorite food blog. My mom's too. We read it all the time! We make all of his recipes! You're like—you're a celebrity! I can't believe it."

"Sometimes," said Lu, "I can't believe it either."

"Mom!" This was Sebastian now, calling from upstairs. "*Mommy!* It's important."

"*What is it?*" She couldn't keep the irritation out of her voice.

"I had a really big poop and the toilet is all clogged!"

Oh, for heaven's sake, thought Lu. She smiled ruefully at Maggie. "You can't tell anyone, though, okay? You can't blow my cover."

"Wait, but—how did you? How do you—?"

"The longer version I'll tell you another time," said Lu. "But the short version is: I just took a chance," said Lu. "If you want something badly enough, sometimes you just have to take a chance."

Chapter 39
Anthony

"Would you read something I wrote?"

This was Anthony, age twenty, home from Dartmouth the winter holiday of his junior year, let into the sanctum of his father's study, clutching a copy of the story he'd written for his fiction workshop. It was just before five o'clock and the sky had surrendered its color, graying before their eyes. Anthony approached his father with an uncertainty so thick it felt as though it covered him like a cloak.

By way of an answer Leonard gestured to the straight-backed chair in the corner of the room and then, still without talking, made a motion with his arm to indicate that Anthony should move the chair closer. He held his hand out for the story, and Anthony, with a trepidation so great it deserved a different name, a stronger name, handed it over. Maybe it was terror. It felt to him like he was handing over one of his organs, his very soul.

The Uttermost table clock in the corner struck five, and here was Anthony's mother, knocking softly, carrying the scotch.

"Anthony has brought some writing to show me," said Leonard significantly, and Dorothy, understanding immediately, departed and returned with a second glass of scotch, this one for Anthony.

Anthony, whose drinking experience at that time was limited to keg beer at the Sigma Alpha Epsilon house and a bottle of shared Pinot Grigio on a date with Lindsay Hendricks at Peter Christian's in Hanover, accepted the glass somberly and sat holding it while his father read the story. He was far too nervous to sip it. Even smelling it, he felt a little drunk.

Those were the longest fourteen and a half minutes of Anthony's life. The only sounds in the room were the soft tick of the Uttermost and the light rustling of the printed pages. Anthony took a cautious sip of his scotch, just to have something to do, then another, then a third, trying not to shudder like a child swallowing cough medicine.

Finally—finally! after an *eternity*!—Leonard put the story on the desk and tapped the edges of each page into place. He blinked down at the pages for a long moment before he spoke, and Anthony wondered if a fairly fit twenty-year-old could possibly suffer a heart attack, because he felt something in his chest squeezing and squeezing. (There was heart disease in his father's family, it wasn't out of the question!)

"You might be better at this writing thing than I am," said Leonard Puckett. He was squinting, first at the pages, and then up at Anthony, and he wore an expression that combined consternation and pride, perhaps with a small dose of disbelief mixed in. There had been an early snow that year, and the spot in the garden where the roses would bloom come summer was overlaid in a white that was scarcely visible in the diminishing light. Anthony could feel the scotch building a fire in his chest. "There's just so much in here—" Leonard's voice broke off and he took a long sip of his own scotch. "You might be a prodigy." He said it softly, as though he couldn't quite take it in himself. "Look, we'll work on this together . . . We'll polish it here and there, and then, well."

"Then what?" asked Anthony. He'd meant to breathe the words but instead, because of the scotch, he'd ended up sort of yelling them. Together? He couldn't remember a moment when his father had suggested that they do something together.

"Then you really should send it out," said Leonard. "You must."

With those words, whether he meant to or not, he laid the mantle upon Anthony's shoulders.

Granta accepted the story, and it happened that a literary agent named Huxley Wilder read it and took a particular liking to it, calling the magazine, the way the agents do, to secure Anthony's contact info.

The first thing that happened after Anthony's crime was revealed was that Anthony stopped running. He stopped eating fruit; he stopped eating vegetables. He developed a soft pudding of a stomach. At night he couldn't sleep; he prowled the house like a cat burglar. *I'm sorry,* he whispered, over Max's sleeping figure. *I'm sorry I'm sorry I'm sorry.* He watched all five seasons of *Homeland,* even the third season, which most people agreed was terrible. (Anthony thought it had its good moments and had been too harshly judged.) When Cassie was in her studio working and Max was at preschool, he slept for hours on end, burrowing deep into his bed as though the covers were a rabbit warren and he an eastern cottontail. *I'm sorry,* he said, when he woke up, to Cassie, to Max. *I'm sorry I slept so long. I'm sorry, I'm sorry.*

Sometimes he woke in the night, sweating, to find Cassie's place in the bed empty. She was working, she said, when he inquired in the morning. And yet she was always freshly showered, smelling like a summer garden. She was with Max, or she was driving back and forth between home and the art gallery in the South End, where she was helping Glen Manning "mount a show."

Anthony thought about all of the potential different uses for the word *mount*. He poured another drink.

More dreams. His father as Jupiter, holding a lightning rod, raising it toward Anthony. *Why?* Leonard Puckett thundered. *Why, why, why?* His father as Jesus, nailed to the cross, and Anthony kneeling at his feet along with Mary Magdalene and the rest of the sinners, Leonard pausing in his great suffering to deliver unto Anthony a look of great consternation and disappointment.

He tried his very hardest with Max. Oh, he tried so hard! He did! He wanted to be a good father. He didn't want Max to see him break down. But one night, while he was reading *The Runaway Bunny* at bedtime, the words reached out and choked him.

Max was concerned. "Why are you crying, Daddy?" He plucked a Kleenex from the box on his nightstand and began to wipe at Anthony's face. It was all very organized and businesslike, and that made Anthony even sadder.

"It's just a sad story, buddy," Anthony said.

"It's not that sad," said Max reasonably. "The mother gets to keep her little bunny, doesn't she?"

This only caused Anthony to cry harder.

One day he came home from the liquor store—although, if anybody had asked, he was at CVS, picking up cough drops for a tickle he was starting to feel in his throat—and discovered a suitcase packed and sitting by the front door. He found himself smiling expectantly for the first time in, oh, how long? He thought Cassie had planned some sort of trip for them, an overnight where they could talk over a bottle of Sancerre, the way they used to. Or maybe they wouldn't talk at all—maybe they'd get drunk and have shower sex, which was also something they used to do. He was willing to bet Max was going to stay with his parents. Dorothy Puckett always welcomed a visit from her only grandson.

He heard Cassie's soft footsteps on the stairs—she walked lightly, like a ballerina, one step below floating.

"You need to pull yourself together," said Cassie. She didn't look like someone who was about to go on an overnight; she was wearing running shorts and a tank top and a baseball hat, and she was sweating prettily.

"I know," he said. "I'm trying. Tomorrow I'm going to—"

Cassie cut him off. "Not here." Her voice was crisp and sure, like a kindergarten teacher directing the class to the story circle.

"But . . ." The set of her eyes caused in him a physical reaction, like a punch to the stomach would. "But I live here."

"I can't do this anymore, Anthony."

For the first time in his life Anthony understood—more than that, he inhabited—the phrase *completely struck dumb*. They were not going on an overnight. There would be no shower sex. He waited for some time, until he was un-struck, and then he said, "You can't do what?"

"I can't watch this shitstorm unfold anymore. It's not good for anyone here. It's not good for Max to see you like this."

"Where am I supposed to go?" He cringed at the plaintive note in his voice. "Where am I supposed to go, Cassie? I live *here*. With you and Max."

"Not anymore," she said. "Not right now, you don't."

If ever there was a bender, Anthony Puckett was on it. He had a rum concoction at Captain Nick's. Two

Narragansett IPAs at Ballard's. A Cocktail Crush at Mahogany Shoals, where he listened to a guy from Galway singing Irish sea chanteys. Before the guy sang, he quoted Yeats, which Anthony thought was a nice touch. *How far away the stars seem, and how far is our first kiss, and ah, how old my heart.*

When he stumbled home sometime later—who knew how much later; he had forgotten about the way time stretched and bent when you were drinking—he tripped over something just outside his front door. He almost kept going without checking what it was, but then he saw that it was his cell phone. He'd forgotten about his phone halfway into his second IPA. It had been sort of refreshing, to be out of touch, not to have wondered if Joy was trying to call, if anyone was trying to call.

He had twenty-seven missed calls and thirteen text messages from Cassie, and they all said different versions of the same things. His heart lurched and every dream he'd had about Max came shooting to the surface.

Max and Dorothy were missing.

Chapter 40
Lu

This had better not be you, Nancy, thought Lu, when the doorbell rang after Maggie had gone. It was too late for Nancy to be out and about anyway. She tended to stay on her own side of the island once Henry had fixed her her first gin and tonic, and very wisely so.

Sure enough, Nancy was not on the other side of the door. It was Anthony, smelling like a brewery that made very hoppy beer and looking like he'd just crawled out of a Dumpster. His eyes were bloodshot, his hair was messed, his signature gray T-shirt had a stain on it in the shape of a cumulus cloud.

"Sorry to bother you." He was slurring. Oh, boy. Anthony had fallen off the wagon, and he'd fallen really hard.

"No bother," she said. "Come in."

"My son took my mother and is missing." He shook his head. "No, that's not right, my mother took my son. They're missing. And I can't get home, because there's no more ferries."

Lu glanced at the clock. Nine-thirty. It was a Tuesday; the last ferry departed at seven forty-five on Tuesdays. "Missing?" she said. "What do you mean, missing?"

"I mean *gone*," Anthony said. He made a move to sit on the couch but misjudged and ended up on the floor. Lu helped him up. She took off his shoes. "Kidnapped."

"Kidnapped?"

"Maybe." Anthony wrinkled his forehead. He looked confused.

"Did Cassie call the police?"

"I don't know."

"Did she put out an Amber Alert?"

"I'm not sure." Anthony rubbed his face. "I'm—"

"I know," said Lu. "Drunk. I can tell. Here, sit down on the couch. Let me see your phone, maybe I can figure it out."

Obediently Anthony handed over his phone. Lu scrolled through the texts. The first one said, Have u heard from ur mother?!!?!! The second one: She and Max are gone. It went on and on from there. I called to tell her I was coming 2 get him and by the time I got there she was gone. Toward the end, R u ever going 2 answer ur phone. And, Ur mother is a psycho.

"Oh, boy," said Lu. She glanced at Anthony. He was standing in the middle of the living room, swaying like a newly cut tree that had not yet landed. She led him to the couch. "Sit down," she said. "I'll be right back." She took from the refrigerator two of the leftover banana pancakes she had given the boys for dinner two nights ago (*Breakfast for dinner always cheers up Charlie and Sammy if they've had a rough day!*) and spread them with her homemade almond butter (she had unearthed a Cuisinart from the basement—it was ancient, but it had done the trick). She poured a glass of milk—an old college trick, or maybe just an old wives' tale, something about the protein soaking up the alcohol—and she sat next to Anthony while he ate and drank everything.

"I need to call Cassie back," he said. Anyway, that's what she figured he meant to say. What he said sounded more like, *I peed in the closet sack.* He couldn't keep his words going straight, even though he looked like he was concentrating very hard on each of them.

"No, you don't, not now," she said. "You're not exactly making sense."

"I'm not?"

"Not at all. Lie down for a few minutes. You can call when you've sobered up a bit. Give me your phone. I'll hang on to it, and if you fall asleep I'll wake you when there's news."

Anthony obediently lay down. Lu found a white cotton blanket covered with blue seashells and draped it over him. She put Anthony's phone on the table next to her. She thought about texting Cassie back, but what would she say? I'll call you when I'm sober? That wouldn't engender confidence. No, she'd just have to wait, and hope that news came by text or that Anthony would be ready to talk soon. She checked on the boys upstairs; both were sleeping in disorganized lumps. She poured herself a glass of wine and tapped her fingers on the side of the glass, then sat on a chair near the couch and made sure Anthony's eyes were closed, that his breathing was deep and even, until she could see his eyes moving rapidly behind his eyelids.

PART 4
August

Chapter 41
Anthony

Anthony was dreaming, but the dreaming was more like remembering: a movie of his life playing out on the screen of his sleeping brain.

"Believe me," said Huxley Wilder. "*Nobody* gets this attention the first time around. Nobody."

It was five years ago, and *A Room Within* was on the cusp of publication.

"Seriously, nobody," said Huxley. "Your occasional Jonathan, a Josh here or there." *Safran Foer*, thought Anthony. *Ferris*. And: *Holy cow. This is my life.*

There was a profile in the Sunday *New York Times*, an article in the *Boston Globe* Style section, a cover reveal in *Entertainment Weekly*. Blurbs that other writers had to chase came to him like a cow to a bell.

Every review came with a star, every mention with a rave.

Especially—especially!—the one that counted the most.

"The book is excellent," said Leonard. All the doubts Anthony had about his father vanished, all the weirdness between them. Leonard took Anthony and his mother to dinner at Asta on Mass Ave. in Boston to celebrate. They clinked the glasses of champagne that came automatically at the beginning of the meal and the brandy that came at the end. Anthony couldn't believe the way his father was looking at him: he couldn't believe the *paternal approval* that was washing over him.

Anthony couldn't believe any of it.

The book came out.

"It hit the list," said Huxley. "Right out of the gate. I knew it would."

"I can't believe it," said Anthony. He couldn't! He couldn't believe how many people showed up at his readings. Lines out the door. MFA students, older women, teenagers. Middle-aged men. Men his father's age. Book clubs full of young mothers who'd left their children with babysitters.

And, in Chicago, one Cassie Fontaine, from Burlington, Vermont, by way of the South End, Boston: a vision in her mid-twenties, gorgeous, with full pink lips and a lithe yoga body and a celestial voice that sounded like silver and gold spun together and poured into a crystal goblet. Cassie was visiting a former college roommate and was amazed to find that Anthony was in town too. She'd rushed right over to the bookstore as soon as she saw the poster. She *loved* the book. She leaned in close as she presented her copy for signing. She smelled like a midsummer garden. She slipped Anthony a piece of paper with her phone number on it.

Anthony thanked her. He was dating someone at the time, in New York City, where he lived. He wouldn't call this woman, this stranger with the dizzying beauty! Of course not. But still. The thought that things like this *actually happened* made him giddy. He put the piece of paper in his pocket. He forgot about it, but not really.

Cassie came to another reading, this one in Boston, at the public library. His parents were at the reading. His father sat in the back row and nodded occasionally—approvingly!—as Anthony read from the first chapter and answered questions. Cassie bought three more copies of *A Room Within*, and had Anthony sign them all to her.

Anthony's publisher had put him up at the Lenox. Anthony invited Cassie to have a drink with him at the hotel bar. Then another. Anthony was drinking Dark 'n' Stormys and Cassie was drinking rosé sangrias. Her fingers were long, like the fingers of a pianist. They went upstairs.

In the morning, he couldn't believe it all over again. She was even more beautiful in the light streaming in from Boylston Street. She had literally no physical flaws. She was perfect.

"I have to go to work," said Cassie, once she was showered and dressed. She worked as an assistant at a gallery on Harrison, in the South End, and concentrated on her own art after hours. She was beautiful *and* creative. Anthony had won the lottery.

"Don't go," said Anthony. He was still in bed, rejoicing. She leaned over him and her long blond hair tickled his bare chest. She'd used the toothbrush that came in the overnight kit in the hotel bathroom; her breath smelled minty, pure. Her skin looked like snow and felt like butter.

"But I'll see you again, Anthony Puckett."

His sort-of girlfriend called, and called again. When Anthony was cagey on the phone, the sort-of girlfriend said she wasn't interested in a long-distance relationship: Anthony was away so much! Distracted all the time, with the book. Was there really a future for them?

Anthony agreed: He was away. He was distracted. "You shouldn't have to put your life on hold, waiting for me," said Anthony. "It's not fair to you."

She sighed, relieved. "So, we're cool, then?" she asked.

"Very cool." He thought about the way Cassie's enormous eyes tipped up at the corners.

Huxley Wilder reported in. The publisher was very, very happy with the sales numbers.

Anthony's publicist was a nervous young man with a twitch in one eye. "This is going phenomenally well," he told Anthony. "We're booking you into more venues. You're available, right?"

Available? He was available. He was on top of the world.

"I'm pregnant," said Cassie, six weeks later.

Something turned over in Anthony. He felt a click that told him everything was falling into place. "Marry me," he said. He got down on one knee, though he had no ring. He'd buy one! He'd buy the nicest one. The book was selling and selling. Number eight on the list, then five, and then it cracked the top three. Then one.

He called his mother. "I'm going to be a dad," he told her. "I'm going to be a husband and a dad."

"Are you sure?" asked his mother.

He'd never been more sure of anything.

He and Cassie got married under a wildflower arch and walked down a path made of cedar chips. Now Anthony was a husband. They bought the house in Newton, because the schools were excellent and Cassie wanted to keep her job at the gallery, working for a visionary named Glen Manning. Anthony could work anywhere, and was ready to leave New York. Now they had a garage, neighbors, real estate taxes.

After a seventeen-hour labor with no epidural, in the obstetrics wing of Newton-Wellesley Hospital, Max was born. Max came out blue and Anthony thought he was going to lose his mind. Then Max started crying and his color developed: he scored 9.6 on his second Apgar test. He was perfect. Anthony had never known a fierce and unshakable love like this.

Anthony and Cassie brought Max home to a nursery that belonged in a magazine shoot: everything was white. Anthony was scared to touch anything for fear of messing it up.

"I know it seems hard to believe," said Huxley Wilder, "but someday *A Room Within* will stop selling. Do you have your next idea ready?"

But it didn't seem possible that the book would ever stop selling. Anthony got royalty checks every six months, enormous royalty checks. The view from the top was distorted, sublime. The money that had come pouring in poured right back out again. Cassie quit her job to care for the baby and to concentrate on her own art. Her taste, once unleashed, was impeccable, expensive. She needed an art studio. They could build one in the back of the house, detached. They had an acre! They may as well put a pool in, why not? And a pool required a pool house. The master bath was outdated. Good shoes cost a lot.

"Even *Gone Girl* fell off the list eventually. Even *The Help*," said Huxley. "Now's a good time to pitch the next one."

Anthony wrote a first chapter, an outline. "It's called *Simon's Rock*," he told Huxley.

"I love it," said Huxley. "Let's present it."

A deal was proffered. A number so big it made Anthony feel anxious. What if he couldn't follow through? What if he wasn't capable? He tried to express his doubts to Huxley, but Huxley didn't want to hear about doubts. Huxley said, "You know what two words a publisher most wants to put on a book jacket?"

Anthony thought about it and said, "*Stephen* and *King*?"

"Ha!" said Huxley. "Hilarious, man. But, no. *Debut* and *novel*."

"But this isn't a debut."

"Exactly! You had those two words last time. You never get them again, not in your whole career, not ever."

Anthony was confused. "I don't understand how that helps me."

"It doesn't help you. That's exactly my point. Debut novels are what every publisher wants. Nothing sells a book like the promise of new blood. So if they're offering you this fucking insane amount of money for a second book you would be an idiot not to take it."

"I'm just nervous," said Anthony. "About selling something before I've written it. Does that make you nervous at all?"

"You'd be an *idiot*," repeated Huxley. "Not to take it. Let's do this. Let's sign, and then let's go celebrate another amazing Puckett book. Sign now, write later, my man. That's how the game is played, in the big leagues."

"It is?"

"Absolutely it is."

Anthony signed.

Anthony showed Huxley a few more chapters of *Simon's Rock*. Huxley took a little time to call back. "It's good," Huxley said. But was there a hitch in his voice? "You keep the fuck writing, man. You just keep it up."

Max turned one. The publisher established a deadline.

"I need more time," Anthony told Huxley. The deadline was pushed back.

Max turned two. The words wouldn't come the way they had the first time around.

A Room Within fell off the list.

"We knew it would happen," said Huxley. "That's why we took this deal."

Max turned three. It was hard to remember what it had felt like to be on top of the world.

Ferocious dreams visited Anthony in the night. *You're not good enough!* thundered his father. *You had just the one book in you, and now it's over. You've spent it!* Anthony was going to be a one-hit wonder: the "Tainted Love," the "Come On Eileen" of the literary world.

Max turned four.

"They need to see a draft," said Huxley. "They're getting antsy. Whatever you have, let's send it."

How many books do you have in you? dream Anthony asked his dream father.

His dream father laughed so long and so hard Anthony could count his fillings: two on one side, three on the other. *I have an unlimited number,* said his father. *They just keep coming and coming.*

Anthony cowered under the covers, a little boy

afraid of monsters in the closet. *But you said I was good enough, that night when I was in college. Remember? When I brought you the story?*

I never said that! Leonard Puckett's voice rose and rose. *I never ever ever ever said that. I never would. That story was nothing special.*

Huxley emailed: *How's it going?*

Great! emailed Anthony back.

Anthony took up drinking—it had always been a casual habit, weekends mostly, but now it felt like a second job. Alcohol softened the sharp angles of his stress, blurred the lines between *can* and *cannot*.

Geez, Dad, Anthony said in his dreams. *Writing a book is hard!*

Not for me, said dream Leonard. *You're not good enough. Not good enough not good enough you can't do it you're not good enough.*

Only when Anthony was with Max did he feel okay. Max wrapped his arms around his neck and held on tight. "I love you, buddy," Anthony said. "You can do anything you put your mind to," he added.

"I know," said Max easily. "I know I can, Daddy."

The deadline drew closer and closer. Anthony thought about the book all the time. The plot curled itself around his thoughts like blood vessels around a tumor.

Huxley checked in: "The publisher is super-excited!"

"Great," said Anthony. "I am too." His voice was a stranger's.

"We're going to hit that deadline, right?"

"Of course we are."

It was never too early to get some buzz going for a big book. Anthony's editor sent him copy for Amazon, even though she hadn't read a word. The long-anticipated follow-up to *A Room Within*! A second book that was better than its super-smash-hit predecessor!

Anthony dabbled in energy drinks, in caffeine pills. They made him too excited, so he dulled them with more alcohol.

His draft was almost complete. He wasn't happy with it.

Huxley emailed. *We need to send what we have.*

One night Cassie went out for the evening. "Girls' night out," she'd said offhandedly. "Super-casual, dinner and drinks." Her dress didn't look casual, and she had on her highest heels. Anthony didn't have the energy to figure out if she was lying. Thinking about the book took up every ounce of him.

Anthony put Max to bed, and then he sat down with his incomplete manuscript and a glass of scotch. There was an elephant sitting on his lungs, and on top of that elephant was another elephant, and the elephant on top was holding a large refrigerator.

He finished the scotch and opened a bottle of good Cabernet—why not? He wouldn't write anything new; he'd focus on tying up all the unfinished bits. A glass of wine (or two) would help with that, help him find the connections he knew were missing.

He couldn't end a crucial scene. He couldn't get it right. The scene was halfway through the book, when the main character, Simon, was confronting his sister about the family secret they'd both kept hidden for decades. The sister was on her deathbed. It was a critical turning point for the narrative, and everything—*everything!*—that followed sprang from that single interaction. Anthony had already written the scene, but he hadn't ended it properly. He hadn't ended it beautifully, in a way that would knock a reader's socks off. It didn't feel right, the way *A Room Within* had felt when he was writing it. Nothing felt right.

One glass of the Cabernet gone, then two, then a third. Anthony prowled the house, thinking. He checked on Max: sleeping. Back downstairs, in his office, his eyes fell on his old copy of *There Comes a Time*. His mother had given it to him in high school— her own copy, already dog-eared, and Anthony dog-eared it further. (Leonard, who read only commercial fiction, fast-paced, sometimes un-beautiful commercial fiction, had never taken the time to recognize its allure.)

Anthony took the book from the shelf. He flipped through it. What a perfect book. How had O'Dwyer *done* it? Everything about it was enviable. The dialogue rang true, the transitions were seamless, the chapter endings were perfection.

The chapter endings were perfection.

No, Anthony.

The bottle of Cabernet was empty. He stowed the bottle in the recycling bin in the garage, under yesterday's copy of the *Boston Globe* and a doorstop catalogue from Restoration Hardware. Good thing they'd gone to single-stream recycling; easier to hide a bottle.

The chapter endings were perfection.

Just this once, he thought. *Just this one paragraph. That's all I need to finish off the chapter.*

I'll go back, he told himself, as he took—no, as he borrowed—O'Dwyer's words. *I'll go back and take out that paragraph a little later, when I've had a little more time to think. I'll put it in my own words. I just need to turn it in.*

He turned it in.

He got back his editor's notes on the draft. And what did it say *right there*, right after O'Dwyer's words? *This is beautiful! Don't change a word.*

There was a second, more ominous note: *More like this!*

A couple of other chapters required work in the next revision. And so it turned out it wasn't just one paragraph Anthony borrowed—it was, as the *Times* article noted, about twelve hundred words. It was a few pages in total, scattered throughout the book. *Unbelievable!* wrote his editor. *I'm practically crying, this writing is so gorgeous.*

His editor circulated the manuscript in-house. She called Anthony. "They're going wild for this book," the editor said. "Especially the deathbed scene, with the sister. Brilliant stuff, Anthony. Brilliant, brilliant stuff. I was worried there, for a while! But you pulled it off."

"Okay," said Anthony. He couldn't believe it was possible for a heart to beat as fast as his was beating. The elephants shifted. Another elephant was added on top of the first two.

"They're talking a very big print run," Huxley Wilder told him. "Some people are talking *prizes.*"

Anthony drank more. He poured vodka into his morning smoothies. Cassie stood at the door of his office, shaking her head. She had a meeting with Glen Manning while Max was at preschool.

"But you're not working for him anymore," said Anthony.

"Other way around," said Cassie. "He's interested in some of my pieces."

Anthony's mind was too addled to ask out loud if that was a euphemism.

"What are you working on, anyway?" she asked. "I thought the book was done."

"Revising," he said, sweating.

Galleys were printed; they began to circulate. Cassie thought they should hire a freelance publicist to redouble the already robust efforts of the publisher.

"I don't think we need one," said Anthony.

"I think we do," said Cassie. "I think we should really invest in this book."

The publicist's name was Shelly Salazar. She'd worked with some big names. "I am going to get you to the next level," said Shelly. She named a very large number. Cassie agreed to it.

"Fine," said Anthony. He had no energy for arguing. He hid a bottle of Monkey Shoulder in his sock drawer, and one in the basement, near the hot water heater.

Huxley Wilder called. "Puckett," he said. "We have a problem."

Anthony's editor emailed. *A strange thing has come up*, she wrote. *Let's talk about it with the attorney. An* anonymous source, who'd read one of the early galleys that was circulating, had leveled a pretty serious charge.

"Who was it?" asked Anthony.

"Could be anyone," said Huxley. "Once those galleys are out, anyone can get their hands on them. You know how it is."

I'm sorry, he said, again and again, to his editor, to Huxley, to Cassie. But Cassie didn't want to hear it; nobody wanted to hear it.

He called his mother. "It's going to get pretty bad," he said. "It's going to get messy."

It was confirmed. The *Times* article came out. "Everybody knows," said Cassie. "Everybody knows now. You've ruined everything, Anthony. You've ruined *everything.*"

There was the sense of a thing having been done that could never completely be undone.

Chapter 42
Lu

Early the next morning Anthony's phone rang, making Lu jump. Cassie's name showed up on the screen. Lu waited a fraction of a second, unsure if she should answer or not. But the alternative was waking up drunk Anthony. She had to answer.

"Hello?"

A woman's voice. "I need Anthony."

"I'm sorry," said Lu. "He's sleeping."

"He's *sleeping*?"

"He, ah . . . wasn't feeling well."

"I'm sorry to hear that," said Cassie. The sarcasm dripped from her words like sauce off barbecued ribs.

"But you can pass any message to me, and I'll give it to him," Lu said hastily. She had slid a pillow under

Anthony's head and his cheek was squished against it. He was drooling.

"Who are *you?*"

"I'm Lu. I'm his friend."

"Anthony doesn't have friends who are girls." That seemed like a rule that must be of Cassie's making, not Anthony's. Anthony was quite a good friend.

"He does now," said Lu.

"If he cares," said Cassie, "please tell him the police found a note."

"Of course he cares," snapped Lu. "What did the note say? I mean, if you want me to pass on the message."

Cassie sighed. "It said, *Don't worry, we went on a little trip.*"

"A little trip!" said Lu. "That seems innocuous enough. What a relief. So we don't need to worry anymore?"

"You never needed to worry, Lu-whoever-you-are," said Cassie. "Because this doesn't concern you."

Chapter 43
Joy

Bridezilla's mother, Linda, was wearing the silver Birkenstock Gizeh sandals that every woman over forty on the island seemed to own. She was also wearing a printed maxi skirt with a generous helping of pinks and blues and a knit top that matched the pink of the skirt. All in all, it was a very rosy getup. Something that was not rosy, though, was her expression. Her normally placid face—as innocent, as sweet as a dairy cow's—looked drawn and anxious. Well, who could blame her? It must be exhausting to be the mother of the bride! Especially *that* bride. Joy was beginning to hope that if Maggie wanted to get married she might be so kind as to elope and save Joy the trouble. Maggie could wear a funny bride-themed T-shirt and a pair of white Converse high-tops. She could marry a boy or a girl. She could marry anyone, or no one! (As long as she didn't marry Hugo from the Roving Patisserie.)

"Linda!" said Joy. "Such a nice surprise, to see you in the shop. What can I get you? A coffee? Whoopie pie? Yesterday Maggie and I were experimenting with a double-chocolate fudge flavor, and we have some left over. I can give you a sample if you'd like."

"No, thank you," said Linda. She sighed as if the very idea of a whoopie pie made her feel weary. "We ate at the Spring House Hotel last night and if you can believe it I am still stuffed to the gills."

"Ooooh!" said Joy. "I believe it. Their menu is fantastic this summer. What'd you have? Did you try that cod special?"

"I had a little bit of everything," said Linda. "The rehearsal dinner is there, you know, in the Barn, and we were sampling." She put a hand over her small pouch of a stomach. "But anyway, I didn't come to talk about that. I came to apologize." She pulled out a chair and sat at an empty table.

Joy's stomach dipped and flipped. "Apologize? For what?"

Linda sucked in her cheeks and looked down at the floor.

"For what?" repeated Joy. "Linda. Apologize for what?"

"Kimberly had a change of heart," Linda whispered to the floor.

"A change of heart?" Joy repeated. "You mean, she and Michael aren't getting married?" It was more likely, in Joy's opinion, that *Michael* had had a change of heart. And who could blame him? Even so, this couldn't mean . . . could it? Joy had so much riding on this wedding! No, this wedding couldn't be off.

"Oh, nothing like that," said Linda. Joy allowed herself to exhale. "Although how Michael puts up with that daughter of mine day after day I will never know. He is really and truly a saint. I keep telling her, *Someday, Kimberly, your collagen will be gone and you'll put on a little bit of weight and you will not be able to act like this.* But she doesn't listen. Who am I? Only the woman who changed every one of her diapers. Who held her while she cried when those awful girls in seventh grade were so mean to her."

"Seventh grade can be difficult," said Joy. She made sure she sounded sympathetic, although she was getting increasingly anxious. If the wedding wasn't off, what was the apology for?

"She didn't even go to the seventh-grade dance, you know! It was awful, we stayed home and watched *50 First Dates* on the television." Linda paused. "Such a silly movie." (Joy didn't concur; *50 First Dates* was no *When Harry Met Sally*, but certainly it was watchable.) "Anyway . . ." said Linda. She tapped her fingers on the table.

"Linda?" said Joy. A very bad feeling was blooming inside her. "What'd she change her mind about?"

"The whoopie pies!" said Linda. She threw her hands into the air. "Can you believe it? She doesn't want them anymore, for the wedding. She wants to get those macarons from the Roving Patisserie instead!" Linda pronounced it wrong; she said *macaroons*. But Joy was far too busy deflating to correct her. "I said we should do both, but then Robert put his foot down. Wasteful, he said. *Now* he's worried about money, after two decades of buying Kimberly anything she wants? But there it is. So I came to cancel the order, Joy. I didn't feel right doing it on the phone, after all you've done for us."

"I'm sorry to hear all of this," said Joy. Inside she was crumbling and seething, but she was hoping that if she could keep her cool Linda might still change her mind. "I mean, those macarons are okay, you know, but—"

"I don't care for them at all," said Linda loyally. "To me, they taste like cardboard. But Kimberly just went crazy for them. Apparently they're very hip these days, macarons. And you know young people, always chasing the trends."

"They may be hip," said Joy. "But the Roving Patisserie is not a true island business, you know. They've got no roots here. They're from New York! If what you're after is a true island wedding, then you need true island fare." Holly had been right to worry for Joy after all. How fickle people were! So distractible, their heads turned so easily by the next new and shiny thing, by free shipping or thirty percent off. Just yesterday a mother had come in with her three young children and asked what she got if she bought ten pies. *You know what you get?* Joy wanted to say. *You get the chance to buy your eleventh one. That's what you get after you buy ten.*

"I'm really, really sorry, Joy. I truly am."

Unfortunately, thought Joy, *sorry is not going to pay for my rental increase. Sorry is not going to populate Maggie's 529.* She swallowed around the lump of panic in her throat. "Linda," she said. "How can I get you to reconsider?"

Linda held up her hands, palms up. "You've met Kimberly, right?" Rhetorical question, obviously. "So the answer is you can't get me to reconsider. As much as I'd like to say that you could."

Perhaps Kenny Rogers had said it best, all those years ago. You did have to know when to fold 'em. Joy sighed. "We can ship all over the country. So if you happen to know anyone who might want to put in a large order, you know, for a future event, I hope you'll pass my name along." She wondered if a food truck mysteriously burning down in the middle of the night would cause much suspicion.

Linda rose from her chair and grasped both of Joy's hands in hers. "Of course I will," she said. "And really, again, I'm so sorry about all of this."

"I understand," said Joy, even though she absolutely didn't. Where was the loyalty, the appreciation for another person's hard work? It was gone; it had evaporated into the ether. Amazon had sucked it out of every creature with a Prime membership.

"I want you to keep the deposit," Linda said. "I insist."

Joy hadn't taken a deposit. She'd known Linda for years; she was going to take payment in full one week before the event, in time to pay her suppliers. "About the deposit," she began. "You never—"

"Oh, I *insist*," said Linda, cutting her off. "Really, it's the least I can do." And with a swish of her maxi skirt, out she sailed into the summer morning.

Chapter 44
Anthony

Anthony woke up with two small faces very close to his own face. They were so close that he couldn't immediately identify them, but he could feel their warm breath on his face, smell their bubble-gum Crest.

Then he heard Lu's voice. "Move back, boys." And, "Hi, there, sunshine." The faces receded, and he recognized them as belonging to Chase and Sebastian.

Anthony looked around. He was on a couch in Lu's living room, and sunlight was streaming in through the windows. It took a minute for him to process everything from the night before. Max and Dorothy, missing? He, asleep on Lu's couch? He had a distant memory of many IPAs, of some Irish sea chanteys, of Yeats . . .

Lu held out his phone to him. "I charged your phone," she said. "I didn't want to wake you until I had to. When Cassie called last night I talked to her. She texted just a minute ago. And then she called. So I told the boys to wake you." She hesitated and said, "Cassie should probably tell you this. But your mother left a note."

"A *note*?" He must have looked as stricken as he felt. "What kind of a note?"

"*No!* Not that kind of note! Cassie's going to call back any second. Here. Drink this." She put a mug of coffee on the table in front of him. Steam rose from the mug, along with a wonderful aroma. The mug said I'm Kind of a Big Deal in Rhode Island in block letters. It looked like something one of Maggie's shirts would say.

Anthony's head was sore. His mouth felt like the inside of a sofa cushion. His stomach quivered. He took a cautious sip of the coffee. It was dark and rich and flavorful, with just a hint of . . .

"Coconut oil," said Lu, watching him, nodding. "And just a little bit of grass-fed butter, all blended with the coffee. It's supposed to make you bulletproof. It's a whole thing."

Just then Anthony's phone rang, and Cassie's name appeared on the screen. Anthony couldn't hit the answer button fast enough. "Cassie!"

"I'm sorry to interrupt your time with your girl-friend," Cassie said, brisk and businesslike. "But I thought you might be interested to know that your mother has taken our son and disappeared. In case you didn't get my messages."

Lu shooed Chase and Sebastian away into the kitchen, and followed. "My girlfriend?" Anthony whispered. "No, Cassie, she's not—" He stopped; that wasn't the line of conversation that was most pressing. "My mother left a note, though, right?" he asked. "Lu said she left a note. Lu said everything is okay."

Cassie ignored his question. "Your mother has never liked me."

If Cassie had the wherewithal to complain about Dorothy, she couldn't have been too worried about Max. "What'd the note say, Cassie?"

"It said, *Don't worry, we went on a little trip.*"

"Where was the note?" Anthony said.

"At her house. I went to pick up Max, and all that was there was a note. Which, by the way, it took me some time to find."

He set that part aside for later. "Where'd they go?" he said. "On this little trip?"

Cassie sighed. "The note didn't say. I'm not sure. I'm hoping she calls one of us. Your mother did this to spite me, you know. I know she did."

Cassie was right about one thing. Dorothy had never liked Cassie; she'd never trusted her. She'd tolerated her as the mother of Dorothy's grandchild, whom she loved to the moon and back, but she had gone no further than that. Dorothy didn't understand Cassie's art or her shopping habits or her disinclination toward sugar and wheat or her decorating tastes. (*A white nursery?*) She didn't understand anything about her at all.

"She did," prodded Cassie, when he didn't immediately answer.

Anthony took another sip of the coffee. It tasted like somebody had blended in a little bit of heaven along with the coconut oil and grass-fed butter. He really did feel bulletproof. Thus emboldened, he asked, "Why was Max at my mom's in the first place, to be taken?"

"Abducted," said Cassie.

"Semantics," said Anthony. "Where were *you*?"

He could imagine Cassie looking the way she always looked when hit with a question she didn't want to answer. She'd tilt her head a little to the side, like she hadn't quite heard the question, and she'd furrow her brow, which in fact preventative Botox treatments had made unfurrowable. "Your father is on a book tour, I thought it might be nice for Dorothy to have the company—"

Anthony believed that about as much as Democrats believed Trump had no ties to Putin. He couldn't help unleashing a gentle snort. "You drove Max from Newton to Marblehead out of the goodness of your heart, because you thought it would be nice for my mother to have Max's company?"

"Yes," said Cassie staunchly.

"And you turned around right after dropping him off, and found him gone?"

"Not exactly," said Cassie. "That's not exactly how it happened."

"How'd it happen?"

"On the second night, when I called your m—"

"Second?" Anthony said. Now they were getting somewhere.

"The plan was for Max to stay two nights. But I changed my mind, and I called your mother to say I was picking him up on the evening of the second day, which was yesterday, and that's when she absconded with him."

"Ah," Anthony said. "And you yourself had no specific plans, nothing you wanted Max out of the way for?"

She paused. "No."

"You just thought a two-night visit was called for?"

"Yes." Her voice took on a strange timbre. "I thought two nights would be more fun for your mother."

"Bullshit. Were you with Glen?"

Another pause, this one pregnant. "Maybe," Cassie whispered.

"I *knew* it!" He was less bothered by this than he would have been two months ago.

"But it's not what you think—we had a fight—we broke up. It's over, Anthony. I promise it's over between Glen and I."

"It's over between *Glen and me*," said Anthony. He couldn't help it. It was a reflex.

He had her on her back foot now, defensive. "There have been a lot of things I needed you to do, Anthony, but correcting my grammar was never one of them. How can you talk to me like this, after all I did for you?"

"All you did for me?" Anthony was incredulous. "All you did for me, Cassie, was rack up one hundred thousand dollars in credit card bills. For starters. All you did for me was kick me out of the house *I* paid for!"

"Some of that stuff was for you! For your image! Some of that money I spent on Shelly Salazar, to promote you!"

"Shelly Salazar," he said, "is an opportunistic millennial nightmare."

"She would have done wonders for you, if you hadn't messed it all up." Cassie sighed. "I don't want to fight about this now. What do we do? Should we call the police? File a missing person's report?"

"Of course we shouldn't," said Anthony. "They're not in danger."

"Your mother is probably feeding him ice cream for breakfast."

"That's nutritional danger. Not real danger. Anyway, she wouldn't do that."

"She's done it before! She called it Upside-Down Day. They ate everything in reverse, and had pancakes for dinner. Max threw up twice before bed."

"Cassie, I know my mom wouldn't let Max get hurt. I'm sure Max is fine. I'm sure they'll resurface soon."

He thought he heard sirens in the background. "Cassie?" he said. "Is everything okay?"

"Oh, this is all I need," she said. "This is all I fucking need. I have to go. I'm driving. I just got pulled over. I'll call you back."

After the call ended Anthony drained the last of the bulletproof coffee. He needed to get back to his own cottage. He needed to take a hot shower, clear his head, brush the disastrous night from his molars. He called goodbye and thank you to Lu and the boys and slunk out of the front door of the house.

And there, outside Fitzy's uncle's front door, stood a sight for his sore eyes, his sore head, his devastated, fractured soul: Dorothy Puckett, and, next to her, the biggest missing piece of Anthony's heart. Max.

Anthony couldn't believe that after such a long time Max was here, in front of him, in the flesh. Anthony crouched down and opened his arms and Max went straight into them. Anthony hugged him so hard and so long that after a certain amount of time had passed Max whispered, "Daddy, I can't breathe!" and so Anthony released him. He held him at arm's length, smiling so hard his face hurt.

Max had grown. He was sturdier. He had had a recent haircut, which made him look a little older and more serious, but his cowlick still stood proudly. He smelled like fresh-cut grass and suntan lotion and clean childhood sweat; he smelled like a little boy's summertime. He was perfect.

Dorothy looked well rested and confident. She wore a tasteful taupe dress; a pair of sunglasses pushed back her silver bob.

"*Mom*," Anthony said. "I couldn't be happier to see you both, but what were you thinking?"

"I was thinking it was time to come for a visit," Dorothy said unapologetically. "All summer I've been asking you! We really need to talk, Anthony. And you yourself told me Cassie was keeping Max from you. I thought it was time to rectify the situation."

"But why didn't you ask Cassie first? She was frantic."

Dorothy chortled. "Cassie would never have said yes to this! So I used one of my old favorite rules: Sometimes it's better to ask for forgiveness than permission. Anyway, I left a note. No reason for her to be frantic. May we come in? I brought you a coffee." She bent down and retrieved from the ground a cardboard tray holding two cups that said Joy Bombs across them in the bakery's signature font. Of course. Where else would Dorothy have stopped for coffee?

Anthony opened the door for his mother and his son (his son! in the flesh!) to enter. Dorothy put the coffees on the coffee table and looked around, delighted.

"Go explore, buddy," Anthony told Max. To his mother, he said, "How'd you even know where to find me, specifically?"

Dorothy beamed and held up her phone. "I've known where you were all along. I use the Find My Friends app. I use it for your father too, so I can keep his schedule straight. He hasn't been home in twenty-one days. This is the book tour to end all book tours. He did Books Inc. last night."

"I love that store," said Anthony. (He couldn't keep the wistfulness out of his voice.) "Which location?"

"Alameda, I think. No, Laurel Village. Oh, who can remember? But, Anthony, that's also why I brought Max here: your father's coming to Block Island next week."

"I know."

"I thought we could have a bit of a vacation—a family reunion of sorts."

It took some negotiating, but Cassie agreed to let Max stay. She had commitments at the gallery the next several days, and then she'd come to Block Island on the sixth. She would stay one night, in a hotel if she could find a room, leaving with Max on the afternoon high-speed ferry on the seventh.

"Ground rules," said Cassie.

"Anything," said Anthony. Max had finished his exploration of the house and had come to sit next to Anthony, pressing his shoulder into Anthony's chest.

"Watch him near the water. He can't swim without a bubble. And don't give him sugar after three p.m. If he gets water in his ears you have to use these drops to dry them out or he could get swimmer's ear. He really needs to be asleep by eight-thirty. And sunscreen! Lots and lots of sunscreen. And a hat."

"Sunscreen," said Anthony. "Roger that." He was so happy to have Max for a few days that he would have gamely applied sunscreen to an entire rhinoceros, even getting in the wrinkly nooks and crannies. In the shower, all he could think about was showing Max around Block Island. He wanted to take him to see the alpacas at Manisses Animal Farm and Mohegan Bluffs and the colorful stones at Pebbly Beach. He wanted to buy him ice cream at Mia's and fried clams at Finn's.

When he returned to the living room, refreshed, Max was pointing the remote at the television. Dorothy was standing in the kitchen looking at the slice of ocean just visible from the window. "It's such an adorable little cottage!" she exclaimed. "So old-fashioned." She returned to the living room and settled herself on the couch. Then she rested her eyes on Anthony and said, "*You* look better than you've looked in some time! A suntan, a new haircut, you're looking very fit and dapper."

"Dapper?" asked Anthony.

"Oh, *very* dapper. Your belly is gone too."

It was true, Anthony knew. He hadn't stepped on a scale since he'd arrived—Fitzy's uncle didn't have one—but he knew he was slimmer and fitter from all of the hiking he'd done with Joy, and the swimming, and the bike rides. In the sea air, the salt air, abstaining from alcohol (the previous evening violently excepted), his body had tightened and grown stronger, more like it used to be. "It really is beautiful here," continued Dorothy. "I can't believe I haven't been to Block Island before. The water is so blue! It looks like . . ."

The Caribbean, anticipated Anthony.

"The Caribbean!" finished Dorothy. "And, Anthony, when I stopped in for our coffees there was the sweetest young girl working behind the counter, she must have been twelve or so."

"Thirteen," said Anthony softly.

"She had the funniest T-shirt, Anthony, you would have loved it. You always did love a pun. It said— Now, let me see, let me get it exactly right. It had a picture of a bear, and then a picture of a deer, and the bear was saying, 'Oh dear.' No, wait, that can't be right. That's not funny at all!"

Maggie was wearing the shirt he'd bought her! The knowledge made him immeasurably happy and enormously sad at the very same time. He felt the weight of his fight with Joy, of all of their almosts, anew.

"'I'll fight you with my bear hands,'" said Anthony morosely. "And the deer says, 'Oh deer!'"

"That's it!" said Dorothy. "How'd you know?"

"Lucky guess."

His regrets about deceiving Joy, and about the fight, were fierce, palpable. He wanted them to meet Max, and he wanted to show Max the island with Joy and Maggie. But Joy's final words sat there, like a boulder he couldn't move. *No more. We're all done here. Forever.*

Chapter 45
Maggie

Maggie is allowed to go back and forth to Lu's to work, because Maggie's mother values commitments and remembers what it was like when *she* was the mother of a young child and occasionally dependent on other people for help, and she's allowed to help in the shop, but other than that, she is stuck at home. No beach, no clamming, no nothing. No recreational phone use, although her mother hasn't been very good about enforcing that one. She keeps forgetting to take the phone.

But tonight Joy comes home from the shop and disappears into the bathroom and then into her bedroom and comes out wearing a turquoise sundress Maggie has never seen before; she announces that she and Holly are going to dinner. "Holly?" says Maggie.

"Not Anthony?" She is still hoping, despite her earlier nastiness, that he and her mother will get back together. She liked Anthony: he was funny and interesting and curious. It was fun to show him around. He let Maggie teach him to clam; he seemed to enjoy her mother's weird and occasionally lame sense of humor; he even bought Maggie a T-shirt that was not half bad.

Her mother sighs and says, "Not Anthony. You know that, Mags. No more Anthony." She says that Holly and Riley's father, Brent, had a reservation and at the last minute Brent couldn't go. Her mouth droops in a sad way and Maggie almost feels bad for her until she remembers that her mother is the reason she is grounded. She steels herself and says, "Okay."

Maggie watches out the window as her mother's turquoise dress disappears into the summer evening foot traffic. Left to her own devices, Maggie wanders through the house, switches on the TV, turns it off when she realizes there is nothing she wants to watch. It is day four of the grounding. There is no way she is staying in this house, alone, all night. She checks her phone: no texts, nothing. Even the "Videos You Might Like" on Instagram are videos she definitely does not like. She considers taking Pickles on an adventure but decides that her mother loves Pickles more than she loves Maggie right now, so should Joy come home to find Pickles missing Maggie would probably be charged with dognapping, and that is a headache she does not need.

In the end she grabs her bike and heads up Spring Street. She thinks she might bike all the way around the island. That will show them. (Who it will show, and what, she isn't one hundred percent sure of.) She leaves her phone at home because she knows her mother can track her location when she has her phone with her. She has considered turning off all location services, but leaving them on is part of the deal she struck with her mother when she got the phone and she's not about to risk her phone for longer than the grounding period.

Maggie's anger at the injustice of it all is a smoldering fire, ready to ignite. Riley is not grounded, which just goes to show you that Riley's mother is nicer than Maggie's. Riley was not pleased that Maggie threw her under the bus regarding the vaping equipment, and she did lose her phone, so she is currently not speaking to Maggie. If they don't make up by the time school starts, it's going to be one long year. Of the five girls in Maggie's class at the Block Island school, Riley is the only one Maggie can stand. The rest she thinks of like siblings she hasn't chosen but is more or less stuck with for the rest of her life.

Riley also has a crush on Hugo, but it is Maggie he has been giving leftover macarons to at the end of the day, and Maggie to whom he's been offering his e-cigarette. (*I declined every single time except once, Mom,* she thought, and the injustice of her grounding boils anew.) It would be so like Riley to use Maggie's incarceration as an opportunity to pursue Hugo.

Maggie knows that sunset will be at 8:11 and last light at 8:43, which is something that, as an island kid, she looks up most mornings if she hasn't seen it posted around town. She's not worried about darkness because her bike has lights on both the handlebar and the seat post and she knows enough to turn them on. She *is* worried about what will happen if her mother comes home from dinner with Holly to find her gone, but they are eating at the Spring House, which is not known for its fast service—it is where couples go when they want to gaze at the ocean over cocktails before they even order an appetizer.

It's a tiny bit of a risk taking the route she's chosen because she goes right by the Spring House, but she holds her breath and rides extra-fast as she takes the curve by the restaurant, which sits on a hill above the road, and nobody calls out to her. The reservation is for seven o'clock and so her mom and Holly have probably completed their ocean-gazing by now and are likely settled at one of the back tables in the dining room.

All thoughts of her mother are put on hold when she sees Hugo's little red sports car passing her, moving considerately into the other lane to give her plenty of space. Her pulse starts to race. She follows it—why not? If he is in his car, and he is going this way, he is not anywhere near Riley.

Maggie pumps her legs hard to make it up the hill on Spring Street, and after a good mile or so she sees Hugo's car in one of the parking spaces at Mohegan Bluffs. She follows, and tips her bike into the rack. There's nowhere to go here but down the little path that leads to the steps. The sun has begun to set.

Maggie, like every Block Island kid, knows the history of the clay bluffs that rise up like great monsters on either side of the steps. She knows that in the middle of some long-ago century (sixteenth? seventeenth?) two Native American tribes, the Niantic and the Mohegan, battled it out for supremacy of the island. She knows that the Niantics forced the Mohegans over the bluffs to their deaths. She knows that on a clear day, you can see all the way to Montauk, on the tip of Long Island. She knows that there are 141 steps leading down to the beach below and that you can see all five of the offshore windmills from here and that in the summer bunches of small white flowers line the steps. But she does not know why Hugo has come here, alone. She gives him enough time to make it all the way down, and then she follows.

Then all at once, she knows.

Down on the beach, which spreads out like a half-moon below the steps, stands Olivia Rossi. She has her hand on the back of Hugo's neck, and he holds her cheeks in the flat of his palms, and they are kissing each other so passionately, and the sunset is illuminating them so beautifully, that Maggie, who has never seen a *real kiss* like this *in person*, feels an ache in her center. She doesn't have time to think yet (she won't for some time) that this kiss, with the ocean air and the sunset and the great gray Mohegan Bluffs, will be the paradigm for all of the kisses to come in her still-young life. She doesn't know if she starts to creep down the steps to *stop* the kiss or to see more of it or just to impress upon herself how very wrong she's been about Hugo, about what he might have thought or not thought about her.

She also doesn't have time to figure it out, because her sneaker catches and she tumbles down, down, down the last five steps. She lets out a little wail. The rest of her fall is surprisingly silent, but it is the wail that makes Hugo and Olivia disengage and turn in her direction.

"Maggie!" cries Olivia. She makes her way over the rocky sand, graceful even in this journey that would be awkward to just about everybody else.

"Olivia!" croaks Maggie.

"What de hell?" says Hugo. He does not look happy to see Maggie, and his French accent is less charming than it once was. He is the same boy who works the crepe machine masterfully, who could sell a half dozen macarons to a poverty-stricken anorexic, but tonight he seems older, different, harsher.

"What are you doing here?" asks Olivia.

Maggie checks herself for injuries. She has miraculously avoided landing on the bigger rocks, hitting mostly soft sand, though there is a smaller rock wedged under her knee, and she landed with her palms flat out. She pulls herself into a sitting position and tries to hold back her tears. "I was on a bike ride, and I saw—I saw—" She can't get any more words out. Finally she says, "Never mind."

Olivia Rossi fixes Maggie with her chocolate caramel eyes. Maggie finds there a mixture of sympathy and pity and she suddenly feels very, very young, and very, very stupid. She closes her eyes for an instant and when she reopens them Olivia is still gazing at her. Olivia is wearing a beautiful white sundress with spaghetti straps. She has a flower—a real live flower—

tucked behind her ear; with her suntanned skin and her long perfect hair she looks like Moana. Maggie, in her T-shirt that has one atom saying to another I Lost an Electron and the other one answering Are You Positive feels like Heihei, Moana's bumbling rooster sidekick. She is such a loser. (She has not one but two science shirts! The other one features the periodic table of elements and the words I Wear This Shirt Periodically.)

"Come on, Mags," says Olivia. "Let's get you out of here."

They climb all 141 steps together. Maggie notices that Hugo is panting and lagging behind and she considers the possibility that vaping and the actual cigarette smoking haven't done him any favors. Every now and then he kicks at one of the steps.

"Hugo," says Olivia. "Put her bike in the back of your car. We'll drive her home."

Hugo says, "In dis?" and looks doubtfully at his small red car. Then, "What de fuck?" His accent, which Maggie once found charming, now sounds ominous.

"Yes," says Olivia firmly. "We'll put the bike in the back and leave the hatchback up." They accomplish this quickly, and Maggie is grateful that Olivia says nothing when a grease stain from the pedal appears at the hem of her beautiful white dress.

"Okay," says Olivia. She seems so in-charge and efficient, so adultlike, that Maggie can hardly believe she is only three years older than Maggie is. Olivia flashes Maggie her megawatt smile (no wonder Hugo has chosen her) and says, "Where to? Home?"

There is a physical pain attached to Maggie's shame: it scorches like a sunburn, and she feels sore and tender all over. Every time Hugo looks at her, his glare seems to deepen. Also, there is an actual physical pain in her wrist.

"Maggie?" says Olivia. "We'll take you home, okay?"

Maggie isn't sure if her mother is back from dinner yet but she can't take a chance on finding out. Her mother will re-ground her, or double-ground her. Can you be double-grounded? She's not sure, but it doesn't seem out of the question.

"Actually I'm supposed to babysit," she says. "Can you take me to Corn Neck Road?"

Chapter 46
Lu

Lu couldn't drive Maggie home because the boys were asleep upstairs. She'd wanted Maggie to call her mother, but Maggie wanted to ride home on her bike. She said she'd be fine; her bike had headlights.

"No," said Lu. "I'm sorry, but I'm not letting you ride your bike home. Not until you have some of my chocolate Heath bar ice cream and tell me what happened."

It came out in fits and starts at first, and then, as Maggie spoke, she became more animated, or more indignant. Poor thing.

"Oh, Maggie," said Lu. "I'm sorry."

"Do you think— I mean, is it possible . . . ?"

"Yes?" said Lu encouragingly. "Do I think what?" She spooned more ice cream into Maggie's bowl.

"Never mind," said Maggie. "It's stupid."

"Nothing is stupid," said Lu. "Nothing you can say right now, right at this minute, in this house, is stupid."

"Do you think I have a broken heart?"

It was such an in-between age, Maggie's age. Painful from the inside, of course, to Maggie, but really rather miraculous from the outside, like watching a caterpillar emerge from its chrysalis as a butterfly. While Maggie ate, Lu studied her. Her braces. The little bit of childhood pudge left in her cheeks. Her completely adorable T-shirts that were probably mass-produced in Nepal but that Maggie firmly believed were one-of-a-kind.

Lu tried to speak carefully. She considered Maggie's question. "I don't think you have a broken heart. But I understand why you're asking. I do understand."

She understood that while Maggie's escapade at Mohegan Bluffs seemed humorous to Lu, to Maggie it was possibly the most important thing that had happened to her that summer.

"I feel like such an idiot," said Maggie. "What should I do?"

"I think you should go home and you should talk to your mother."

Maggie rolled her eyes.

"You know I adore you, and the boys adore you, you're practically part of the family. But your mom knows you best. She should be the one talking to you about this. She would *want* to be the one talking to you about this."

"I doubt it," snorted Maggie. "All she wants to do is get mad at me. She's *looking* for the slightest mistake so she can jump all over it."

"I guarantee you that's not what she's doing."

Maggie pushed her ice-cream bowl away and winced.

"Maggie?" Lu asked. "What's wrong?"

"It's nothing," said Maggie. "I just bumped my wrist."

"Let me see it." Lu frowned at Maggie's outstretched arm. "Hang on a second," she said. "Is it tender here?"

"Ouch!"

"What about here?"

"*Yes.* Ow. Super-tender."

"I think this might be broken. I think we need to call your mom, Maggie."

Chapter 47
Joy

First I lose the only boyfriend I've had in ages, thought Joy. *Then I lose Bridezilla's wedding. And now I'm losing my daughter.* She'd also lost the half of her dinner she hadn't had time to finish.

Maggie's bike was leaning against the side of Lu's cottage. Joy stomped up the steps, being careful not to look over at Anthony's. She stood outside the door for a moment, torn between rapping loudly to display her displeasure and knocking very, very softly because Lu's little boys might be asleep. In the end she chose in favor of the boys, and when Lu opened the door, her cute little ponytail swinging, her snub nose snubbing, Joy wanted to shake her by the throat and growl, *Give me back my daughter.* Thankfully she'd had only a single cocktail at dinner—a Moscow mule. She hadn't expected to be driving tonight; any other time she would have had another, but she was very conscious of the fact that Holly was paying, and she didn't want to be greedy.

"Come in," said Lu. She swung the door open and Joy stepped inside.

"What's going on?" Joy asked. "You weren't very clear on the phone."

What Lu had actually said was, "Everything's fine, Joy. Maggie's here and I think you should come and pick her up." In retrospect, Joy appreciated that— mothers, well-trained babysitters, and school nurses all knew to begin a phone call with *everything's fine*, unless, of course, it wasn't.

"Come into the kitchen," said Lu. She was speaking in a near whisper. "The boys are sleeping," she added. She pointed toward the stairs, where Joy could see a hall light turned down low.

The first thing Joy noticed was how natural Maggie looked. Maggie wasn't supposed to look natural in other people's kitchens! In front of her was an empty bowl with a spoon and traces of chocolate in it. "I'm sorry, Mom," she said immediately. Her mouth was set in a defensive grimace.

"You're supposed to be grounded," said Joy. She hated the way her voice sounded, desperate and tight.

"What's going on, Maggie? Why'd you leave without telling me?"

"I'm sorry," said Maggie again, without answering any of the questions.

"Ice cream?" Lu suggested brightly. She was watching the two of them carefully, her eyes moving back and forth. Joy saw now that there was a second bowl with a spoon in it on the counter. Wasn't that lovely: a nice little ice-cream party for two.

"No, thank you," she said curtly.

"It's homemade," said Maggie, too eagerly. "Lu makes her own."

I'm sure she does, thought Joy. *Which she has plenty of time to do, because she doesn't have a job and she has a doctor husband, a helpful mother-in-law she complains about for being too helpful* (Maggie had told her that), *and her very own babysitter.*

"Sounds so good," she said. *I'm sure she churns her own butter too.* "But I had a big dinner. I'm completely stuffed."

Maggie had a strange look on her face. It reminded her of the look Maggie had had that time she flew off the swing at Ball O'Brien Park and had the wind knocked out of her—there had been an excruciating few seconds before she opened her eyes when Joy was positive she had died. "Maggie?" she said. She could hear the way her own voice cracked. "What's the matter?"

"I hurt my wrist," said Maggie, at the same time that Lu said, "I think her wrist might be broken."

Now Joy could see the unshed tears in Maggie's eyes. She hadn't noticed the way Maggie was sitting, with her right palm over her left wrist. She'd been too busy thinking snarky thoughts about the ice cream. She was suddenly reminded of her daughter at age five, when Joy had forgotten to put the money under Maggie's pillow for a tooth and Maggie, struggling to be very brave, had said that she understood and that the Tooth Fairy probably missed the last ferry and would have to come the next night.

"I think you should have it looked at," said Lu.

"Let me see," said Joy, more gently. Maggie moved the hand that was covering her wrist and Joy bent over it. Lu was right: she could see the swelling. "Oh, sweetie," she said. "How'd this happen?"

"I fell off my bike," said Maggie, at the same time that Lu said, "She fell down the steps at Mohegan Bluffs."

"You *what*? All of them?"

"No. Just the last few."

Small consolation. "What were you doing out there at night?"

"It's a long story," said Maggie.

"I wish Jeremy were here," said Lu quickly. "He could have a look. You see how it's starting to bruise there, just near the bone? And I didn't want to have her try to turn it, but I don't know if she could."

"I can't," whispered Maggie.

"Oh, *honey*," said Joy. She was a terrible mother, not to have noticed immediately that something was wrong. "We do need to get this looked at. In the car."

"My bike—"

"I'll come back for it tomorrow. In the car, okay?"

Still Maggie stood there, and then Lu said, "Maggie, let me talk to your mom for a sec." It was then that Maggie decided to get in the car. Of course she listened to Lu.

Once Maggie had left to get in the car, Joy turned to Lu and said, "I still don't understand what happened— why she— Oh, never mind. It's not important now. What's important is that she's okay. Thank you for calling me."

"Of course." Lu hesitated. Then: "Do you mind if I say something?"

Very much so. "No," said Joy.

"Don't be too hard on her."

Joy set her teeth together.

"About the grounding," said Lu. "She's had quite a night. I'm sure she'll tell you all about it."

I'm sure she won't, thought Joy grimly.

Lu touched Joy lightly on the shoulder, and there was something about the touch that made it all come roiling to the surface—all of the disappointments of the summer: her disappointment in Anthony, and her terror at the thought of Maggie growing up and leaving her alone, and her worries about her business and the money and the goddamn macarons, and how she might one day *in the very near future* be an old lady who lived alone with one or more cats, without even the benefit of the grave of a loved one to visit, as Mrs. Simmons had.

It took every ounce of Joy's self-control not to slap away Lu's hand. But she did flick it. "In the future," she said coldly, enjoying the look of dismay on Lu's face, "if my daughter comes here, and she's hurt, I'd appreciate if you'd call me right away. Maybe forgo the ice-cream celebration."

"I'm sorry—" said Lu. "I just thought . . ."

Joy didn't let her finish. She made her angry way to the Jeep. Maggie was already in, seat belt on, eyes straight ahead. If Anthony were to have looked out his window he would have seen the Jeep reverse and start down Corn Neck Road on the way to the Block Island Medical Center, where Joy knew from Olivia Rossi that her mother, an ER nurse who had trained at Johns Hopkins in Baltimore, was on the overnight shift.

Chapter 48
Lu

Lu had missed a call from Jeremy while she'd been talking to Maggie and Joy, but she wanted to sit for a few minutes before calling him back. She wondered if she'd done right by Maggie. It felt like a privilege and a responsibility, being trusted by a girl Maggie's age—a girl right on the cusp. She hoped she hadn't messed up.

While she was mulling that over she checked her email. Abigail Knowles was back from vacation. *I'm back from Italy! Sono tornato dall'Italia! Totally jet-lagged but ready to get to work! Give me a call when you have a chance to chat! I am so super excited about this project!*

Lu couldn't put off a phone call much longer. Abigail Knowles's trip to Italy had been a welcome reprieve, and now it was over. *Era finito.* (Lu had taken two semesters of beginning Italian in college.) She logged on to the website of the Wilder Literary Agency, and clicked through to Abigail's bio. There was a photo there. It showed a young (very young!) woman with a humongous smile and long brown hair. She lived in Manhattan; she had a German shepherd named Mogley. Her biggest sale was a nonfiction book called *The New New Feminism.* Lu didn't know what that meant, but she was intrigued.

(*Feminism is a luxury,* Lu's mother used to say. *A luxury for women who have time to worry about such things.* Lu's father had walked out on her mother when Lu was seven and her sister was eight, and from then on they'd all fought to keep their heads above water, the three of them. Almost everything was a luxury.)

Lu cleared the ice-cream bowls, loaded them into the dishwasher, and sat down again. She wondered if the new new feminism of today's wives and mothers might be more difficult to articulate and so it came out in silly quibbles about who unloaded the dishwasher last and whose turn it was to bring in the garbage cans. (Lu always did the dishwasher and the garbage cans because Jeremy was never home.) Really it was only after she'd become a mother that she saw the invisible shackles so many women wore. Even pretty Jessica, with her workout clothes and her cozy relationship with her MIL, wore shackles. She just might not have admitted it to herself.

But Lu admitted it. She felt her shackles tightening. She felt them in the set of Jeremy's jaw. She felt them in the way Nancy's eyes pinched together when she disapproved of something Lu had done or (more likely) when she disapproved of something that she hadn't done. She felt them when Chase had a nightmare and she stroked his hair until he fell asleep. When she prepared to creep out of the room and his little hand reached out and clutched at hers—even in sleep trying to keep her there.

Maybe, if she told Jeremy about the blog, she could continue working on it as a hobby, maybe Jeremy would be okay with that. But she didn't want to be a casual blogger, treating conferences like an excuse to get a new outfit and paint her nails and get drunk while the husband stayed home with the kids. Not that Jeremy could stay home with the kids: he had to work. Lu wanted to *speak* at the conferences. She wanted to develop really good recipes, produce the splashiest cookbook, identify the next rung on the ladder and climb it. She wanted to be the best. And to be the best she needed to treat Dinner by Dad like a job, not a hobby.

Enjoy them while they're young! her mother would

tell her if she were here. *They won't be young forever,
it goes so fast.*

But the career years go by fast too, Lu wanted to
scream. *Those are also finite. All of it goes by too fast,*
life *goes by too fast.* By the time Chase was off to college she'd be—well, old. Older. Old. Over fifty. She'd
be tired. She'd definitely be out of touch. She'd have
no connections; she'd be starting from scratch. She felt
the shackles tightening around her. And if there was a
third baby, she'd never get going.

When Joy saw Lu come into Joy Bombs the next
day she stiffened visibly. "Hey," Lu said. She tried
to sound both upbeat and nonchalant—a tricky balance. She placed a large order: a dozen whoopie pies.
She'd bring them to Nancy, who was taking the boys
to lunch. Maggie had texted to say she had a hairline
fracture in her wrist but that her cast was waterproof
and she'd be back tomorrow. Lu also ordered a triple
decaf cappuccino with a shot of almond syrup, and a
raspberry whoopie pie to eat there. She didn't want
the almond syrup, but it cost seventy-five cents extra,
and she wanted to spend as much money as she could,
because she noticed that it wasn't very crowded in the
café. The Roving Patisserie probably *was* a legitimate
threat.

When the pies were boxed up and the coffee was done, Lu asked Joy to sit with her for a minute.

"I don't know," said Joy. "I'm sort of busy."

"I'm sure you are," said Lu, looking at the empty tables. "I can tell. But I won't keep you long. I promise."

"Okay," said Joy. She slid into the seat across from Lu. "Shoot." She was fiddling with a coffee stirrer. Her hair was tied back in a messy bun, and she looked tired.

"Listen," said Lu. "I want to apologize to you for the other night. I'm sorry I didn't call you sooner, right when Maggie showed up. I'm sorry I was the one to hear her story first. Did she tell you what happened?"

"She did," said Joy. "After a while. And I felt like such an idiot, there was a text I had seen earlier in the summer, something about *going for it*, about someone *who was older*, and I got caught up in everything else, and I completely forgot. I let this happen. I basically broke her wrist for her."

"No, you didn't," said Lu firmly. "You didn't." There was something else she'd come to say too. "I'm sorry I took her away from you so much this summer. I'm sorry if I did anything—*anything*—to offend you."

Joy's face underwent a transformation. Her tight lips loosened; her eyes drooped. Her shoulders slumped forward. She looked like a blow-up doll whose air had suddenly been taken out. "No," she said. "You didn't do anything wrong. I should be apologizing. I over-reacted. I think . . ." She swiped at her eyes, and tied a knot in the coffee stirrer. "I think she likes you better, and that's why I got so mad." She started to cry.

It was funny how certain actions really showed your genetic heritage. Joy looked just like Maggie when she cried, in the same way that Lu and her sister laughed alike because they both held their hands over their mouths the same way. (Lu had decided that this was because they were always trying to hide the gaps in their front teeth.)

"No!" Lu cried. "Of course she doesn't. Of *course* she doesn't like me better."

"She does." Joy nodded. "She does."

"It's not that. It's not *you*. It's just the nature of mothers and daughters, that's all."

"How would *you* know?" asked Joy. "You have sons. Dear little sweet, loyal sons." She wiped her eyes with a napkin.

Lu considered this. "You're right," she said. "I don't have a daughter. But I *was* a daughter, don't forget. A thousand years ago, I was a teenage girl with a mother."

Lu's mother would have been over the moon if Lu had confided in her, and Lu refused to tell her anything. What had Lu's mother ever done to Lu, except for at one time know her so intimately that Lu couldn't bear to expose her to all of the humiliations involved in her growing up?

"Did you tell *your* mother everything?" Lu asked Joy. She sipped her drink. The almond syrup turned out to be a really nice addition, well worth the extra cash.

"Definitely not." Joy tied another knot in the coffee stirrer. "My mother was far too busy keeping up with my brothers to pay much attention to what I was doing. I was sort of a wild child, on the streets of Fall River."

"There you go!" Lu felt triumphant. "See? It's not that different."

"I don't know. It is, though. I have all these brothers, and I have a dad—it was chaos, all the time. Nobody was focused on just me, it was nobody's job to do that. And that was fine. But Maggie is my responsibility, she's all mine. I mean, Dustin exists, obviously. But he's . . ." She paused. Her eyes flashed.

"Negligible?" offered Lu.

Joy smiled, a little. Progress. "Right. His influence is pretty negligible. It's all on me, when you get right down to it. And I don't think I'm doing a very good job. I've been taking my eye off the ball. For part of the summer I was caught up in Anthony, who turned out to be a jerk and a liar . . ."

Lu winced. Anthony had told her about what had

happened with him and Joy. She understood why Joy was angry, but she also thought Anthony deserved another chance.

"Sorry. I know you're friends with him. But he did turn out to be that way. And at the same time I've been obsessed with my business, which has been sucking wind, and also with the Roving Patisserie, which I think was put on this earth in general and specifically this island to torture me. And Maggie slipped through the cracks. For the first time ever, she slipped through the cracks. I've never let that happen before." Joy's voice broke. "I've *never* let that happen."

Lu thought about her first crush, her first kiss, her first time having sex (with Sean Townsend, on his decrepit brown basement couch, with a runaway spring sticking into her back the whole time). She thought about the time she and two of her friends had been thrown out of a seven p.m. showing of *Fargo* for pouring wine coolers into their soda cups. "Don't you think it's possible that she slipped herself through the cracks?" she asked. "Like, on purpose? Because she's growing up?"

"I don't know. I think I deserve the blame. I overreached. My expectations were too high. It's too hard to do all of the things I was trying to do and be any good at them." Joy pulled a face that was wry and self-mocking. "Isn't this essentially the argument women have been having since time began? Whether or not we can have it all? I thought we were *done* with that question. I'm exhausted by it."

"Me too," Lu said softly.

"And now I know the answer, for sure. The answer is, we can't."

"No!" said Lu, sudden tears stinging her eyes. "No, don't say that, *please* don't say that!"

"Whoever said we could was not a single mother or had a high-end nanny or only needed four hours of sleep a night or something. Because the rest of us, the ones with credit card debt and Bridezillas? And vet bills and college to save for, and a seasonal business that operates at a loss every single winter? We can't have it all. We have to pick." Joy looked so sad and defeated that Lu felt herself crest a wave of indignation.

"You're wrong," Lu said. "You have to be wrong."

Joy shook her head sadly. "What would you know about it?" she said. "You have no idea."

Lu felt like Joy had slapped her. "You have to be wrong," said Lu. She tried to tamp down the vehemence in her voice, but it escaped anyway. Lu realized how difficult it would be to explain everything to Joy, how Lu looked to her as a role model, a success story.

A trailblazer, in a very real way—someone who had struck out on her own, and made it work. If she wasn't actually making it work, what did that say to those who hadn't yet had the courage to strike out?

"And now I'm zero-for-three. I messed up all of them, in one summer. Kid, job, relationship."

Lu let an appropriate amount of time pass, and then she said, "Public service announcement. I don't think Anthony is a jerk."

Something flashed across Joy's face. "What is he, then?"

Lu leaned back. She took another sip of her cappuccino and considered the raspberry whoopie pie on the plate before her. She thought for a long time about the answer to this question. She didn't speak until she felt that she had it right. "A guy who got messed up by his mistakes," she said. "A guy who sometimes panics and does the wrong thing. Like all of us." She shrugged and popped the whole whoopie pie into her mouth.

Joy snorted, but there was something glittering in her eyes. It could have been anger or indignation, but it also could have been hope.

Chapter 49
Joy

Maggie and Joy were making a Thai mango salad with peanut dressing, courtesy of Dinner by Dad. Maggie had relaxed her silent treatment soon after the neon-green plaster cast had been applied to her wrist and seemed to have accepted her punishment with something approaching equanimity.

Joy, despite what Lu had told her, had stopped looking for Anthony around every corner, behind every coffee cup, and was trying to focus on her business and her mothering. She had recently listened to a podcast about the teenage brain and had decided to try to remember in all of her dealings with Maggie that Maggie, like everyone her age, was operating without the full use of her frontal lobe and would be doing so for another full decade. (Astonishing, Joy thought; how was it that the *driving age* was sixteen and the *drinking age* twenty-one when the *one hundred percent thinking age* was twenty-five? Only the rental car companies seemed to understand this.)

Of course, they were still on precarious footing—more provisory détente than signed peace accord. Dinner by Dad had posted this particular recipe weeks earlier in the summer and Joy had bookmarked it but hadn't made it yet. Dinner by Dad had given them the option to add crispy baked tofu or grilled chicken to the salad.

"Which do you think Charlie would choose?" asked Maggie. She speculated about Dinner by Dad's boys like they were celebrities. Which they were, sort of. They were the most famous foodie children you've never seen, except in charcoal drawings.

"Definitely chicken," said Joy. "Sammy would choose tofu. And Jacqui would have whatever Leo is having, because that's how she rolls."

"She'd be tired from work," Maggie surmised.

"She'd just be happy to have someone put a meal in front of her!" Joy added.

Together Joy and Maggie debated the merits and drawbacks of each protein source. Chicken might be faster; tofu might be healthier. But there was the thing about the soy and the estrogen, so maybe not.

In the end, chicken emerged victorious. "Actually, un-victorious, if you're the chicken," noted Maggie. Maggie's sense of humor was coming back!

"Nice job with the pepper," said Joy a few minutes later. Maggie's knife skills were excellent, even encumbered by the cast. Joy gave herself partial credit for that because she'd taught Maggie to use real knives, sharp knives, when she was six. But the rest of it was Maggie's particular blend of instinct and confidence, the stuff you couldn't teach. "I'll do the dressing," added Joy, "and you do the jalapeños. Don't forget the—"

"Seeds and membranes," said Maggie. "I know." She went at the jalapeño with grace and precision. A moment later, Maggie started to hum a song from *Hamilton.* "Helpless." Her favorite. A good sign.

They kept at the salad: Maggie washing the lettuce, Joy seasoning the chicken to grill. *Genius is patience,* wasn't that what Isaac Newton had said? Joy would be patient.

"Let's go outside and sit for a minute," Joy suggested. "While the chicken is grilling." She poured a glass of wine for herself and a seltzer for Maggie. They sat on the love seat on the deck, with its view of Old Town Road. It was a glorious summer evening, and there was foot traffic and bike traffic and car traffic. Joy heard a child yell something about ice cream. She heard a car horn honk. She put her arm over the back of the love seat, cautiously, like a teenager on a first date at the movies, and she waited for Maggie to stiffen and pull away. But Maggie leaned against Joy, the way she used to, when she was young and her heart was whole and open. Joy was scared to breathe too hard.

Maggie got up to check the chicken on the grill. Her legs were so brown and skinny in her denim shorts, and her black Converse sneakers were so . . . well, it was all just so *Maggie.* It was too much. Joy's heart seized. What a lot the world asked of us, when it asked us to love another human being.

What made Joy say what she said next? "So, listen," Joy said. "Do you want to talk any more about Hugo?"

Maggie flinched. "No," she said.

Joy had said the wrong thing, she was always saying the wrong thing. "I just want to make sure you know just how big the difference between sixteen and thirteen is. I don't want you to feel embarrassed about . . . about what happened."

"Nothing *happened.*" Maggie's face closed up like a morning glory after sundown.

"Well, about what you may have . . ." Joy pushed forward, casting about for the right thing to say. "About what you may have expected. Hoped for." (What *had* Maggie hoped for, exactly?)

"I said, I *don't* want to talk about it." Maggie stiffened. "Geez. I *knew* this would happen! I knew you'd bring this up, to embarrass me. I *knew it*. I'm going to Riley's. Unless I'm still grounded. Am I still grounded?"

Joy studied her. "No," she said finally. "I guess you're not still grounded." It was hard, deciding these things alone! She wished she had another grown-up to bounce the question off of. Was the grounding she'd given Maggie overdoing it, underdoing it, or just right? She was Goldilocks, with no guidance about which chair might fit. "But we haven't eaten."

"I'm not hungry," snarled Maggie.

"We did all this work!" said Joy. "It's almost ready!"

"I *said, I'm not hungry*," said Maggie. "You can't make me be hungry." And with a stomp of one Converse and a curl of her lip she was gone.

Joy poured herself more wine and considered the possibility that in short order she had driven everyone away from her: Anthony, Maggie, even Bridezilla. The great alienator, that was Joy. On the way to the kitchen to pick up her cell phone she tripped over Pickles. Pickles looked up, possibly resentfully. "Not you too, Pickles," she pleaded. "Don't you turn on me. You're my only hope." Pickles raised one of her ears. She was probably wishing she had a bike so she could follow Maggie to Riley's.

The phone at the auto shop rang six times before Joy looked at her watch. It was the end of the business day, of course they'd be closed. Finally her mother answered and Joy presented her question.

"You were awful to me!" said her mother cheerfully. "Of course, I had the boys, so that helped. As long as I fed them they were perfectly nice to me."

Joy felt pained. "Well, what'd I do, exactly?"

"Where do you want me to start? There was the time you snuck out in the middle of the night and set off the car alarm when you were trying to turn the car on. The time you took the good whiskey my sister had brought me from Ireland and brought it to a party. Oh! And the time you said four days in a row you were going swimming at Lisa Costa's house and your bathing suit came home dry every night. I never did find out where you'd been."

"Well, I'm not telling you *now*," said Joy. (She couldn't remember.) "Did I at least apologize, for any of that? Please tell me I apologized."

"Of course you didn't." Her mother laughed. "You were a teenage girl. The world revolved around you and only you. It was natural. But that doesn't mean it wasn't infuriating. Just a moment, darling." She put down the phone and called, "The second drawer down." Then, to Joy, "Sorry, I'm at the shop. Well, you know that. You called me here."

"So how did you ever forgive me? How'd you even stand me?"

"*I said the second drawer down!*" screamed her mother. "Honestly, that man couldn't find an ear of corn in a cornfield. Your brother is just like him."

"Which brother?"

"All of them, come to think of it. And I'm only here today because Mariana had to take Hunter to his baseball game. How did I forgive you? How did I stand you? It was my job to stand you. And I forgave you because that's what parents do."

Joy was hovering somewhere between relief and despair. "What do I do, though, Mom? I feel like I have to be so careful, but I'm never sure what I'm being careful of."

"You wait her out," said Joy's mother. "You wait her out, and she'll come back to you soon enough. You'll see."

Chapter 50
Anthony

Cassie was wearing pale pink gloss and a hint of shadow on her eyes when Anthony and Max met her at the ferry on the sixth. She had somehow scored a room at The 1661 Inn for the night (unheard of, in August; who knew what strings she'd pulled), and she wanted Max to stay with her. Her tank top was taupe, silk, pristinely pressed. She was carrying the Sonia Rykiel weekender bag she'd given herself two birthdays ago. Anthony reached out to take the bag from her. She bent to hug and kiss Max. "Are you okay, sweetie?" she asked. "That must have been very scary for you."

"What?" Max asked, confused.

"Getting taken like that."

"Taken on a *fun trip*," Anthony corrected, casting a warning look at Cassie.

"I wasn't scared," said Max staunchly. "I was with Grandma."

Cassie's gaze took in the swarm of people by the ferry, the crowded veranda of the National Hotel, the glimpse of Fred Benson Town Beach. It was a glorious summer day, the pick of the litter. She nodded slowly. Her smile was tight and insincere. "I see how it's been," she said. "While Max and I have been at home alone, you've been having yourself a vacation."

"It wasn't a vacation," Anthony said.

"You even have better weather than we have at home. You know we're getting a big storm, right? At home? Practically a hurricane. I had to move in all of the pillows on the outdoor furniture by myself."

Anthony was sure Cassie was exaggerating. "I haven't heard about any storm," he said.

"Of course you haven't. You've just been here, in your little island paradise, not worrying about the rest of the world. Aren't you lucky. Well, for your information, coastal Massachusetts is supposed to get pummeled."

"It was the only place I could go for free, Cassie! Fitzy's uncle has a cottage—"

Cassie straightened and said, "Oh, *Fitzy.*" She said it like a curse word. Fitzy had been at their wedding; he hadn't accorded himself very well. He'd left the heart of one of Cassie's friends in shreds on the ground.

"I had no choice," Anthony said.

"Well," she said. "I wonder if Max is hungry. Are you hungry, sweetie?" Max nodded somberly. He was holding tightly to Anthony's hand. Max's hand was small and warm and certain, with an overlay of in-offensive childhood stickiness. It was a perfect hand. "Is there somewhere around here we can get some lunch?"

"Yes," said Anthony. "Of course." It was Block Island in the middle of summer: there were dozens of places to get lunch.

They went to Dead Eye Dick's and sat on the deck overlooking Great Salt Pond. The harbor was lousy with boats and kayaks and Jet Skis and clammers and swimmers. You had to wonder how so many boats could move around safely in a relatively small space but they seemed to have it figured out, like dancers in a well-choreographed number.

"Should we share salt-and-pepper calamari to start?" Anthony suggested. It would have been a peace offering if calamari was something Cassie would eat.

Cassie shook her head. "Nothing fried."

Anthony ordered a grilled fish sandwich with a side of fries and Cassie ordered a summer shrimp salad without the onions. Max ordered grilled cheese and a chocolate milk. Cassie said, "How about white milk?"

and when Max said, "No, *chocolate*," she sighed and flicked her hand: *What did it matter?*

"A drink?" suggested Cassie. She ran her forefinger up and down the cocktail menu. "The Summer Sunrise sounds good."

"I haven't been drinking," said Anthony. The amber liquid in the decanter, and all the drinks that came after, had left him with a headache that remained for days.

"Fine," said Cassie. She sighed. "I'll have a seltzer."

"Can I go look at the boats?" asked Max.

"Yes, but stay on the deck," said Cassie. When Max had gone, she tented her fingers and said, "So."

"So," said Anthony.

"After what your mother did, honestly, I've been very worried. I wonder about the stability of your family. I wonder about your *genes*, Anthony."

"My jeans are very fashionable, thank you very much. No need to worry about them."

"I'm *serious*, Anthony. This isn't a joking matter. Your mother *kidnapped* our son."

"She didn't kidnap him. She took him on a vacation! She left a note. It will be a memory that lasts him for the rest of his life. No harm done."

Cassie squinched her eyes shut. "I disagree," she said. "Ice cream for breakfast: That's a terrible idea.

Breakfast should be protein and fresh fruits or vegetables, plus, for a child, a serving of whole grains." She rubbed her eyes and added, "Full-grown adults can generally get by without the grains."

"It's okay to do crazy things on vacation!"

Cassie snapped her eyes open. "It was *child theft*. It was not vacation."

A woman in a blue bikini jumped into the water from one of the boats docked nearby. She let out a little whooping sound before she hit the water and three other people on the deck of the boat cheered.

"Anyway," Cassie said. She tapped the saltshaker against the table. "I didn't come here to talk about your mother. I came here to collect Max. And I wanted you to know . . ." She paused, then straightened her already straight back. "That it's over with Glen. Like I said on the phone. It's over."

Suddenly all Anthony could think of was Joy on her deck, fiddling with her little grill, turning to talk to him with the tongs in her hand. *And then this guy wants four iced lattes*, he imagined her saying. *So I told him . . .*

"Anthony?" said Cassie. "Did you hear me, did you hear what I said?"

"I heard you."

Cassie moved her hand over so it was covering his on the table. Her nails were freshly done in a steel-gray polish. Her hands were unblemished. Joy had small scars and burns all over her hands.

"And?" When Anthony stayed silent she put a little pressure on the top of his hand. "And I was thinking that since you and I have both made mistakes, well, I thought you might be able to come back home now. Max needs his father."

Anthony opened his arms expansively. "He has his father. I'm right here."

"He needs you home. We need you." Cassie sighed and unrolled her silverware from the napkin. She said, finally, possibly reluctantly, "I need you."

He knew what it must have cost her to say that. And yet. "What about all of those things you said to me before I left? You said some terrible things, Cassie."

"I know I did." She lowered her gaze and gave him the full view of her long, full eyelashes. There was a time when that view would have sent him into paroxysms of desire; there was a time when he could have spent the better part of a morning on one of those eyelids.

Then she lifted her gaze. "I know I did, and I'm sorry. I'm so sorry, Anthony. I was too hard on you. I should have supported you. I never should have . . ."

She paused. Did she really not know how to complete the sentence? "You never should have slept with Glen Manning," he offered.

She colored briefly; that delicate, porcelain skin had always been her tell. He could almost see her internal struggle through her skin, behind the lavender veins that showed under the surface of her wrists, along the temples. "You're right," she said finally. "You're exactly right. I never should have. I wish I hadn't. I wish I hadn't thrown away what we had, Anthony, for . . ."

"For an arrogant asshole?"

She let a small sigh escape. "Yes. For an arrogant asshole. But more than that, I wish I hadn't hurt you."

For so long he'd waited to hear her say those words. And now that she had, the funniest thing happened. He didn't need to hear them anymore.

"I wish you hadn't too, Cassie, but the fact is, you did hurt me. Not only that stuff with Glen Manning, which was pretty terrible in its own right. But what's worse is the fact that you gave up on me. When all that shit with *Simon's Rock* went down. You gave up on me, and you stopped loving me."

She shook her head fiercely. "I didn't stop loving you."

"You stopped showing it."

She nodded. "Yes. Yes, I guess I did do that. But I won't again, Anthony. I won't again. You'll see."

He felt not the vindication that he was expecting to feel. He felt only a great sadness, a tightening in his chest. The realization hit him like a wrecking ball, like a stream of cold water pointed straight at his forehead. Anthony and Cassie were not perfect in any sense of the word, either of them, but each of them was better apart than they were together.

Cassie had been the most beautiful bride, her hair in those flower-woven braids, her simple dress that accentuated the utter gloriousness of her skin. He'd felt so lucky to be walking down the aisle with her at the end of the ceremony. (*What aisle?* his mother would have said. *I just saw cedar chips.*)

He shook his head. "I'm sorry, Cassie."

"You're not going to come back?" Her voice cracked.

"I don't think so."

"Even for Max?"

He thought about Joy. She'd shown him that a certain kind of connection was possible—was as necessary to his happiness as food and air. He had never loved Cassie the way he loved Joy; he'd been drawn in by the shiny gossamer fabric that covered her, and then he'd been too caught up in his own problems to notice when it tore.

"I'm not going to come back *especially* for Max. Because living with unhappy parents would be the worst thing for Max, way worse than having divorced parents."

"Divorced." Cassie seemed to be turning the word over and over in her head, and then in her mouth. She put the emphasis first on one syllable and then on the other. *Divorced. Divorced.* It was a funny word, once you kept repeating it. But then again, weren't all words funny, repeated again and again? *Tangerine. Hiatus. Incandescent. Rhinoceros. Blue. Plagiarism.* "Are we going to be a divorced couple?" she asked.

"Eventually," he said. "Eventually, I guess we are."

"And then what?"

"And then, I don't know, maybe I'll start writing again."

Cassie let out a sharp, mean laugh. "Right," she said. "Like that's going to happen." But it didn't hurt him, not anymore, not the way it would have a few months ago.

"It could," he said. "I've been doing a lot of thinking. Lots of walking on the beach and thinking."

"Alone?"

"Not always. I started— I've been—" He cleared his throat. "That is to say, I was seeing somebody."

"Somebody *here*?"

"Yes," he said. "Somebody here."

"Wait a minute. You have a girlfriend?"

The word seemed inadequate for his relationship with Joy—the word *girlfriend* implied youth, transitoriness. Joy deserved another word, a freshly minted, spectacular word. But: "Yes," he said. Then, "No."

"Which is it?"

"It's complicated."

"You'll have to end it. Like I did with Glen."

"Did you end it with Glen, or did Glen end it with you?"

Cassie didn't answer, thereby making the answer clear. "I don't think staying apart is the right thing for anyone," she said instead. "We need to be a family unit again."

"But we're not, Cassie. We can't be." He believed that both he and Cassie were good parents—that was one piece of knowledge that had sustained him through his Max-less days, the certainty that Cassie would do right by their son. But they were not better together than they were alone, the way parents were supposed to be. In fact, they were worse.

He thought of Joy, bent over the account books in her office. He thought of Maggie teaching him to clam. It was so unlikely, so impractical, this little life they'd carved, really out of nothing, out of sand and sea and grit and determination and whipped cream. And yet. It was what he wanted, more than anything.

"Are you planning to stay with her? This girlfriend? On this . . . *island*?" She spat the word in a way that made Anthony feel protective of Block Island. "What about us? What are Max and I supposed to do?"

"We'll figure it out," said Anthony. "Max is priority number one. We'll figure it out."

At exactly that moment the waitress returned with three plates balanced on her arm. Cassie's face assumed a smooth mask, and all traces of suffering and distress vanished. Cassie never showed vulnerability in public. She smiled at the waitress. "Max!" she called. "Honey, come and eat! Come and eat!"

A boat sailed past, heading to the estuary that would take it to the Sound. The woman in the blue bikini jumped once again off the deck of the boat, landing beautifully, with scarcely a splash.

Chapter 51
Lu

"Abigail Knowles," said Anthony, when he came over, at Lu's request. He told her that his almost-ex-wife Cassie had taken Max to stay with her at The 1661 Inn the night before, so it was a good time to make the phone call. "Why does the name Abigail Knowles sound so familiar?" he asked.

"I'm not sure," said Lu. She was hoping to get Abigail's voice mail. She had written everything Anthony was supposed to say on a yellow legal pad. "She's part of a bigger agency. She represents mainly nonfiction. *The New New Feminism*? Ever heard of that book?"

Anthony shook his head.

"Me either," said Lu. "Anyway, she says she's the low man on the totem pole. The head of the agency is some guy named Huxley."

Anthony blanched. "Huxley?"

"I know," said Lu. "It's a wacky name. Only in New York, right?" She felt a buzz of excitement. She had an agent! In New York! She was going to publish a cookbook! It all seemed unreal.

"Is his full name, by any chance, Huxley Wilder?"

"Yes! I think that's it. He's the head of the agency. WLA, Wilder Literary Agency."

"Oh, boy," said Anthony.

"What?"

"Nothing," he said. He studied the paper. She watched his lips move as he went over the words, like he was an actor running some very important lines.

They had an agreement that if Abigail *did* answer her phone Anthony would put the phone on speaker and Lu would scribble down answers to any questions he couldn't answer. It would be like *Cyrano de Bergerac*, food-blogger-style, and hopefully without the tragic ending. Anthony assured Lu that the agency would have an assistant taking calls, so if the assistant didn't offer Abigail's voice mail but instead transferred the call directly to Abigail they'd have a few extra seconds to prepare.

Lu pictured a sleek Manhattan office, sleek Manhattan assistant—a brave, single young woman in a summer dress and the knockoff version of expensive wedges, a young woman who was beginning to make her way in the world. Of course, maybe the assistant would be a frazzled mother of three who took the train in from Jersey City every day, but in her mind, Lu whispered, *You go, girl, you do your thing. You figure out your path.*

"Okay," said Anthony finally. "Okay, I think I'm ready."

"You sure?" said Lu.

"I'm sure. Ready."

And then, all of a sudden, he didn't look ready at all. Something in his face shifted. "Anthony?" Lu asked. "Is everything okay?"

Anthony sat down at the kitchen island and tapped his fingers on the granite. "I'm not sure we should do this. The phone call."

Lu's pulse started to race. "Why not? You don't want to? I'm sorry, Anthony. I didn't mean to put you in an uncomfortable situation."

"No, no, it's not that. I don't mind making one phone call for you. That's not the issue." He laughed glumly. "I mean, *I'm* not standing on some moral high ground, we all know that."

"So what is it?" Everything had felt so within her reach . . . but maybe it wasn't. Maybe it was slipping away.

"It's that . . ." He hesitated. Lu poured Anthony a glass of water and set it in front of him. He nodded to thank her. "I want to be careful to put this the right way. It's that . . . I think you need a real plan here. I'm not sure how long you can kick this can down the street, even if we make one phone call today and that works out. Then what?"

Then what? It was a fair question. Lu hadn't let herself think too far ahead.

"There are lots of things I wish I'd done differently, but the main one is I wish I'd never started deceiving anyone," said Anthony.

"Anthony," said Lu. "At some point you have to stop beating yourself up over this."

"I don't," he said. "I don't have to stop yet, because I never really started. I made a huge mistake, and I didn't own it, and then I got swept up in this whole mess, and it ended up taking me down. I still haven't owned it, not really. I've just been hiding from it."

Lu considered this. Maybe Anthony was right. But wasn't her situation different? *Was* it different?

"I think you need to find out sooner rather than later if you can do this book as Lu Trusdale, the former Dinner by Dad. Or, I don't know, Lu Trusdale writing as Dinner by Dad. Or something." He drank the water and watched her over the rim of the glass.

She sat for several seconds with what Anthony had said, letting it settle into her.

"I don't want you to be right," she said slowly, "because I'm scared. But I do think you're right. I do. I do think I need to think carefully about what to do next."

Impulsively, Lu hugged Anthony. She was just so grateful to have someone on her side—someone who listened without judging, someone who understood the complications of her situation and who was genuinely looking out for her, counseling her away from her worst instincts. She whispered, "*Thank you!*" into his soft gray T-shirt, and she took a deep breath, and she got ready to think.

Just then there came a sharp, bossy rapping on the cottage door. Lu pulled away from the hug and looked at Anthony, and Anthony looked at Lu.

"Who could that be?" asked Anthony.

The rapping came again. The door to the cottage opened, and into the room, like a hunk of seaweed flung upon the sand by a wave, came Lu's mother-in-law.

"Nancy!" Lu said. "What are you doing here? The boys are at day camp!"

"I know perfectly well where the boys are," snapped Nancy. "And here's what else. I know what *you're* up to too. And you are sorely mistaken if you think you're going to get away with it."

The three of them stood as if at opposite points of a triangle, staring at each other.

"With all due respect," said Lu (though privately she didn't think any respect was due), "you have no idea what you're talking about."

"Don't I?" said Nancy. She pointed a finger at Anthony. "Do you think I don't know that you've been sleeping with him? I saw him sneaking home the other morning. This has been going on all summer, probably. In the house that Henry and I are paying for. Leaving your boys unattended, probably hooked up to screens." (Lu did not point out to Nancy that the boys weren't "hooked up to screens," whatever that meant, you didn't hook up to screens these days, you just tapped on them.) "Sneaking around behind Jeremy's back while he works his *fingers to the bone* to support you all?"

"I'm not sleeping with anybody!" cried Lu. (She was scarcely sleeping with her own husband.) "Anthony was just helping me with something."

"I bet he was," said Nancy. "I'm going to get in touch with Jeremy to let him know."

"To let him know *what*?" said Lu, starting to laugh. It was so wildly improbable, all of it.

"To let him know that something untoward was going on. He's on his way home right now."

Lu stopped laughing.

"How do you know that?" she asked.

"Because he told me."

"Why didn't he tell me?" Lu looked to Anthony, confused.

"Maybe he couldn't get hold of you. Maybe you were . . . otherwise engaged."

Lu's stomach flipped and dropped. This was it, then, the end of her charade. If she didn't want Jeremy to think the very worst thing, the thing that would end her marriage, she was going to have to come out with the rest of it. She was going to have to tell him about the blog, the book deal, the blogging conference, the imaginary family. She was going to have to tell him all of it.

Chapter 52
Anthony

Cassie had asked if she could take Max to a late breakfast alone, and Anthony had agreed. Now that he'd left Lu with her tyrant of a mother-in-law (he hadn't wanted to, but Lu and Nancy had each, in their own way, suggested that he leave), he was trying hard not to think about the fact that his father had a reading scheduled that afternoon at Island Bound Books. Even so, he knew his mind would keep going there all day: *Now my father is getting off the plane. Now he's on his way to his hotel. Now he's eating lunch.*

"What do you want to do now, Mom?" he asked, to distract himself. Dorothy was sitting on the small deck, frowning at her iPad. There was a mug of coffee in front of her. "What is it? Mom? What are you looking at?"

"Just reading the weather," she said. "It looks like we're getting some really heavy rain."

"When?"

"Today. Later this afternoon." She peered at the screen. "Goodness, this looks serious."

"What kind of serious?"

"Very heavy winds. Lots of rain."

He remembered what Cassie had said the day before about the weather at home.

"I hope your father gets in safely. I'll just send him a text to let us know when he's arrived." She tapped at the screen and then looked up at Anthony. "Anthony? I was thinking we could talk. Maybe inside?" She carried her coffee into the living room and took a seat on the couch.

Anthony followed her, confused. His mother had been in his cottage for nearly a week now. They had exhausted nearly every one of Block Island's sights, and most of their topics of conversation, to boot.

"Talk?" he said.

"About your father," she added. "We haven't *really* talked about your father."

What was there to say? He took a comb to his mind. His father hadn't spoken to him since the *Times* article. His father was so disappointed in Anthony that he couldn't even stomach a short conversation with his only son. Then he thought of one thing he hadn't told his mother. He said, "Shelly Salazar thinks I could get my career back on track if I did a photo shoot with Dad."

Dorothy picked at a thread in the worn-out sofa. "Who on earth is Shelly Salazar?"

"That publicist Cassie hired. Before—before all of the rest of it. She wants me to do a photo shoot with Dad, something big and splashy. She's talking about getting Annie Leibovitz to do it!" For the first time since Shelly Salazar had mentioned Annie Leibovitz, Anthony added an exclamation point to the thought.

"Heavens." Dorothy bit her lip. "Don't you think we should ask your father if he's interested? Do you think it would help you?"

"Probably. But he won't be interested, Mom. He wants nothing to do with me. I think he might hate me."

"Nonsense! Of course he doesn't hate you."

"Then why hasn't he talked to me since February? Why hasn't he tried to get in touch at all? *You* called me. *You* checked up on me. *You* answered if I called. But he never did."

Dorothy waited a long time before answering. When she spoke, her voice was clear and steady, authoritative, as though she were speaking to a roomful of Anthonys and not just one.

"It was more complicated for your father than it was for me."

"Why?"

"He was envious of you, Anthony. He has been, ever since he first read your writing. I don't think he liked that part of him, the part that could envy his own flesh and blood, but it was there, and it was tenacious."

"No—"

"*Yes*, Anthony. Yes."

"For how long?"

"Well, I think it started when you brought that story home from Dartmouth." She nodded. "Yes, it started there for certain. He was really taken aback by how good that story was."

"But he encouraged me . . ."

"He did. Of course he did. But he was always conflicted about your career. Always."

Anthony sat for a long time with that knowledge. Lu had been right. Anthony had been Katherine Mansfield to Leonard Puckett's Virginia Woolf.

"Did you talk about . . . what happened?" He lowered his voice like he was about to utter a curse in front of a child. "The plagiarism?"

"Only once. We had a big fight." Dorothy paused, and in that pause Anthony thought he felt the very earth reverse its rotation. "We're none of us exactly who we say we are," Dorothy said finally.

That seemed like a non sequitur. Anthony considered his mother: his dear, familiar mother, with her stylish bob, and her lipstick, and her beautiful posture. Look at her even now, her legs crossed at the ankles. "You are," he said. "You're just exactly who you say you are."

Dorothy sipped her coffee. There was something almost aggressive about her sipping, something combative. "There's something I want to tell you," she said. "I've been trying to tell you this all summer." She stood and crossed the living room. She examined the crystal decanter, ran her finger along the rim of one of the glasses. "Really, in some ways, I've been trying to tell you your whole adult life. But I never could quite get up the nerve." She turned back to Anthony, and there was something about the way she was looking at him—there was a shrewdness in her gaze, a clarity that made him take notice.

"What?"

"I always thought you'd figure it out on your own," she said. She sat back down. She sat with her hands folded together, very politely, like a theatergoer waiting for the curtain to go up. Softly she said, "Think about it, Anthony. I know you're not a thriller writer, but there've been clues all around you, all of the time, about your father, and about me."

Anthony gasped. "Am I adopted?" It didn't seem likely. He had his mother's small ears, and his father's nose.

"No," she said. "But keep thinking." She nodded encouragingly. It was the same way he'd seen her nod at Max when she was helping him sound out a word in one of his picture books. (They both particularly liked the one about the bear and the mouse who visited the library together.) "Where was your father, when he was writing?"

"In his study."

"And where was I?"

Kitchen. Garden. Car. "A lot of different places."

"Where was I when I wasn't a lot of different places?"

Dorothy brought Leonard Puckett a scotch every day at five o'clock. Sometimes she put it on the desk and went back to the kitchen to make dinner, but sometimes she didn't. Sometimes she brought a glass of white wine in and closed the door. There was that stretch when he was in high school and she'd taken up knitting. She'd knit fifteen different blankets to donate to a homeless shelter; she'd knit baby hats to give to the hospital; she'd knit a sweater for Anthony that he'd never worn (he'd been in high school! Who wore a hand-knit sweater in high school?) and one for Leonard, which he did wear, though not in public. Where did she do the knitting? Not in the living room or in the easy chair in her bedroom or on the cushioned bench in the breakfast nook in the kitchen. No, she sat on the leather sofa in his father's study.

"You were in the study," he said.

Vacations, which they always took to locales where Leonard was setting a book. *A Wolf's Cry* (Manitoba). *We Are Berlin* (Germany). *Rats in the Cellar* (Nassau). *The Bearded Lady* (Romania).

When Anthony was old enough he went off on his own to roam the hotel, to swim in the pool, to peruse the shops. His mother stayed with his father more often than not. Doing . . . what?

"You're getting warmer," she said. "I can tell."

"You—" he breathed.

"Yes," she said.

The sound was almost audible, the pieces of the puzzle falling into place. "You wrote the books," he said. "You're Leonard Puckett. That's it, isn't it?"

She tipped her head forward just a fraction of an inch. A concession. "Not all of them," she said. "But it's been a partnership for a long time. That's why we fought, Anthony. Your father was so upset about what you did. Beyond upset. And I told him he was making too much of it. I told him that in the end it wasn't so different from what he was doing, putting his name on our work. My work."

"I can't believe this," said Anthony. "I just can't believe it."

"There's one more thing, Anthony—"

"Just a second," Anthony said. "I need some air." He went through the kitchen and opened the back door and stood on the cottage's small deck, then he followed the path to the beach.

There was a figure walking along the sand, a figure in blue scrubs.

Jeremy. He looked out of place, walking on the beach in his scrubs; he looked like a jungle animal wandering a glacier.

"Jeremy," Anthony called. He walked down the steps of the deck and toward the beach. He couldn't believe his voice could sound normal. Nothing was normal.

Had Nancy already gotten to Jeremy? He had the idea that he could save Lu if he could get to Jeremy first.

"Hey!" said Jeremy, waving. The wave was innocent, neighborly—Nancy couldn't have gotten to him already.

"Where you headed?" He tried to make his voice sound normal, even though his mind was spinning.

"On my way home," said Jeremy. "Didn't you hear? Ferries stopped running. There's a storm coming." His mother's storm, thought Anthony. From her iPad. And the storm Cassie had mentioned, the one that was supposed to hit Massachusetts. "The purple flag is up!" said Jeremy.

The purple flag was up? Anthony had thought the purple flag was mythical, like a unicorn. He'd never heard of it actually going up. He'd never *seen* the purple flag. The water was so flat. Then again, storms could be like that. They could sneak up on you. That's why there were so many metaphors surrounding them. The eye of the storm. The calm before the storm. Maybe only two metaphors: he couldn't think of any more. Maybe *Dorothy Puckett* could think of more. Dorothy Puckett the writer.

"How can there be a storm big enough to stop the ferries?"

"I listened to some guy on the ferry explain it," said Jeremy. "It has to do with the offshore winds, and what the pattern is in the Caribbean, and then the angle of the winds as they head toward the island. I don't remember all of it exactly. But basically it can be really calm here, and a mess out there, and then—*bam*, everything can change direction. And it hits. A hurricane."

"A hurricane?"

"That's what they're saying."

"Geez," said Anthony. He'd have to track down Cassie, make sure she and Max were safe. Were they back at their hotel? Had anyone told them a storm was coming here?

Then Jeremy's phone must have vibrated, because he held up a finger to Anthony, indicating he should wait, and put his phone to his ear. He walked toward the ocean and when he turned back the set of his jaw had changed, and his posture had changed. Nancy.

Lu had been a good friend to Anthony this summer— a calming, next-door presence, just like Amanda Loring had been in fourth grade. He remembered how much trouble he'd had with place values and rounding that year, and how much Amanda had helped him. He remembered the crook of her neck as she bent over the paper, chewing the eraser on her pencil. Everything had been so uncomplicated in fourth grade, so clear and right.

Anthony steeled himself and called, "Your mother has it all wrong, you know."

"Sorry?"

"Your mother. Your mother has it all wrong. Whatever she told you about Lu, it's not right. It's not what's going on."

"I'm not really sure what's going on," said Jeremy. "But I'm about to go figure it out."

Plot twist, thought Anthony grimly. He turned to go inside.

His mother was still on the couch, with her hands folded and her gaze pointed straight ahead, steady, staring at nothing.

"I don't understand," said Anthony. "What do you mean, specifically, about the writing? What was your involvement in the work? Are you talking about a few suggestions here or there . . . the untangling of a knotty plot point? That's not really *writing*, with all due respect, Mom. That's simply editing. Helping. Pick whichever words you like best. But lots of writers need to bounce ideas off somebody else sometimes . . . you know, just to see if things make sense."

"I did pick the word I like best," said Dorothy. "The word is *writing*."

"You wrote the books for him? Mom, are you telling me you wrote Dad's books for him?"

Dorothy nodded crisply. "It differed somewhat, here and there. Sometimes we would work together—he with his legal pad, I with mine. We'd each take a chapter or a scene. Maybe they were different viewpoints. For example . . ." She tapped her forehead. "Ah, yes! For example, the *Drug Me Tender* books. I'm sure you remember that those were written in alternating points of view, the detective and the killer."

"Yes." It had been a trilogy to start with, but the *Drug Me Tender* books sold like crazy. The publisher wanted more, and it became a series of seven, released every six months for three and a half years. A gold mine. That series had sent Anthony to college with plenty left over.

"Well, your father was the detective. And I"—she brandished an imaginary knife—"was the killer."

"Holy cow," whispered Anthony. The killer points of view in the *Drug Me Tender* series were all written in second person—a nearly impossible voice to sustain over one book, never mind seven. He'd always been impressed that his father had pulled it off. But his father hadn't pulled it off. His *mother* had pulled it off.

"There are many more examples," Dorothy said. "*The Beauty's Beast. Red as Rubies. Jury of Peers.* I'd have to look at a bibliography of all of his work to sort it all out."

"Not *his* work," said Anthony. "Your work too. Your collective work. Mom, I still don't get it. Can you explain it to me further, so I can understand, how you could be doing this all this time, how you were okay with it, and how *he* was okay with it?"

"I'm not sure I can completely explain it, Anthony. Marriages are complicated." She paused, and looked up to the ceiling for several seconds. When she met Anthony's eyes again she said, "I've loved your father forever, Anthony. *Forever.* Since before leggings counted as pants. Since before the Beatles broke up, and the wall came down."

The Beatles broke up, and the wall came down. That was beautiful. Poetry. His mother did have a way with words.

"And you didn't mind," said Anthony. "You never minded."

"Who said I never minded?" There was something in her gaze he'd never seen before. "Maybe that's one of the reasons why I'm here right now, Anthony, why I took Max and fled. Maybe it's because all of a sudden I minded."

Plot twist, Anthony thought.

"Maybe it's because I'm tired. Maybe it's because I want to finish our current contract, and be done."

"You do?"

"I want to stop."

"You should stop, then, Mom."

"I'm ready. I'm ready for our current contract to be our last. But he's not." *Major plot twist.* There was so much to absorb. Anthony's head was spinning.

"And also, Anthony?"

The purple flag was up. A storm was coming. His father might be on the island. He needed to make sure Cassie and Max were safe. And there was only one person he wanted to talk to about all of this.

"Anthony?" his mother said again. "There's something else, something really important. There's one more thing—"

Anthony's thoughts were flying; there was a surge of adrenaline flooding him. The flag. The storm. The father. Joy.

"Mom—let's talk later, okay? I have to do something. I'll be back, as soon as I can be."

Chapter 53
Lu

"Where are the boys?" Jeremy asked. Nancy had gone home. She'd spoken to Jeremy, she told Lu, and now it was up to the two of them to talk it through.

Lu was too nervous to sit still, so she puttered around the kitchen. "They walked over to the club," she said. "There's melted crayon painting today!" She tried to make it sound as if melted crayon painting were something to celebrate.

"I see," said Jeremy. "Did they walk over to the club *by themselves?*"

Lu shook her head.

"They couldn't have walked over to the club with my mother, because my mother called me, and she was here, she wasn't with the boys."

"Right," whispered Lu.

"So . . . who'd they walk over with?"

"Maggie." She watched a small muscle in Jeremy's jaw clench and unclench.

"Maggie, who you said you weren't going to use anymore?"

"It's not what you think," she said. "It's not even remotely what you think. It's not what your mother thinks." And then she took a deep, deep breath. She said, "It started a while ago, when the boys were little." It occurred to her that this could also be an explanation for a love affair. Then, in a voice that was so shaky and uncertain it didn't even sound like hers, she told him all of it.

Chapter 54
Anthony

He had the feeling that if he could only talk about everything with Joy it would all make sense—he could recapture the sense of peace he'd felt those weeks with her. But he couldn't find her. He couldn't find Maggie either. The Jeep wasn't outside the cottage and nobody answered the door. He could hear Pickles sniffling and snuffling on the other side, though, so he let himself in. Pickles greeted him joyfully, like he was a sailor who'd been at sea for six months. Anthony couldn't get over how much Pickles licked his face and pawed at him and nibbled at his ears. It felt like the dog wanted to climb right inside his shirt with him.

"Well, that makes one of you," he told Pickles. Pickles wriggled her hindquarters so hard Anthony thought her tail might fall off.

"Joy?" Anthony called. "Maggie?" The cottage was quiet and immaculate. Nobody answered.

He called Cassie: she didn't pick up her phone. She didn't want to talk to him; she was hurt and angry. He texted her. Storm coming. R u someplace safe? No answer.

He tried Joy Bombs—Olivia Rossi was there, but Joy wasn't. Olivia told Anthony the shop was closing early because of the storm; Joy had called to tell her but hadn't said where she was calling from. Anthony looked for Joy's Jeep at Mansion Beach and Scotch Beach. He drove up Spring Street. He lucked out with parking at Mohegan Bluffs, arriving just as somebody else was leaving. He ran down all 141 steps. Nope. He jogged back up. He didn't have to stop even once to catch his breath, but little good that did him now.

He drove all the way out to Corn Neck Road and checked out Settlers' Rock. All he found was a family of five having their photo taken by a kid in a blue sweatshirt that said Art Academy of Cincinnati. "Say, 'Christmas!'" said the photographer. "Think snow! Let's get this done before the storm starts!"

"Christmas!" said the family members obligingly. They smiled.

Anthony didn't want to think snow. He wanted to think about Joy. He wanted to talk to Joy. Where was she? His head was spinning. He stood for a moment and gazed out at the water, and he thought about what a different person he was from the one who had first driven up this road in June, thinking that the island was too small to hold his regrets and his grief on its shores. How wrong he'd been.

The fact was, he hadn't had enough confidence in himself. That was where this had all started. The success of *A Room Within* had seemed like a fluke, not a beginning. So he'd sold a second book he didn't believe he could write; he'd undertaken a career he didn't feel qualified to see through. He'd panicked, and he'd made a big mistake. The fact that he was going to correct his mistake down the line really had no bearing on the truth of what had happened.

All summer he'd been looking to cast blame: on the *New York Times*, on the anonymous source, on Cassie, on the pressure of his father's reputation. Even now, when Dorothy had told him what she'd told him, he'd wanted his father's deception to somehow excuse his own. But it didn't. What he viewed as his father's sin of publishing Dorothy's work under his own name did not absolve Anthony of his. This was what he'd been trying to get at earlier today with Lu, before they were interrupted by Nancy. He'd hidden from what he'd done, but he'd never really owned it, and now he could.

He did. There was nowhere else the blame belonged, other than on Anthony's own shoulders.

Oh, sorrow, he thought. *Oh, Joy!*

He looked at his phone. No reply from Cassie. Text me back! he typed in. Right away, Im worried!

Chapter 55
Lu

"Let me get this straight. You have a secret food blog, where you pretend to be a man."

Put that way, it sounded like an odd little hobby, not the makings of a food empire. Of course, Jeremy wouldn't know anything about food blogs; the second-to-last thing he would be interested in would be recipes, and the very last thing would be exhaustive write-ups of how and why the recipes were created.

"A *successful* food blog," Lu said. "A very successful food blog. I'm getting two hundred and fifty thousand page views a month." (Over the summer, even with the limited cooking supplies in the cottage, her page views had increased. The momentum was there; everything was coming together beautifully.)

"But a secret."

She held off for a long moment before answering. Finally she said, "Yes. A secret."

Even then some optimistic, idiotic part of her felt proud of what she'd accomplished. No, feeling proud wasn't idiotic of her. Expecting Jeremy to feel proud on her behalf, that was idiotic. He wouldn't think she was clever or entrepreneurial. He wouldn't be impressed by her signature charcoal drawings or the fictional life she'd created for her fictional family. He'd feel like he'd been made a fool of by not knowing. He'd think she'd taken her attention away from the boys unnecessarily. He'd focus on the fact that she'd hidden so much from him.

They were in the kitchen. When Anthony had come over to make the phone call to Abigail Knowles she'd been laying out ingredients for a strawberry and arugula salad. She wanted to add jalapeño and radishes to it, and she wasn't sure which cheese would be best: goat or feta. She'd wondered if the peppery tang of the arugula would complement or do battle with the radishes . . .

But all of these questions seemed pointless now, with Jeremy pacing back and forth across the kitchen like this. He opened the door that led to the back deck.

"Where are you going, Jeremy?" Was he going to go back to the mainland, sleep at the hospital, find a hotel? She felt short of breath. Was she going to hyperventilate? "You're not going to leave the island, are you? Please don't leave the island."

"I. Can't. Leave. The. Island." The way he spoke, each word parceled out like a noxious gift, gave her chills. She'd seen him angry before—of course he yelled, everybody yelled sometimes, she did too—but this anger was so quiet, so neatly contained. "Because of the storm."

"Storm?" Lu looked outside. She didn't see any storm.

"It's coming," he said. "Apparently offshore the winds are really picking up. Hurricane-force. Should be hitting the island later today. They've shut down the ferry."

"They've shut down the *ferry*?" All she could do was stand there like an idiot, repeating his words. "Should I call back Maggie and the boys?"

Jeremy shrugged. "Apparently you know what's best for the boys, I'm sure you'll figure it out."

The words stung, as he'd meant them to. He was waiting for her to say something else. He was waiting for an apology, she realized. She started to gather one up but then the words lodged in her throat, or maybe even deeper, in her soul. It wouldn't be true to say them, because she wasn't sorry. She lifted her chin and waited for him to say something else.

"I'm going for a walk," he said finally, in that same strange, cold voice. "On the beach." He held out his phone. "But first, before I do. Can you please tell me how I can find this blog?"

Lu took his phone. Her hands were shaking so much that at first she couldn't open the browser. Then she typed in the address and handed the phone back to Jeremy.

He was going to read all of it now. He was going to read two years' worth of her posts, and he'd see all the wrong things. He wouldn't see the artistry behind the cooking or the beauty in the charcoal drawings.

"Okay," he said. He was still wearing his scrubs, but he kicked off his shoes and left them at the door. He disappeared.

He was gone more than an hour. When he came back, he went right up to the bedroom, not saying a word, walking by Maggie, who was delivering the boys back after arts and crafts.

"Do you mind hanging out for a little bit?" Lu asked

Maggie. "Just a few minutes?" This conversation with Jeremy needed to happen now, not after Maggie had gone. Now.

She knocked on the bedroom door. There was no answer, so she pushed it open. Jeremy was sitting in the straight-backed chair by the window. To Lu's knowledge nobody had sat in the straight-backed chair all summer.

"I can't believe you would keep this from me," he said, without preamble. "Something so big. A whole *job*. You had a whole secret job, and you never told me about it."

He said *had*, and the tense made her a little bit nervous. "I thought you'd be mad," she said in the world's tiniest voice. "I thought you wouldn't support it."

"I *don't* support it, Lu. I don't. I am mad."

A flame of self-righteousness licked up at her. "I knew it."

"Can you blame me? Can you *blame* me, Lu? We had an agreement. For four years, ever since Sebastian was a baby, we've had an agreement. I would do that"—he gestured toward his scrubs, and maybe toward a hospital filled with unseen patients a great distance away—"and you would do *this*."

"By *this*," she said, "I suppose you mean every single thing that has to do with the care of the boys."

He sighed: he was exasperated. "That was the deal, Lu. I'm sorry you're sad your life isn't the perfect fantasy you've created in your blog, but no one's life is perfect. We had an agreement. We agreed that it was best for the boys to be raised by a parent. Don't you think I would like more time with the boys? Don't you think I would love the luxury—and let's call it what it is, it's a *luxury*—of these long summer days at the *beach* with *my boys* instead of being inside a hospital all of the time?"

Lu drew herself up to her full height, wishing it were fuller: she was a perfectly average-sized American woman, five feet five inches. "No," she said. "I'm not sure you would." Full-time family time was one of those things that sound lovely in the abstract, but wait until Chase cut his foot on a clamshell and then got sand in the cut and had to be carried back to the house. Wait until Sebastian came home from a birthday party high on cupcakes and Capri Sun and turned into a wet puddle of emotions.

Jeremy tented his fingers together. "I do the work I do so I can provide for this family. I thought we were working for something together. Your part, my part." He made motions with his hands while he was saying this, as though he were marking out different sections to be constructed later with plywood and nails. "I thought we were going to have another baby, Lu."

She had the sensation of standing on the high dive at the community pool she used to go to as a child. (She only went there when a friend's mother could drive, because her mother had to work.) She closed her eyes, and she jumped. "My part isn't enough for me, Jeremy. It's just not. I wish it were, I really, really wish it were. But it's not." She inhaled, then let the breath out slowly. "You wouldn't be *you* without your work to make you complete, and nobody expects that you would be. You told me once that being at the hospital is like a drug for you—that you actually feel like you get high on it sometimes! I can't . . ." She paused, trying to make sure she was saying the right thing. "It's not enough for me, being with the boys all the time. The blog is really important to me."

He wasn't absorbing what she was saying. He shook his head. "Maybe when they're older, when they don't need you as much, you can pick it up again." He rubbed his eyes; he looked like Sebastian did when he was tired. "I want you to shut it down," he said. "We never talked about spending money on a babysitter, when we still owe my parents, when we have a lot of expenses, Lu. We had an agreement, where for now I make the money and you take care of the kids. You can't just opt out of the agreement."

"But that agreement is four years old. Things change!"

"I *don't want some stranger raising our boys*," said Jeremy. "Neither did you, when we would've had to find a new nanny for Sebastian. And a new baby? I don't want a stranger taking care of a baby. For now, you're going to have to shut down the blog."

Lu thought of all the sponsors she'd gathered, the cookbook deal, the invitation to the conference, the advertising dollars, the momentum. She'd never get it back, not years from now, not if she turned it all down now. She had to build her empire before she could live in it—she couldn't show up in ten years or more and say, *Where's my empire? I thought I left it right here.*

"I can't," she said. "I can't do that, Jeremy. I've given a lot to the family, but I can't give everything. I won't."

And then she left the room, closing the door behind her.

Chapter 56
Anthony

The events coordinator at Island Bound Books was a small young woman with a wide smile and sun-tanned skin. If eyes really could be said to sparkle, hers did (cliché). She was wearing jeans and a T-shirt that said I'm a Bad Girl. I Read Past My Bedtime and a name tag that said BRIDGET. The T-shirt made Anthony think of Maggie.

"Oh, I'm sorry! We've had to cancel our event for this afternoon!" Bridget said when Anthony rapped on the door. It had taken him some effort to get to the store. The wind was whipping off the water something fierce, and there was a point on Water Street where the air seemed to be pushing him back just as strongly as he was pushing himself forward. Bridget pointed dramatically at a handwritten sign that said

AUTHOR EVENT CANCELED. "With the ferries stopped, it just seemed silly to continue." She leaned toward Anthony as though she were about to divulge a great secret. "We don't always get such big names here, you know, and the owner understandably would rather postpone until we can really fill the house."

"And then some, I'm sure," said Anthony. "I mean, Leonard Puckett! He's a big deal." He tried to make his voice sound affable, but really he was thinking, *Fraud.* He was thinking, *Liar.*

"One of my favorites," Bridget confirmed. "I've just had a few minutes to speak with him. A real treat! An *unexpected* treat, I might add. Sometimes the big ones just blow in and blow out without so much as a sideways glance. But he's quite the gentleman."

"He's here?" asked Anthony. His heart started to beat very fast.

"Oh, yes," said Bridget. "He came in on the last plane this morning. As luck would have it! That's why I feel so bad postponing the event. He was so gracious about it. A big name like Leonard Puckett! I know authors way less successful who'd never be willing to be flexible."

"That's great," said Anthony. He was sweating. His father was *here*. He wondered if Bridget had made the connection between his own face and either the *Times* article or the book jacket of *A Room Within*—she worked in a bookstore, after all, wasn't it possible that she'd recognize the author of a bestselling novel? But there was the fact, as incontrovertible as the weather, that a certain amount of time had passed since the publication of his debut. Bridget looked awfully young, even though she sort of talked like a forty-year-old.

"Well, well, well." Leonard must have come from the author version of an actor's green room, which in Anthony's experience was more often than not a storage room filled with galleys and unpacked cartons of books and the occasional snack bin.

"Hello," said Anthony cautiously. He stopped himself before saying, *Hello, Dad.*

"Oh!" said Bridget. "You two know each other. I hadn't realized . . ."

"We do," said Leonard, at the same time as Anthony said, "Only very casually." *I Don't Want to Taco 'Bout It*, Anthony told himself softly. *It's Nacho Problem.*

Bridget hovered uncertainly, bouncing back and forth from one foot to the other like a tennis player preparing to return a serve. "Well, then," she said at last. "I don't expect anyone to come in with the storm we're getting, and I've posted the cancellation on the door—why don't you sit and talk for a few minutes while I close up?" She lowered her voice, although nobody else was around. "There are twelve bottles of wine we bought for a little reception after the reading. I didn't bother refrigerating the white once we decided to postpone, but help yourselves to the Cabernet. They told me it's a nice one!"

Besides a small table, there were two chairs in the back room: a floral armchair that looked like it had been recovered from somebody's basement, and a swivel desk chair. Leonard took the latter, which left Anthony no choice but to sink into the armchair, giving him a distinct feeling of being on uneven ground, looking up at Leonard.

"So!" said Leonard expansively. "So, this is where you've been hiding out all this time." He used almost the exact words Cassie had used, and Anthony resented them exactly the same amount.

"Mom told me," Anthony said, without preamble. "She told me everything."

Leonard's face was inscrutable. "And what do you mean," he said slowly, "by everything?" He took his time opening the wine and pouring a healthy amount into two plastic tumblers he selected from a stack on the table. At first Anthony wasn't going to have any— it seemed like an admission of complicity, to join in a friendly drink, and it was still afternoon—but in the end he needed it to calm his shaking hands, his shaking nerves.

"Everything about your career. Your *collective* career. She wrote as much of the books as you did. More, in some cases! *The Beauty's Beast. Red as Rubies. Jury of Peers.*"

"Ah," said Leonard. He sat back in the desk chair and regarded Anthony.

"Well?" said Anthony. "Is it true?"

Leonard said, "So, with this little tidbit, you think you know everything. You think you know the whole story."

"I think I know most of it," Anthony said. He felt like they should be drinking something more manly— bourbon, scotch—but the wine went down easy and he began to feel more relaxed.

"I bet you don't," said Leonard. "So why don't I tell you when it started?"

"Okay," said Anthony. He hated how compliant he sounded.

"I was sick with the flu," said Leonard. "I was so sick, for almost a month. I don't know if you remember that. You were in middle school. My last two books had done *extremely* well."

"I don't," said Anthony evenly. He did, but he wanted to hear his father tell it. The year of the flu, seventh grade. Some particularly virulent strain had appeared, and half the school was out for days at a time. Then his father caught it. Anthony and Dorothy somehow escaped. He remembered his mother disappearing constantly into the master bedroom. Tending to the sick, Anthony had thought at the time.

"Sick or not, the deadline didn't go anywhere. There was no leeway. You wouldn't understand, you haven't been doing it like I have. You're not the same kind of writer. One novel to your name."

"Two," said Anthony. "And the short stories."

Leonard raised an eyebrow. "Not quite two, is it? And I don't count the short stories. Short stories don't sell."

"Well, I understand the concept of a deadline," said Anthony evenly. He drank more wine.

"The pressure to produce, to keep producing, on the schedule the publisher had set up. It was enormous. But to stop, when I was just getting that momentum—that simply wasn't an option. I never would have become what I became if I'd stopped. So I was trying to work on the book when I was quite ill, and I couldn't keep the thoughts straight in my head. They kept—" He made a whirling motion with his hand. "They kept moving around. Every morning while you were at school your mother would come in with a pad of paper and take notes for me. My hands were too shaky to write. I'd say the lines of dialogue, and she'd write them down, and every now and then she'd make a suggestion. What if the killer said *this* instead of *that*? What if the child appeared in the scene in the restaurant, or the argument took place on the boat? And so on. On we went like that, for days and days and days, and when I was better, and I was back in my study, I realized how helpful she'd been to me. I started calling her in when I had a question, a doubt. Her suggestions became more and more integral to the book. That book did better than any of them, and when it was time to start the next book, it just seemed natural that we would work on it together. So we did." He looked down at his hands, then took a long pull of the Cabernet. "And we've simply never stopped."

"Because all this time she's been—she's been your slave."

"*No.*" Leonard sat up. "No, not my slave."

"Your beard, then."

An almost-smile played at Leonard's lips, but he swallowed it back.

"That's ridiculous."

"It's not."

It was very strange to be talking to his father while surrounded by such a large selection of his father's (mother's?) books. The store had stocked up, naturally, on dozens and dozens and dozens of copies of *The Thrill of the Chase*, but also trade paperbacks and mass-market paperbacks of some of his earlier titles. Anthony picked up *Escape the Unknown* and flipped it over to look at the author photo, then he did the same with *Grasshopper*, which was published three years later. (In between were three more Gabriel Shelton books.) Leonard Puckett got a new author photo taken every two years ("Whether I need to or not!"), so Anthony could trace the evolution of his father's face, of his aging, simply by looking through a vast collection such as this one.

"I want to stop," Dorothy had said. "I'm ready. But he's not."

"So why don't you stop?"

"Stop?" Leonard, a man of letters, appeared not to understand the meaning of this very basic word. "Stop what?"

"Stop *writing*, Dad. Why don't you stop writing? Mom wants to. But she said you don't."

"We can't stop. We're under contract." So now it was *we*, Anthony noticed. Now that the cat was out of the bag, it was first-person plural all around.

"For how many more?"

"Two. After this one."

"So why don't you stop after that? She told me she wants to be done. You can take her on a trip around the world."

"Your mother," Leonard said, "has been around the world."

"Only in bits and pieces. And never on *vacation*, apparently. All this time I thought she was out and about, gazing at the *Mona Lisa*, touring the Kronborg Castle, but she was working. The two of you were working. And you took all of the credit."

"Don't talk about credit." Leonard slammed his hand down onto the table. "This has nothing to do with credit. Why must you fight me on this?"

"I won't stop," Anthony pressed on. "I'm fighting for Mom, who nobody ever fights for. Why not put her name on the last two books? Why keep going after that, against her wishes? You have more money than you'll ever spend. How much more do you need, Dad? To make you happy?" The twenty grand he owed Huxley reared its unattractive, inconvenient head once again.

"Need?" Leonard Puckett seemed to consider the question. He looked around the room, peered into his tumbler, then said, "Well, none, I guess. No more. But it's not about being happy."

"What's it about, then?"

"I don't know what else I'd do, if I stopped." His entire being seemed to sag. "Die, I guess."

"Oh, Dad," said Anthony. "Come on, now."

For the first time in his life, at the tender age of seventy-two, his father looked weak and old. It wasn't just the way the skin of his lower face slumped; it wasn't the unfamiliar veins that throbbed at his temple. It was something internal turned outward: it was the revelation of the long-held secret.

Leonard emptied his tumbler, and then refilled it. Anthony did the same. Leonard Puckett regarded his son, unblinking. "You have no idea what it's like, son." Anthony couldn't remember if there'd ever been a time in his life when his father had addressed him as *son*. No, he decided, there hadn't been.

"You've made that clear," he said. "I have no idea what it's like to be as successful as you. I know that, Dad. I get it. I know I don't have what you have."

Leonard was looking down at his cup, and when he raised his head again his eyes were damp. Was Leonard Puckett . . . crying? "That's not what I mean," he said. "You understand, presumably, what it's like to have your talent—your *immense*, your *enviable* talent—without the career. But you will never know what it's like to have the career without the talent. To be merely a hack. To need your wife to do half the work because you simply can't keep up with it yourself."

It was the regret in Leonard's voice that gnawed a pathway through to Anthony. Regret was such a painful and permanent thing. He felt a twinge of pity for his father. "You've written more books than any other writer in this store," Anthony said, indicating with the wave of an arm the bookstore that lay beyond the storeroom. "In any store! You're *immortal*." Did he mean to say *immortalized*? He paused, uncertain, then let his decision stand.

"But the truth . . ." said Leonard. He hesitated. "What I mean to say is—the truth *you* got at, Anthony . . . In all of your writing, from the first work of yours I ever read, you had a way of getting at the truth. A way of just—grasping it. Piercing it. In all of my years of writing, I've never been able to do that, to get at the truth." He sighed, and pressed his hands to his temples. "How I've envied you that, son— right along, how I've envied you. The quality of your writing, the masterfulness, the beauty, the insight. And you didn't have to work for it."

"Yes, I did. I worked for it." His father was trying to negate Anthony's blood, his sweat and tears, with a single furrow of his famous brow. "I worked like hell for it."

"Not like I did," said Leonard, shaking his head. "Not like I did."

Why, then, did Anthony begin to feel a terrible sense of foreboding, as dark and heavy as a cloak laid about his shoulders? Then, so quietly that Anthony had to strain to hear him, Leonard said, "That's why I did what I did."

"What do you mean? What did you do?"

"I'm not proud of it."

"Of what? *Dad?* Of what?"

Chapter 57
Lu

Lu dismissed Maggie, paid her, and went back up to the bedroom. She told Jeremy, "I need to go and think for a few minutes. You're in charge of Chase and Sebastian." She walked down to the beach.

The day Lu had told the partners in her firm that she wasn't coming back after maternity leave, there had been a terrible rainstorm. She'd found a day when Jeremy, then a resident working who-knows-how-many hours a week, was off, so he could drive Lu in and stay in the car with the boys. Sebastian nursed too often to be without her for long, and it had felt very important to Lu that she do this errand in person. (Though in hindsight a phone call would have been perfectly fine.)

Chase was just beginning to be toilet-trained, and some error of judgment or timing had resulted in his leaving the house in his big boy underpants—a privilege he hadn't yet earned.

The partners were dismayed by Lu's decision (she had been very good at her job) and they tried to woo her with talk of flex-hours and work-at-home Fridays. Lu was stalwart, firm. She knew those promises always lapsed and that at her firm there really was no such thing as flextime. The only real choice was all the time.

Leaving the office, she'd come upon a third-year law school recruit who was being given a tour of the building. She was probably only five years younger than Lu but at the time Lu—dark crescents underneath her eyes, nine pounds of baby weight lodged somewhere between her pelvis and her rib cage, breasts ballooned to three times their normal size, her whole body as unfamiliar as a foreign language on her tongue—felt like a dowdy spinster chaperone standing next to the season's most desirable debutante. The envy she felt of this girl was palpable, breathtaking.

"Well, that's done," said Lu when she got back to the car. She tried to keep her voice brisk and nonchalant.

"How do you feel?" asked Jeremy. He looked even more tired and worn down than Lu felt.

"Great," she said untruthfully. She gazed at Sebastian, sleeping in the car seat. "So relieved. It went really well." She sniffed. "Did something . . . ?"

"Less well in here," said Jeremy at the same time.

"I made a giant poop," said Chase. A proud grin snaked dangerously across his face. "Right in my big boys!"

As if given a cue, Sebastian stirred in the car seat. He opened his eyes and began to suck frantically on his fist. A tiny spasm wracked his small body, and then he broke into a wail. Lu's breasts simultaneously filled and began to leak. A great crack of thunder shattered the un-silence, and then the skies opened up.

Now, on the beach, Lu thought about that day and looked up at the sky. The wind was picking up. There must be a storm coming after all. Of course there was. They wouldn't have stopped the ferries for nothing.

Lu had never walked out on Jeremy like that before. It was out of character. She wasn't a passive fighter—she always saw a fight through to the bitter end, like a *GLOW* character with a mouth guard and a story to tell. Just ask her mother, her sister, or any of her ex-boyfriends. Jeremy had always been more cerebral, more measured in his approach to conflict, more willing to take a step back and think before speaking.

Was this going to be the end of it—was her marriage going to end not with a bang but with a whimper, not over wild adulterous sex and lipstick on the collar but over arugula salad?

People broke up over less. People stayed together after more.

Sex was a kind of power. Everybody knew that—look at Harvey Weinstein, look at Steve Wynn and Matt Lauer! But work was a kind of power too, and people didn't always look at it that way. Who got a career, who didn't, and what you did with yours once you had it—these were all their own kind of power plays.

Lu looked north toward Mansion Beach. Maggie had told her that Mansion Beach got its name because a mansion had once sat where the parking lot was. You could still see the outline of the foundation.

Here Lu was, nearly a century after Virginia Woolf had told women to procure some money and a room of their own. But what was the point of having the room if you couldn't figure out how to get to it? If you had to clear away a half-built Lego set before you used it?

If her college roommate, Sandia, were here she'd say something like, *Rise up, girl!*

Lu was astute and, yes, privileged enough to realize that Jeremy wanting her to shut down the blog wasn't a life-or-death situation. But it was hundreds of little deaths, all the time, every day: like death by a thousand cuts. Missed chances. An atrophying brain. Time passing. Added up, put together, those cuts made a real injury.

Why do we have to rise up? Lu wondered. The word *up* implied against. *Why, for heaven's sake, can't we all just rise?* Lu watched a lone surfer make his way toward the water—he was either brave or stupid, heading in when everyone else had left. The water was churning now, a dark gray, and the sky had turned a strange color, not dark, exactly—more like a sickly yellow, the color of a stomachache.

She thought again of Virginia Woolf, who had written, *Money dignifies what is frivolous if unpaid for.* And she knew she had to finish the conversation. As Lu walked back toward the house she could feel it in the atmosphere. It was the storm coming, but it was something else too, all around her—a reordering of the molecules. The way everything was changing.

Chapter 58
Joy

Come to the shop, Joy texted to Maggie. Storm coming.

Joy had heard from Mitzy Collins, who owned a T-shirt shop on Water Street, that the offshore winds were now nearly hurricane force and all flights to Block Island were grounded indefinitely. Mitzy Collins had learned this from her cousin Joe, whose ex-wife's new husband worked for New England Airlines, which made daily flights between Block Island and Westerly. So Joy, who had been out at Stevens Cove, had come into the shop and sent Olivia home.

Joy Bombs had been lucky during Hurricane Sandy in 2012, but other island businesses hadn't fared well at all. Ballard's had ended up with inches of sand inside the restaurant, which had to be removed wheelbarrowful by heavy, painful wheelbarrowful. The Beachhead (along with much of Corn Neck Road) had sustained heavy exterior damage. Old Harbor Bike Shop lost a fleet of scooters.

Joy was on the floor behind the counter, boxing up the for-here coffee mugs, whose shelf was precarious in the balmiest of weather circumstances, when she heard the door rattle. "Sorry!" she called. "We're closed!" (Had she forgotten to turn the sign?) The door continued to rattle; in fact, if anything, the rattling increased in intensity. Joy popped her head above the counter to see if it was anyone she knew—a friendly fellow shop owner, perhaps, comparing notes on storm preparation. No, it was a woman with a small boy, nobody from Block Island. "Tourists," Joy muttered. They probably wanted to come in for a hot cocoa and a front-and-center seat for the storm. She glanced at her phone. Maggie hadn't answered.

Answer me now, Joy texted. She hated to resort to these tactics, but clearly they were called for. If u don't answer me I don't pay the cell phone bill. No reply. Wonderful. Ghosted by her own daughter.

The door-knocker hadn't gone away. "Fine," growled Joy. She made her way to the door, opened it a little bit, and said, "Sorry, we're closed." She glanced down at her phone, whose screen showed the three little dots that meant the person you had just texted was texting you back.

"Oh, I don't want to buy anything," said the woman. "I'm looking for Anthony Puckett. I thought you might know where he is."

The dots disappeared.

Joy looked up then and gave the woman her full attention, and as she did so her heart did a funny little jump and she realized she was staring right at Cassie, Anthony's ex-but-not-really-ex-wife. She looked much the same as she did on her Facebook page: the full lips, the perfect blond hair, the silk dress. Joy looked down at the pint-sized version of Anthony standing next to the woman. This would be Max. He was (of course) as adorable as his mother was gorgeous, with a red T-shirt on which was printed a dinosaur and the word Max-o-Saurus. He had a Norman Rockwellian cowlick and the sturdiest little legs you could imagine. She couldn't help smiling at such a delectable specimen of little boyhood, and Max smiled back. "You thought I would know where someone named Anthony Puckett is?" she said to Cassie. "Do I know you?" Better to pretend innocence than admit to a Facebook stalking habit.

"No," said Cassie (sort of haughtily, Joy thought). "But my husband knows you."

Joy pretended confusion. In high school, during her brief flirtation with the theater department, she'd played Abigail Williams in *The Crucible*. It had involved a lot of hysterical screaming, and she'd nailed it.

"My husband definitely knows you."

"Hmm . . ." Joy tried to look as if she were searching among the many, many names and faces in her memory, and was coming up short.

"I'm hungry," said Max. He pulled gently on his mother's hand.

"They're closed, sweetie. We're just here for a minute."

"We are closed," conceded Joy. "But I might be able to find him a little something." No reason to punish the little boy for the sins of the mother and the father. "Does he have any allergies?"

"No," said Max.

"We try to stay away from processed sugar," said Cassie.

"Good luck with that," said Joy. "You're in a bakery." She was reminded of the untimely, damaging visit from Shelly Salazar, book publicist. She went into the kitchen and returned with a plate of leftover pies in assorted flavors—she'd been planning to bring them home to Maggie. But Maggie, who still had not answered Joy's text, clearly did not deserve any whoopie pies.

Joy put half of the pies on a plate for Max and half on a plate for her and Cassie. She pulled out three chairs at one of the four-tops, but Cassie said, "I'm just going to let him sit at a different table, if that's okay."

Joy shrugged and said, "Suit yourself." Then, relenting a little, she pointed toward the kids' table that had a basket of toys next to it. "He's welcome to sit there," she said. Without meaning to, she kept stealing surreptitious glances at Cassie. She was *so pretty.* Her skin was porcelain, and her hair was perfect, and her clothes fit perfectly. She looked like an adult version of a super-Caucasian American Girl doll.

Cassie set Max up at the small table. "Can I have your phone?" he asked.

"No," she said. Then, "Oh, I guess, why not?" To Joy: "I'm normally very strict about electronics. But I kind of feel like everything's gone out the window this summer."

"I know what you mean," said Joy.

Cassie rooted in her handbag and said, "Oh, shoot, I must have left it at the hotel. Max, play with the toys." She rooted some more. "Found it! But I'm sick of it. Turning it off."

Joy indicated the plate. "Help yourself."

"No, thank you."

Joy took two and bit into the first one ostentatiously. For a moment the two women stared at each other. Cassie's eyes were a light icy blue. Looking at them felt to Joy potentially dangerous, like looking directly at the sun during an eclipse.

"I do know who you are," said Joy. "And it's over between Anthony and me, so really, you have nothing to worry about."

"That's not what I'm worried about," said Cassie. "That's not what I'm here for. You know what? Fuck it." She glanced guiltily at Max, but he was absorbed in a picture book from the toy box and he didn't react. She took a peanut butter surprise pie (the surprise was the bits of Heath bar in the filling) and allowed herself the smallest bite possible. "Oh, my *God*. These things are *amazing*."

Joy was starting to like Cassie a tiny bit better. "So what *are* you here for?" she asked.

"I've been married to Anthony for five years," said Cassie. She blinked her annoyingly long eyelashes (and so dark! with Cassie so blond! extensions?) and pursed her glossy lips at Joy. "And I hate to say it, but I haven't seen him this happy in a long time. Maybe ever."

"Well, I haven't seen him since July. He's probably happy because we broke up." Joy stood. Max, from the small table, looked up, alarmed, and pulled the plate of whoopie pies closer to him.

"No," said Cassie. "Sit back down. I can't believe I'm saying this. I mean, overall, his health, his stress level, his potential for happiness . . . they are all greater than they ever were with me. He's always been . . . so worried. With this big weight of a book on him. I didn't make it easy on him. I wanted his success as much as he did. Maybe more."

Joy regarded the other woman. She hated to admit that a seed of hope had sprouted deep in her soul, which had for so long been too dry to support any growth.

"That's the only time I'm ever, ever going to say that," continued Cassie coolly. Her face was a smooth mask, devoid of wrinkles, blemishes, emotion. "I'm not going to beg you to get in touch with the man I married. But it's too late for us, for him and me. That's very clear. And maybe I didn't do right by him, and maybe this is the way I think I can make it up to him." She glanced over at Max and lowered her melodious voice. "He doesn't want me," she said. "He wants you." She rose from her chair and said, "So you really don't know where he is?"

He wants me? thought Joy. She felt the blood rush to her face. She was happier to hear that than she was willing to let on. "I really don't know where he is," she said evenly.

"Figures," said Cassie. "Come on, Max."

Max looked up from the book. There was a swipe of filling on one cheek, and his left sneaker was untied. There was something about his expression that reminded Joy so much of Anthony: it was hopeful without being needy, and sweet without being guileless.

Chapter 59
Lu

Lu came into the house on nervous little cat feet. The boys were watching TV, and Jeremy was still in the bedroom. He had moved from the straight-backed chair to the bed. He was lying on his back, the back of his head resting in his hands, his long legs stretched out in front of him. He was staring at the ceiling.

"Do you remember when I was working at the firm?" Lu asked. "Before kids."

"Of course." His voice was gentler than it had been, more conciliatory.

"You were just starting your residency, remember?"

"I do."

"Working *crazy* hours."

"Crazy."

"And our schedules almost never matched up."

"I know. You were alone a lot."

"I didn't mind." She had never minded being alone when Jeremy was at the hospital. She had a new job. She had friends, and plans, and she could go for drinks or dinner any night of the week if she chose to. Sometimes she didn't choose to. Sometimes she poured a glass of wine and put on her pajamas at eight-thirty. She was always tired after a day at work—they worked the young attorneys to the bone—but it was such a good kind of tired, a satisfying emotional and intellectual fatigue.

"But every now and then, we'd match up perfectly, on a Saturday! We'd both have it off. Remember that? Remember those Saturdays?"

Jeremy had a faraway look in his eyes. "I remember," he said.

"Jeremy?" Lu sat cautiously on the edge of the bed.

"Yes?"

"I liked me better then."

He narrowed his eyes at her, considering. "I liked you then too."

"Better?" she asked. She was scared of his answer.

"No . . ." he said slowly. "Not *better*. But you were happy. I liked you happy." He hesitated. "Do you know what I thought when I read your blog?"

Lu leaned back a little bit, so that her upper back was against Jeremy's legs. "What?"

"I thought that you don't love us anymore. The way you wrote about this other family—like you wanted us to be them, not us to be us. Like you like them better."

Lu could see how it came across that way. She could see how that hurt Jeremy. "Of course I love you. I love you just the way you are, I don't want you to be Jacqui and Charlie and Sammy. But I can't love *just* you."

Jeremy sat up and pushed his back against the headboard. "*Lu*—"

"No. You have to listen to me. Nobody has ever asked that of you, Jeremy, to love just your family, and not your work, and not all of the things you can do that have nothing to do with this household. You don't know what that's like. You can try to imagine it, but you can't really know it, not the way I do." She watched him, wondering what he was thinking, and she kept talking. "It's not enough, Jeremy. I can't do this . . . forever, just this. But I also can't do the other thing if you're thwarting me at every step. If you . . ."

"If I what?"

"If you're not proud of me." No, that wasn't even it. "If you don't take it seriously. To do it the right way takes hours every day."

"Okay," he said. "I get that."

"You do?"

"I do. I'm trying to. So maybe you have someone, Maggie or someone like her, two mornings a week. You can do a little bit more every day while the kids are napping. We can afford a little bit of babysitting, if it's what you really want."

Tears of frustration sprang to Lu's eyes. It was a concession, but it was all wrong. He didn't really get it. "Chase hasn't napped for two and a half years, Jeremy, and Sebastian is in the process of giving his nap up. If you ever had charge of the boys on your own you would know that." Her voice came out sharper than she'd realized it would. "To do this thing the right way takes hours every day. The people who are successful with this are doing it as a full-time job. I can't do it if I don't take it seriously. If you don't."

She thought again of Virginia Woolf. *Money dignifies.* And she told him about the money, all of it: what she had in her secret account, and what she was making from affiliate links, and how many potential advertisers she'd found just this summer, and what her agent thought she could make in a book deal. She watched something change behind his eyes as she spoke—as fleeting as a flame, as undefinable. Was it hope? Desire? Disbelief?

Then she knew. It was respect. The money was changing it for him.

You go, Virginia, Lu thought. *Nearly nine decades ago you wrote those words, and you hit the nail on the goddamn head.*

"I didn't realize," he said.

"Of course you didn't. I never told you. It's another secret I was keeping from you. But with this kind of money, we can do a lot. We can pay your parents back. We can hire a nanny. We can get that awful wallpaper out of the basement bathroom."

Jeremy smiled at that. "That wallpaper is horrendous." She waited. The wallpaper was the least of it, obviously. "The money is a big deal, Lu. I get that. That's huge. But even so, a nanny isn't going to replace *you* giving them your full attention. Despite everything you're saying, I still think one of us should. They're still so little. That's what we believe in. That's what we always agreed on. Don't you see?"

Again, the sensation of the high dive, the closing of the eyes, the jumping. "That's not what I believe anymore. I'm sorry, Jeremy, no. I don't agree." She shrugged, and there was an apology in her shrug, but at the same time there was no apology at all. "I just don't agree."

"What do you mean?"

She stood and walked over to the window, which faced Anthony's cottage. "If you think one of us needs to be home full-time with Chase and Sebastian, then you need to quit your job and be home with them."

"Quit my job? I can't quit my job. You can't really mean that, Lu. People don't quit jobs like mine."

She whirled around. "Of course I don't want you to stop being a doctor. Of course not. I'm trying to point out how ridiculous that would be, for me to ask you to do that. Priorities change, Jeremy, and needs change, and our priorities about this aren't the same anymore. They just aren't." Jeremy's mother had been home with him, and he'd loved it; Lu's mother hadn't, and she wished she could have been more. But she was finally able to articulate the exact thought that had been eluding her all summer: her need to be more than a mother now outweighed her belief that a parent needed to be the primary caretaker. "What you want me to need and what I need aren't the same."

There, she'd said it. Everything but the big one.

Jeremy got off the bed and came to stand beside her.

"But that won't work, Lu. A full-time job for you? I just don't see how we could possibly swing that right now, not without creating chaos. When we have another baby—" His voice was pleading with her, and his eyes were too.

Now it was time for the big one. She had climbed

the ladder for a third time; she jumped again. "I don't want to have another baby, Jeremy." There.

"Lu! No, please don't say that."

"I have to say it. It's true. I don't want to. I'm not going to."

"Lulu." Jeremy's voice cracked. "I want three kids so badly. I've always wanted three kids. I was always clear about that. So were you! *You* used to want three kids."

It was true, long ago she'd said that. "That was before."

"Before what?"

"Before the whole burden of child care fell on my shoulders. I'm only willing to give up so much anymore, Jeremy."

His eyes were pleading; his whole body was pleading. "If I could have the baby for us, I would."

"And I would say, be my guest." Lu believed that Jeremy *thought* he meant that, but she also believed that if it came right down to the uncomfortable reality of it he probably didn't want to perform surgery pregnant, with swollen ankles and distended veins, and then stay home from the hospital for twelve weeks while he milked—sorry, *nursed*—the new arrival.

He took her hands in his. His long-fingered, sexy surgeon hands, hands that knew how to bring people back to life. "I just want us to want the same thing, that's all."

She shook her head. "No, you don't. You don't want us to want the same thing; you *want me to want what you want*. That's different." He let her hands drop. She could feel the moment growing beyond its own size—pushing out of its casing, ripping the seams. "Does that mean we can't be married anymore?"

"I don't think it means that," Jeremy said. Jeremy, who never looked scared, looked scared. "Does it?"

What if it did? The flood of hot tears came on so quickly then, and she put her hands to her face.

"Shhhh," said Jeremy. His arms found her; he wrapped her up the way he used to. Lu couldn't stop crying. "Shhh," said Jeremy again. Lu closed her eyes and for just a minute allowed herself to believe they were themselves more than a decade ago. She was sitting on Main Street in Hyannis with a bleeding knee. Their futures were bright. It was all far enough ahead of them that they couldn't yet get to it. But it was there. They were trying, pulling, reaching for it, arms out, wanting everything.

Chapter 60
Maggie

There is an eerie quiet to the downtown. Maggie is pushing her bike along Water Street with her good arm. Water Street is nearly deserted, and the people who are out are moving with a purpose, looking at the sky or out in the water every now and then. Though there *are* people on the long white porch of the National Hotel, under the American flags, gathered as if for a movie that will be shown on the surface of the harbor. People love a weather event until it becomes an inconvenience or a catastrophe.

Maggie is close to the end of Water Street, near the post office, the bookstore, and the statue of Rebecca that stands at the intersection of the four Old Harbor roads. Like all the island kids, Maggie knows that

Rebecca was erected in the late 1800s by a women's Christian temperance group to remind people to limit their alcohol consumption. Like all the island kids, Maggie also knows that it's really hard for Rebecca to do her job in the summertime. Whenever the Patriots win a Super Bowl (which is often) Rebecca wears a Pats jersey.

On her wrist (Maggie's, not Rebecca's) is a neon-green cast applied at the Block Island Medical Center by Olivia Rossi's mother. It makes it difficult for Maggie to ride her bike. But not impossible. And it's waterproof, at least.

Maggie checks her cell phone. She has three texts. One is from Riley, the first in several days. When she'd gotten her phone back, she'd given Maggie a good dose of the electronic silent treatment, but this text, even though it just says Hey, is a sign that the friendship is on the mend. There is another text from Olivia Rossi, confirming that Maggie will pick up one of Olivia's shifts next week, and a third from her father, asking if they can switch her planned weekend visit to the weekend after.

Hey, she texts back to Riley. To Olivia she texts the thumbs-up emoji, and to her father she texts NP. In the summer she doesn't like to leave the island any more than she has to, so the change in plans is fine with her, but she wonders what's behind it. Most likely her stepmother, Sandy.

On Maggie's last visit she overheard her father and Sandy talking about a potential move to Laguna Beach, California, where Sandy is from. Sandy has hated New England from the moment she married Maggie's father and isn't afraid to talk about it. Maggie hasn't told her mother about the move—she isn't sure if this is a legit plan or just one of those things that Sandy says when she gets mad. (Sandy has a temper, and gets mad a lot; Maggie's father, whose temperament Maggie's mother has always labeled *artistic*, adding theatrical air quotes, seems relaxed and even-keeled by comparison.)

If her father moves to California, Maggie will miss him, some, and she'll miss her little sister, Tiki, a lot. Tiki is unbearably cute, even more so now that she has learned how to say Maggie's name. When she says it, and puts her chubby little arms up to Maggie, Maggie feels a definite melting sensation. It's lucky Maggie's name doesn't contain the letter *s* because Tiki has a lisp and she says *s* like *th*. Sandy has already contacted a speech therapist, who told her that Tiki is too young to begin receiving services.

Maggie won't miss Sandy (Thandy) if her father moves to California. Sandy often looks at Maggie the

way someone looks at an exotic but possibly dangerous zoo animal—you know it can't hurt you, because
it's behind glass, but you're going to keep a close eye
on it anyway. Sandy doesn't like it when Maggie cooks
in her kitchen. She won't let her use the sharp knives
(Maggie is *thirteen! And knows how to fillet a fish!*)
and she won't let Tiki try anything spicy because she
thinks it might offend her young palate. Tiki eats
mostly carrot sticks and chicken nuggets shaped like
dinosaurs. Dinner by Mom, Sandy is not.

While Maggie is answering the first three texts, a
fourth one comes in. Her mother, asking her again to
please report to the store. This text Maggie ignores
again because she is still angry with her mother: for
the grounding, for probing the sore spot that Maggie's
humiliation in front of Olivia and Hugo has left on her
soul. Possibly her mother wants to make sure Maggie is
safe, but it's more likely that she wants to put Maggie
to work, like some sort of child laborer.

Maggie wonders if Pickles, who is terrified of
storms, has taken up her spot in the center of the
bathtub—she's better than a barometer at responding
to changes in weather. She almost feels bad enough for
Pickles to go home, but an angry part of her wants her
mother to sweat it out a little longer. She wonders, if
she went home, if her mother would be there making

her coconut-oil stovetop popcorn, which is miles better than the microwaved crap that Riley's mother makes. By then Maggie realizes that she's actually missed hanging out with her mother this summer.

Lately Maggie has been considering packing up all of her T-shirts and replacing them with some plainer but stylish tops from American Eagle and Hollister. Once she has decided to forgive her mother all the way, maybe they can take a trip to the mainland for some shopping before the beginning of the school year, which, hard to believe, is now just less than three weeks away. This summer has been the fastest of Maggie's life.

"Excuse me!"

Maggie looks up. A very pretty blond woman is heading toward her at a trot, waving her arms frantically. "Excuse me!" she calls. "Excuse me! Have you seen a little boy with a red shirt? Four years old, dark hair?"

"No," says Maggie, looking around. "No, I haven't."

"I was on the phone for just a minute," the woman says. "Not even a minute, for a second. And he was gone . . ."

The woman's phone rings. She answers it. "Not now, Glen," she says sharply. She listens for half a second and barks, "*Now* you want to talk about it? I can't. I'm in the middle of an emergency. I can't find

Max. What? Well, yes, again, but the first time wasn't my . . . Oh, never mind! I have to go." She ends the call and emits a little puff of anger or frustration. She scans the horizon frantically.

Maggie says, "I can help you look for him." When she was little, her mother taught her never to help a strange man who told you he'd lost his dog, because he might actually be trying to kidnap you. This woman, besides being female, is clearly legitimately distressed—most likely not a kidnapper. Also, she is even skinnier than Maggie, and Maggie figures she can take her physically if necessary.

The woman says, "I wonder if he wandered off down the road . . . though I don't think he would do that . . ."

"You never know," says Maggie. Before she started working for Lu, Sebastian had walked himself right down to the beach; if Anthony hadn't rescued him, who knows what might have happened? "Here," she says suddenly. "Why don't you take my bike and do a loop? I can stay here and look around for him. You should call the police too." Two summers ago a seven-year-old girl had drowned in the ocean. Bad things happen, even here. You could lose someone in the blink of an eye.

"Okay," says the woman slowly. "Yes, okay." She looks at Maggie's bike like it might bite her. She is wearing a spaghetti-strap sundress and her hair is beautifully curled just at the ends—the kind of hair Maggie and Riley used to call princess hair—and for a second Maggie thinks she is going to turn down the offer. But then she says, "Thank you," and reaches out for the bike. She mounts it steadily enough and off she goes, cycling up Water Street, calling out, "Max! Max! Max!"

The wind picks up. The gray clouds that were on the horizon are now scudding across the sky. The scene reminds Maggie of *The Wizard of Oz*, with Miss Gulch riding her bike in the cyclone. And what happens in that movie? Miss Gulch, of course, turns into a witch.

Chapter 61
Anthony

"You're not proud *of what, Dad?*"

"Earlier this year," Leonard whispered. "When was it—February?"

February was when—was when—was when. Anthony knew that because the days were so short, and it got dark so early. There was no reason to get out of bed when his waking time amounted to only three hours of daylight. The publication was set for September, so the galleys would have been bound and circulating.

Suddenly it made sense. It all made sense. The final puzzle piece fell into place; the key slid into the lock.

"You did it," he said slowly. "Anonymous source," the in-house attorney had said. "We didn't think anything would come of it, of course, but we're obligated to check out everything that comes our way." "It wasn't anonymous at all, was it?" He kept his eyes on his father's face the whole time he spoke. "It wasn't anonymous! It was you."

Leonard looked so like Dorothy had, just the tipping forward of the chin. The acquiescence, the concession.

"I made myself believe it was a well-read editorial assistant," Anthony said. "Or maybe even some long-lost O'Dwyer relative, out to get some money for the estate." He waited for Leonard to tell him it had been one of those. He didn't. "But you didn't know O'Dwyer, Dad. He was Mom's guy, mine and Mom's."

Leonard shrugged. "You did something dishonorable." His expression was implacable. "It deserved to be discovered, son. Righted."

"*Mom* put you up to it?" His mother had been trying to tell him in the cottage earlier. Something else, she'd said, something really important: one more thing. His own *mother*?

"No. Of course not. She pointed it out to me, when she was reading through the galley. That's all. She was . . . concerned. She was going to talk to you about it, son."

"Don't call me *son*," said Anthony through clenched teeth.

"But before she talked to you, I took matters into my own hands."

A red rage filled Anthony's field of vision. "You're supposed to wish me well. But you didn't. You didn't wish me well because you couldn't stand to think that I was going to publish something better than what you could write. So you exposed me. You ruined me. When all along, *you weren't even writing your own books.*" Anthony got up, banging his hand on the table.

Bridget's voice came sailing in from the other side of the shop: "Everything okay in there?"

"Fine," said Anthony in a strangled voice. "Just knocked over some books, sorry, I'll pick them up."

"No worries! Just wanted to make sure!"

"You took the credit for all of Mom's work," Anthony accused his father, biting off each word, "all of this time. And you're calling *me* dishonorable?"

"It wasn't her work. It was shared work. And we've already talked about this. It wasn't about the credit. Your mother doesn't care about that. She didn't mind."

"How do *you* know she didn't? Because I think she minded. I think she fucking minded. She told me she minded."

"She didn't."

"She did!"

"I don't believe you. We were a team. Arc. We are a team. The level of success we've reached together was possible because we both had our roles."

Anthony snorted, and Leonard held his hand up in a gesture of instruction that forced Anthony to stop and listen. "I didn't make your mother do anything she didn't want to do, Anthony. She wanted to be a part of it, and she was good at it, and I needed the help. So we worked together. We *work* together."

"Then why is it your face on the book jacket, and not hers? Why is it you who gets up in front of the crowds of people? You on television?"

"Because we both have things we excel at. She's a master of plot, a true master. She never wanted to be on *CBS This Morning*! Anyway, it was better this way. Women thriller writers don't sell the way men do. Maybe now it's changing, but back then—no, even now. Look at the list, Anthony. Patterson. Le Carré. Stephen King."

"Sue Grafton!" cried Anthony.

"Maybe," conceded Leonard. "But no doubt she was an exception, not the rule. So, your mother's brain, my face, together we won. We built a life together. We traveled. We raised you! We have enough money to do anything we want, for the rest of our lives."

"I think that's a bullshit argument."

"Think what you want, son."

"*Stop* it. Stop calling me that." Anthony sat for a moment. His rage was a monster, a Demogorgon, growing before his eyes. It became clear to him what he had to do: "If you thought it was okay to out me for what I did, maybe I think it's okay to out you. I can see the article now: 'Leonard Puckett Has Sold Millions of Books. But Who Really Wrote Them?' Or, this would be a good one: 'Is Honesty the Best Policy? Top Thriller Writer Says No!'"

Anthony had seen his father in many guises: angry, confident, arrogant, pleased, displeased, impatient, kind, tired, energized. But until this moment he wasn't sure he'd ever seen him afraid.

Leonard refilled their glasses. "You might do that to me," he said quietly. "But I don't think you'd do it to your mother."

Anthony knew on the deepest level that his father was right. This wouldn't be what his mother wanted. She wouldn't feel grateful. She'd feel ashamed and exposed. He hesitated. "I might," he said.

"You won't."

There was a pause. Then Leonard said, "Don't question things you don't understand, Anthony. That's my advice to you. Father to son."

"Stop saying that. That father-and-son crap. Think about Mom."

"I am thinking about her. Long marriages are complicated. You wouldn't know, because yours wasn't long. Yours didn't have what it takes to make it."

Anthony thought of all of the things he'd lost after Anonymous Source had contacted the publisher. The money, of course. *So much money.* His marriage. Time with his son. His future. Even if he wrote another book one day, there would be a stain forever covering his name, an asterisk attached to it. He had committed the crime, and he was finally able to own that in a way he hadn't been. But his father's exposure of it had compounded it by a hundred. He couldn't in a million years imagine hurting Max in the way his father had hurt him. He turned to his father and he was ready to . . .

But something didn't look right. "Dad?" he said. "*Dad.* Are you okay?"

"I'm—" said Leonard. "My heart is beating quite fast."

"Dad?" said Anthony. "Dad? Daddy?"

"I can't—" said Leonard. Outside, the wind picked up, screaming and whirling around the building. "I never could—" he said. "Not like you."

And the great man fell.

"Oh, dear!" sang Bridget. "That sounded like quite a pile of books this time! We do stack those galleys up pretty high. Do you need some help back there?"

The world shrieked and howled. Three boats that weren't properly secured in New Harbor swirled out to sea. Other boats, those that were tied up, pulled against their moorings, straining like recalcitrant dogs at their leashes.

All across the island, the lights went out.

Chapter 62
Maggie

The Inn at Old Harbor, like many of the buildings on Block Island, is from the Victorian era and looks like an old-fashioned gingerbread house. One side of it faces Water Street and the other side faces the Old Harbor, where the ferries come in. A set of steps leads from the ground level to the second level of the hotel, and it is behind those steps that Maggie thinks she sees a flash of red. She draws closer to investigate. The red is part of a shirt, and inside the shirt is a little dark-haired boy with his knees drawn up to his chest and his chin tucked into his knees. He seems to be employing the principle (of which Pickles is also fond) that if he can't see anybody, nobody can see him. He's very close to where Maggie and the woman had been standing; he must have heard his name being called. Therefore, Maggie surmises, the little boy is not lost. He is hiding.

"Are you hiding?" she asks. The boy looks up at her. He nods slowly.

Before this summer Maggie hadn't known anything about little boys. Now, after so much time with Chase and Sebastian, they are familiar to her: their little-boy smells, their quirks, their morning bedhead. She's pretty sure she could tell this boy a fart joke that would land. She crouches down. "What are you hiding from?" she asks.

He shakes his head, not bending.

"Wait, let me guess. You're hiding from a giant green monster with furry teeth. From a purple shark that can walk on land. From a super-evil puppy?" The last one brings a tentative giggle. He shakes his head. "No?" says Maggie. "I'm not on the right track? Hmmm." She cups her chin in her hand and acts like she's thinking.

That's when the boy blurts out, "From Mommy!"

"From Mommy!" Maggie pretends to be very shocked. "Well, my goodness, what did Mommy do to deserve being hidden from?"

"She made Daddy mad."

It occurs to Maggie that she has no way to let the blond woman know her son is safe. She should have taken her cell phone number—but, since she didn't, she will wait with Max until she returns. She figures they should come out from behind the steps and sit on the porch of the hotel, where they will be in plain sight of Max's mother.

"Are you all done hiding now, Max? Are you ready to come out?"

He nods somberly.

"Why don't we sit over here," Maggie says. "And wait for Mommy. She went to look for you. But she'll come back!"

They were sheltered from the wind when they were behind the steps, but once they emerge they can feel how much it is picking up. Maggie glances at the sky— it has taken on a yellowish tinge—and shivers. She's seen the skies over Block Island a lot of different ways, but never yellow.

She settles Max on the top of the short set of steps leading to the sandal store and sits beside him. She knows from Chase and Sebastian that it's best to keep talking. "You don't live here, do you?" she asks. "Because I know everyone on this island and I don't think I've seen you before. You must be a very important visitor. Are you a very important visitor, Max?"

He looks uncertain. "We're visiting Daddy. I think he lives here now." He sighs, world-weary. "But I don't know."

"What are the names of your parents?" Maybe she can call the police station and submit a report; that way, if the mother calls the police, they'll have Maggie's phone number.

"Mommy is named Cassie. And Daddy's name is Anthony."

"Ohhh!" says Maggie. Could it be? She has known, of course, that Anthony has a son he never told her mother about, and that the not-telling was the cause of the breakup. Grown-ups are both confusing and exhausting. "Is there any chance," she says, "that your last name is Puckett, Max?"

He nods. He seems unsurprised that Maggie knows this.

"Max," she says, "is your dad an author? Does he write books?"

Max nods. "Only some. But my grandpa writes lots and lots and *lots* of books." He holds his arms out as if he is holding the books. Maggie's mom told her all about the other secret part of Anthony's life too—the ultra-famous thriller-writer father. "Daddy doesn't live with us anymore," says Max.

Maggie supposes it's not out of the question that Anthony's wife and son would come to the island at some point during the summer. Maybe they have come to woo Anthony back. She hopes not. She doesn't want Anthony to get wooed away.

"I'm sorry," says Maggie. "Does that make you sad?"

Max nods again. "But before there was lots of fighting," he says. "I didn't like that."

Maggie was so young when her parents split up that she doesn't remember any fighting. "No," says Maggie softly. "Of course you didn't." She thinks about how badly she wants her mother to be the kind of happy she was with Anthony. For her mother to be that happy, this kid will see less of his father. For Sandy to be happy, Tiki will grow up hardly knowing Maggie. It suddenly hits Maggie that there's only a certain amount of happiness in the universe, and if you take what you think is your fair share, somebody else might have to give up theirs.

From far down Water Street she can see a figure on a bike. Driving next to the bike is a police car, and, as the car draws closer, Maggie can see that behind the wheel is Bret Holyman, one of the island's four full-time police officers.

"It's going to be okay, Max, you know that?" She suddenly feels very old and wise. "I promise you that everything is going to be okay, even though sometimes it seems like it isn't."

He nods solemnly. He has a cowlick—adorable. She's not sure how this kid would react to a hug: some kids are huggers, some aren't. (Sebastian is and Chase isn't, for example.) She settles for a friendly shoulder rub, which is what Chase prefers. Max leans into her, the way Pickles does when you hit the perfect spot on her back, the one that makes her left hind leg twitch.

"Do you mind if I pick you up, Max, just for a sec?" Max shakes his head. He seems firm and sure of himself, like a survivor.

She raises Max into the air. It's hard with the cast, but not impossible. He is heavy and solid in her arms, like three Tikis put together, or one Sebastian plus half a Chase. "He's here!" she calls, as the bike comes closer. She'd wave an arm if she could, but she needs both to hang on to Max, so she instructs him to wave, which he does. "I got him!" Maggie cries. The wind picks up; the sky turns, almost instantly, from yellow to black. A bunch of trash funnels down Water Street. Then the rain comes.

Chapter 63
Block Island

People stood in line every Friday to get a copy of the *Block Island Times* as it arrived on the ferry from the printer in Springfield, Mass. The Friday after the storm the line was especially long. That issue of the *Times* contained photographs of the damaged boats in New Harbor, and an article about the cleanup at Ballard's, and an interview with a well-known meteorologist who explained the weather patterns that allowed a storm of such force to strike with very little warning.

And the following two items:

OBITUARIES
Helen Simmons, 84, died peacefully at home on August 7. She joins her beloved husband, the late

Jack Simmons. She is survived by her sons, Jack Simmons II (and wife Joanne), of Stamford, Connecticut, and Joe Simmons (and husband Bart Winslow), of New York City, and her daughter, Lila Simmons Griffin, of Providence. Born on Sept. 8, 1934, in Woonsocket, R.I., Helen graduated from Salve Regina University with a degree in nursing. She served as a nurse in the U.S. Army during the Korean War, after which she moved to Block Island with her husband, a native islander, to raise their family. She has been a proud island resident for most of her adult life. Funeral services are pending.

FAMOUS NOVELIST DIES DURING STORM

Bestselling thriller author Leonard Puckett, author of dozens of popular thrillers that have sold millions of copies worldwide, was in town to give a reading at Island Bound Books when he collapsed and was taken to Block Island Medical Center, where he was pronounced dead.

Leonard Puckett's son, Anthony Puckett, who had also been a celebrated novelist in his own right until a plagiarism scandal sullied his reputation earlier this year, was with the elder Mr. Puckett at the time of his collapse. Mr. Puckett's reading had been postponed due to the storm. "He was such a nice man," said Bridget Fletcher, an employee of the bookstore. "So gracious, and very kind."

Mr. Puckett's latest book, *The Thrill of the Chase*, has held a spot on the *New York Times* bestseller list since its publication this spring. Mr. Puckett's publisher issued the following statement: *It is with tremendous sadness that we hear of the loss of our beloved author. In his long career Leonard Puckett has proved himself to be an unrivaled talent who never wavered from his prodigious and punishing schedule. The literary world has lost a great man.*

Chapter 64
Joy

All in all, they'd been lucky, with their cottage spared any damage. At Joy Bombs, one of the front windows had been knocked out by a bicycle pump that had blown down the street: could have been worse. Block Island Power expected to have service restored by early afternoon; for now, the shop was closed, Joy never having invested in a generator the way some of the big restaurants had. Joy was trying not to think of how many lost dollars each hour out of business was costing her. Just before the storm Harlan Nichols had sent a reminder of the increase in rent in writing.

The Friday after the storm, Joy and Maggie were wearing gloves and picking up the larger pieces of glass so that the smaller ones could be cleaned up with the shop vacuum. The day before, Joy had taped cardboard over the broken part of the window, but she decided to wait for the power to come back before doing the real cleanup. Maggie had said that she and Riley would be happy to decorate the cardboard later if Joy wanted, using miniature spray-paint cans they'd procured in sixth grade for a history project on the Wampanoag tribe. Riley, for all her questionable decisions with the vaping and the boys, was a pretty good artist, so Joy figured she'd probably take them up on that. Later that day, she hoped, she could reopen Joy Bombs and everything would go back to normal. Mostly normal.

"When we're done here, Mags, can you zip down to the terminal to pick up a copy of the paper?" In all of the frenzy Joy had forgotten. She wanted to see the storm photos.

"Sure," said Maggie. She seemed affable and compliant. Most likely she'd been more scared in the storm than she'd ever let on.

Joy had been terrified for a good long time too when the lights first went out and the wind picked up and the whole island seemed to be shrieking and wailing. She'd closed up the shop and taken refuge at home, texting Maggie to please please please come home or let her know where she was so Joy could collect her. There had been a solid twenty minutes when she'd imagined Maggie swept out to sea, never to be seen again.

When Bret Holyman brought Maggie home and told Joy Maggie had helped find a missing little boy, Joy had gotten so dizzy with relief that she'd had to sit down. Her head was actually spinning. When she learned it was Max—Anthony's Max, the Max who had just been in the shop while his mother told Joy, in so many words, that Joy made Anthony happier than Cassie ever had— she'd gotten even dizzier, and then, in an unexpected display of emotion that had made Maggie wince and cringe, she'd sobbed.

"You did all the right things, you know," she said now to Maggie, to keep the conversation going. "With that little boy. Max. Keeping him calm."

Maggie shrugged. Her shrug said, *Whatever*, but her smile said, *Thank you*: the contradiction of the teenager.

"What'd you talk about with him?" asked Joy.

"Oh, nothing." Maggie didn't meet Joy's eyes, and Joy wondered if her name had come up. Then Maggie asked, "Was Dad a good singer?"

Joy paused to consider this non sequitur. When she'd first seen Dustin with his early band, the Chiclets, she'd thought he was fantastic. She'd watched him up there, tossing around his hair, his eyes closed, a trickle of sexy sweat traveling down from his temple to his slender jaw, and she'd thought, *That guy is something special.*

The Chiclets became the Unbecoming, which morphed into the Stellars. They won a Battle of the Bands here and there; they played around New England in dive bars and hip basement venues. They scraped together enough money to do their own studio recording and waited for their big break. And waited and waited and waited. Joy went from groupie, to young wife and mother, to single mother, to single mother and business owner. Dustin capitulated; he got a job at a tech company that did something nebulous with storage. He married Sandy; they had Tiki. Joy imagined that life for Dustin became both exciting and pedestrian.

"Not good enough to go anywhere with it," she said finally.

"He told me that," Maggie said.

"He did?"

Maggie nodded. "Last time I was there. It makes him sad."

"It does?"

"Yup."

A small seed of sympathy sprouted somewhere inside Joy's heart. She tried to dislodge it, but it stuck there, refusing to budge. All these years Joy had wished bad things for Dustin. The revenge plots she'd hatched in her mind, the ill fortune she'd visited upon him in her imagination. *See what you've done?* She wanted to say that to him a thousand times in the beginning. There was the time when the heater in her car broke and it was the middle of winter in Fall River and she'd had to layer blankets over Maggie's car seat to keep her warm. There was the time she had a meeting with the small business loans department of a bank in Narragansett and she'd prepaid for Maggie to stay two extra hours at day care and ten minutes before the meeting she'd received a phone call saying Maggie had just projectile-vomited in the sandbox and could Joy please come pick her up immediately. The time when Maggie's school had held a father-daughter dance and Maggie had cried herself to sleep because she hadn't been able to go. *See what you've done, Dustin? To your daughter? To me? So you could chase your silly little dream! See what you've done.*

But now she wouldn't say that. Now she'd say this: *Thank you.* If Dustin hadn't left her she would never have known how *resourceful* she could be. In the literal sense of the word: how full of resources.

"He was good," Joy said now. "He was very good, really, Mags." (She could tell that Maggie really wanted him to have been good.) "But the music business is hard. There's talent but that's not all it takes. There's a certain amount of luck. You have to be in the right place at the right time, that sort of thing. And if it doesn't happen by a certain point, well, you sort of have to accept that it might never happen."

"Yeah," said Maggie. "Okay."

"I'm sorry he's sad about it," she said.

"You are?"

"A little."

After a while Maggie said, "I miss Anthony."

"You do?"

"Yeah." Maggie looked sidelong at Joy. "Don't you?"

"Sometimes," said Joy, as nonchalant as you please. (*All the time*, she thought.) And it wasn't just the sex! (Though that was at least thirty-eight percent of it.) Just the other day she'd been thinking about how Anthony let Maggie teach him how to clam, even though he didn't eat clams. She'd been thinking too about the way he held the back of Joy's neck when he kissed her, like if he let go she might fly away. She was thinking about the time Pickles had picked up a tick walking in Rodman's Hollow and Anthony had gone out and bought a magnifying glass to make sure they'd gotten the legs out too. "I think we're doing fine on our own, Mags."

"I don't," said Maggie. "Not really."

Maybe because she wanted to change the subject to something less close to her heart, and maybe because

Maggie seemed open to conversation in a way she hadn't been in a long time, Joy said, "Bridezilla changed her mind, Mags. She wants macarons for her wedding, not whoopie pies."

Maggie looked up. "No! Really? That's awful. From the Roving Patisserie?"

"Yup. Of course."

"Ugh," said Maggie loyally. "That's a really bad idea."

"Maybe it's not," said Joy.

"It is! Those macarons are terrible." Maggie stood up and brushed her hands on her tiny shorts. "You have to do something! You can't let her get away with that!"

"There's not much I can do. The contract was only verbal, so I don't have a lot of recourse. Except not to make that mistake ever again. Not to trust a verbal contract." You couldn't trust anyone, that was the real and true lesson of Joy's summer.

"But you have to do *something*." Maggie reached up and pressed a piece of the tape holding the cardboard on the window, while Joy closed the paper bag. The shop vacuum would be able to get the rest of the pieces. "Do what you always tell me to do."

"What do I always tell you to do?"

"You tell me to figure it out!"

"Ah," said Joy. "Excellent advice from the Phone It In School of Parenting."

"It's actually good advice," said Maggie. "Anyway, I'm sure you *will* figure it out. You're tough."

"I am?" Joy looked around to make sure there wasn't somebody else in the shop Maggie might be addressing. "Me?"

"You're the toughest person I know."

"Careful," said Joy. "That almost sounded like a compliment."

Maggie rolled her eyes and said, "Well, it wasn't."

"What was it, then?"

"It's just a fact." Maggie bent over and inspected something on the floor, but even with her face pointed downward Joy could see that she was smiling. "It's just a fact."

Joy figured that in present circumstances that was good enough.

Chapter 65
Lu

Two days after the storm the ocean was still wild and angry. To Lu it seemed like it was holding a grudge. There were a few surfers visible far down the beach; Lu could see their wet-suited bodies appear and disappear with the movement of the waves. It was high tide—very high. Giant clumps of seaweed littered the sand where the Trusdale family was walking, and pieces of driftwood, and the occasional bird feather. The seaweed made it look like a bunch of mermaids had taken off their wigs and thrown them ashore.

Chase and Sebastian ran ahead of Lu and Jeremy, then back toward them. They had a lot of pent-up energy after a day and a half full of solid rain and no electricity.

After their beach walk they were going to see which breakfast places were open in town. The island was still getting its feet back under itself, but they were hoping at least to find a bagel.

Chase and Sebastian had discovered big sticks on the beach and were using them to poke every mound of seaweed they came across.

"I bet there's a seal in one of these!" called Sebastian. Optimistically, he kept poking.

"Maybe," said Jeremy. "Keep looking, you might find something."

"I'm looking for a whale," said Chase firmly. "Sometimes after a storm you get a visit from a friendly whale."

"I don't think—" said Lu. Then, "Oh, never mind." She had been about to say that any whale washed up on a beach was probably not alive, but maybe Chase was right—maybe after a storm you *did* get a visit from a friendly whale, and who wouldn't like that?

The sky was pale, with stripes of white clouds that seemed as if they'd been laid out in lines. Sebastian found a piece of driftwood that looked exactly like antlers. "These could have fallen off a moose," he reported, holding them up.

"Could have," said Lu.

When Sebastian ran ahead to show Chase, Jeremy said, "So."

Lu said, "So."

"I've been thinking."

Lu couldn't find her voice to ask what he'd been thinking.

"I think we should make this change . . ."

She held her breath. "What change?" she whispered finally, nearly drowned out by the sound of the waves.

"This change to make your thing possible."

"You do? You really do?"

There was a wild smell to the air too—raw, a post-storm, briny, alive smell.

Jeremy took her hand and squeezed it. "I do. If this is what you really want."

Lu let go of Jeremy's hand and stopped walking. She faced the ocean. She was terrified. This was it: Her chance to say, *No, I don't want it. No, I'm too scared. Let's go back. Reverse. Keep things how they are, don't change.*

She watched as each wave crashed onto the sand and then pulled itself back out before the next one came. They were endlessly repetitive and also different each time: enduring and capricious all at once.

A seagull screeched and dipped and then settled briefly next to Lu before flying off again. The waves looked like each time they came ashore they were taking giant breaths and then releasing them. Lu took her own giant breath and let it out slowly.

"Okay," she said, turning back to Jeremy, who had come to stand beside her. *You can't ask for things and not take them when you get them, Lu,* she told herself. *You can't wait for everything to be perfect. Sometimes you have to jump first and think later.* It was time; she was ready.

"Okay?"

"Yes. Okay."

Chapter 66
Joy

Joy had to wait in a line fifteen people deep and spend upward of seventy dollars to do what she did while Maggie was off getting the paper and walking Pickles. It was insane, really, how many people were lined up at the Roving Patisserie. Well, summer wasn't over yet—it had just been briefly interrupted. She noted with some satisfaction that the boy who was taking orders—this would be Hugo, of course—was flustered, overworked. Maybe he was hungover.

Finally it was her turn. "Hello!" she said brightly. "I'll have . . . let me see. A salade Niçoise." Hugo had an iPad for order-taking; he tapped on it and then looked up at her, half expectant, half annoyed. Good. She wanted both. "Oh, and also a macaron," she said, giving the word a bit of a French twist, just for fun.

(She'd taken two years back at B.M.C. Durfee High School in Fall River, but rarely trotted out her accent, which Madame Girard had called "impeccable.")

Hugo didn't seem impressed. "What flavor?" He yawned.

Behind Joy the line thrummed with impatience. "What flavors do you have?" she inquired.

"They are all listed right there." Hugo pointed to a sign bearing a list of the twenty-four flavors.

"Hmm," said Joy thoughtfully. "Raspberry. Oooh, that sounds good. Mocha, *yum*." She kept going. (She heard someone behind her say, "What's the holdup up there?") "Orange cream," she read. "Boysenberry. Wow." Across Hugo's face passed a look of irritation, quick as a lightning strike. Finally she said, "You know what? I'll have one in every flavor." This had been her intention all along, of course. "Also, may I please speak to the owner?"

Hugo glanced behind him. "He is . . . occupied. Busy."

Joy flashed Holly's Chamber of Commerce ID. "I'm so sorry, but I'll need to speak to him anyway. I work for the town. It's an important administrative matter." She felt gleefully, ridiculously important saying this.

"One minute," said Hugo. He went to the small window on the side of the truck and called a string of

French words too fast for Joy to understand. "Wait over there," he said, pointing.

When Joy had her order—it had cost her seventy-two fifty—she stood off to the side and waited until a short balding man wearing a white apron appeared. He was such a stereotype of a French chef that Joy wanted to pop him right into a cartoon. She wanted to put him on Instagram. But what would she say for her caption? *@Joybombs. Ran this guy out of town today. #Majorwin.*

His name was Luca. She had to put the bag with all her food on the ground to shake his hand. Again she showed Holly's ID. At first Luca thought she was there to assess storm damage, of which, he assured her, the truck had sustained none: they were within their rights to be open for business.

Joy chortled gracefully, professionally. "That's not why I'm here," she said. She explained her mission. She'd been charged with overseeing the proper use of all summer business permits. Then she shook her head regretfully and told Luca that the Roving Patisserie had been found to be in violation.

"But why?" asked Luca. He looked so genuinely perplexed that Joy almost felt sorry for him. But then she thought about her little shop. She thought about the fingers-to-the-bone effort she'd been putting in for a decade now. She thought about the time the compressor on the walk-in freezer had failed and the repair had cost so much that she'd had to beg Harlan for an extension on the rent payment for three months until she could get herself back on track. She thought about Harlan's mother moving into her long-term care facility.

"Yes," she said firmly. "You have a permit. But according to our records, you do not have a *roving* permit."

"Eh?" He began to glower. He looked like he might start to chase a villain around while waving a rolling pin, with his chef's hat lifting off of his head and following several inches behind.

Joy glanced down at the place where a clipboard would have been if she'd thought to bring one. "My records show that your permit is a single-use, single-space permit." She'd made that up.

"Pardon me?"

"That's right." She decided to repeat it, because it sounded so legitimate. "You were issued a permit for a single location, and each time you move your truck you are in violation of the permit."

Luca blinked at her and shifted his weight from one foot to the other. "What is the . . ." He paused, maybe searching for the right word. He looked worried. She almost felt bad for him, again, but then she thought about Bridezilla, and Harlan, and Dustin's uselessness, and she kept going.

"The penalty?"

"Yes, this is it. The penalty. What is it that you want?"

"Well," said Joy. It had not occurred to her to think too much past this point. And she knew Luca was asking the question literally, but she found that in her mind she was answering it in the abstract. *I want my island back*, she wanted to say. *I want you to take your golden-skinned son and your twenty-four flavors and your high-end truck and the backing of your New York financiers and I want you to go back where you came from, because if you aren't going to stick around and put your kid in the school and your tax dollars in the coffers and your butt in the bleachers at basketball games that our kids take hour-long ferry rides to get to, then you don't deserve to be here right now.*

"We are almost done here anyway," Luca said. "It has been—how do you say it?—a shit summer for the business. And this is the . . . what is it, the ultimate straw."

Now *she* was perplexed. "But how can you say that? I drive past your truck all the time. There's always a line."

"Lines, yes. But the overhead is high, and the profits are low. So many expenses! You can't imagine what it costs, to get the ingredients here."

Oh, she thought, *oh, but I can.*

"All of the ferry times and the missed shipments and the timing and the spoiling." He waved his hand toward the line, which was now only five deep. "And people wait and wait and they buy only one or two macarons, and that is not enough to sustain us. My boss has lost money on us this summer. I have lost money for him." Luca looked disappointed in himself and Joy felt her sympathies begin to shift.

He shook his head sadly. "We are only, what do you call it, men for hire, my son and I. It is a man in New York who has the money, who owns the truck, who made the plan. If it is not a success this year"—he made a *poof* motion and the accompanying sound—"then we will not be back next year. We knew that from the start. And it is not a success this year."

"So what will you do?" Joy asked.

"We will go back home."

"New York?"

"No, no. No. *Home.* Paris. France. So the penalty for this—this permit situation. Can you tell me more about that? I will have to let my boss know. I was not aware . . ."

Joy felt something change then, a shifting of the tides. "You know what?" she said. "I'm just the messenger here. But let me put in a word with *my* boss and I'll see what I can do about making this just a warning. Since you're leaving soon and everything, it really doesn't seem right to shake you down for a fee."

His relief was almost palpable. "Really?" he said. "I would be so grateful. You would do that for me?"

She nodded magnanimously. It was such fun to wield power! Perhaps she should run for public office. "I would, Luca. I would do that for you."

After Luca had returned to the bowels of the truck, Joy opened the container and took a peek inside.

Instead of a composed salad, the way a Niçoise was often served, the Patisserie had cut up the beans into bite-sized pieces, pan-fried the boiled potatoes to leave little crispy bits in the salad, and done the eggs in a medium boil, so that the yolks hadn't gone all chalky. Besides the usual suspects—the olives, the cherry tomatoes chopped in half—she thought she spied some chopped fresh herbs, and a deep sniff told her she was right. Tarragon? Chervil? She didn't see any anchovies in the salad, but when she dabbed her index finger into a piece of the (she had to admit, *beautifully torn*) butter lettuce and put it to her lips, she thought she tasted anchovy. The bastards must have minced it and put it right into the dressing.

Even though Joy was about as loath as could be to say it, it sort of had to be said: that food truck had turned out a genius of a salad.

Chapter 67
Anthony

Anthony, walking down Water Street, turned when he heard his name. Joy. His heart thumped and turned over, once, twice, experimentally, like an engine trying to start in the cold. He turned around. He'd missed her so much, but now here she was in front of him, and his heart was still full of his father's death. It was hard now to find room for anything else.

"I just heard about your father, Anthony. I'm sorry. I'm so, so sorry." She held up a copy of the *Block Island Times*. Leonard's author photo was on the front page. "I wish I knew sooner. I just found out. Anthony—" She raised an arm like she was about to hug him, but something in his face must have stopped her because she let it fall.

Every time Anthony forgot for a fraction of a minute and was then reminded, he broke anew with the realization. His father was gone. "Thank you," he said formally.

"Can you come by the shop for a minute? Can I make you a coffee?"

He hesitated. "I don't want to leave my mother for too long. And I don't really want to see anyone."

"Just for a minute? We just reopened."

"Okay. Just for a minute." They made the short walk to Joy Bombs in silence. Olivia was working behind the counter, doing her usual thing. There was a small line. Anthony didn't want to see any people. He felt raw. His sleep had been fractured; his organs felt swollen and tender.

"Here," Joy said. "Come back to my office. I'll get you a coffee and bring it to you."

Anthony sat in the corner of the kitchen at her desk, which was piled high with paper and order forms and a manila folder that said INVOICES in Joy's beautiful, crooked handwriting.

When she returned with the coffee, Joy said, "Your mother was able to come. That's really great." She squeezed his hand.

"My mother's been here for several days," he said. "Even before . . . It's a long story. It's a very long story. Cassie and Max were here too. My mother and I are leaving on the last ferry today. The funeral is on Sunday. My mother—" He was supposed to be good with words, but, of all of the words in the universe, there were none that felt right for Dorothy.

The kitchen smelled like the remnants of that day's baking (chocolate, lemon) and also like something surprising (basil?), and even besides that there was something else, something particularly *Joy*, something as wild and unsettling as the ocean itself. The way the light caught Joy's face and her hair: his heart lurched. He might never have an opportunity to say what he wanted to say.

"Listen," he said. "Give me one more chance to say I'm sorry about the whole mess. I'm sorry about my secret past. I just need to say that, before I go."

"I just need to say that I don't care that you plagiarized." Joy's voice was gentle. "I never cared about that. I cared that you lied to me, Anthony, that you didn't even tell me you had a son."

"I know," said Anthony. He shook his head. "I know. It's terrible. And I love my son so, so much. You don't even know."

"Of course I know. I'm a parent too. I'm divorced. I have a daughter. You didn't have to hide any of your things from me. You didn't have to be ashamed of them."

Anthony looked around the kitchen. The giant mixer, the prep tables, the cart that held dozens of empty trays waiting to be filled—it was all so familiar, so strangely intimate. He felt an ache in his throat.

"I was ashamed of everything, Joy. Ashamed of my whole life before. When I came here, I just wanted to hide out. I didn't even want to talk to *anyone*, never mind fall in love with someone. I wasn't expecting any of this—I wasn't expecting *you*, Joy Sousa. And once I met you, and Maggie, and even Pickles—and you all liked me the way I was, the guy without a past—I didn't want to suddenly become the guy with a past."

Joy smiled. "I'm pretty tough, Anthony. I can *handle* a past. It wouldn't have mattered to me."

"I know that now," he said. "I even knew it after the first ten days with you. But by then it seemed like it was too late."

"It wasn't."

They were both quiet for a moment.

"I had this whole *When Harry Met Sally* list ready for you. The day of the storm. I looked for you, but I couldn't find you. And then, my father—" His voice broke.

She squeezed his hand again. "A *When Harry Met Sally* list? Like at the New Year's Eve party?" The corners of her mouth turned up, just a little. He nodded. "I want to hear it."

"Now?"

"Yes, now. If that's okay with you. If you feel up to it."

"Okay, then," he said. He took a deep breath. He'd had this list ready since they'd fought out by Settlers' Rock. "Here goes. I love how tough you are. I love that your daughter is fierce and independent because that's how you are, Joy. Heck, I love that your name is Joy and that you pull it off. I love that you picked this island out of all the places in the world and you said, *I'm going to set up shop here*, and you did it. I love how you look in just your underwear. I love that you make fun of the tourists even though they're the ones who buy most of your whoopie pies. I love that you drove that old neighbor of yours to the doctor once and instead of pretending you didn't notice his shirt was on inside out, you told him so he could fix it before he embarrassed himself. Speaking of shirts: I love Maggie's T-shirts, and I love that you actively seek out more of them for her. I love that you brush Pickles's teeth." He took a deep breath. He was surprised by how readily everything had come out. Grief could do that to you, though. It could open all of your pores, let all kinds of emotions escape, not just the sad ones. "I love how you brush your own teeth, for that matter, the way you come at them so earnestly, like you're doing the most important job on the planet."

Joy was smiling. "But I don't go too rough on the gums," she said. "My dentist is very clear about that."

"No," he said. "You're totally gentle on the gums."

She nodded crisply. "Okay," she said. "That's a decent list."

"Now you say, 'You say things like that, and you make it impossible to hate you.'"

"Oh, brother," she said. "I'm not going to say that."

"Because it's not true?"

"No," she said. "Because I'm going to do this instead." She kissed him, long, deep, and then he drew back, and then he kissed her. *This* was what he needed. This was solace.

"Do you think you could come?" he asked, when they paused. "To the funeral?"

She hesitated. "You don't want me there. Do you?"

"I do."

"Well, then I'll be there. Of course I'll be there. If you want me."

"Max won't be there," he said. "He's too young. But Cassie will. It might be strange for you to meet them. But then again, it might not."

"As it turns out," she said, "I've met them both. Sort of accidentally."

"Really?"

"Really. I'll tell you the whole story, another time."

"Okay."

Her smile was whole and open. Her eyes were a mix of fondness and kindness and possibly—dare he say it?—love. She didn't know about Dorothy, and what he'd found out about his father's career. She didn't know everything that had happened in the bookstore. There was so much left to talk about, so much left to say. "Definitely," she said. "Another time."

Taken alone, they didn't mean much, those two words: *another*, and *time*. But together—oh, the promises they held.

Epilogue

Five days after the storm, Helen Simmons was laid to rest next to her beloved husband in the Island Cemetery, where, visitors to the cemetery noted, the most beautiful flowers were left every year on both graves in late June.

Later people said that if the winds hadn't been so strong because of the storm, if the lights hadn't gone out, things might have turned out differently for Leonard Puckett. If the rescue squad had been able to get there sooner. If, if, if.

"It was just—life, and then no life. Just like that," Bridget Fletcher said for a long time after that, to anyone who would listen. "No matter what anyone tried to do. The life was just *gone*."

When Bridget began the first semester of her MFA

program at Boston University in the fall, the first story she attempted was about witnessing the death of a great man. Most everyone in her seminar dismissed it as maudlin, or flat, or insipid. Unrealistic. Bridget, unused to the evisceration that was an MFA seminar, felt hot tears rise. "But it really happened," Bridget insisted—which, everyone in that program came to learn, was *not* a defense of a poorly done story. She put the work away for a long time.

Years later, when Pauline Morrison would read the debut novel by the hot new entry on the literary scene, one Bridget Fletcher, she'd recognize a small scene in the middle of a chapter—not crucial to the overall plot—in which a young shop owner performed CPR on a customer, thereby saving his life. In fiction, Pauline (who was no writer herself) understood, we can sometimes change that which we could not change in real life.

Lu Trusdale's agent, Abigail Knowles, was at first worried and disappointed when she learned that Dinner by Dad's creator was a woman. "I don't know, though," she said. "You know what, let me talk to my boss." She spoke more quietly into the phone, like she was the one with the secret. "I'm actually really quite low down here. I'm just starting out. Huxley has the real power. I'll have to talk to him."

Forty-five minutes later she called back. "Huxley reminded me about Elena Ferrante," she said. "Nobody knew who *she* was for the longest time but that didn't keep those books from selling bazillions of copies." It was a basic tenet of human nature, Huxley had reminded Abigail, that people loved secrets and scandal more than they loved almost anything else. "In fact, he said the mystique was partly why the Ferrante books sold so well. Also they were brilliant. But anyway, Huxley says we organize a PR campaign around the idea of this mystery dad. We'll keep with the charcoal drawings. Once you get really big, we'll do a reveal."

Abigail gave Lu the names of a couple of PR people who might be interested in helping. "The first one is pricey," she said. "But we've had a few authors who have used her, and she's supposed to be the best. Her name is— Hang on, I'm just looking it up. Okay, here it is. Do you have a pen? Shelly Salazar."

It took a long time for the Trusdales to find a good nanny. Sebastian bit the first two, and Chase scared away the next one when he put the pet hamster in her sneaker. When they were in between nannies Lu had to call on Nancy's help, which Nancy managed to offer both willingly and judgmentally. Sebastian's first trip to the emergency room happened when Lu was in New York, meeting with the designer for her cookbook. Chase's soccer playoff game was the same day she had a photo shoot scheduled with three other up-and-coming food bloggers for the *New York Times* to be used as part of the big reveal. Chase scored, and he looked immediately for Lu, and Lu wasn't there. Lu missed Sebastian's school play when she was speaking at Sapor! in San Francisco.

Sometimes Lu had to speak directly to herself in the mirror, out loud. She had to say, *You. Wanted. This. Now go and get it.* Testing recipes for a cookbook was painstaking and time-consuming, and she had to rent industrial kitchen space and hire an assistant to do it, because it was too difficult and disruptive at home. It was a lot of work to keep up the blog and at the same time manage advertisers and affiliate sponsors without letting them take over. As Dinner by Dad's visibility increased, so did Lu's (and Leo's) responsibilities. The social media alone sometimes felt like a full-time job. The money helped, of course, although it didn't do all the heavy lifting, because money never did. There were rocky days in the marriage and there were smooth days, but overall there were far more smooth than rocky. When Lu was in the thick of it, cooking, writing, tweeting, thinking, learning, responding to readers' comments and queries, it felt like she was on the only correct path, and that it was straight and sure.

In March on Block Island you might have a series of rainy days followed by an early spring stunner, sunshine all over, crocuses thinking about poking their heads out. The next day you could have a wind kicking up from the southeast, holding the ferries back. Temperatures could be in the forties or in the sixties or the thirties or the seventies.

Almost nothing was open. Well, Joy Bombs was, from seven o'clock to ten o'clock each morning so the locals could get a cup of coffee before they walked their dogs on the beach or caught the ferry to the mainland for some shopping or took their places in the various year-round island businesses—the schools, the police station, the medical center. The post office was open full-time, as was the diner at the airport, and the bookstore managed to find enough customers three days a week. The Spring House Hotel served dinner Wednesday through Saturday.

Maggie's school hours were regular, and she was surprisingly busy with after-school sports or other activities. On the weeks when Anthony retrieved Max from Cassie on the mainland and brought him to the island they felt like a real family, the four of them. They went sledding in front of the Spring House Hotel and iceboating on Sachem Pond.

It took Anthony some time after his father's death to convince Dorothy that theirs was a story that needed to be told. In the abstract, she was uncertain. Her grief was tremendous, all-consuming, palpable, and complicated, like all grief is. Then he showed her the first three chapters when he was home for a visit. She poured a glass of scotch, disappeared into Leonard's study, and turned up the Puccini. An hour or so later she found Anthony in the kitchen and pressed the pages into his hand.

"Do it," she said, her eyes damp. "Keep going. Write it."

And he would. He did. Finally, after such a long time of trying and failing, Anthony Puckett had something to say.

Fame and Infamy: A Memoir of a Father and a Son was harder to write than both of Anthony's novels combined. He showed an early draft to Huxley Wilder, whose belief in Anthony returned once he had his twenty grand and a promising new manuscript. After he read the draft, Huxley swooned. (Not literally.) Huxley was eager to start shopping the book around.

He began dropping hints about it during his various lunches with editors. He had nine editors from six different houses drooling over it before the manuscript was ready to submit. And they both knew that early attention like that could drive a book up and up and up, all the way to the sky.

Chococoa Baking Company Chocolate with Creamy Vanilla Buttercream Filling Whoopie Pie

½ cup (1 stick) unsalted butter, softened

1 cup dark brown sugar

1 tsp vanilla extract

1 large egg

2 cups all-purpose (or gluten-free) flour

½ cup Dutch process chocolate

1¼ tsp baking soda

Pinch of salt

1 cup buttermilk

Preheat oven to 375 degrees (190 C). Line 3–4 large baking sheets with parchment paper.

Place the butter, sugar, vanilla extract, and egg in a large bowl and beat together until light and fluffy.

Sift flour, chocolate, baking soda, and salt into the bowl and mix together.

Add buttermilk and stir until combined.

Using a level 2-inch (5 cm) ice cream scoop or heaping tablespoons, make 24 scoops. They will vary in size.

Leave at least 3 inches (7.5 cm) of space between each one.

Bake in oven 10–12 minutes, until firm to the touch. Transfer to a wire rack.

Creamy Vanilla Buttercream Filling

¾ cup (1½ sticks) butter, unsalted, softened

¾ tsp vanilla extract

3½ cups confectioners' sugar

1 tbsp milk or cream

Place butter and vanilla extract in a large bowl and beat together with a wooden spoon until combined (or use electric mixer on low speed).

Sift in the confectioners' sugar. Add the milk or cream and beat together until light and fluffy. Use immediately or store in refrigerator.

Take two cooled whoopie pie lids of about the same size and place flat side up. Using a small ice cream scoop, place a scoop of vanilla filling on one lid. Place together gently, being careful not to press too hard.

Makes enough for 12 whoopie pies

Adapted from the award-winning Chococoa Baking Company recipe.

Acknowledgments

I have experienced neither the crazy highs of Leonard Puckett's writing career nor the abysmal lows of Anthony Puckett's, but I have been around the block enough to realize how lucky I am to be here. Elisabeth Weed of The Book Group has been my tireless, optimistic, hardworking, and clever agent from the beginning, and I am grateful. My new editor Kate Nintzel's brilliant, indelible mark is all over this book, and thank goodness for that. It improved by leaps and bounds with her touch. Thank you to Vedika Khanna for steering me through the nitty-gritty details. I'm still getting to know everybody else at William Morrow, but I feel so warmly welcomed. To borrow a phrase from that famous redheaded orphan, I think I'm gonna like it here. A big thanks goes to Jenny Meyer for handling foreign rights.

Pam Gasner of the Block Island Historical Society was kind enough to give me a tour of the island and share some tidbits about life there. Kate Butcher, Molly Fitzpatrick, and Vincent Carlone answered various island-related questions for me. Michael Oppenheimer of Princeton University helped me sort out the details of weather events on Block Island. Block Island is truly a special place and such a rewarding location to set a book. Though I don't live there, I did my best to understand it and to honor it. I tried to keep geographical liberties to a minimum, but I may have taken a few, especially placing a couple of imaginary cottages close to the water in service of the story. I hope the island understands. Kathryne Taylor of one of my favorite food blogs, Cookie and Kate, answered my many questions about food blogging, and many of her recipes inspired my fictional food blogger. Dianne Jacob also helped me understand the industry.

The inspiration for Joy Bombs came from a local whoopie pie shop in my town of Newburyport, Massachusetts. Julie Ganong and Alan Mons of Chococoa Baking Company and Café, who reinvented the whoopie pie long before Joy did, generously gave me insight into their fabulously successful business. (If you visit Newburyport, you really need to stop by.) Joy Bombs' motto, "Reinventing the whoopie pie," is a twist on Chococoa's "A twist on the classic whoopie pie."

My friends and neighbors, Marc and Cindy Burkhardt, have been beyond generous with keys to their beach house to allow me some writing time away from home. (I especially appreciate the upgrade to an ocean view this year.) Newburyport wouldn't be the same without my mom squad, who have never met a cocktail menu or a dance floor they didn't like, and my mental stability wouldn't be the same without my frequent runs with Jana Schulson.

Jennifer Truelove, always a willing researcher, this time helped me find the right T-shirts for Maggie to wear and create the perfect titles for Leonard Puckett's body of work. The other third of our trio, Margaret Dunn (along with Wally Dunn), let me pretend to be a playwright for a weekend to join her retreat in Maine when I was working on the first draft of this book.

My parents, John and Sara Mitchell, and my sister, Shannon Mitchell, have never been ashamed to make up ninety percent of the audience of a book reading all on their own, and for their love and unwavering support, and that of the Moore and Destrampe families, I thank them.

Addie, Violet, and Josie: you are turning into such

smart, interesting, independent, funny, talented young women right before my very eyes. I am so fortunate to have a front seat to your show, which often requires a good amount of audience participation. In this case I don't mind.

A bookseller recently dubbed my husband, Brian Moore, my "number one fan," and not only do I feel incredibly lucky to be able to agree with that, the sentiment goes both ways, forever.

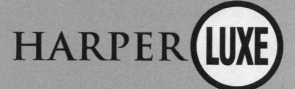